SIX FEET DEEP DISH

SIX FEET DEEP DISH

MINDY QUIGLEY

St. Martin's Paperbacks

First published in the United States by St. Martin's Paperbacks, an imprint of St. Martin's Publishing Group.

SIX FEET DEEP DISH

Copyright © 2022 by Mindy Quigley.

For information, address St. Martin's Publishing Group, 120 Broadway, New York, NY 10271.

www.stmartins.com

ISBN: 978-1-250-79243-3

Our books may be purchased in bulk for promotional, educational, or business use. Please contact your local bookseller or the Macmillan Corporate and Premium Sales Department at 1-800-221-7945, ext. 5442, or by email at MacmillanSpecialMarkets@macmillan.com.

Printed in the United States of America

St. Martin's Paperbacks edition / September 2022

10 9 8 7 6 5 4 3 2 1

ACKNOWLEDGMENTS

So many thanks to Charlotte Morgan, Danna Agmon, and Jessica Taylor for lending their insights on the manuscript and sharing their opinions about everything from proper cat behavior to whether eggplant belongs on a pizza. Tanya Boughtflower's awesomeness deserves special mention. There is so much of her in this book, and in all my books. Big ups to Tracee de Hahn for plot and recipe help, and writerly advice.

To the members of the New River Writers Group, thanks for reading many draft chapters, and for taking "pizza cat" every bit as seriously as literary fiction.

Big thanks to my parents, aunts, sisters, in-laws, and other members of my big, fantastic family for cheering me on. Shout-out to my aunt Sandra Heyer. We were on a boat on a lake in the Poconos when you asked me, "Have you ever thought about becoming a writer when you grow up?"

Sonya Steckler, Laura Rettberg, and the real doctor Mara Sittampalam kindly lent their names. Mara, remember how you promised to buy a million copies of the book and give them out as gifts?

To Montez Vaught, Dr. Meghan Shepherd, and Dr. Lauren Dodd, without whom there would have been no Fat Cat

Study, and therefore no Butterball. I'm lucky to have you and the rest of my vet school colleagues, especially Brian Huddleston, whose help with Puerto Rican slang is much appreciated.

LaDale Winling *finally* put his Ph.D. to good use to help me choose appropriate hometowns for Delilah and Capone. Thank you. Thanks to Todd and Kelsi Jones, proprietors of the legendary BT's in Radford, VA, for letting me tour their restaurant, and forgiving my ignorance. Cheers to Jane Goette, Heidi Dickens, and my special cronies, the Crones, for believing in this concept even when the whole storyline consisted of something-something cat, something-something pizza . . . and a murder!

Big ups to LynDee Walker, who remembered little old me at an opportune moment. Thanks to our shared agent John Talbot for getting this book safely into the capable hands of Hannah O'Grady at St. Martin's. Hannah, your support and guidance has been invaluable. Thanks, also, to the whole Macmillan St. Martin's team, especially Sara Beth Haring, Sarah Haeckel, John Rounds, and John Simko. Thank you to blurbers *extraordinaires* Vicki Delany, Julie Lindsey, Edith Maxwell, and Paige Shelton.

Special thanks as always to Paul, Alice, and Patrick for listening as I spew out the million and one ideas that are perpetually tumbling around inside my head, and for gamely trying out my recipes.

SIX FEET DEEP DISH

CHAPTER 1

The problem with perfection is that it doesn't exist. Somewhere, deep down, I knew this. But in the high-end hotel kitchens and Michelin-starred restaurants where I honed my cooking skills, the name of the game was churning out perfection on a plate. Dish after dish, night after night. No mistakes. Ever.

I opened the doors of my new top-of-the-line Everest three-door commercial fridge and allowed the chilly blast of air to wash over me.

"It's all there, Delilah. Nobody's touched anything since the last time you checked an hour ago."

I jumped at the sound of my sous-chef's voice. "Oh, hi, Sonya," I began. "I just needed to get—"

"What? A life?" Sonya Dokter nudged past me with her hip.

She pointed to different sections of the refrigerator as she spoke. "Fresh organic spinach. Check. Locally grown red and white onions. Check. Metric tons of the finest quality Italian sausage from pigs whose lives were more pampered than a Kardashian's. Check. Parmesan, pepperoni, provolone, peppers, prosciutto, pepperoncini, and pineapple. All present and accounted for. Cheese so fresh it'll slap your backside and call you 'Sweetie.' Check-er-oo." Sonya put her arm around my shoulder and gave it a reassuring squeeze as she pulled me away from the fridge. She gently pried my hand from the handle and shut the door. "Relax. We're ready."

Part of me knew she was right. I'd tested the new appliances dozens of times. I'd spent the previous day polishing the stainless steel worktops until they sparkled and scrubbing the floors until I could practically hear them begging for mercy. But a bigger part of me wanted to make one last practice pizza before the guests arrived for my new restaurant's soft opening.

I reached for one of the huge bowls where that night's already-risen pizza dough was resting. Sonya slapped my hand away. "No more dough for you. Tonight is for you and Sam to enjoy. No pressure. Let the rest of us worry about the execution. A soft opening should be a celebration. I, for one, am ready to get this pizza party poppin'."

Sonya shimmied her hips and twirled in her vintage rockabilly polka-dot dress. Her hair—chopped into a midnight black bob with high-cut bangs—swished as she spun.

Pizza making is a floury, saucy business, and Sonya and I usually sported matching chef's whites and hairnets while we worked. For tonight, though, I'd wrestled my wilderness of coppery chestnut hair into a sleek up-do. I had opted for a low-cut wrap dress, which I hoped accentuated some of my curves and camouflaged others, while Sonya rocked her plus-sized pin-up model look.

"You're a walking party," I said, smiling at her. "Just add champagne."

"Or better yet, bourbon," she replied, striking her best Bettie Page pose and blowing me a red-lipped smooch.

I walked through the kitchen again, ticking off items from my mental checklist for tonight's party and tomorrow's grand opening, while Sonya threw on an apron and began mustering little battalions of red and green peppers to chop. Bins of semolina and flour, industrial-sized cans of crushed San Marzano tomatoes, and jars of oil-cured Spanish olives lined the shelves. Garlic-infused tomato sauce gently burbled on the stove. I dipped a tasting spoon into the sauce and brought it to my lips—balanced, comforting, rich. The same adjectives could probably be used to describe my fiancé and business partner, Sam Van Meter. I tasted it again. Something was keeping it from being one hundred percent right, but I couldn't quite identify the flaw. Alas, the same thing could probably be said about my relationship with Sam.

Moving to Geneva Bay, Wisconsin, and opening a restaurant was more my dream than Sam's. The resort town was only about an hour and a half north of Chicago, but it felt worlds away. I'd spent most childhood summers next to the lake's inviting blue depths, sunbathing and gobbling down titanic-sized pistachio sundaes during our annual family vacations. Whenever I was overwhelmed by the constant din, clanging pots, and expletive-laced tirades of the Chicago restaurant kitchens where I'd worked, my mind traveled to Geneva Bay. Living here full-time was a wish come true.

On those childhood trips, my family always stayed at my great-aunt Biz's quaint waterfront cottage. Small houses like hers were increasingly rare, many of them razed to make way for the lake houses of the nouveau riche or dwarfed by the legions of imposing, turn-of-the-century estates that ringed the lake. Those older mansions had been built as summer getaways for the biggest names in Chicago business: Wrigley, Schwinn, Vicks. In Geneva Bay, the names were attached to fabulous homes instead of well-known products. As a kid, I'd fantasized about living in one of the breathtaking mansions, and now that dream, too, was coming true. Sam and I were midway through remodeling a hulking Queen Anne mansion built during Prohibition by one of the many Chicago tough guys who'd minted a fortune running illegal booze from the Canadian border to the Windy City via Wisconsin.

Sam knew how much Geneva Bay meant to me, and he'd been the one to offer to bankroll our move and invest in my restaurant. As a sophomore in college, Sam had created an app to allow users to access baseball stats in real time, which apparently is (1) a thing some people feel the need to do, and (2) very lucrative. He sold the majority stake in his company, Third Base Analytics, for a small fortune when he was twenty-six, allowing him to devote the last decade to spending some of the money he'd amassed.

After sprinkling a smidgen more crushed red pepper into the tomato sauce, I tasted it again. A smidgen closer to that ever-elusive goal . . . perfection. My fingers brushed the smooth stacks of three-inch-deep round steel pans that would hold our new restaurant's signature menu item: Chicago-style deep-dish pizza. My twist was to draw on my years in top restaurants to create innovative recipes using top-notch ingredients, rather than the typical sausage, peppers, and cheese pies churned out by Chicago's old guard deep-dish establishments.

I checked the sauce again. *Good. Very good. But . . .*

"Stop with the sauce already. We're not going to have any left for the pizzas if you keep taste-testing it," Sonya said, giving me a not-too-gentle shove toward the door that led out to the dining room. "Why don't you check the setup out front?"

With one last wistful look at the pizza dough, I walked into the thirty-seat dining space. The windows facing the lake seemed almost like gigantic landscape paintings, revealing a dazzling palette of watery blues and arboreal greens. Every time I saw this view, I had to pause for a moment to let my eyes take a deep, long drink of it.

No one would guess that a few short months ago, this building had been derelict, in danger of demolition. It had fallen into disrepair years before, after the Feds raided the previous tenant's business—a pizza-place-cum-mob front called Rocco's. The eponymous Rocco, Rocco Guanciale, was now serving time instead of pizza, twenty-five to life at a federal prison upstate for crimes that included running an illegal gambling ring, extortion, and fencing stolen goods, with the odd bit of pimping and drug dealing thrown in just for kicks. He ran his criminal operation from the small apartment over the restaurant, an apartment Sam, Butterball—our oversized butterscotch tabby cat—and I were temporarily living in while our new house was being remodeled.

The restaurant was slightly removed from downtown Geneva Bay, fronting a narrow inlet and a modest pier—convenient for criminals, but also perfect for diners seeking serenity. While other potential buyers had been deterred by the building's unsavory connections, I'd thought of it as a selling point. Growing up on the rough-and-tumble South Side of Chicago, my sister Shea and I had been raised on our father's stories of wise guys and beat cops. Chicago had its fair share of big-city problems and unsavory history, but no one had more affection for the grit, ingenuity, and openheartedness of the place than our father did. When he'd passed away the previous year, I'd decided that opening a restaurant with a Chicago theme and a unique spin on the city's signature dish would be my way of honoring him.

As I made my final inspection of the dining room, Daniel, my old friend and newly hired bartender, glided into view outside the windows, rowing his kayak toward shore. Even from a distance, I recognized his athletic frame and neon green boat. Like many Geneva Bay dwellers, during the warmer months, Daniel commuted around the large lake by watercraft. Unlike the well-heeled residents who tootled back and forth in deluxe powerboats, though, our ultra-fit bartender paddled in a sleek kayak, which he stored at the small dock just on the other side of the tree-lined parking lot from the restaurant.

Banished from the kitchen, I continued to busy myself with restraightening and recleaning the dining area for a few minutes until Daniel strode in, unzipping the top of his wetsuit to reveal his bronzed pectoral muscles. He removed his Ray-Bans and blinked the late afternoon sunshine out of his eyes. As his vision adjusted, he stopped and stared at the canvases that hung from the ceiling.

"Cool, huh?" I said, gesturing at the artwork. "They went up this morning."

He raised an eyebrow and ran his hands through his close-cropped black faux-hawk haircut. "It's a statement. I'll give you that."

The interior space had finally been finished earlier that day. Shiny gunmetal gray wallpaper and gleaming honey beige wood floors formed a subdued backdrop for the funky, mismatched bubble-gum pinks and maraschino reds of the dining chairs. A warm, beechwood bar paralleled the back wall, while seductively lit bottles of alcohol perched on the shelves behind it. Huge, vivid portraits suspended from the high ceiling added a sense of drama.

I'd commissioned the new artwork for the dining room from an up-and-coming student painter at Chicago's Art Institute. I'd asked for something that would "put Chicago's past and present in perspective," instructions the artist took quite literally. The canvases depicted famous Chicagoans, with a twist. One featured Oprah Winfrey and Harry Caray in vivid colors, pushing a miniature sepia-tone Al Capone in a baby carriage. Another had Michael Jordan and Jane Addams holding hands with a tiny, pigtailed Bugs Moran. The city's old-time gangsters were made into children—smaller than life—while its more reputable citizens were rendered as towering adults.

"You don't like it?" I asked.

"You got Capone up there with a pacifier and Pampers. Maybe you're playing with fire a little." Daniel wobbled his hand back and forth. "People can be touchy."

"It's art," I huffed. "I moved here to escape the grind of the city, but that doesn't mean I don't still love Chicago. Besides, who's going to defend the reputations of a bunch of crooks from a hundred years ago?"

Just then, Melody, our hostess, ducked through the vestibule and slipped past Daniel.

"Ready for the big day, chef?" Melody chirped in her cheery Upper Midwest accent. "I'm having, like, an excitement heart attack right now." Sometimes Melody's nonstop optimism grated on me, but I had to admit that my heart was feeling a little fluttery, too. She looked up at the newly installed artwork. "Cripes! Baby Face Nelson as an actual baby. Too funny," she squealed.

I raised my eyebrows at Daniel in a silent "I told you so."

"It's pretty edgy, 'n so?" Melody continued, using the Wisconsinese contraction for "isn't it so?" "People are still sensitive about that stuff." She removed her sunhat, sending her blond curls springing out in every direction. "My grandpa lives in Manitowish Waters—where the big Dillinger shootout was? Dillinger's gang went on the lam up there, took an innkeeper and his wife hostage, and shot six people. The whole town's still traumatized. Even a tiny, baby Dillinger would be . . ." Melody looked at me and dragged her index finger horizontally across her throat. She shrugged. "I'm sure it'll be fine, though."

Now it was Daniel's turn to give me an "I told you so" look.

An apron-clad Sonya burst through the kitchen door, carrying a steaming spoon in one hand and cupping her other hand under it. "I knew you'd need to taste it again, and change something, even though you tasted it literally five minutes ago."

"You make it sound like I'm some kind of crazed control freak." I looked to Melody and Daniel for support. Melody suddenly found urgent bits of napkin folding and centerpiece arranging to do.

"I need to get changed now," Daniel said, quickly slipping away toward the restrooms.

I grabbed the spoon from Sonya. Melody edged closer, still not making eye contact, waiting for my verdict. I took a slow sip of the sauce. I paused, letting the blend of garlic, oregano, basil, spices, and tomatoes meld in my mouth. "Perfect," I declared.

"Really?" Sonya asked. She tipped her head down and shot up a black-penciled eyebrow. "Nothing you'd change?"

"Nope, it's perfect." I bit my lower lip.

"Nothing?" She waved the spoon back and forth like an orchestra conductor's baton.

I shook my head, pressing my lips tightly together.

"Ok-a-ay," she sang, still looking doubtful. She turned back toward the kitchen, walking in slow-motion strides. With every step, she cast an expectant glance over her shoulder.

Just as she reached the kitchen door, I broke. "Maybe just a pinch more oregano," I blurted. "And by 'pinch' I mean three-quarters of a teaspoon."

"I knew it!" she said triumphantly. By now, Daniel had rejoined us, looking causally spiffed up for the evening's festivities in black trousers and a tight black T-shirt. He and Melody each handed Sonya five-dollar bills.

"I am *not* that predictable," I protested.

"I could set my watch by you," Sonya said with a wink.

It was hard to deny. Sonya and I had roomed together when we were students at the Chicago Culinary Institute almost twenty years before, and we'd overlapped in restaurant and hotel kitchens for years afterward as we climbed through the ranks. She probably knew me better than my actual sister did. When I decided to open my own place, Sonya was my first hire.

Sonya turned to head back to the kitchen, but stopped to say, "Hey, I noticed the new sign still hasn't gone up outside. Is it going to be ready in time?"

"I hope so," Melody added. "It's confusing for people that the Rocco's sign is still out there. I've already had a couple of sketchy guys drop by looking to put money on next Sunday's Cubs-Brewers game. I told them we just do pizzas now, not, you know, all that other stuff."

"Sam's taking care of the sign," I replied. "And for your information I haven't micromanaged him at all."

What I didn't say is that Sam and I had had a pretty epic blowup about me micromanaging every single other aspect of the restaurant, and that he'd gone as far as packing a bag and heading out the door a few weeks prior. In the past, when we argued, one of us—usually him—would quickly back down and apologize. While our personality clashes were nothing new—I was Type A and Sam was Type *Zzzz*—our arguments lately had taken on a sharper edge. Honestly, I was scared. Sam's unshakable calm had buoyed me through many a rough patch over the past three years. To prove that I trusted him and to prevent a breakup, I'd agreed to hand all the marketing over to him with the added concession that I would stay completely out of it.

Through the windows that overlooked the parking lot, we watched a large yellow truck emblazoned with the words Lundqvist & Son rumble to a stop. "Speak of the devil. I think that's the sign people now. Melody, can you run upstairs and let Sam know?" I held up my hands, palms out. "This is me, *macro*managing from a healthy distance."

Though I was dying to take charge of the sign installation,

I busied myself helping Daniel work out some kinks in the bar's electronic point-of-sale system while we waited for Sam. Sonya went back to the kitchen to get the first of the night's pizzas baking. Even in our blast furnace of an oven, the heavily layered pies would take at least thirty minutes to cook, so if we were going to be ready when guests arrived, the cooking needed to get underway. A few moments later, Melody came back, followed by Sam.

"Smells great in here. And looks great, too," my fiancé said, eyeing me up and down. "That's quite the dress."

He twinkled his toothpaste-commercial grin and let his gaze skim the low neckline of my dress. As he leaned in to give me an unhurried kiss on the lips, a week's worth of stubble grazed my cheek. His long, brown hair was gathered into a loose man bun on top of his head. The hairstyle had become an off-limits topic between us—he was strongly pro man bun, while I felt that it made him look like an out-of-work samurai.

Despite his less-than-fastidious grooming, it was hard to deny that Sam was a mouthful of man candy. We sometimes got looks from women on the street, radiating wonder at the fact that I—a freckly, queen-sized working-class gal with exaggerated facial features—had landed this stylishly disheveled hunk. And that was *before* they learned that Sam was a gazillionaire. Truth was, I didn't totally understand it myself. Closest I could come to an explanation was that mellow, passive Sam craved both my cooking and the whip-cracking structure I brought to his life. Our yin-yang dynamic, plus good, old-fashioned romantic chemistry, had gotten us through a lot.

Sam clapped his hands and rubbed them together. "Are you ready for the big sign reveal?" He moved his hands to my shoulders and squeezed, like a coach trying to pep up a player for the big game. His voice boomed out, "Sam and Delilah's Deep-Dish Pizza."

I'd initially been opposed to Sam's idea of having our names on the restaurant, thinking the play on the biblical Samson and Delilah was too kitschy. But everyone we'd run the idea past loved it, so in the end I'd relented.

"Looks like Butterball liked your outfit as much as I do," Sam smirked, pausing to pick at a thick cloud of creamy-yellowish fluff that clung to the dark material of my wrap dress.

Daniel, who was standing nearby, chimed in, "With the amount of fur that cat sheds, you'd think he'd be lighter."

I glared at Daniel. My staff knew that Butterball's weight was a point of contention between my fiancé and me. Sam, who'd brought the tubby rescue cat with him into our relationship, was forever trying to restrict Butterball's calories to get him to shed some of his excess tonnage. Even when Butterball bleated pathetically for nom-noms at four a.m. or stalked his food bowl like a prisoner of war, Sam's resolve held firm. I, on the other hand, had trouble controlling my natural chef's instinct to see that everyone is happily fed, and snuck treats to our famished fur-baby when Sam wasn't looking. I had to admit, though, that even I was beginning to find Butterball's increasing porkiness troubling. Recently, Sonya had mistaken the snoozing feline for a fur-covered footrest.

The push-pull of Sam constantly trying to rein in Butterball's diet and me constantly indulging him meant that our cat had a very obvious favorite parent; Butterball made his preference for me known by rubbing fur onto every piece of clothing I owned. Sam claimed that I'd stolen his cat's heart with an endless buffet of tasty bribes, the truth of which stung, especially since I often wondered if I'd won Sam the

same way. After all, food is love, but too much food is heart-
burn and diabetes.

Sam and I walked outside to find an ancient, rake-thin man
edging slowly out of the passenger's side of the sign truck.
Watching him climb down was like watching the Tin Man
from *The Wizard of Oz* try to move without being oiled. Seconds stacked into minutes as we waited for the old man to
fully dismount. The sun dipped lower toward the horizon. At
last, he creaked over to where we stood underneath the old
Rocco's sign.

He stuck out a cadaverous, liver-spotted hand for Sam.
"Tommy Lundqvist."

Sam returned the handshake. "I'm Sam Van Meter. We
spoke on the phone. This is my fiancée, Delilah O'Leary."

"That was my old man you spoke to. Tommy Senior."

I tried to catch Sam's eye. This relic was the "& Son" half
of Lundqvist & Son? Sam, for his part, didn't appear to register anything weird. That was his style. Sam could be watching our restaurant burn to ashes and he'd comment on how
cheerful and toasty fires are. When we'd met three years
earlier at a fundraising event I'd catered, his gentle, easygo-
ing nature had seemed like the perfect foil to my more . . .
structured personality. The months leading up to the restaurant launch had definitely been a test of the theory that op-
posites attract.

Tommy Lundqvist Jr. circled to the back of the truck,
where he was met by a man who, by the looks of him, could
probably have given a first-hand account of Moses parting
the Red Sea. With all the swiftness of sediment forming into
rock, the two of them lowered the truck's lift gate and rolled
open the rear door. I had to grip Sam's hand to keep myself
from jumping up into the truck and knocking them out of
the way. I was dying to see the finished sign, while Sam, as

usual, seemed content to let events unfold naturally. *I will not micromanage*, I repeated in my head like a mantra.

By now, Daniel, Sonya, and Melody had joined us outside. Finally, Lundqvist the Elder and Lundqvist the Even Elder hefted the cloth-wrapped sign onto the sidewalk in front of the restaurant.

"I'll get the ladder, Pops," Lundqvist Jr. said.

"Eh?" his father replied.

"I said, I'll get the ladder!" the son shouted as he walked back toward the truck.

Sonya gave her upper arms—one decorated with an image of a joyfully knife-wielding Julia Child and the other adorned with a rainbow jukebox surrounded by flowers—a brisk rub. "Is somebody going to unveil this thing or what?" she asked. "This lake breeze is going to blow my tattoos off." Thank goodness someone shared my impatience.

"Delilah, why don't you do the honors?" Sam ushered me forward.

Without a moment's hesitation, I pulled back the cloth to reveal our new sign: Sam and Delilah's Deep Dutch Pizza.

I blinked hard. "Deep *Dutch* Pizza?" I enunciated each word through clenched teeth.

"Um, Mr. Lundqvist," Sam said, tracing his fingers over the letters. "I think there may have been a mistake."

"Eh?" the older man said. His son rejoined the group, holding a ladder and a toolbox.

"This should say deep-dish pizza. Sam and Delilah's Deep-*Dish* Pizza," Sam explained, his voice even.

"I wondered about that," Lundqvist Jr. said, leaning the ladder against the exterior wall of the restaurant and resting his hand under his chin. "Pops is a little hard of hearing. We thought it was maybe one of them new fusion restaurants."

"A Dutch pizza place?" I tried to keep my voice calm, but

my fingers curled into fists. I forced my lips to constrict into an expression I hoped resembled a smile. "Sam, honey, you said you were taking care of this. You did double-check the proof, didn't you?"

"We'll get it straightened out. It'll be fine," Sam soothed.

I took a few steps to one side and motioned for Sam to follow me.

"It really won't be fine. We can get through the soft opening, maybe, but we're going to have to open to the public tomorrow with no sign, the old Rocco's sign, or"—I punched the air in the direction of the new sign—"*that*. We've got press coming later this week for a photo shoot. Couldn't you have found a sign maker whose age doesn't need to be measured in geologic time?" I hissed.

Sam's brow furrowed. "I'm sure you'll figure something out."

"So now that it's gone belly-up, *now* it's okay for me to take charge?" My voice rose to a pitch so high I half expected it to summon a pack of neighborhood strays.

Sonya appeared behind me and took hold of my shoulders, steering me into the restaurant before I could shift into full Hulk Smash mode.

While Sam remained outside talking things over with the sign makers, Daniel and Melody scuttled inside after Sonya and me.

"What on God's green earth is a Dutch pizza anyway?" I stormed, probably loudly enough to be heard through the plate glass windows. "A pizza topped with . . ." I searched the air with my hands. "I don't even know! What do Dutch people eat?"

"Tulips?" Melody ventured.

"Gouda?" Daniel offered.

"How am I going to—" My anger train screeched to a temporary halt. "Actually, Son, make a note to try aged Gouda on a pizza. That would be good with caramelized onions and wilted spinach."

"*Oui*, chef. Already doing it," she replied, pen and note-pad in hand.

The door of the restaurant swung open, and our server, Carson, loped in. He sported a pair of trendy headphones over his mop of blond-tinged curls. "I've gotta leave early tonight, okay?" he bellowed over the *thump-thump* of his music. "My friend's band is playing the Flat Iron."

Carson had been late to every training session since he'd been hired and had missed a mandatory health and safety briefing the day before because of a "scheduling conflict" with his intramural *Call of Duty* gamer league. I'd already tried to fire him twice, but Sonya had convinced me that we'd struggle to replace him this close to opening. Geneva Bay's high season kicked off the next weekend with the Memorial Day holiday, and finding reliable waitstaff was no mean feat. But tight labor market be damned, I pivoted to face the boy with balled fists, no doubt looking like some pagan Goddess of Anger. Sensing danger, Sonya signaled to Melody, who shuffled the oblivious server out of the dining room.

I heard the engine of the Lundqvists' truck start and looked up in time to catch Sam ambling toward the side of the building, where an external staircase led up to our apartment. Clearly, he intended to avoid me.

"Oh, hell no," Sonya mumbled.

Hell no, indeed. This was textbook Sam. Any time a conflict arose, he fled. Once, he'd sold his apartment and moved rather than simply asking the next-door neighbors to stop storing their bikes in the shared hallway. His conflict phobia made it impossible for the two of us to truly resolve disagreements. I raced out of the restaurant, rounded the corner, and rocketed up the stairs. I took them two by two, catching the door just before Sam closed it.

As I stomped into the entryway, Sam spun to face me with his hands on his hips. "You projected so much negativity toward Mr. Lundqvist and his son. I apologized on your behalf, but you should call them."

Butterball oozed around my legs, and I stooped to hoist the lovable lardball into my arms.

"You swore you'd take ten cleansing breaths before talking when you're mad," Sam continued. "What about those breathing exercises from the Ashtanga yoga retreat I took you on for your birthday? Did you even try the visualizations or cognitive reframing?"

"That's your takeaway from the situation? That I need to be more Zen? Because *my* takeaway is that I've been working my tail off for months to open my restaurant and you totally botched the one thing I put you in charge of."

"*Your* restaurant?" Sam said. He remained as composed as ever, but a harsh edge crept into his voice. "Did you forget who's bankrolling the whole thing?"

I gasped and took a step backward. I felt like I'd been slapped. "You said you wanted to . . ." Tears welled up as I struggled to form words. Sam had always insisted he was giving me the money so I could realize my full potential. I hadn't wanted to take his money, but he'd been adamant that I had a gift that I should share. I never thought he'd be the kind of person to hold it over me. I bit the inside of my lip. *O'Leary women don't cry. Crying is for weaklings.*

Sam took a step toward me. "I'm sorry, Dee." He reached for my hand, but I drew it back and tucked it into Butterball's fur. "That came out wrong. I only meant that you've never considered me a full partner in this. Sometimes, I feel like all I'm good for is my money. You'd never let anyone be a real partner."

The sting of his words seeped into my blood like poison.

How dare he? I'd fallen for him before I had any clue about his money. "You know I'd never use you," I growled.

"You're not listening to me," he said, throwing his hands in the air. He walked into our open-plan kitchen/living/dining room and perched on the edge of a bar stool at the kitchen counter.

I took a deep breath and began to count to ten. I got to about four before yelling, "Oh, I heard you, all right. Until you met me, you had zero direction. You kite-surfed and did ten different kinds of yoga and tended your man bun. You have no idea what it's like to really work for something. You had one good idea in college and you've been milking that cash cow ever since. As soon as you had to try running Third Base as an actual business, you sold it. This means nothing to you. If this restaurant fails, you'll just move on to the next thing. I'm not going to apologize, to you or to the Lundqvists. Getting angry is what normal people do when they care about something." Startled by the volume of my voice, Butterball leapt from my arms and landed with a graceless thud on the wood floor.

Sam stalked to the bedroom and pulled a suitcase from the closet. "You know what? You're right. It is your restaurant. Your dream. Clearly you care about it way more than you care about our relationship."

After an ungainly failed attempt, Butterball successfully launched his ample mass onto the bed. He looked back and forth with a forlorn *Why are Mommy and Daddy yelling?* expression in his wide, green eyes. Usually, Butterball was better at defusing my anger than the most seasoned hostage negotiator. This time, though, Sam and I both ignored our cat's baby doll gaze and continued our march down the warpath.

Sam pointed to the cat. "He gets it from you, you know."

"Gets what?"

"His anger issues."

"What are you talking about? He's a love muffin."

"To us he is." He pointed to Butterball's torn ear. "But he took a swipe at your aunt the other day, and he was in another catfight last week. He's very sensitive, and negative karma affects him."

"That fight wasn't his fault," I said, rushing over to cradle the cat. "That Maine Coon provoked him. You can't blame Butterball for standing up for himself. And my aunt can be very hostile toward him."

Sam let out a disdainful exhalation as he began to fill his suitcase with clothes.

"What are you doing?" I sputtered. I followed Sam as he walked to his dresser and gathered more things.

"I'm leaving. The new house is too much of a construction site for Butterball, so he'll have to stay here for the time being." Sam zipped his suitcase shut. He moved toward the door, but stopped to point to a container of bocconcini I must've left out on the counter earlier. "Were you feeding him cheese again? It gives him hairballs."

"Dairy doesn't cause hairballs. I googled it. Besides, fresh mozzarella balls are his favorite food," I bristled.

"Everything is his favorite food," Sam countered, wheeling his suitcase to the door.

"You're really going to leave now? We have sixty people arriving any minute for the soft opening. How's that going to look?"

Sam huffed again and rolled his eyes.

"What?" I demanded.

"Typical Delilah. I tell you I'm breaking off our three-year relationship and the only thing you're worried about is appearing less than perfect to the outside world."

"Typical Sam," I countered, "running away every time there's a problem without even trying to resolve it."

Sam paused and looked at me, his expression softening. "I wish you luck, Dee, I really do." His voice cracked, and his eyes brimmed with sadness. I reached out and took hold of his hand as he trailed his fingers along my cheek.

"Sam . . ." I began, pressing the smooth skin of his palm against my face.

He shook his head and pulled away. "I can't do this anymore. This time I mean it."

My mind searched for a counterargument, but even after the door had clicked closed behind Sam, I kept circling back to his accusation—that the only thing I cared about was the outward appearance of perfection.

Feeding my misery, I popped a couple of mozzarella balls into my mouth and walked over to where Butterball perched on a leather cushion in the bay window that looked out toward the lake. Together, we scrutinized the breaking waves. If Butterball was watching for Sam to return, I was pretty sure he was in for a long, fruitless wait. After months of low-grade squabbling in the lead-up to opening night, Sam's and my relationship had grown so brittle that a single typo was enough to shatter it.

The cat pawed the container of bocconcini in my hand and meowed loudly, his not-so-subtle snack-time cue. I resisted, thinking about what Sam had said. Maybe it was time to make some changes.

Butterball caterwauled and threw a series of kitty-paw uppercuts at the cheese. The small white mozzarella balls bobbed up and down in their packaging water like shipwreck victims. When I moved the cheese out of reach, he climbed over me, his hungry eyes trained on the container. Then he restarted his campaign of screeching and punching. We played this out three or four times. My resolve defeated, I broke off a nugget of cheese and fed him as he purred contentedly.

"There you go, Bud," I whispered. I stroked the cat's wide span of fur and buried my face in the soft folds of his body.

Suddenly Butterball sprang from my arms. His pink tongue poked from his mouth and his abdomen began a rhythmic gyration. He retched and hiccupped for a few seconds until at last a gelatinous mass of congealed hair and spittle splatted onto the leather cushion next to me.

Perfect.

CHAPTER 2

Despite the (literal and figurative) hiccups, by nine p.m., the soft opening was well underway. My staff—God bless them all, even Carson—had pulled things together. Pizza slices were being passed, champagne corks popped, and selfies taken. I'd selected a music playlist to orchestrate the vibe of the party, starting with jazz and acoustic classics to facilitate relaxation. We were now nearing a tempo change: Spice Girls, Lady Gaga, and Madonna to ramp things up. I felt, if not exactly calm, then at least tipsy enough to keep from having a total meltdown. Everything was back under control. I downed my glass of champagne and swiped another one from a nearby table.

"Where's that fiancé of yours? Shouldn't he be here?" Auntie Biz's voice cut through the background noise of the restaurant like a buzz saw through butter. Elizabeth O'Leary, aka Auntie Biz, weighed all of 92 pounds, but her voice had more decibel power than a trumpeting rhino's. She gripped my hands and pulled me down to the level of her wheelchair. Her strength always surprised me. "Your head waiter's a weasel."

"When did you get here?" I asked, dodging her provocations as I leaned in to kiss the papery skin on her cheek.

Her thinning white hair was puffed into a wispy dome, and someone—probably Jeremy, her caregiver—had applied *Whatever Happened to Baby Jane?* squiggles of lipstick and eyeliner to her pale face. "Where's Jeremy?"

"He's always disappearing somewhere. I've been here for over an hour," she said. "Stuck over in that corner facing a wall until the little blond girl rolled me out." She gestured toward Melody.

"Do you need a drink?"

"Based on your rosy glow, it looks like you're taking care of that for the both of us," Auntie Biz said.

"Where could Jeremy have gone?" I asked again. Questions about Sam and comments on the quantity of alcohol I was consuming were not on tonight's menu.

I hadn't seen my aunt's caregiver, but I assumed he must've brought her. I scanned the crowded room for Jeremy's balding, pink head and round, cherubic cheeks, but he was nowhere to be seen.

Auntie Biz had lived in Geneva Bay her entire adult life. In her prime, she'd traveled from her modest lakefront cottage all around town by snowmobile, rowboat, and cross-country skis, but now even walking to the end of her driveway was a challenge for her. She hadn't driven in almost a year, after having blacked out and wrapped her ancient Buick LeSabre around a fire hydrant, and summoning an Uber was light years beyond her technological capabilities. This was a woman who dismissively shunned "fancy gadgets" like microwaves and electric mixers. There was no way she'd gotten here under her own steam.

Although Auntie Biz acted sharp as a pin for the moment, her increasingly teeter-totter mental state was a big part of the reason I'd left Chicago for Geneva Bay. Auntie Biz, my father's aunt, was the last living relative on my dad's side of the family. My sister tended to give our cantankerous and outspoken relative a wide berth, but I had a sweet spot for the old gal. She was a fantastic cook, and had been extraordinarily patient with me as I discovered my love for cooking. I can still remember her standing me on a stool in her kitchen during one of our summertime lake visits—I must've been three or four years old—and letting me smell and taste every one of the four dozen herbs and spices in her spice rack. Even though she'd never admit to a human weakness like familial affection, I knew the affinity was mutual. One of the only times she'd left the state of Wisconsin in her life was a trip to see me graduate from culinary school.

In the past year or so, our weekly phone calls had revealed worrying slips in her memory. Instead of swapping recipes with me and mercilessly hounding me about my personal life, she'd begun to need more and more prompting to keep the conversation on track. Where just a few years ago she'd zipped all over town, she was now afraid of falling, afraid of thieves, practically afraid of her own shadow. The change broke my heart. The ever-solicitous Jeremy had been with her since her decline began—at first part-time—and he'd recently moved into the spare bedroom of her cottage to provide more support.

Even though I assured myself that Auntie Biz was in good hands with Jeremy and the local elder care agency he worked for, as she declined it felt more and more wrong to leave her totally dependent on hired help. She tolerated Jeremy's presence, but grudgingly. She'd never married and had no children. With my parents dead and my sister Shea wrapped up in her high-powered career and high-achieving children, it seemed natural for me to be the one to lend a hand. And Geneva Bay was a dream location to unfurl my pizza ambitions.

"Thanks for coming, Auntie Biz," I said, resting my hand on her shoulder. Her bones felt as delicate as spun sugar.

"Where else did I have to be?" she shrugged.

My sister hadn't been able to attend the opening, and I had yet to make any close friends in my new home, so despite her characteristic grumpiness, Auntie Biz's being there was especially meaningful. I'd mainly packed the room with vendors, fellow restauranteurs, and others whose presence I thought might confer some advantage to the pizzeria. This type of glad-handing came naturally to Sam. For me, it was the social equivalent of a Pap smear. I wanted desperately to throw on a hairnet and get elbow-deep into some pizza dough.

"There you are!"

I turned toward the sound of Jeremy's lilting, sing-song voice. He pressed through the crowd and knelt near us, taking hold of Auntie Biz's hand. He was out of breath and slightly sweaty. Jeremy was one of those round-cheeked men whose age is impossible to tell. Could be thirty. Could be fifty. Although he wasn't overweight, his body had a certain Jell-O-like formlessness about it.

"It's about time you showed your face," Auntie Biz snapped.

"I was getting your seltzer water, and I had to stand in line by the bar, and then I couldn't find you," Jeremy offered. He looked plaintively at me. "She never eats or drinks enough. I'm afraid one of these days a strong wind is going to blow her into the lake."

It was true. For a woman so passionate about cooking, Auntie Biz ate like a sparrow, never tasting more than a mouthful or two of whatever she made. If I had her self-discipline, maybe my clothes wouldn't be so snug.

Auntie Biz took a few sips from the proffered glass and then commanded, "Help me out of this contraption. I've been staring at butts all night."

I hooked my arms under my aunt's armpits and guided

her into a standing position, as Jeremy tucked Auntie Biz's wheelchair away behind a nearby table. She steadied herself against me, planting her feet firmly underneath her. Auntie Biz was still capable of walking, but with her increasingly frequent dizzy spells, we'd insisted on the wheelchair as a precaution.

"I didn't mean to be gone so long. I got caught up with—" Jeremy began.

"Elizabeth, my dear! You look marvelous. And Delilah, this little place is just darling." A well-manicured older woman had elbowed her way through the crowd in Jeremy's wake. As she joined us, her floral perfume loudly announced its presence over the competing aromas of garlic and baking crust wafting from the kitchen. The dimensions, color, and gloss of her fawn-colored hair hinted strongly at a wig. Around her neck, she wore a string of faux pearls the size of ping-pong balls.

"Lois Gorman," Jeremy finished, with a smile so forced it bordered on rigor mortis.

I remembered now. Auntie Biz and Lois were part of a weekly duplicate bridge club that met at the Grand Bay Resort. I'd met Lois a few weeks before when I'd accompanied my aunt there. From what I could tell, no one, including Auntie Biz, seemed particularly fond of the woman, and yet she always seemed to be lurking around. When I'd commented on it to my aunt, she remarked, "When you get to be my age, all the good people are dead. You make do with whatever's left." I hadn't invited her, and I wondered how she'd even heard about the party.

Lois turned to Auntie Biz. "Isn't it sweet that my grandson and your grandniece are working together here?"

"Your grandson?" I scanned the room, confused.

"Why, yes. Carson is my daughter Tambria's boy. Didn't your aunt tell you?"

"I only listen to about a quarter, maybe half, of what Lois says," Auntie Biz deadpanned.

Lois laughed as if Auntie Biz had made a joke, but I saw no hint of a smile on my aunt's face. Lois wiggled her fingers in the direction of my negligent server, trying to catch his eye. That explained her presence—I'd told my staff they should ask their families to the opening. Carson's attention, however, was glued to Veronica Tanaka, the attractive consultant sommelier whose services I'd engaged to help Daniel build the restaurant's wine list. Carson was flagrantly hitting on the poor woman. She seemed decidedly unamused. Meanwhile, all around him, dirty plates stacked up and empty glasses went unfilled.

"I had no idea you and Carson were related," I said. *But clearly being irritating runs in the family*, I added silently.

Auntie Biz wobbled slightly. Before I could reach out, Jeremy's steadying arm was around her. "Have a little more water," he urged, offering her the glass. "Do you need to sit down?"

"Are you okay?" I asked. "Do you want something to eat?"

"Stop fussing. Of course I'm okay. It's stuffy in here. That's all," Auntie Biz replied.

A tight cluster of partygoers now blocked my path to the table where I'd parked Biz's wheelchair. "Carson!" I yelled, snapping to get his attention. "Bring my aunt's wheelchair over here, please."

I could practically hear the server's melodramatic eye roll as he broke away from Veronica and maneuvered the wheelchair near us. "My pleasure," he said, flashing a petulant smile.

"Thank you, sweetie," Lois said, patting her grandson on the arm.

I eased my aunt into her chair. "Maybe Jeremy could take you out to the boardwalk for some air?" I suggested.

"Are you sure that's a good idea?" Lois asked officiously. "It looks like rain."

"I'm sure it'll hold off. We'll be back in a jiffy," Jeremy replied.

I turned back to chastise Carson for ignoring his duties, but the slippery jerk was already gone.

"You're so lucky to have a fiancé who supports your hobbies," Lois said, watching Jeremy and Biz zigzag their way toward the door. "You hang on to that man. You don't want to end up alone in your old age like your poor aunt."

"My aunt isn't alone, Mrs. Gorman. She has Jeremy to look after her around the clock, and now I'm here, too. And this restaurant isn't a hobby," I said, smiling through gritted teeth. "It's a dream I've worked hard for my entire life."

"Still, it must be nice not to have to worry about money. I read somewhere that upward of sixty percent of restaurants fail in their first year, but you won't have that problem. And you must know that this town needs another restaurant like I need a hole in the head."

I opened my mouth, but before the creative string of expletives that were forming there could take wing, Sonya materialized at my side. "We need you in the kitchen, chef." She seized me by the shoulders and steered me away from Lois, through the press of bodies, and toward the bar. Magical Sonya. She seemed to have a sixth sense for when I was about to go ape on somebody. Without her, no doubt I'd have a body count higher than Al Capone's whole crew combined.

Sonya signaled to Daniel with a snap of her fingers. "Delilah needs a glass of wine. *Es una emergencia médica*," she said, easily slipping from English to Spanish to describe my medical emergency. Like most American restaurant workers, Sonya and I had learned to speak in the patois of French, English, and Spanish that grew out of the cultural mixing of the various kitchens' staff and the classical origins of many cooking techniques. Neither of us could write a word of proper Spanish or French, but we definitely knew a diction- ary's worth of Spanglish slang and foreign swearwords.

Daniel walked down the bar and stood in front of me. He leaned across, cradled my chin, and studied my face. I'd met the handsome Puerto Rican years before on a trip to San Juan. He'd been slinging cocktails out of a tiny beachside ca- bana and served me a piña colada so good it was practically a religious experience. We'd kept in touch on social media over the years, and I was delighted when he took me up on the offer to move to Wisconsin and bartend for my new res- taurant.

"What seems to be the problem?" Daniel asked. He peered into my eyes. "Looks like heart trouble to me."

I nodded. "Sam . . ." I swallowed hard. I'd given Sonya the rough outline of what had happened, but I wasn't prepared to say the word "breakup" out loud yet. "Sam and I . . ." My lip quivered. I tried again. Better to channel the pain I felt into something constructive. Like rage. "Carson's grandma called my restaurant a hobby. A hobby!"

Daniel put his finger to my lips. "Say nothing more. Wine can't cure this," he said. "This calls for a time-tested rem- edy I like to call"—he whipped a couple of amber-colored bottles off the shelf behind him—"hard liquor."

"Where does she get off?" I snorted. "Does she really think anyone opens a restaurant just for kicks?"

Sonya shook her head. "Some people, right?" She paused as she handed me the glass of whatever fiery potion Daniel had concocted. "Still, though, I did kind of wonder . . ."

"What?" I demanded.

"Well," she continued, "Sam was bankrolling this place, right? What does it mean, now that you two are—?"

"We've always gotten back together before," I said, interrupting her. My voice sounded hollow, the untruth of what I was saying obvious even to my own ears.

Sonya squeezed my hand. Even if I could've fooled myself, there was no fooling her. Sonya's romantic history was so checkered it could've doubled as a NASCAR flag. If anyone knew about bad breakups, it was her. "Dee, I know this is hard, but you need to protect yourself. He put a lot of cash into the renovations. What if he asks for it back? Did you guys have any kind of written agreement?"

"Sam's not the vindictive type," I said. *Or at least I hope he isn't.*

"Well, even if he doesn't come after what's already been spent, what about the future? How long can Sam be expected to finance his ex's restaurant? Even our optimistic projections forecast that it could be a year before we can cover our expenses and start turning a profit," she said.

I swallowed my drink in one gulp, letting the alcohol loosen my brain from its moorings. Truth was, I had no idea what Sam's leaving meant for the restaurant, but I was pretty sure it didn't mean anything good. No doubt what Lois Gorman had said touched a raw nerve because it hit too close to the truth. I knew all too well what the restaurant was up against. Without the cash-stuffed cushion of Sam's tech fortune, I could be out of business in a month.

"I'll take out a small business loan or something," I said. "Or I can sell my ring." I glanced down at the 3.5-carat vintage-style diamond and emerald ring Sam had given to me when he proposed. "It'll be fine."

Daniel poured me another drink, which I transported to my liver post haste.

While Sonya and I were talking, Melody had sidled up to the bar next to us. She waited until I had finished my drink, rocking back and forth on her heels. "Um, I'm sorry to interrupt. I can see that you're"—she looked at the empty glasses—"busy."

"What now?" I said, shoulders slumping.

"It's just that the dishes are stacking up and I can't get them cleared and refill the buffet fast enough by myself."

"Why isn't Carson helping? Don't tell me he's on a break," I said.

Melody grimaced. "I'm sorry. I don't want to be a tattle-tale."

I put one hand on each of her shoulders. "Spill it. Nothing you could say would make me angrier at him than I already am."

She shifted on her heels and hung her head. "Well, I think he went down to the dock with that woman who did our wine list."

Sonya shot me a look that was the visual equivalent of flame retardant. "Melody, honey, can you please go clear dishes on the patio? I'll be out in a sec to give you a hand." She watched the blond hostess bounce through the crowd toward the patio door and then turned to me. "Why don't you let me handle Carson?"

"Not a chance," I said.

I intended to stand up from the barstool in a very authoritative, commanding way. Instead, I listed slightly starboard, and Daniel had to stretch across the bar to realign me. I pushed past Sonya. "I have a can of whup-ass that's full to bursting, and it's getting opened on that little jerkwad right now," I said. "I'd rather have Butterball wait tables than look at Carson's smug little face for one more minute."

I rammed myself through the crowd, dodging the well-wishers who tried to congratulate me on the restaurant opening or compliment the pizzas. Suddenly, the music on my epic playlist was way too loud. The voices of my guests grated. The clinking of glasses and silverware sounded like an explosion at a cymbal factory. If I were being honest, the best place for me at that moment would've been submerged in one of those sensory deprivation tanks. But I wasn't being honest; I was being intoxicated, angry, and in deep denial about my relationship ending and the precarious future of my restaurant.

The floor seesawed a little as I walked, and the contents of my stomach threatened to travel upward rather than down, but I persevered. I was going to fire Carson if it was the last thing I did. Bursting out the door to the lakeside patio seating area, I stormed past the small clusters of partygoers who'd settled outside.

I stopped for a moment to get my bearings and let my eyes adjust to the darkness. The boardwalk that ran from the restaurant to the dock was dark, lit only by a wispy slice of moon and the globe lights strung around the patio. The lake swished uneasily as the wind changed direction. Inside my head, liquor-addled thoughts traveled at half speed. *What was I doing? Oh, yeah, kicking Carson to the curb.*

The nearby sound of a car's engine backfiring jolted my brain back into gear and set me off like a starting pistol. I shivered as a gust of wind kicked tiny darts of precipitation against the bare skin on my arms. Although the weather report had been calling for thunderstorms for several days, the predicted deluge had yet to materialize. I hoped the worst of the storm would hold off, because I was unsteady enough on my feet without adding wet terrain.

My eyes struggled in the low light. The shadows deepened as I moved away from the building toward the line of trees on the far side of the restaurant's parking lot, near the dock. One of my high heels slid between the wooden planks of the boardwalk and I nearly pitched forward. I managed to steady myself and pulled off my shoes, taking hold of them like a pair of nunchucks. *Must not break ankles until Carson is fired.* I didn't care if I had to walk barefoot across a river of flaming tar, this punk was getting what was coming to him. I teetered toward the dock as I scanned the area for Carson.

Sure enough, deep in the shadows of the dockside trees, I saw two figures pressed close together. It looked like one of them was already halfway to the ground. Ugh. Carson was handsome enough, but surely Veronica Tanaka could do better. She owned her own wine consultancy and, based on her designer clothes and the BMW X5 she drove, seemed to be doing very well at it. Why give the time of day to that worthless slacker?

"Ahem." I ostentatiously cleared my throat as I stepped toward them. "I need to speak to Carson. Now."

"Delilah?" The voice carried toward me by the wind wasn't Carson's or Veronica's, but it was all too familiar. What was unfamiliar was the hesitancy. The voice was meek, frightened, submissive. "Please, help."

My heart froze. I realized that the shadowy figures I'd seen weren't Veronica and Carson. The alcohol-induced haze promptly evaporated from my brain as I threw my shoes aside and moved into a full-on sprint.

I caught the tiny figure as she released her hold on the other person and staggered backward. Her companion slumped sideways and hit the ground at our feet with a thump. A flash of lightning ruptured the sky, and I could see with sickening clarity Jeremy, my aunt's sweet-natured caregiver, laying at my feet, his mouth agape, a little rivulet of blood running into the crease of his cherubic cheek. His eyes stared up into the cloud-filled sky, vacant, seeing nothing. A perfect circle of gore adorned his forehead.

Auntie Biz leaned into me and searched my face with help-less, puppy eyes. She held out a shaking hand. The glint of metal caught my eye as I reached out to take the object from her. A handgun, warm from her grip.

CHAPTER 3

Melody, Sonya, Daniel, Biz, and I hunkered down in the living room area of my darkened apartment. They looked as dazed as I felt. Through the floorboards, the singalong crescendo of my carefully selected party soundtrack was still thumping—Neil Diamond's *Sweet Caroline* slid into Queen's *Bohemian Rhapsody*. This was supposed to be peak party time.

The events of the previous hour cycled through my brain like a demonic slideshow. Jeremy's slumped, lifeless body. Auntie Biz collapsing into my arms. Me screaming for help, holding onto her and gripping the still-warm gun. Partygoers streaming from the restaurant and thronging around us in a horrified ring. Sonya cutting through the melee, ordering someone to call 9-1-1, and directing Daniel to carry Auntie Biz inside. Melody taking hold of my shaking hand and guiding me along after them. It wasn't until the apartment door had shut behind us that Melody pointed out that I was still holding the gun.

Now, across the open-plan living/dining room, I watched as a uniformed officer lifted the weapon with gloved fingers and dropped it into a plastic evidence bag. First responders filtered in and out of the apartment, while outside the burly, mustached officer who'd been the first one on the scene was probably still gathering home addresses and phone numbers from our guests before allowing them to leave. Flashing red and white lights signaled the arrival of an ambulance, presumably to take Jeremy away.

Officer Mustache had ordered Auntie Biz and me to stay put. Not that Auntie Biz was in any shape to flee anyway. The poor woman looked brittle as a dried-out husk, and we'd barely been able to get a word out of her. The paramedics concluded that she was stable enough for the time being to avoid hospital admission.

Butterball, with his usual knack for cozying up to people who weren't fond of cats, nestled against the curve of her hip and laid his paws across her midsection as she dozed in the armchair next to me. If she'd have been awake, no doubt she would have shooed him away, complaining about his fur getting everywhere and making her eyes water. My mouth formed a sad smile at the way his soft, bulky body sheltered my aunt's fragile little frame. I could never tell if Butterball's over-the-top affection for Auntie Biz meant he was trying to win her over or messing with her. Knowing him, probably both.

Sonya drummed her fingers on the arm of the couch, while Melody nibbled at a ball of bocconcini the size of a quail's egg. I watched for a moment as she took squirrely little bites of the soft mozzarella.

"I got those out for Butterball," I pointed out.

Melody put the cheese down and began to chew her thumbnail instead. "Sorry, I eat when I'm stressed."

I, too, was a stress eater, but as I considered Melody's petite size-2 frame, I couldn't help but think that her life must be about sixty pounds less stressful than mine.

I sighed and popped two cheese balls into my mouth. I let their creamy saltiness bathe my tongue. I used a larger and firmer mozzarella on most of my pizzas, but I'd have to figure out a way to incorporate these little orbs of deliciousness into the menu. *Maybe marinated in citrus and herbs and served as an appetizer?* I silently chastised myself. A man's dead body was being loaded into an ambulance just below. How could I be thinking about recipes at a time like this? *Maybe something with an arugula pesto . . .*

The officer who was holding the now-ziplocked gun removed his latex gloves, and Sonya whispered, "You should have thrown the gun into the lake."

I pivoted my glare from Melody to her.

"Trust me, having your fingerprints on a murder weapon is never a good look," she continued. "The cops'll twist you into knots and the next thing you know, you'll be doing twenty-five to life. You can't let them think they have anything on you."

"Well, they don't. I didn't kill Jeremy and neither did Biz," I huffed. I suppose I should've been more circumspect. After all, I'd literally caught my aunt holding a smoking gun. She had been a little addled lately, and she'd definitely grown increasingly cagey and suspicious. But I knew down to the bones of my baby toes that she was not a killer. I mean, this woman had taught me to coddle custards in a bain-marie and pamper my puff pastry into flaky divinity. She was the closest thing I'd had to a mother since my own mom died when I was twelve. If I'd had even a sliver of a doubt about Biz's innocence, it was tamped down seeing her slumped and helpless next to Butterball. No way would my fur-baby cuddle a murderer.

"I'm telling you," Sonya murmured. "Never talk to cops without a lawyer."

"We don't need a lawyer. We're witnesses, not suspects. We're going to tell the truth so this can all be cleared up quickly," I said.

"My cousin Seth could be up here in an hour," she countered.

"Your cousin Seth who hit on me outside the synagogue at your aunt's funeral?" I rolled my eyes. "No way I'm calling that smarmy ambulance chaser."

"Hold the phone," Melody said, practically bouncing off the couch. "Sonya Perlman-*Dokter*." She sounded out each syllable of Sonya's name. "You're related to *the* Dokters?"

I shushed her, and pointed to Auntie Biz, who was still slumbering.

"Who are the doctors?" Daniel whispered.

"D-o-k-t-e-r. Their last name," I explained. "You know when you're driving from O'Hare on I-94, those big billboards that say 'Medical malpractice? Time to call the Dokters!'? That's them. Sonya's cousin Seth and her uncle Avi."

Sonya continued, "They also do a fair amount of criminal defense. My mom and dad are lawyers, too, but they only do white collar stuff, like tax evasion and insider trading."

Daniel smirked. "So the Dokters are all lawyers."

Sonya crossed her arms again and shot Daniel a withering look. "Your last name, Castillo. That's Spanish for 'castle,' right? Unless your family is a bunch of Puerto Rican dukes and duchesses, I don't want to hear another word."

The Dokter/doctor thing had always been a sore spot for Sonya, especially given all the grief she got for becoming a chef instead of going into the family business.

I held out my hands, trying to calm the waters. "Focus, people. The fact is that either Jeremy shot himself or there was some kind of crazy accident." I lowered my voice, both to keep from waking Biz and to keep from being overheard by the policeman lurking in my kitchen, who seemed tuned in to our every word. "Or someone shot him and ran away."

Melody suddenly gasped and pointed to the floor. "What if it's them?"

Our eyes followed her finger to the wide-planked oak floors.

"Who?" Sonya prompted.

"The canvases on the ceiling downstairs." When we continued to look at her blankly, Melody hissed, "*The mob.* I told you about those guys asking about putting bets on the baseball game. What if 'friends' of Rocco Guanciale are trying to sabotage the restaurant?" Melody's voice sank to a whisper.

"Why would they? Rocco's been locked up for years. If any of those guys wanted to do something with this building, they would've done it a long time ago," I said. "It's not like this property was in high demand."

A knock sounded and the apartment door swung open, carrying in the smell of rain and a tall, well-built man. The new arrival held out his hand. "Detective Calvin Capone," he said. His voice was a slick, melty baritone.

As I shook his hand, I got a close-up look at his honey-colored skin, close-cropped black hair, amber eyes, and full lips. His jacket was speckled with rain. *Zing.* Touching his hand made me feel like I was swimming in a pool filled with champagne bubbles. Yes, I'd very recently discovered a dead body and broken up with my fiancé, but I'm not made of stone.

"Delilah O'Leary," I said.

"O'Leary? Like the fiery cow," Capone replied.

"What . . . How dare . . ." I sputtered, my cheeks reddening with a mix of anger and shame. It was true that my size-14 jeans had gotten a little tighter recently. In fact, the size-16 clothes I'd designated as my go-to monthly bloat wear were also a little on the snug side. And I would be the first to admit I had a temper. But a "fiery cow"?

"Your name," Capone ventured, offering a bemused smile. "O'Leary. Like Mrs. O'Leary's cow who kicked over the lantern and started the Great Chicago Fire. Sorry, I thought for sure you'd know the reference."

I quickly rearranged my features into something resembling politeness. In my fluster, I'd forgotten that the fire that had destroyed most of Chicago in the 1800s was supposed to have been caused by a high-spirited cow whose owner happened to share my last name.

"Without that fire," Capone continued, "Geneva Bay as we know it wouldn't exist. All the big-name Chicago families moved up here and erected their luxury getaways while the city was being rebuilt."

"Of course," I said, feeling myself relax a bit. "My sister and I used to get teased about it when we were little."

I'd never been questioned by a police officer before, and I hadn't known what to expect. Based on TV shows I'd seen over the years, I wasn't anticipating Capone's wry wit or calm, easy presence. And I certainly wasn't expecting him to be a straight-up hottie. Still, I tried to keep my guard up. In the neighborhoods I grew up in, cops weren't always seen as the good guys.

"I heard you're from Chicago, so I figured you'd know about the cow," Capone continued. "Blue Island, right?"

I nodded at the mention of the section of the city I hailed from. The name Blue Island sounded like some tropical paradise, when in fact it was a working-class neighborhood of modest bungalows, crisscrossed by train tracks and dotted with dive bars.

He placed his hand on his chest. "Hyde Park. Fifteen years with the CPD until I moved up here the summer before last." He scanned the room. "Is there somewhere private we can talk?"

His uniformed colleague, who I now realized had probably been tasked with keeping an eye on us until Capone arrived, touched the brim of his hat and promptly left, toting the bagged gun.

"We'll wait downstairs," Daniel said, nudging Melody, who otherwise seemed quite content to stay put and gaze at the gorgeous detective.

Sonya rose with them. As she passed me, she whispered, "Let me know if you want to lawyer up. And don't cop to anything."

CHAPTER 4

"Has your aunt said anything about what happened?" Detective Capone asked once the apartment door closed behind the departing trio. We both looked over to the armchair where Biz and Butterball slumbered. Butterball had cracked his eyes open when Capone came in, but Auntie Biz hadn't budged.

I shook my head. "She's been pretty out of it. The shock, I suppose."

Capone gestured for me to take a seat next to him at the kitchen island and opened up his laptop. "My colleagues who've set up camp downstairs already filled me in on the basics, but I'll need to speak to both you and your aunt. We can let her rest a little longer, though. Why don't we start with you telling me everything you remember?" He took a small device out of his pocket. "Okay to record this?"

I nodded. *You have nothing to hide*, I reminded myself. "I don't know where to start. It's like a nightmare."

"Of course. Take all the time you need."

I hugged my chest and shivered.

His brow furrowed in concern and he placed a hand on my arm. "You're like ice," he said. He walked over to the tea-kettle on the stove. "May I?"

I nodded. Usually, I was highly selective about who I allowed to touch my appliances, but watching him switch on the burner, locate a pretty china cup, and decant herbal tea leaves into a strainer bordered on hypnotic. I was used to seeing male cooks lumber around kitchens like gorillas or carry on like prima donnas. Capone was . . . effortless. Nothing showy. Nothing clumsy. No need to speak.

After a few minutes, he handed me a steaming cup. I inhaled the woody, sweet scent of it and instantly felt calmer. I hadn't realized how tight I'd been wound. Slowly, I began to speak, picking up steam until the story gushed out of me. Capone stopped me occasionally to clarify details and keyed in a few details on his laptop. Mostly, though, he sat very still, watching me. I thought that being questioned by a detective was supposed to feel like having a klieg light beamed into your face. Instead, Calvin Capone's attention felt like glowing firelight.

"And that's when my aunt handed me the gun," I finished, a little breathlessly.

He was silent for a long moment, waiting to see if I would add anything. "And nothing seemed out of the ordinary during the party? Did Jeremy seem frightened? Agitated?"

I thought for a moment. "He was a little . . . sweaty, maybe? And I did wonder why he'd left Auntie Biz marooned for so long. The line at the bar moved quickly all night." I shook my head. "It was pretty hot in there, though, and he wasn't in the best shape."

"Anything else odd or unusual?"

I raked over the coals of my memory. "I really don't think so."

"I noticed security cameras at the doors," Capone said. "Those working?"

I nodded. "Sam set them up. All the footage is stored in the cloud. I'm not very tech-savvy, but I think you can download a copy of anything you need." Capone pushed his laptop across to me and watched as I accessed the website. I scrolled through the time-stamped reels until I found the relevant hours.

He took over the mouse. "Looks like you can see people walking from the front out onto the patio, but can't see them once they're out there."

He let a section of video play. Jeremy came into view, wheeling Auntie Biz out the door and captaining her wheelchair toward the shore path, but the two of them quickly disappeared from the frame. I swallowed hard. The clip couldn't have been more than two seconds long. The last two seconds that would ever be recorded of Jeremy's life. The poor guy had no idea he was minutes away from his doom.

I spun the screen away, regretting having watched that clip. It would no doubt be burned in my memory along with all the other horrors of the night.

"That's right," I said, bringing my attention back to the matter at hand. "The cameras only monitor who's coming in and out of the doors. They're to deter after-hours break-ins. I didn't see any reason to set up cameras outside to watch the diners while they're eating on the patio. Once people are outside, they're out of range pretty quickly," I explained. "It's the same behind the restaurant. You can see the back door and a little bit of the dumpster, but that's it."

"Still, it should be helpful to know who was out of the building when the shooting took place," he said.

"It may not capture everyone," I said. "The patio is fenced in, but there's a gate that leads straight from the parking lot to the patio. Once we open, we plan to have that latched so that diners have to come inside to the hostess stand to be seated. But that night we had it unlatched and open. That's the route I took when I went down to the shore path."

"I see," he said. "It's possible some of the partygoers never went inside at all. They could've gone straight from their cars to the patio. And it's possible someone who was on the patio could go straight to the shore path without passing through the camera's view."

"Right. Unless they wanted a drink from the bar or had to use the bathroom, they could have stayed outside the whole night. We had a buffet station set up out there in addition to the one inside. And maybe whoever shot Jeremy wasn't at the party at all. Maybe someone was hiding in the trees down by the shore path," I said. I desperately hoped Jeremy's death would turn out to have no connection to my restaurant.

"Good to keep an open mind," Capone said. He slid the laptop back toward himself, and looked at it for a moment. Then he steepled his fingertips under his chin. "Thank you. I appreciate your time."

"Uh, you're welcome," I replied.

I suddenly felt exposed, almost as if I'd been dumped after a promising first date. I realized I'd told Capone *everything*—my anxieties about opening night, my anger at Carson, even the details of my breakup with Sam. I'd agreed to have my apartment searched and to bring Biz down to the station so we could both be fingerprinted. He had soothed me into some sort of obedient trance. I probably would've let him read my junior high school diary if he'd asked. I should have listened to Sonya.

"Delilah?" a weak voice called from the couch.

"Auntie Biz." I rushed to her side. I helped her sip some water, and eased a pillow behind her back.

Butterball shifted from his sentry post next to Biz and edged cautiously toward the detective, who crouched down to cat level. Capone held out a hand, rubbed his fingers together, and waited for the cat to approach him. "Hey, pretty kitty," the detective soothed. "Who's a good kitty?"

Butterball, sucker for flattery that he was, was immediately won over. He pressed his head into Capone's hand, purring shamelessly. I'd have to talk to him about playing it cool. Then I'd have to have the same talk with myself.

"You must be Elizabeth O'Leary," Capone said, rising to greet Auntie Biz. "Detective Calvin Capone."

"Ah, I heard about you a while ago from the girls at my bridge club," Auntie Biz replied, her voice taking on a smidgeon of its customary pep. "Scarface's great grandkid, right?"

"I'm sure the name's just a coincidence," I began apologetically, certain that Auntie Biz must still be drowsy and confused. Of course, I, too, had noticed the detective's last name, but what were the odds that a direct Al Capone descendent would be here, in Geneva Bay, investigating a murder outside my organized-crime-themed restaurant? Surely, Calvin Capone was no more related to Al Capone than I was to Mrs. O'Leary and her flaming cow.

"No coincidence, I'm afraid," Capone answered. "My dad was Al's grandson. I never met either one of them. My father died before I was born, and of course the big man himself died in the forties."

"Oh," I sputtered, realizing with horror that Capone had mentioned speaking with his colleagues downstairs. He must have been in the restaurant dining room. "The artwork," I sputtered. "With Capone as a baby. I didn't mean any offense." Clearly, Daniel and Melody had been right to warn me that the gangster connections might be fresher than I'd realized. The chiseled hunk before me shared a significant slice of DNA with the chubby-cheeked Mafioso in the painting right below our feet. I squinted. Maybe the dreamy full lips I'd attributed to some exotic ancestor actually came from his notorious great-grandfather.

"I made peace with it a long time ago. I was raised by my mother, who's a perfectly law-abiding jazz singer."

"Wait a second, is your mother Lola Capone?" I asked, my mouth dropping open. "When I lived downtown, I used to go to the Green Mill sometimes after work to listen to her. I'm not much of a jazz buff, but her voice is something else."

"That's her all right. She still sings three nights a week in the city. Lives here with me the rest of the time. I like to think that all I inherited from the Capone side was the name."

"That's quite the pedigree," I said. "My parents' only claim to fame was winning the St. Donatus Parish couples' bowling league trophy three years running."

"Notoriety isn't all it's cracked up to be. You're better off inheriting bowling skills than the name of the world's most famous criminal." His fingers unconsciously brushed across the badge that hung from a chain on his neck. He directed his attention back to Auntie Biz. "Are you up to telling me what happened, ma'am?"

"Can't it wait until tomorrow?" I asked. "She's been through a lot, and she hasn't been in the best of health."

"I'm afraid not. A man is dead, and your aunt may have been the last person to see him alive. Either we can talk here, or I'll need to take her down to the station." He softened, no doubt seeing the shock on my face. "I wish it didn't have to be like this, but I need her to try to remember while everything is still fresh."

"Can I at least stay with her?" I asked.

Capone paused and then nodded. "Promise to stay quiet, okay?" He settled onto the couch near Biz. "Do you need a glass of water? Another blanket?" he asked her.

She shook her head. "No. Let's get this over with."

I held my breath as she began to recount her story. Although I was sure she couldn't have killed Jeremy in cold blood, I also had no idea what she was going to say. What had happened in those terrible moments between the time they left the restaurant and the time I found them? Slowly, she related the events she could recall—getting ready for the party, being wheeled into a corner and stranded there, Jeremy pushing her along the lakeshore path in her wheelchair. The whole thing felt like a hideous countdown. Mundane event after mundane event building toward the horrific finale that Jeremy never saw coming.

"Just as we turned toward the dock . . ." She paused for a long moment and closed her eyes. I could almost feel her scraping the walls of her brain, trying to unearth an elusive nugget of memory. "Jeremy saw someone at the edge of the woods," she said, her eyes still closed. "He called out, 'Who's there?' Then he said, 'Oh, it's you.' I think he walked toward the woods, and then . . ." Her face clouded. "Then I heard the shot."

"Could you see anyone?" Capone asked.

"No. My chair was facing the lake." She paused, her brow furrowing.

"He didn't say a name, or give any indication of who it was?"

"No. Just 'Oh, it's you,' and he stepped toward the person, then I heard the shot. I'm not sure what happened after that. I'd been feeling a little woozy. Maybe I blacked out?"

Capone paused for a moment, making notes on his laptop. In the silence, the reality began to sink in. Someone else had been there. So much for my theory that the shooting was a suicide or an accident. Murder was looking like the only possibility.

"What's the next thing you remember?" Capone asked.

"My gun was in my lap and I held onto it. I pushed up out of my chair, walked to where Jeremy was. He had sunk to his knees, and I saw that he'd been shot. Then he flopped to the ground right at my feet. I guess that must been have when you showed up, Delilah."

"*Your* gun was in your lap?" I blurted out. "*Your* gun?"

"One of my guns, yes," she sniffed. "My Beretta. I recognized it right away."

I looked at Capone, but he betrayed only the merest hint of an eyebrow raise. By contrast, I was pretty sure my eyes bugged out like a Looney Tunes character.

"*Your* gun?" I repeated.

Capone held up a steadying hand. "If you don't mind, Ms. O'Leary." He turned his attention to Biz. "Please, continue."

"I have no idea how it got into my lap," Biz said indignantly. "I always keep the Beretta in my purse and the shotgun and the twenty-two locked out in the shed. I haven't been hunting in years, so those stay out there in the gun safe."

Capone picked up his laptop again and clicked the mouse pad a few times. "Is that your purse? Hanging on the back of your wheelchair?"

I peered over their shoulders, and saw that the image on the screen was taken at the crime scene. Thankfully, it was a close-up of the wheelchair, and nothing else was visible.

"Yes, that's my purse," Biz confirmed.

"And you're sure you didn't remove your gun?" Capone prodded.

Auntie Biz shook her head. "No, I didn't."

"And no one to your knowledge removed anything from your purse?"

Again, she shook her head. "No."

"You weren't in your wheelchair the whole night, remember?" I interrupted. "Right before you went out, you got up to stretch your legs for a few minutes and I rolled it out of the way." I turned to Capone, my voice verging on desperation. *If the murder weapon was really my aunt's, there had to be another explanation.* "Anyone at the party could've taken the gun."

Capone shot me another warning look for butting in, but I noticed that he typed a note on his laptop.

"How long have you been carrying a gun?" he asked.

"My whole life. I have a permit, you look it up and you'll see. I'm a single lady and these roads get dark at night. Rocco Guanciale wasn't the only lowlife that ever called Geneva Bay home. When I was younger, we had bears, too."

"She used to walk everywhere," I explained.

"Who knew that you kept a gun in your purse?" Capone asked her.

"No one," Biz said.

"Not even Jeremy?" Capone prompted.

She shook her head vigorously. "He wouldn't have let me keep it if he'd known. When I told him about the hunting guns in the shed, he took the keys. For safekeeping, he said."

"Well, he was right," I said.

"That's enough from you, missy," she snapped.

"And you're sure it was in your purse this evening?" Capone asked.

"I always bring it when I go out. Someone went through my purse. That's the only explanation."

"Was anything else missing?" Capone asked.

"I don't think so," her voice wavered a little. "I'll have a better look when I'm less tired. It's time for my pills." She curled her fingers around the edge of the blanket and pulled it over her chest. "I've told you everything I remember. I didn't do it, and I don't know who did."

"Just one more question, please. It's a short one," Capone said, "but it's important. Did you trust Jeremy?"

Auntie Biz thought for a long moment, dropped her gaze and then said simply, "No."

The word hit me like a sucker punch. How had I left my aunt in the care of someone she couldn't trust?

"Can I ask why not?" Capone said.

"He was a faker," she said, her voice growing quieter. "Treated me good as gold when we were in front of people, but back at home, he was usually looking at his phone or swanning off on little errands that I didn't send him on." She met my worried gaze. "He wasn't unkind to me. Nothing like that. My meals were on the table on time and the house kept clean. But he was"—she searched for the word— "phony."

"Why didn't you say anything?" I asked.

"I can handle my own affairs. You had enough going on without having to worry about me." Auntie Biz lifted her chin and thrust out her thin chest. The look on her face wasn't one of pride, though. It was far away, lonely.

In the silence that followed, a heavy brick of guilt settled into my stomach. Once my sister and I had helped Auntie Biz settle on Jeremy as her caregiver, I'd taken their arrangement for granted. Jeremy had come highly recommended and had an impeccable résumé. When my aunt needed more care a few months back, and Jeremy suggested that a live-in situation would be better, I'd encouraged her—no, I *pushed* her to accept it. I was busy with my job, the new restaurant, and with Sam, and my batteries were drained by the aftermath of my father's death. I'd wanted to get her situation settled so I could tick it off my to-do list.

I'd visited Auntie Biz as often as I could, which, if I was honest, wasn't all that often. She didn't seem very fond of Jeremy, but that was natural enough. Of course someone as independent as Auntie Biz would object to having a stranger living in her home taking care of her needs. I hadn't wanted to pry into their arrangements, I'd told myself. Truth was, I hadn't wanted to know. Deep down, I, too, had sensed that Jeremy wasn't as great as he seemed. Part of my reason for moving to Geneva Bay was to be able to supervise things with Auntie Biz's care a little more closely. But once I'd arrived, I'd stayed busy and stayed out of it, for the most part. Fundamentally, I knew I'd ignored my gut so I could get on with my own life. Hearing this strong, feisty woman describe her misgivings about her caregiver so meekly, almost fearfully, made me realize that I'd left her powerless in the hands of a stranger. The little brick of guilt in my stomach grew into a cinder block.

Biz's voice cut through my dark thoughts. "Now, Detective Capone, if you're not going to arrest me, it's late and I'd like to go to bed." She squeezed her eyes shut and turned her face away from us.

Capone clicked off his voice recorder, closed his laptop, and rose, signaling for me to follow him to the kitchen area, as far out of earshot as we could manage in the small apartment.

"What happens now?" I said.

"Your aunt is right. It's late. You should both get some sleep."

"So that's it?" I asked, dumbfounded.

"For today," he replied. "We'll know more in the morning."

"You're not going to arrest us?"

He arched an eyebrow. "Should I?"

"Well, no. I mean I didn't do it, and there's no way Auntie Biz could've, either. There must be some mistake about the gun. Maybe it just looked like her gun."

He nodded but said nothing. I should've felt relieved that

Capone had treated us so well, but I couldn't shake the feeling that behind those beautiful amber eyes, his wheels were spinning a hundred miles an hour. He maintained the same calm, open expression he'd had since he walked in. I'd seen brick walls give away more than he did. I didn't expect him to spill the location of Jimmy Hoffa's body or anything, I just wanted some indication of what he was thinking and what was likely to happen. I wasn't used to being so completely clueless. He handed me his business card and took a few steps toward the door.

"You're just going to leave now?" I asked. Despite my earlier insistence that everything was going to be fine, deep down I wasn't convinced that an interrogation could be as simple as telling the truth and being believed, especially now that Auntie Biz had admitted to not only holding the murder weapon, but owning it.

"I'll leave an officer outside to watch out for you two," Capone said.

Watching us as much as watching out for us, no doubt. Why hadn't I listened to Sonya about getting a lawyer? Maybe because I'm as good at taking advice as I am at taking criticism. Which is to say, terrible.

"Thanks," I said, not really sure what I was thanking him for. Stationing a jailor outside my door?

"I'll see you soon." He shrugged his jacket over his broad shoulders.

Without thinking, I stepped toward him and plucked at the tufts of golden cat hair that flecked the dark blue material. The detective and I stood face-to-face for a moment, so close I could feel the heat from his body. "A token of Butterball's affection," I said, stepping back, willing my cheeks not to turn crimson.

Capone petted the cat, who had moved on to the back of

a chair near the door. "Thanks, big guy. Next time, you can just send flowers."

I hesitated, but as Capone turned to leave, I blurted, "You're probably going to think this is crazy, but my hostess thought maybe there could be some connection to the mob, or to Rocco Guanciale, given our location and all. Maybe it was a whack job." I paused, realizing the implications of what I'd said. "No offense to your forbearers."

"First of all, 'whack job'?" He raised an eyebrow. "Nobody says that. Second, there's no organized Mafia, no Cosa Nostra, in Geneva Bay. That kind of system requires a huge amount of violence and intimidation to maintain itself. What we have here in Geneva Bay, like in most places, is *dis*organized crime. People think the Chicago mob from the twenties and thirties was a well-oiled criminal machine—a crime version of Microsoft—but that's almost never the case when you're dealing with criminals. The criminal world is chaos. It's hard to run a smooth operation when your workforce is all violent people, desperate people, greedy people, amoral people, and, frankly, dumb people. Even if Jeremy's death was part of something bigger, I can promise you that the killer made a mistake. Probably ten mistakes. And we will find him."

He took a deep breath and put a hand on my arm. "I'll be in touch. Soon. Until then, be careful, take care of your aunt, and call me if either of you think of anything you didn't mention. The medical examiner only had a quick look at the body, but based on the angle of the shot, she was already thinking that suicide seemed improbable. You just heard your aunt say there was someone out at the dock with them, maybe waiting for them. Jeremy knew the person. You and your aunt both swore to me that you didn't pull that trigger. I hope that's true. But if it is . . ."

"Then there's a murderer on the loose." I searched his face. I was getting a little better at reading the subtle variations in his muted facial expressions, and I thought I saw a whisper of worry behind his eyes.

CHAPTER 5

I pried my eyelids open one at a time and then slowly peeled my sweaty body off the couch. The wall clock read eight a.m., and the morning sun blazed in through the cracks in the curtains.

I had a patchy recollection of Daniel, Sonya, and Melody coming back upstairs after they'd been interviewed by Detective Capone. Seeing the concern on my face, Daniel had offered to stay over. In addition to being a world-class drink-slinger, he'd recently finished a six-year stint in the Army National Guard. He knew how to handle himself in a crisis. As appealing as the thought of a buff ex-soldier as my personal bodyguard was, I shooed him and the others out. I just wanted to lock the door and be alone. Well, almost alone. Biz and Butterball had settled into my bed, and were so deeply asleep at that point that they practically counted as furniture.

I reached for my phone on the coffee table, half hoping there would be a message from Sam. Although I was still fuming after our blowup yesterday, I craved his unshakable calm. I had never quite learned to believe him when he told me everything was going to be all right, but hearing the words would've done me a world of good right then. My phone held the usual garbage notifications from social media, but nothing from Sam. I supposed he was holed up in the new house, probably breaking in his custom-designed yoga and meditation room. The only real message was from Sonya, asking me to call her when I woke up.

I zombie-shuffled to the espresso machine and made myself a double. I inhaled the bright, woody scent of the coffee, hoping it would rouse my sluggish brain. I had a feeling it was going to be the first in a continuous line of caffeinated beverages that day. Once I'd downed my caffeine, I tiptoed to my bedroom and peeked in through the door. Biz and Butterball were curled up together, their breathing synchronized.

I returned to the living room, retrieved a stack of financial papers that included the restaurant's invoices and profit and loss statements, and opened my laptop. I set everything on the coffee table as I sipped my second espresso. Usually, once I'd gotten the necessary jolt from my first cup of coffee, I savored my second cup, noting how subtle differences in the grind affected the taste. Today, though, I was too distracted for my customary tasting ritual. A glance through the restaurant's QuickBooks accounts left me queasy. Sonya had been right—without Sam around to bankroll the restaurant, we were in dire straits. I clicked over to the restaurant's social media accounts, updating them to announce that our grand opening had been postponed. Until when, I had no idea. Even once the detectives finished hunting for clues, I couldn't imagine anyone wanting to eat a meal while looking out on a fresh crime scene.

My stomach sank as I realized that all the marketing and promotion we'd set up had been under the "Sam and Delilah's" brand. That would need a rethink, too. Which meant spending even more nonexistent money. Maybe the Dutch pizza sign mix-up had been a different kind of sign—an omen of doom. I was definitely in deep *something*, and it sure wasn't deep-dish pizza. Next, I texted the reporter who was doing the feature on the restaurant's opening to let her know that now might not be the best time for a big photo spread in the local paper. Who was I kidding? We were probably all over the local paper anyway, and not on account of our enticing menu.

"Delilah?" Auntie Biz called in a shriveled little voice.

I hurried to the bedroom and perched on the edge of the bed. Butterball immediately moved to my lap and began a frantic chorus of mews. I recognized the pattern as his hunger cry. Usually, his "Starvation Anthem" started around four a.m. and escalated in volume and desperation until five thirty or six when either Sam or I finally got up to feed him. This morning, though, I had fuzzy memories of batting him away and pulling a pillow over my head. I must've been practically comatose for him to give up on his demand for nom-noms.

"How are you?" I asked my aunt.

"Feeling like something the cat dragged in," Auntie Biz said, shifting up to a sitting position. She still had the slightly gray, sickly look she'd worn the previous night, but I thought I could see a glimmer of light in her eyes. I made her sip a little water as Butterball snuggled up by her legs.

"Butterball isn't allowed to drag anything in," I said, giving him an affectionate pat. "At least not until he heals from his last brawl." I gently took his face in my hands to show Biz where a chunk was missing from his ear.

"Got your butter-butt kicked, eh, cat-so?" Biz said.

"He's always on the losing end." I turned my attention to Butterball. "Sam says you have anger issues, but you're a lover, not a fighter, aren't you, Bud?"

"Maybe the other cat was making fun of him for being a mama's boy."

I ignored her and continued, "And you still love Auntie Biz even though she's mean to you and calls you names, don't you?" The cat let out a defiant meow.

"He only sleeps here because I'm a warm body. Cats will start eating their owners even before they're dead." She nudged him with her foot. "And this one looks like he could eat you and me both."

"You'll win her over yet," I said to Butterball, and then in a mock whisper I added, "She's just intimidated by your good looks." I rose and addressed my aunt. "I'll make you something to eat, and I should feed this beast. He didn't get any dinner last night. I don't think he's ever gone this long between meals."

I called to Butterball, who under normal circumstances would've knocked me over racing to his food bowl. Now, though, even though his eyes were signaling that starvation was imminent, he seemed reluctant to leave his sentry post at Biz's side even as she continued to try to nudge him away with her foot.

"All right, Butterbuddy," I said. "You can have breakfast in bed, too."

A quick survey of the pantry and fridge revealed that I was out of bread, butter, eggs, and just about anything else that would form the basis of a human or feline breakfast, unless I was planning to serve black coffee with a side of bour-bon. Good thing I had my very own fully stocked restaurant kitchen downstairs.

I was suddenly aware that I was still wearing my sexy wrap dress from the previous night. Mercifully, it didn't seem to have any bloodstains on it, but it was still one hundred percent destined for Goodwill. Last night was not a memory I'd ever want to relive. I pulled a pair of jeans and one of Sam's yoga T-shirts out of the laundry and threw them on.

"I have to run down to grab a few things for breakfast," I called to Auntie Biz. "Don't go anywhere."

"Where am I going to go?" she called back. "Waterskiing?"

I smiled as I climbed down the outside steps, glad to hear sass rather than helplessness coming out of her mouth. The morning sun soaked into my skin. With a sky as blue as this one, today had to be a better day than yesterday.

As I rounded the corner of the building toward the back door of the restaurant, I hit a thick fog of cigarette smoke and almost ran into the pale, wiry man at the source.

He turned toward me, his face etched with premature wrinkles. His eyes looked desperate and wary. My heartrate picked up speed, and my body stiffened. I didn't need any surprises today. And I didn't need scruffy mystery men hanging out next to my dumpsters.

In Chicago, I'd become a pro at shooing off the shifty people who often lurked in the back alleys of the restaurants and hotels where I worked. I'd seen fifty shades of shadiness—dealers, drunks, and ne'er-do-wells of unspecified provenance. If the alley-lurkers seemed like they just needed to catch a break, I might give them a to-go box and send them on their way. If they seemed menacing—well, I'm not a small woman, and I can usually be found with a sharp knife in my hand. I'm not fearless by any means, but growing up where I did and choosing the career I had, you learned to carry yourself.

That morning, though, I wasn't feeling up to bluster or confrontation. I thought I'd left the grittier parts of city living behind when I moved to Geneva Bay.

"Can I help you?" I demanded.

The guy quickly stubbed out his cigarette and removed his baseball cap, revealing a graying buzz cut and a receding hairline.

"I'm Rabbit, uh, Robert. Robert Blakemore. Lots of people

call me Rabbit," he stammered, thrusting out his hand. The gesture was so awkward I guessed Rabbit wasn't in the habit of shaking hands. He looked around. "Do you know a guy named Sam Van Meter? I'm supposed to meet him about a dishwashing job."

I sighed. Of course. In addition to marketing, Sam had been in charge of hiring a dishwasher/busser. His first hire had ghosted after two days, his second one's roving hands "accidentally" bumped into Melody one time too many. Not that the poor HR track record was all Sam's fault. Restaurants aren't particularly known for employing a legion of saints. The work is hard, the hours are long, and the pay is usually rotten. Dishwashing, being at the bottom of the restaurant totem pole, can attract even more rough-and-ready types than the rest of the industry. I'd started my restaurant career as a washer/busser, and I knew it took a special kind of glutton for punishment to stick with the job.

Why couldn't Sam have remembered to get in touch with Rabbit to reschedule? Or at least have given me a heads-up? Sam wasn't exactly Mr. Attention to Detail, but it wasn't like him to go completely AWOL. Then again, none of our previous breakups had ever seemed so final.

"I'm Delilah O'Leary, the chef." I opened my mouth to explain that we weren't going to need him after all, since our grand opening was indefinitely postponed. Before I could get a word out, though, he launched into a monologue.

"The agency sent me over. I'm real grateful for the opportunity. Not many people will give convicts a chance, and we got bills to pay same as everyone else. I got a kid, too—Everleigh, she's six—and her mom's after me for child support. Says she'll get my visitation rights taken away if I don't pay up. I must've applied for fifty jobs or more. Before I got the call for this, I didn't know how I was gonna get the money together . . ." He trailed off, but immediately picked back up. He tugged a folded piece of paper out of his shirt pocket and handed it to me. "That's my résumé. I was assigned to the kitchen at Oakhill, so I got five years' experience. I can even cook a little, if you ever need me to."

Oakhill. I recognized the name of the correctional institute a few counties over. I also recognized the desperation in Rabbit's eyes. They were green and round, the way Butterball's get when he *needs* nom-noms.

I ran my eyes down the crumpled paper. Rabbit was upfront about his criminal record; he had a variety of convictions—shoplifting, arson, a drug offense—so I supposed he wasn't wrong to list "flexibility" and "willingness to do anything" as strengths. As references, he'd listed his AA sponsor, a parole officer, and his mother. I sighed again. Sam was always the softie in situations like this, but a pang of conscience zinged my solar plexus at the thought of unceremoniously kicking Rabbit to the curb. I at least owed him an explanation of why I couldn't hire him now.

"Let's talk inside," I said. "I've got to make breakfast for an old lady and a cat."

He raised his eyebrows, but followed me inside without a word.

Sonya had come back downstairs to put the food away and tidy up after the police left last night, but here and there, little things were out of place. A heap of white side towels lay unfolded on the counter. The pizza pans were stacked off-kilter and in uneven numbers. The kitchen was Sonya clean, but it wasn't Delilah clean. Through some sort of OCD telepathy, Rabbit moved to the heap of towels and began to fold them, quickly and meticulously.

"I'll just get these," he said. "Don't know about you, but I get a weird feeling when there's a mess that needs cleaning. Gives me a sense like something cold touching my teeth, n' so?" He grimaced at the imagined sensation.

"Exactly so," I replied, with a knowing smirk.

I sorted out the pans and wiped up a few stray splatters from the stove, while Rabbit folded and tidied. Once everything sparkled, I could begin breakfast prep. I moved around the kitchen, firing up the gas stove, cracking eggs into a bowl, seasoning them, and whisking them until they foamed. The added air gives scrambled eggs a fluffy texture, which I amped up even more by adding a teaspoon of water to the pan. Next, I laid a piece of leftover Italian bread under the broiler to toast.

"Want me to grab some juice or something?" Rabbit asked. "Since you're making breakfast?"

"Uh, sure. There should be some in the fridge behind the bar."

Rabbit disappeared through the swinging door and re-emerged a few moments later with a tray laden with glasses of orange and pineapple juice, along with a dish of kiwi, mint, and strawberries he must've put together from Daniel's cocktail garnish and infusion stash. He'd folded a napkin into an elaborate fan and even included a little arrangement of flowers taken from one of the floral centerpieces that had adorned last night's buffet table. Setting the tray on the prep counter, he began wiping down surfaces and tidying away the debris of the party.

"Who's the old lady you're cooking for, chef?" Rabbit asked.

"My aunt Elizabeth."

His eyebrows pressed together. "Hang on a minute. Your name's O'Leary, ain't it? Your aunt isn't Miss Elizabeth O'Leary is she? Who taught GED classes at Oakhill?"

I nodded. Up until her recent decline, Auntie Biz's active post-retirement schedule had included volunteer teaching at the prison.

"I can't believe she's your aunt. She's the reason I got my

life together," Rabbit continued. "Well, her and Everleigh. Miss O'Leary made me feel like maybe I was worth something after all."

Dang. This man must've earned a music degree in playing the heartstrings along with his GED. The longer I waited, the harder it was going to be to send him packing.

"Here's the issue, Rabbit," I explained, as I mixed together a bowl of Butterball's favorite breakfast combo: salmon chunks with chicken livers. "We had an . . . incident here last night."

"The shooting." He nodded his head solemnly.

"How did you know about that?"

"Word gets around Geneva Bay fast," he said. "And even if I hadn't already heard from Jeff at the Quik Stop, I'd probably have guessed that something wasn't right when I saw the crime scene tape over by the dock. Plus, it was on the front page of the paper, a big headline about a possible homicide at Rocco's."

So I'd been right about the local paper picking up the story. I started to correct Rabbit about the restaurant's name, but I realized it was pointless. Hard to believe that up until yesterday, the idea of being associated with crime seemed part of the attraction of this property. I thought about all the gangsters on the dining room artwork. Ugh.

"You can see the problem," I said. "I don't know when we're going to be able to open. And without any customers, we're not going to have any dishes to wash." Seeing no change in his expression, I added, "We also have good reason to believe the murderer is on the loose. It might not be safe here."

"I shared a cell with a murderer for two years. Killed his boss in cold blood and shot one of the cops who tried to bring him in." He opened the broiler, and slid the toasted bread onto a plate. He pulled two condiment cups off the shelf. After digging in the fridge for a moment, he filled one with butter. "To be honest," he said, continuing to rummage in the fridge, "I almost didn't show up this morning after I heard what had happened. The last thing I need is to get mixed up with a murder. If I get caught associating with felons, my parole officer will have me back inside before you can say . . . fig jam." He pulled a jar of the sticky preserves out of the fridge, filled the other condiment cup to the brim, and added it to Auntie Biz's breakfast platter. "So I hope nobody here pulled that trigger. But, like I said before, I need this job real bad, so it's a risk I gotta take."

Much as the practical side of me wanted to tell Rabbit that there was no work, no money, and maybe no restaurant, and that I wasn't too sure I needed to add a thick slice of ex-convict to this catastrophe sandwich anyway, what I found myself saying was: "Aprons are over there. I suppose you can start by clearing up the dining room."

CHAPTER 6

I made my way up the stairs, balancing the breakfast tray on my shoulder. In the parking lot, Officer Mustache from last night sat vigil in his patrol car. I hoped he'd keep any curious lookie-loos away.

Inside the apartment, Auntie Biz sat on the couch, wrapped in my velvety red dressing gown. Given our size difference, she looked like a child dressed up to go to a Renaissance fair. My laptop was open on the coffee table where I'd left it, and Butterball was, as usual, perched on top of the keyboard. I hoped he hadn't sent any emails with his butt. Auntie Biz was raking through the stack of financial documents I'd left out.

"You're up," I observed, setting the breakfast tray next to her. Butterball did a grateful figure eight around my legs as I placed his bowl on the floor.

"And you're in deep trouble," she said, tapping the top of the papers with her finger. She flicked through the pages and mumbled, "Even if you can amortize your capital expenses to the max and set longer A/P terms with your vendors, we're probably looking at months, if not weeks, till this place goes belly-up."

I mostly thought of Auntie Biz in terms of long-ago

summer vacations and recipe exchanges, but before she re-
tired, she'd taught personal finance and accounting classes
at the local high school for more than forty years. Despite
her recent physical and mental slowdown, she could still
split a check five ways or triple a three-quarter-cup mea-
surement before I could even open the calculator app on my
phone.

"I'm sure we'll figure something out," I said, tugging the
financial statements out of her range and closing my laptop.

"Like robbing a bank?" she said. "Or winning the Pow-
erball?"

Mercifully, a knock interrupted the conversation. I hustled
to the door and practically tore it off its hinges.

Detective Capone stood on the small deck. A round, white
cloud floated in the sky almost directly behind his head,
framing his handsome face like a halo. Man, could this guy
make an entrance.

"I'm sorry to bother you so early," he said. "I wondered if
I could ask a few more questions."

"Come in," I said.

I got Auntie Biz settled at the breakfast bar, and signaled
for Capone to follow me out onto the small balcony that overlooked the lake so we could have a little more privacy. Both
the living room and the bedroom had sliding doors that led
onto the balcony, and even though the space was only big
enough for a couple of chairs, the view made the modest
quarters feel luxurious.

The sun lit up the lake like a giant mirror, reminding me
again why I'd moved to Geneva Bay. Morning walkers were
already below us strolling on the shore path, the walking trail
that ringed the entire twenty-mile circumference of the lake.
Pristine white piers poked into the water from each of the elegant properties viewable from our perch. Practically everyone in Geneva Bay had a boat of some kind. After all, why

pay for primo lakefront property if you weren't going to take advantage of the water access? Capone and I leaned against the railing, taking in the view.

"Sure beats freezing L platforms and bumper-to-bumper traffic on the tollway," Capone said, listing a few of the downsides of Chicago city living.

I smiled. "Can I get you some coffee? I forgot to ask."

"No, thanks. I can't stay," Capone replied. Butterball followed us outside and zoomed to the detective like a heat-seeking missile. Capone bent down to pet him. "Hey, man, I brought something for you." He pulled a little pouch of straw-colored nuggets from his pocket and turned to me. "The bakery in town makes them with tuna and catnip. Okay if I give him one? Brujo loves them."

"Brujo?" I asked, recognizing the Spanish word for "wizard."

"My cat, well, my mom's cat, but my mom lives with us. These are his absolute favorite." He removed one of the small treats for me to inspect. It looked like an oversized Goldfish cracker.

"Sure," I said. "But you need to be aware that Butterball will express his gratitude by covering you in cat fur."

"I've been told gold is my color," Capone replied with a wink.

I watched the two of them for a moment, and then said, "What was it you need to ask me?"

Capone gave my cat a final pat and then rose. "I need to know if you have another way of getting in touch with Sam Van Meter."

"Sam? Why?"

"He's not answering his cell phone or his email, and none of the workers at the house he owns here have seen him since the day before yesterday. They said he comes by most days."

"That's right," I said. "He stops in during his daily jog."

"Well, he didn't show up yesterday or today. No posts on his social media in the last twenty-four hours, and no transactions on his credit card either," he said.

"Why do you need to talk to Sam?" I asked. "He wasn't even here when it happened." It sounded like the police had gone to a lot of trouble trying to track Sam down, considering he couldn't have witnessed anything.

"Well, correct me if I'm wrong, but yesterday, you and your fiancé had a serious argument and broke off your long-term relationship, right?"

I nodded.

"And that conflict was over his belief that you cared about the success of the restaurant more than you cared about him," he said. "Now he's gone completely AWOL."

He paused, as cool and quiet as a snowfall, apparently waiting for me to put two and two together. But the numbers wouldn't compute. Sam couldn't have had anything to do with Jeremy's death. They barely knew each other.

"You can't think Sam did this," I said. "He probably didn't recognize your number, so he didn't pick up the call."

"Could be."

"I'll text him. I'm sure he'll reply if I say it's urgent." I tapped out a text and hit Send without waiting for assent from Capone. Surely, this would all be cleared up in no time. Sam probably wouldn't be too pleased to hear from me—no doubt he was still stewing after our fight. I knew I was. But this was bigger than the two of us. No matter how mad he was at me, Sam would resurface to help the investigation and clear his name. After three years together, I knew him like the back of my hand. The detective and I stood in silence for a moment as I stared intently at the screen. Nothing. I voice-dialed. Maybe he hadn't heard the text alert's *ding*. Straight to voice mail. My heart began to beat a little faster. A few more moments passed.

"You're sure you checked the new house? It's got a lot of rooms," I said. I heard the disquiet creeping into my voice.

"He's not there," Capone reiterated. He paused. "Ms. O'Leary, can you see how this looks? Your fiancé, your business partner, has vanished. I wouldn't be doing my job if I didn't talk to him. Spurned exes have been known to do some crazy things to get revenge."

"There's no way Sam knows anything about Jeremy's murder. He does goat yoga, for heaven's sake. He drinks cucumber-infused water." I was sure of Sam's innocence, but I had to admit that goat yoga wasn't a particularly convincing alibi for murder. First, Auntie Biz admitted to owning the murder weapon, and now Sam had apparently gone on the lam. Guilt settled over me. If only I hadn't blabbed all about the breakup and Sam's jealousy over the restaurant to Capone last night, Sam wouldn't be in the crosshairs of the investigation.

"Um, I've got his dad's number," I sputtered, "but they're not close. I don't think Sam's talked to him since Christmas. Maybe try SilverMoon, his meditation guide? Or his friend Amrit? They hiked the Inca Trail together a few years back. I'll text you the contact info."

I wondered if Capone heard the tremble in my voice. A combination of Capone's charm and the fact that neither Biz nor I had been immediately shackled and dragged to some godforsaken dungeon last night had allowed me to get too comfortable. I'd temporarily forgotten that this was a murder investigation, and we were all suspects. Our lives would be ripped open again and again until the culprit was found.

Capone stood up. "I better be on my way. You've got my number. If you hear from Sam, make sure to let him know I need to speak with him."

I nodded. "Hey," I said, as he turned to leave. "Can I ask you something? Why didn't you arrest Biz last night? The more I think about it, the more I don't get it. I know she didn't do it, but to you it must look like she was caught red-handed."

He shrugged. "She taught the chief of police and half the force when they were in high school. Apparently, some of them still have nightmares about her pop quizzes."

"So the whole force is afraid she'll give them detention if they arrest her?" I was being sarcastic. But only a little.

"In this job, we have carrots and we have sticks," Capone said. "Too often for my liking, Chicago was all about sticks. Geneva Bay is more of a carrot place. You get to know the people here, and maintaining those relationships is important. If I'd hauled your itty-bitty eighty-year-old aunt—the legendary Miss Elizabeth O'Leary, who's taught three generations of Geneva Bay's citizens—down to the station in the middle of the night, and I was wrong about her guilt?" He shook his head and pressed his lips together in a low whistle.

"But aren't you afraid that we'll run off to Venezuela or something?" I asked.

"In my experience, ordinary people don't suddenly develop the capacity to obtain fake passports or access Swiss bank accounts. Your aunt has deep ties here. Her health is delicate. She doesn't strike me as the running-off-to-South-America type." He smiled. "That said, Officer Torvald is going to be stationed outside your apartment until we sort this mess out. He'll be trading off with another officer. I'd appreciate it if you'd check in and out with the officer on duty any time you or your aunt leaves the premises."

So I'd been right to think that the cop "watching over us" wasn't there as a courtesy. The freakishly blond Officer Mustache must be Officer Torvald, our bodyguard/jailor.

"Which leads me to something else," Capone continued. "I wanted to let you know that we're executing a search warrant on your aunt's house."

"You're searching her house?" My whole body went numb as I pictured officers tearing apart the cozy cottage where I'd spent my childhood summers. Apparently, even a carrot place used a stick now and again.

"I'm afraid we don't have a choice. It was Jeremy's last address," Capone replied. He indicated a canvas bag that he'd been shouldering. "I brought your aunt's medications, toiletries, and a few changes of clothes. I'm afraid she won't be able to remove anything else from her house until the search is compete." He crouched down to give Butterball a pat before heading out the door.

After I'd seen him out, I slumped at the breakfast bar next to my aunt, swiped a piece of bread from the breakfast tray, and piled on the fig jam and butter. Biz, in her customary way, had eaten at most ten bites of the meal.

"You should eat more," I chided. "You still look a little green around the gills."

She waved her hand away. "No appetite."

She pushed the tray toward me. Even though she seemed more on the ball this morning than she'd been in a while, there was no doubt that she wasn't entirely well. Her hands had a slight tremor, and her complexion looked pale. I hoped she was up to dealing with whatever lay ahead.

I brooded and worried my way through her leftovers as she silently sipped her tea. Silence. That was one of Auntie Biz's special talents. She could do calm silence, critical silence, contemplative silence—all flavors of silence. I wasn't completely sure which one this was, but I was grateful for it.

There was a knock on the door, and before I could get up, Sonya pushed it open. "Yesterday a murder, and today you've hired a convict? Maybe you should at least consider locking your door?"

"So you met Rabbit?" I asked. "And I guess he shared his . . . eventful life with you?"

"He didn't need to. I recognized the tattoos. And the look."

"The look?" I asked, raising an eyebrow.

"Yeah, you know the one. That ex-con look. Kind of a cross between a baby bird and a pit viper?"

She wasn't wrong. She and I had both worked with enough recently paroled people to see some patterns.

"And here I thought you were hiring only wholesome types now that you had your own place. Daniel, aka Mr. Clean Cut Ex-Military, and Melody who, as far as I can tell, is made of sugar and spice and a ten-gallon bucket of marshmallow fluff."

"What about that Lois Gorman's grandson?" Auntie Biz interjected. She puffed out her lips in disgust. "He's a weasel."

I sighed. "Carson. I never even got to fire him. That was going to have been the highlight of my evening."

"So, my friend," Sonya said, inhaling deeply, "let's talk about the restaurant."

I noticed that she'd edged around to the far side of the kitchen island as she spoke, as if it might be a good idea to put a big piece of granite between her and me before she said whatever she was going to say.

"What about it?" I demanded.

"Daniel and Melody and I were talking. They're downstairs, helping Rabbit get everything shipshape."

"I see."

"None of us can go very long without a paycheck. Daniel's mother lost her home in Hurricane Maria, and he's sending every spare penny back to help her. He took this job because he needed to make more money than he could in Puerto Rico. Melody's family's farm is in bad shape. Without this job, she can't pay her college tuition in the fall. Me, well, I could always ask my parents for money, but I'd rather

die than let them think I couldn't support myself as a chef,"
Sonya said.

"Like I don't know that," I snapped.

"We can't open with all this uncertainty—police flitting
in and out questioning people isn't a good look."

"Neither is having the owner and her aunt as prime suspects," I said. "And apparently Sam is also a person of interest. He's gone AWOL. Even the police can't find him."

"That's not good," Sonya said. "Until you talk to Sam, you
don't even know if we're allowed to operate this place. This
is his building after all. You don't even have a lease."

"I'm aware, but thanks for summarizing the situation with
excruciating clarity," I said, crossing my arms. "Everyone is
depending on me and I'm letting you all down. I appreciate
the friendly reminder."

I was on the verge of tears, but I masked my feelings of
failure with an angry, defensive posture. I'd trained under
some of the most vicious chefs in the Midwest, and it only
took enduring one or two of their expletive-heavy public
haranguings for me to learn that tears had no place in the
restaurant business. Not if you wanted to survive long. I'd
carried that lesson over into my life.

"Dee, that's not what I'm saying at all. You have to stop
thinking you have to do everything alone."

"It's my responsibility, and I'll take care of it. We're going
to open ASAP, and we'll start to get some cash flow going."
Biz coughed, but thankfully said nothing. "Besides, you're a
great cook. You'll always land on your feet. If the restaurant
goes under, I'm sure Quotidian would have you back in a
heartbeat, and they must've paid twice what I can afford,"
I said.

I'd hired Sonya away from one of the most coveted gigs
in Chicago—the nouvelle cuisine restaurant, Quotidian, a

cutting-edge place helmed by celebrity chef Graham Ulrich that touted itself as a "tasting experience" rather than a restaurant.

Sonya rose and walked toward the window. The sunlight framed her figure. "I can't go back there." She spoke with her back toward me, almost too quietly to hear.

I threw up my hands. "Well, if you're sick of Quotidian, you could go somewhere else. A reference from Graham Ulrich is worth its weight in gold." Didn't Sonya realize how lucky she was to have a Plan B?

"I said I can't go back." Sonya's shoulders heaved.

"Son," I said, my tone softening. "What is it?"

"I had an affair with Renee Ulrich."

"Graham's wife?" I sputtered.

Auntie Biz rose, gave me the slightest nod, and wordlessly slid open the door to the balcony. There was that gift for silence again.

The door slid closed behind her, leaving me alone with the sound of Sonya's wrenching sobs. "Oh, Son." I didn't ask the whys and wherefores. As capable as Sonya was in the kitchen, as loyal as she was as a friend, her love life had always been a four-alarm dumpster fire. Her heart seemed to have a homing device that always headed straight for misery.

Sonya turned to me, mascara-streaked tears cascading down her cheeks. Her normally powder-pale face bloomed with pink blotches. "I'd left my phone on a chair in the office. Graham must've seen texts pop up on the screen. He stormed into the kitchen in the middle of service. He"—she sniveled and wiped her nose with her sleeve—"he dumped an entire pot of jellied veal demi-glace over my head and pushed me out, physically pushed me, into the alley," she concluded, a fresh volley of sobs escaping her lips.

I rushed across the room and folded her into my arms. I could hardly bear to think about the implications of that incident for my friend. Graham and Renee Ulrich were *the* culinary power couple. If Graham Ulrich had blacklisted Sonya, she'd never work in fine dining again. Heck, she'd be lucky if she could get a job flipping pancakes at Denny's.

"Why didn't you tell me?" I asked.

"You were dealing with your dad's illness. Besides, I was ashamed of the affair. I didn't want to talk about it with anyone, even you. Then, no one would hire me and I got into debt, and I felt even more humiliated."

"You know I'm always on your side, no matter what."

She shook her head. "You've told me a million times not to get involved with people who are off-limits. I was kind of hoping you'd eventually hear the whole saga secondhand and I wouldn't have to tell you myself," she said.

I sighed. Though I had dozens of industry connections, and most of our mutual friends were in the business, I wasn't surprised nobody had mentioned this fiasco. I'd been out of the Chicago restaurant scene since my father had gotten sick, and I'd barely socialized for months as I grieved for him and then got the new restaurant underway. Most people who knew me knew how tight Sonya and I were and probably assumed I already knew. Besides, as gossipy and inbred as the Chicago culinary community is, most of the scuttlebutt gets passed around during the boozy post-service pub sessions. It would take a brave soul to reach out to me specifically to dish dirt about Graham and Renee Ulrich. It was practically blasphemy.

I hugged her again. "Don't worry, Son. We're going to make this restaurant a huge success. The Ulrichs will be coming to *you* looking for a job in a few years."

She gave me a weak smile. "You know I would've taken this job even if my bank account wasn't circling the drain, right?"

"Gee, thanks."

"Just because this was my only option, doesn't mean I don't want to be here," she added.

"And just because you're the only person alive who'll put up with me, doesn't mean I wouldn't have hired you anyway." I smiled. "As soon as the police clear us all of suspicion and catch whoever did this, it's all going to be fine."

"That's not how these things usually go." She drew herself back and cradled her body with her arms, the smile fading from her lips. "Remember, my parents, my uncle Avi, and my cousin Seth are all lawyers. In my family, babies learn their Miranda rights before they learn their ABCs. Police investigations take time. It could be months until you're in the clear. We'll be lucky if the restaurant is still standing by the time this blows over. It's possible the police won't ever solve the case."

The restaurant. I loved everything about it. The location, the color scheme. I loved the team I'd built, working every day elbow to elbow with Sonya, a chef whose passion for good food rivaled my own. To both of us, creating innovative pizza recipes was every bit as artistic as putting a brush to canvas or chisel to stone. I threw my whole being into my food, and I'd worked for this dream my entire life. Now my best friend's future as well as my own hinged on making it a success.

I took a deep breath. "Well, then. I guess I'm going to have to solve it for them."

CHAPTER 7

By eleven o'clock, Auntie Biz was washed, dressed, dosed with her medications, and settled back into one of the chairs on the balcony. Even as I was still processing Sonya's revelation, I'd been dying to quiz Auntie Biz about her gun and about Jeremy. She'd put me off, saying she was too tired for the third degree. Now she snoozed in the sunshine, Butterball splayed out at her feet. Glad someone could relax.

My mind ping-ponged back and forth, careening from problem to problem. I had a murder to solve, a missing ex-fiancé to find, a friend's career to save, deliveries to rearrange, vendors to pay, and a whole new brand identity and marketing campaign to devise. The first time around, Sam and I had spent almost ten grand hiring a fancy Chicago design firm to come up with a logo, lay out the menus, and establish the restaurant's "visual identity." This time, I'd have to figure it out by myself.

I was used to taking charge, assessing situations, and taking action. I was beginning to wonder how well my skill set was going to translate into becoming an amateur detective. Solving the murder was clearly the most pressing thing on the agenda. If I could do that, everything else would seem more achievable. But how was I going to solve the murder if I couldn't even muster enough concentration to write a social media post about the restaurant?

I paced up and down the breakfast bar—my command center. Ten different tabs were open on my laptop. I stopped walking and clicked on one of them, a list of suspects and motives. It had seemed like a good place to start, but I'd been staring at the document on and off for twenty minutes and no magic solutions had presented themselves. For motives, I'd written "fear? hatred? greed? revenge? jealousy? random act of violence?" So basically every possible motive. For suspects, I had a blinking cursor.

I put my head in my hands. My staff, minus Carson, was downstairs, probably finished cleaning by now. I pictured them. Daniel, who'd left his home island to come here. Melody, who needed this job to pay for her education. Rabbit, who had to find steady work if he had any hope of rebuilding his life. And Sonya, who'd left Chicago in disgrace.

I straightened my spine. *Right. Enough with the pity party.* I didn't get this far by being a quitter. I summoned a memory from my first-ever executive chef gig, a little French-style bistro in Lincoln Park. I'd taken the helm and managed to pull the place up from a neighborhood joint to become one of the hottest reservations in the city. And then, on the same night that the *Chicago Tribune*'s food critic showed up, our hot-water heater decided to give up the ghost and two of my line cooks went down with the flu mid-service. Did I curl up into a ball and cry? No. I'd cooked like a whirling dervish and gotten the plates out on time.

I'd earned the right to be the boss, chosen to hold responsibility over these people's lives. I closed my laptop and marched down the stairs. I may not have had the slightest inkling of how to solve a murder, but I practically had a PhD in taking control and getting things done. If I was going to concentrate on the murder, I needed to marshal my resources.

I found my team gathered in the dining room. Their voices dropped when I came in from the kitchen. Sonya slumped at a table, sipping a Diet Coke. She'd touched up her makeup, but fresh cat eyeliner couldn't hide the gloom in her eyes. Daniel stood behind the bar re-racking glasses, while Rabbit and Melody rolled utensils into cloth napkins. Undoubtedly, they were talking about me and, by the looks on their faces, fretting about the future.

I cleared my throat. "Thanks for coming in today. I know we got off to a rocky start last night," I began. Understatement of the Century award. "Son's probably already told you that we're going to have to stay closed for a bit."

"We got the place all cleaned," Rabbit offered.

"I appreciate that," I said. "But there's still more work to do." I walked over to Sonya and put my hand on her shoulder. "I need you to look through our food supplies and find ways we can economize. Make a list. What we can freeze, what we can preserve, what will keep. Then I'm going to need your help to adjust the menu based on the list."

Sonya turned and looked at me with a confused expression. "Did you just say you're going to need my help? That can't be, because the Delilah I know and love does not accept help. She gives orders, sure, but she doesn't ask for help."

"You must've misheard," I replied, smirking. "I said that you better adjust the menu stat or you're fired."

She smiled. "Phew, that's more like it. For a second there, I thought we were dealing with a body-snatcher situation."

"Daniel," I said, turning toward my bartender, "you'll need to visit our vendors to find out if we can cancel this week's orders and modify our payment schedules."

"I could call them," Rabbit offered. "That would save some time."

I shook my head. "Good suggestion, but most of the accounts payable folks are middle-aged ladies. Daniel's the man for the job, and he needs to go in person."

Daniel melodramatically puckered his lips and gave us his best smoldering Caribbean dreamboat look. "It's true. Tell me you wouldn't give a thirty-day extension for this?"

Sonya rolled her eyes, while Melody stared at Daniel as if she'd fallen into a trance.

"Melody, you're commissioned to design a new brand identity."

Melody jumped at the sound of her name, practically knocking her chair over. "Me?" she squeaked.

"Those display signs you made for the soft opening with the little drawings weren't half bad," I said. "Besides, you're the closest we're going to get to a professional graphic designer with our zero-dollar budget."

Sonya rose from her chair and pinched my arm. "I'm still not convinced that you're not an alien who's taken over Delilah's body. This all sounds suspiciously like delegating."

"Don't make me regret it," I said, slapping her hand away.

I thought back to what Sam had said during our last fight. That all I cared about was the restaurant, as if the restaurant were just bricks and mortar. I looked at my crew. I wish I could have made him understand—*this* was the restaurant. This feeling of leading a great team and coming together to get the work done. I felt a lump form in my throat. I wished I could tell them, too, but that kind of schmaltz just wasn't in my vocabulary.

I swallowed hard and stiffened my spine. "While you all get started on your tasks, I'm going to get some lunch cooking.

Rabbit, can you help me bring my aunt down? She's wobbly on the stairs."

"There's that 'help' word again," Sonya said.

Daniel narrowed his eyes at me. "Definitely a body snatcher."

"We may have to wake my aunt up," I said to Rabbit as I opened the door to my apartment. "She was napping when I left."

Rabbit and I walked into the open-plan kitchen/living room and his eyes ran along the phalanx of Auntie Biz's pill bottles, which were lined up on the counter next to him. "Miss O'Leary got a bad back? Or arthritis?"

"Not really. Just the usual elderly person creaks and squeaks," I said. The balcony door slid open and Auntie Biz and Butterball entered. "Speak of the devil."

"I've been called a lot of things, but the devil?" Auntie Biz said, arching an eyebrow. She made her way slowly into the room. "I thought I heard a familiar voice in here."

Rabbit doffed his baseball cap. "Miss O'Leary. Sorry if we woke you."

"Always glad to visit with a former student, Mr. Blakemore. Delilah told me you'd gotten a job at her restaurant. I'm pleased to see you on the right side of those prison walls. How's your daughter?" Her foot caught on the edge of the rug, and she tottered slightly. Rabbit rushed to steady her, easing her into an armchair.

"She's real good, ma'am." He pulled his phone from his pocket and squatted down next to the chair. "I got about a million pictures of her on my phone, if you wanna take a look."

"I remember you used to carry that one folded snapshot with you everywhere. Nice to have the benefits of freedom,"

Biz said, tapping the screen of Rabbit's phone. "Oh my, she's gotten so big. Such pretty eyes."

Butterball slid across my shins, meowing for a snack. "I came to see if you wanted to lend a hand with lunch," I said to Biz. "It's been a while since we cooked together." Although I did genuinely enjoy cooking with Biz, my invitation had an ulterior motive. Auntie Biz wasn't big on conversation, and I still needed some answers from her about Jeremy and the murder. I suspected that she was going to keep trying to dodge my questions. Throughout my life, the only time we'd been able to really open up to each other was while we were cooking. Maybe if I could get her in front of a stove, I'd be able to get some information out of her.

As Rabbit guided Auntie Biz onto the landing and down the steps, Butterball jockeyed for position, trying to dash through my legs as I stepped onto the landing. "Oh no you don't, buster," I scolded, intercepting the cat and placing him back inside the apartment. "We're all on house arrest, but especially you." I shook my finger at him. "No more brawling." Butterball arched his back and twitched his tail, denying all wrongdoing, past, present, or future.

Officer Torvald strode into view as we reached the ground. The back stairs weren't visible from the parking lot, which meant he must've actively been watching the comings and goings from my apartment. Having a twenty-four-hour police guard would take some getting used to. Still, I supposed it was preferable to wearing an ankle monitor or being locked up in the slammer.

"Everything all right?" the officer called, taking a few steps toward us. "This man bothering youse guys?"

"No!" Biz snapped. "He's helping me."

"Don't worry," I replied, waving the officer and his thick-as-a-brick Wisconsin accent away. "We're not escaping, just going to make some lunch."

"All right. I'm about to go off shift. Officer Stanhope will be taking over soon," Torvald said.

I'd have to bring Torvald a plate before the shift change. He may have been one of our jailors, but he looked tired. The poor guy had been keeping watch all night, and if there was one thing I couldn't stand, it was the thought of someone missing meals on my account.

We entered the kitchen, and Rabbit settled Auntie Biz on a stool in front of the gas range.

"You'll stay for lunch, won't you?" Biz asked him.

"No, thank you." He hesitated, gripping his baseball cap and worrying his hands around the edge of it. "If it's all right with you, chef, I wondered if I could leave a little early today, since the cleaning's done and the restaurant's closed. I got a custody hearing later on this afternoon, and I want to get cleaned up for it and get all my paperwork together and whatnot. Don't need to give the judge any more reason than she already has to think I'm not fit to take care of Everleigh. I swear this won't happen all the time. I'm reliable. You'll see. It's just that all this got scheduled before I knew about the job here."

"It's fine, Rabbit. Thanks for your work today," I said.

He exhaled. "Appreciate it. I'll see you tomorrow morning. First thing."

I bid him goodbye. It seemed that Rabbit was officially part of the team. What was one more salary to add to the nonexistent payroll coffers? If my ship was going to sink, I might as well steer straight for the iceberg with all engines steaming.

I started to pull ingredients out of the fridge.

"Delilah, you know better than anyone that there can

be only one head chef. Today, it's me." Auntie Biz tottered across the kitchen and plucked an apron off the hooks.

"*Oui*, chef. But only if you let me be your sous," I said, pulling on an apron of my own. "What are we making?"

Auntie Biz took stock of our ingredients. "Something light and Mediterranean, I think. Wouldn't want to see all this beautiful produce go to waste. Why don't you pour us some prosecco?"

It wasn't even noon, but like a good sous chef, I followed instructions and got the bubbly flowing. Auntie Biz tasked me with making pissaladière, a French onion tart spiked with anchovies, herbs, and olives. Luckily, we still had some of last night's pizza dough lurking in the back of the fridge to form the base. Deep-dish dough can survive pretty much unscathed for about a day if it's chilled properly after the first rise. After that, it risks being over-proofed—looking like a flatulent Jabba the Hutt and having the texture of a baked sponge.

I formed the dough into a rectangle as I melted a tin of anchovies into hot olive oil. I inhaled the pungent, seaside aroma. Anchovies may be a controversial pizza topping, but cooks know dissolved anchovies are also a surefire way to add a salty tang to sauces, dressings, and pasta dishes. The salt used to can the little fishes breaks down their muscle proteins, giving them the melty, magical properties of gelatin.

"Is there anything else you'll need from your house?" I asked, trying to come to the subject of Jeremy's murder in a roundabout way. Auntie Biz continued to chop tomatoes as if I hadn't spoken. "Or anything you forgot to mention to the police?" More silence. "Anything you want to tell me so it doesn't get sprung on me later? Like, you know, the fact that you own the murder weapon?" By the hard set to her chin, I could tell that she was deliberately ignoring me. "Auntie Biz, if you know something that would help to figure out who killed Jeremy, you have to tell me."

She turned to face me, pointing an accusatory stalk of asparagus. "You want to know if I did it, don't you?"

"No," I sputtered. My hand knocked into a waiting onion and sent it bowling down the counter. "Well, yes. I mean, that's not what I was asking. I know you didn't kill him, but you must know more than you've said. He's worked for you for a year. He's been living in your house for almost two months, for heaven's sake."

She steadied herself on the counter with both hands. I watched her for a moment as she took slow, deep breaths. The kitchen was silent, save for her breathing and the gentle boil of water on the stove. When she spoke, her voice was soft. "Truth is, my memory's gone all spotty. Not just about last night, but about everything." She inclined her head toward me, her voice quavering. "I'm losing my marbles."

I gathered her tiny body into my arms. "I'm sorry," I managed. What could I say? I had a pretty good sense of what it felt like to be on the cusp of losing everything. Quite the pair we made.

"Don't you go all soft, now," Biz said, as she pulled herself away. "Check on your tart. You don't want to overbrown it." She picked up a paring knife and used it to point at the oven.

So much for our heart-to-heart. It was no wonder I wasn't great at mushy emotional stuff. My father would've given John Wayne a run for his money in the strong, silent-type category, and my sister Shea was about as sentimental as a cardboard box.

After a few minutes of chopping and sautéing, I tried again. "What was Jeremy like as a person?" I asked gently. "Did you ever notice anything strange? Romantic drama, anything like that?" Even if my aunt couldn't remember all the specifics, I knew by what she'd told Capone that she'd formed a negative impression of her caregiver.

Biz shook her head and leaned against the counter. "He had some friends who would stop by the house, but they never came inside, and he never went out with them. He mentioned some old flames, but I don't think he had a special someone currently. No family, either. At least not that I can recall. At the holidays, he would stay up in Menomonie," she explained.

"Menomonie? That's up near the Minnesota border, right?" I asked.

Biz nodded. "He must've had a friend there. I can't remember him mentioning any names or details." She shook her head again. "Like I said, the old noggin isn't firing on all cylinders lately."

"How did you find out about the agency where Jeremy worked?" I gave the onions in the pan I was tending a stir as they started to take on a tinge of gold.

Biz took hold of her knife and began to section a bulb of fennel. "Duplicate bridge club. A few of the girls have started needing help around the house the past few years. Some have live-ins. You know me. I didn't want help, even after I started to have these spells. I figured I was just getting old. My doctor said it might be blood pressure. But after I had that fender bender last summer, you and Shea made such a fuss I didn't really have a choice."

I remembered it all too well. My sister and I had gotten a call to say that Biz had been driving the wrong way down a one-way street on her way home from the Grand Bay Resort and had careened into a fire hydrant. I was wrapped up caring for my father at the time, so Shea, with her typical no-nonsense efficiency, had laid down the gauntlet—no more driving, period. Either Auntie Biz could hire some in-home help ASAP, or Shea would start looking for an assisted living facility.

"So I asked around, and everyone seemed to think highly of Glacier Valley Senior Care. It's the outfit Tambria Callahan and her husband own. I taught both of them eons ago. They sent Jeremy over. He was quiet, did what he was supposed to, and he kept himself to himself."

"I wish I'd helped you more," I said. "I can't believe I left you with someone you couldn't trust."

She waived my apology away with a wooden spoon. "Figured I could do worse. I could've ended up with someone who clucked over me all day and tried to make idle conversation."

"You make it sound like polite chitchat is one of the seven deadly sins," I said.

She rolled her eyes. "People today feel like they've got to share every little thought that flits through their brains. They put up those Twitters and their Facebooks. What's it all about? Nothing."

I ignored her "these kids today" diatribe, turning the information about the senior care agency over in my head as I blistered the skin of a red pepper over the gas flame. Despite spending summers in Geneva Bay, I'd never gotten to know many locals. But something stuck in my mind. "Tambria Callahan. Where have I heard that name?" I asked aloud. Tambria wasn't a common name, and I had a hard time believing there would be more than one in Geneva Bay.

"Probably from that weaselly waiter of yours or his grandmother."

Ah, yes. My weaselly waiter, Carson. A weasel who had conveniently sidled off just before Jeremy was killed.

Lois Gorman, the annoying woman from my aunt's bridge club, had mentioned her daughter's name when I talked to her the previous night: Tambria Callahan, boss of Jeremy, and mother of Carson. It was tenuous, but it was a definite connection between my aunt, the restaurant opening, and the dead man. My list of suspects was no longer a blank screen.

CHAPTER 8

By one p.m., lunch was laid out family-style on the outdoor patio at the table closest to the lake. Paying customers might not be able to enjoy waterfront dining in this picture-perfect weather, but there was no reason my staff and I couldn't. The occasional jet-ski or powerboat buzzed across the gray-blue water. The mail boat, packed with tourists, cruised past. A summertime fixture of Geneva Bay, the mail boat ran in the warmer months, hiring spry college students to pop the post into mailboxes perched on residents' private piers. In the early days of Geneva Bay, when the road system was in its infancy, the boat was a vital link to the outside world. Now, it had been upgraded and enlarged to accommodate vacationers who bought tickets to tag along and watch the agile postal workers leap from moving boat to dock, sprint to a mailbox, and race back again before the boat left them behind.

The appetizing rainbow of dishes that Biz and I had cooked up married perfectly with the backdrop: a simple caprese, orange supremes with shaved fennel and arugula, asparagus and feta salad, grilled sardines, and the fresh-from-the-oven pissaladière I'd made using Auntie Biz's recipe.

Daniel, Melody, Biz, Sonya, and I settled into our chairs.

Carson, unsurprisingly, hadn't bothered to check in. More
surprising was that I still had no reply to my half-dozen texts
and messages to Sam. As more time passed with no word
from him, worry crept into my thoughts. While fleeing
from conflict was his MO, I couldn't understand how he'd
dropped off the grid the way Capone described. The scene
before me—the lakefront restaurant, beautiful weather, de-
licious food, and wonderful staff—might look something like
contentment. But it felt like a mirage, a fragile fantasy that
was quickly slipping out of my grip.

As the dishes were passed around the table, Sonya gestured with a serving spoon to a fancy BMW parked on the
far side of the lot. "Isn't that the wine lady's car?"

"Veronica Tanaka? *Sí, se fue.* I saw her heading out on
foot last night," Daniel said. "I served her *quite* a few glasses
of wine." He mimed drinking from a glass.

"Maybe she was shaken up by what happened, or freaked
out by being questioned by the police. It was super stressful," Melody said. Leave it to her to always think the best of
people. "Rabbit found her purse hanging on one of the purse
hooks at a side booth when he was cleaning up. She must've
left in a hurry."

"All the party guests rushed down to the dock to gawp,"
Sonya said.

"Everyone?" I asked.

"I think so," Melody replied. "I was the last one out
because I'd been in the kitchen loading the dishwasher. The
dining room and patio were both empty."

"Then once the police arrived, nobody could get back into
the restaurant because the cops wanted to sweep the place
and make sure it was safe," Sonya said.

"I still can't figure out what Veronica Tanaka would want
with Carson," I said. "Why would they have left together?

She seems like a go-getter, and he's so lazy. She's got a well-established career."

"You have to admit that he's pretty good-looking," Melody said.

"For a weasel," Biz muttered, spearing a sardine with her fork.

I leaned back in my chair, hoping I looked casual. "Speaking of Carson, did anyone see him come back after the shooting last night? Or maybe earlier in the evening, was he acting strange at all?"

"You mean do we have any evidence to link him to the murder?" Sonya deadpanned. When would I learn that she knew me too well to let me get away with subterfuge?

Daniel, Sonya, and Melody shot looks at one another.

"What?" I demanded.

"We want to help," Sonya said. "With the investigation."

"No way." I dropped my cutlery and pushed my chair away from the table. "I'm not having you get involved in anything that could be dangerous or get you into trouble. Concentrate on the tasks you were given."

Sonya inhaled through her teeth. "The thing is, we finished everything."

"Because we're just that good," Daniel added, pretending to polish his knuckles on his lapel.

Sonya handed me a piece of paper, filled with her bubbly, girly cursive. "That's the inventory list."

"What about the menu rewrites?" I asked, raising an eyebrow.

"Flip over the paper," Sonya said. Sure enough, she'd mapped out a number of yummy-sounding ideas.

"And all of our vendors are . . . very satisfied." Daniel winked.

"Even the meat guys? Sujeet and Big Dave?" I asked,

crossing my arms. "Don't tell me you batted your eyelashes, rolled your R's, and made that invoice go away."

"Turns out, I was stationed in Kuwait with Big Dave's son. We're all going fishing next week." Daniel playfully popped the collar of his shirt. "See? I'm not just a pretty face."

"You did all this while I was making lunch?" I turned to Melody. "How about you? I suppose you've already created a whole new brand identity when it took that Chicago design firm a month?"

Melody grimaced and chewed on her thumbnail. Sonya nudged her. "Show her."

Melody popped up from her chair and scurried inside. She returned clutching a sketchbook to her chest. "You'll probably hate them," she said. "They're just sketches."

I wrested the book from her grip and flipped through the pages. They were doodles—rough conceptual sketches—but I could see how she'd cycled through different iterations, zeroing in on a clean, art-deco look that I instantly realized was a perfect fit with our modern mobster interior. One whole page of the book was full of name ideas. Speakeasy Pizza. Deep Lake Deep Dish. Prohibition Pizza. Not half bad. "What's this one?" I asked, pointing to words that had been scribbled out.

She snatched the book back. "Oh, that was silly."

I reclaimed the book and parsed the crossed-out words. "Delilah & Son?"

"See? It's silly."

"It's not," Daniel said. "Your ideas are really good."

Melody blushed so deeply I was afraid her cheeks might burst a gasket. I'd caught her making goo-goo eyes at him more than a few times, and it seemed that his praise meant a lot to her.

She cleared her throat. "I was just thinking about how you always call Sonya 'Son' and how you've been friends for so long. It didn't seem completely fair that Sam had his name on this place just because he paid for the renovations and stuff, when it was you and Sonya doing all the work. It was kind of a play on the whole 'and sons' thing that businesses do. Locals who come here a lot would know it was pronounced 'soh-n' instead of 'suh-n.' Like the password for a speakeasy." She blushed again, took the book back and closed it, hiding it on her lap under the table.

I sat rooted to my chair, staring at the tabletop. I'd delegated, and they'd all risen to the occasion. I'd asked for help, and they'd come through, big-time. Part of me wanted to call Sam and tell him how wrong he was about me. Part of me, though, still didn't quite believe it was possible that giving up control wouldn't end in disaster.

"Look, I appreciate what you've done, but you don't need to be getting mixed up in the murder investigation," I said. "It's my problem, and I'll deal with it."

"But don't you see? We're already mixed up in it," Sonya said. "We know you'd do the same for any of us."

My chin quivered. I was dangerously close to crying, and even in front of those closest to me, that wasn't something I was going to do. *No weakness, Delilah. You're supposed to be in charge.* I bit the inside of my lip and held my head up.

"You doing okay?" Daniel asked, poking me with the handle of his fork.

Before I could respond, the sound of a car made us all turn toward the parking lot. Well, everyone except Auntie Biz, who had dozed off in the warm sun. An Uber pulled up, and Veronica Tanaka, our consultant sommelier, stepped out.

"Hi, all," she called with a broad smile. "I don't suppose my purse turned up? Totally spaced about it last night, with all the commotion."

Melody went to fetch it for her while Veronica waved the driver away.

She walked toward us, her long dark hair shimmering in the sun. Her tailored, pastel summer dress hugged her slim waist and revealed just enough cleavage to make sure all eyes stayed on her. "Oh, thank heavens you found it. I think this is the longest I've ever gone without my phone. I've been feeling phantom limb pains. And Beemer"—she blew a kiss toward her parked BMW—"I missed my baby so much."

"Do you want to join us?" I asked, gesturing to an open chair. "Plenty of food to go around."

"I've already eaten." Probably a lettuce leaf, judging by her figure. "You're so sweet to cook for everyone," she continued. "I'm amazed you're up and about after what happened last night. Finding a body on your opening night. I think I'd be catatonic under ten blankets."

"Dee's a tough cookie," Sonya said.

Melody came back with the purse, a Louis Vuitton model that probably cost more than my first car. She handed the bag to Veronica reverently, as if placing an offering on an altar.

"You jetted out of here pretty quickly last night, I guess," I said.

Veronica shrugged. She somehow managed to make the mundane gesture look elegant. "I figured the last thing the police needed were more useless lollygaggers."

"Useless?" I said. "So you didn't see anything that might be relevant?"

She tapped the side of her forehead and gave a ditzy roll of her eyes. "It's all a blur."

If there was one thing Veronica Tanaka was not, it was ditzy. I'd hired her because she was whip-smart and great at her job. I couldn't understand why she was putting on this empty-headed girl act. "I thought you'd gone down to the dock with Carson. So you would've been there right before Jeremy was shot," I said bluntly.

Veronica's jaw clenched for a millisecond, and then she

broke into a wide smile and rolled her eyes again. "I think Carson's got a little crush," she stage-whispered. "He's sweet, but a little young for me."

She was putting on a convincing performance, but no way had I imagined the hardness of her glare when I mentioned Jeremy's death. Why was she dodging my question about her whereabouts at the time of the murder?

Veronica dug through her bag and pulled out her car keys. "Well, I'd better be on my way. I have an appointment at the Grand Bay Resort. They're refreshing their wine list. Cha-ching, if you know what I mean. Delilah, could I talk to you for a quick sec?"

I rose and followed her toward the parking lot.

"I really hate to bother you about this right now." She looked slightly pained. "Sam said he'd have my check last night for my consultancy fee? Do you need me to resend the invoice?"

I remembered the invoice all too well. A number trailed by a long string of zeros. Sam mentioned that he hadn't paid her yet, but yesterday morning, that hadn't seemed like a big deal. Now, he and his bottomless checking account were nowhere to be found. I gritted my teeth. "No, I've got a copy. I'll get the money to you ASAP."

Her phone rang inside her bag. "You're such a star," she said, pulling her phone out and putting it to her ear. "Be in touch soon," she mouthed to me. "Veronica Tanaka," she chirped into the phone, starting toward her car. She clicked the key fob to unlock it and then turned to wave goodbye before sliding into the vehicle.

I rejoined the others on the patio.

"What was that about?" Sonya asked. "Did she have top-secret evidence to share?"

"Hardly," I said. "But did you notice how she avoided saying where she was at the time of the shooting?"

"That lady was one of Jeremy's friends." Our heads snapped toward Biz, who'd spoken quietly, her eyes still half-closed. I thought she'd been asleep, but apparently not.

"Did you just say that Veronica Tanaka was friends with Jeremy?" I asked.

"I never knew her name. I thought I recognized her at the party last night, but I never saw her up close. None of Jeremy's friends ever came inside the house. When I saw her with that fancy car, though, I remembered. She came around a few times to see him," Biz said.

"If they were friends, she certainly didn't seem too broken up over his death. Why didn't she say she knew him?" I asked, half to myself.

"Who knows?" Biz said. "What I do know is that it's almost time for *Law & Order* and my nap."

"Speaking of law and order, there's another suspect we need to add to the list," I said.

"We?" Sonya raised an eyebrow.

"Another slip of the tongue," I countered.

"Oh, right, because the entire world will collapse unless you personally hold it up one hundred percent of the time." Sonya rubbed her brow as if to ward off a headache. "Dee, listen to my words: *We are helping you.* You can play the iron boss lady all you want, but we know that you know that you need us. This"—she gestured to herself, me, Melody, and Daniel—"is happening."

"But, but . . ." I sputtered like a dying engine. What choice did I have? "Fine," I muttered.

Daniel rubbed his hands together. "*Vámanos, amigas.* Let's begin."

After we'd cleaned up the lunch dishes and I'd tucked Auntie Biz into a comfy chair upstairs for her afternoon rest, Melody, Sonya, Daniel, and I reconvened at the restaurant's bar and got down to business. Now that I'd resigned myself to accepting help, I began to feel my old can-do mojo returning.

I quickly filled the others in on what Auntie Biz had told me about Glacier Valley, the senior care agency that employed Jeremy. "We definitely need to know more about them," I concluded.

"Yeah," Sonya agreed. "I know this is a small town, but it does seem like a pretty big coincidence that the son and mother of the woman who employed the dead guy were both at the party."

"I agree. My aunt said his last words were 'Oh, it's you.' His killer was someone he knew. He knew that entire family and, apparently, Veronica Tanaka as well. I'll go over to Glacier Valley and ask about getting another caretaker for Auntie Biz. That should seem perfectly normal, and it'll give me a chance to check them out," I said. "Task number two is to find out more about Jeremy. We know nothing about him other than that he had a lot of supposed friends who never came inside the house and who he never seemed to go out with. And that he spent holidays in Menomonie," I said.

"Maybe I could go to Menomonie and ask around? Show his picture at some local hangouts?" Daniel offered.

"That's a great idea. Melody, could you go with him? That could be a lot of ground to cover, since we're starting from zero," I said.

"Road trip!" Daniel high-fived Melody, who looked like she'd just won the lottery. Three hours alone in a car with Daniel.

"What should I do?" Sonya asked. "I guess I'm on Biz-sitting duty?"

"If you don't mind," I said. "But could you also see if you can get more info on the investigation from the cop in our parking lot? I think Torvald said his name was Stanhope."

"So, I should sidle up to the patrol car and casually ask him if I can peek at the crime scene report?" she asked.

"Why don't you bring him some food, and do a little, you know, 'Wow, officer, what a nice uniform,'" Daniel suggested, doing the worst Marilyn Monroe impression I'd ever heard.

Sonya raised an eyebrow. "You do know that I'm a lesbian, right? And a feminist?"

He clapped her on the back. "A feminist lesbian on a mission."

CHAPTER 9

When I'd left the others at the restaurant, I'd planned to head straight to the senior care agency. Instead, I found myself heading around the curve of the lake toward the house Sam and I had bought. Correction. The house Sam had bought. Nothing was in my name. Not the house, not the restaurant building, not even the car I was driving. Truth was, my financial situation was worse than even Sonya and Biz realized. I'd taken a months'-long leave of absence when my dad got sick, and insisted he try a Hail Mary experimental treatment that wasn't covered by his insurance. I'd thrown every penny I had at that damn tumor. I'd always been financially independent, working steadily since I was sixteen, but my dad's illness knocked me sideways. I remembered with a pang how Sam's generosity had kept me afloat. And I remembered Lois Gorman's words about the restaurant being my hobby. Maybe she was right. I'd allowed myself to become a trophy wife, only without any of the legal protections of marriage.

I wound my way through the tree-lined streets. The size of the homes increased, as did their distance from the road. The larger the home, it seemed, the more inconspicuous the driveway. Sam's house had a *very* inconspicuous driveway.

As I approached, the trees gave way to a welcoming expanse of lawn. Before me stood Sam's stunning Queen Anne mansion, whose gingerbread details, circular turret, and wraparound porches were the stuff of my girlhood dreams. Two white vans and a truck from the local high-end appliance store were parked near the entrance.

I waved to Julio, the general contractor, who stood on the front porch talking into his phone. His company specialized in the kinds of lavish renovations homeowners in this area demanded—installing media rooms and elevators, indoor basketball courts and outdoor kitchens, ripping out ridiculously enormous pools and replacing them with *obscenely* enormous pools. Julio couldn't have been more than five and a half feet tall, a paunchy sixty-something with a quiet voice and a warm gap-toothed smile. But woe to anyone who tried to get away with shoddy work on one of his building sites. He mandated perfection.

"Hey, Ms. O'Leary," he called, pocketing his phone. "How ya doing? I heard about what happened."

"I'm hanging in there," I replied, wondering if he'd heard about Sam dumping me, or the murder, or both.

From inside the house came the sound of drilling and the thwack of a hammer. Julio and I walked through the large oak double door and into the kitchen. Everywhere, workmen were busy putting the final touches on my dream house, daubing on the subtle parchment paint color I'd chosen for the vaulted entryway, installing sleek kitchen appliances that rivaled the ones I had at the restaurant. I looked around while Julio had a quick word with the appliance installers. Apparently, there was a ding in the vent hood and he was demanding a replacement unit. Sam had hated the renovation process; details drove him crazy and the endless choices bored him. But for me, getting every detail just right had been heaven. I swallowed a lump in my throat.

"Cops came by first thing, looking for Mr. Van Meter," Julio said, walking back over to me.

"I heard. They're checking some routine stuff. Covering all their bases." After I'd cast Sam in a bad light with Capone, I wanted to be sure nobody else got the wrong idea. "Still no sign of him?" I asked, hoping I sounded casual.

"No. We put the bamboo flooring in his meditation room yesterday. I thought maybe he would come by and take a look at the finished product."

We walked toward the back of the house, where almost every room boasted glass doors opening onto a veranda with stunning lake views. In the back corner, down a short hallway, stood Sam's meditation room. I'd kept the decoration in this part of the house understated and natural, with a tatami-room-meets-Victorian-conservatory vibe. Julio opened a set of double doors to reveal the freshly installed bamboo flooring.

"Take off your sandals," he suggested. He crouched down and ran his hand lovingly over the floor planks. "It's like walking on a baby's backside."

I smiled and did as instructed. The floor felt warm and almost pliable underfoot.

"So you were able to seal that crack in the subfloor?" I asked.

"Yeah, that new underlayment should stop any moisture problems in the future, too. It was a bear, but we got it done."

Once upon a time, this part of the house had been used as a ballroom, and I'd had the idea to adapt the original sprung floor to provide cushion and shock absorption for Sam's intensive yoga sessions. Along one wall, built-in cherry cabinets would store mats, yoga balls, cushions, and the other accoutrements of exertion and relaxation. Outside, the landscapers were hard at work, installing a Japanese-style garden to provide a lush, calming backdrop. Surely, Sam would have to admit that my attention to detail and concern over appearances had resulted in a truly magnificent space. Julio and I took in the view for a moment.

"Did you and Mr. Van Meter decide if you wanted more security cameras placed out by the pool?" Julio asked. "The guy finished the ones out front and down by the shore path. Those are active as of yesterday."

"You should probably ask Mr. Van Meter," I said. Techy gadgets were the one area that Sam actually might take an interest in. He'd been the one to insist all the latest "smart" features be included in the design, even if he hadn't been terribly fastidious about overseeing the work. Taking charge often meant finding fault, and finding fault meant potential conflict. I suspected Sam's inability to hold people to account or have tough conversations had a lot to do with why he'd sold the controlling interest in his start-up company.

"What about the paint color in the foyer? You going with the Mourning Dove or the Cotton Ball?" Julio asked.

As tempting as it was for me to take over and make the decision, I knew I had to let go. This was Sam's house, not mine. "Better leave that to Sam, too," I said.

"If you say so," Julio replied. He was quiet for a moment, and then he spoke, seeming to measure his words. "Lots of times, my clients don't care about nothing but having the biggest and newest of everything. The workmanship don't matter to them as long as what they got is bigger than what their neighbors' got. But you're different." He pointed to his eye and then to mine. "I seen how you notice what's quality and what's garbage. I seen how you talk to my guys—respectful when it's done right, no bull when it ain't. You got respect for quality."

I smiled, feeling strangely buoyant. So many times, my quest for perfection had caused problems. It was rare to find a kindred spirit. Someone who knew that the devil was in the details, but so were the angels.

"I gotta check a few things upstairs," Julio said, giving me a jovial clap on the shoulder. "I'll call you if I hear from Mr. Van Meter."

I pulled the doors to the meditation room closed behind me and stood for a moment, trying to absorb some serenity from my surroundings. No dice. Sam strived for years to get me into his hobbies. He'd given me exotic dietary supplements for Christmas, suggested couples' cleanses, and dragged me along to sample every flavor of yoga ever concocted. None of it had taken root. Try as I might, I was never going to be a sit-still-and-munch-herbs kind of gal.

This wasn't my house anymore. I might never see this room again. In our three years together, Sam hadn't come close to understanding that all the perfectly cooked meals I'd lain before him, all the fastidious tidying I'd done of his closet, every element I'd selected for this calm oasis of a space, was how I showed him my love. I sighed. I supposed that his superhuman calm and attempts to get me to join his health-boosting pastimes were his ways of showing me his love. We'd been shouting past each other in unintelligible languages this whole time.

That left me with a choice. I could learn Sam's language, teach him mine, and try to win him back. Or I could cut my losses and move on. Maybe find a kindred spirit like Julio. Well, like Julio only a foot taller, twenty years younger, and with all his original teeth.

I tried Sam's phone again. Voice mail. Friday, today, was supposed to be payday, and I had no way to pay my staff. I'd tried to get Sam to set up a separate bank account in my name for the restaurant, but as usual, he was in no rush to complete the task. He had simply supplied any money I needed and said his accountant would figure it all out later.

I'd never hesitated to express my opinions on anything from Sam's hairstyle to his lifestyle, but money was one area where I felt uncomfortable badgering him. I'd been ashamed of being so dependent on him for cash, so I ignored the issue. But I wasn't going to let my spinelessness mean that my staff would go without a check.

I headed for the outskirts of Geneva Bay, a section of town where fast food joints and big box stores abutted the highway's cloverleaf interchange. Somehow, I had to get the funds to cover the weekly payroll, not to mention to pay the huge sommelier fee Veronica had not so gently reminded me that I owed. I knew that my staff would cut me some slack until I figured things out, but I couldn't stand the thought of them making sacrifices because I'd been irresponsible about ensuring that Sam and I had clear legal and financial arrangements. Regardless of what they said, I couldn't shake the belief that this was my mess, and I'd have to dig myself out of it.

Although Geneva Bay marketed itself as a haven for the rich, working-class Chicago families also flocked to the lake on summer weekends, and the businesses on this side of town catered to them. I pulled into a strip mall that was straight out of central casting for the underbelly of a resort town—tanning salon, nail salon, tattoo parlor, pawn shop. It was the last of these that interested me.

I looked down at my hand. A few years ago, I'd been cooking at one of the luxury hotels on downtown Chicago's Magnificent Mile. Sam and I had been dating for over a year at that point, and we were living together in his "little" 2,200 square-foot condo overlooking the Newberry Library and Washington Square Park. On my walk to work one evening, I'd seen this ring sparkling from a street-front display window at Tiffany & Co.: a diamond and two emeralds set in a platinum band. The vintage flair of the details, the way it stood alone in the display case on a bed of black velvet, the whole thing was clearer than a flashing neon sign—this was THE RING.

Sam wasn't great at keeping secrets, and my Spidey-sense told me a proposal was in the offing. I wanted to be sure the ring Sam chose was just right. I'm not the kind of gal who goes all gooey over jewelry, but once I saw THE RING, I came down with a bad case of diamond fever. After all, if I was going to get engaged, I wanted to be sure that the band I would be wearing 'til death do us part was perfect. I spent about a month dropping hints so heavy they could've anchored a naval destroyer. When Sam at last presented it to me, on a private boat he'd chartered for a midnight Lake Michigan cruise, I put it on before the words "Will you marry me?" were even out of his mouth.

I took stock of my appearance in the yellow light of the visor mirror. Pulling a hairbrush and a tube of coral red lipstick out of my purse, I did what I could to glam myself up. I was glad that I'd showered and changed into a peplum blouse and fitted trousers before I'd left. Just because I was broke didn't mean I had to look desperate. I twisted the ring off my finger and held it in my palm. *'Til death or arguments about incorrect pizza signs do us part.*

Twenty minutes and some painful negotiations later, I'd ransomed my prized jewelry for a paltry few thousand dollars. The pawnbroker said I'd been lucky to get that much, and despite the fact that the sum was a mere sliver of what the ring was worth, I knew it was true. If I'd had time to sell the thing through an upscale consignment boutique in the city, I would've done far better. But time was not on my side. I don't know who I thought I was fooling with my lipstick and fluffing my hair. Anyone who pawns a valuable diamond in a strip mall that sports a view of a soybean field and a Dollar General is, by definition, desperate.

I bucked myself up. *What's done is done.* My eyes flashed briefly to the stack of bills in my purse and then my bare finger as I pushed the ignition button and headed back into town.

CHAPTER 10

Glacier Valley Senior Care was headquartered in the upper level of one of the classic two-story buildings that made up the bulk of Geneva Bay's charming downtown. Given its proximity to the lake, I guessed that the "glacier" in the agency's title probably referred not to Wisconsin's notoriously frosty winters, but to the massive ice sheet that carved out much of the landscape of the upper Midwest at the end of the last ice age. The legacy of the retreating ice sheet sparkled in the sunlight as my Jeep Wrangler crested the small hill that sloped gently down toward the lake. Would I ever get tired of catching a glimpse of the gorgeous lake? I doubted it. If I ever met the glacier that carved this landscape, I'd give it a big kiss.

Even though the tourist season wouldn't officially begin until the next weekend's Memorial Day holiday, the shops and restaurants downtown bustled with life. Luckily, I was able to score a metered spot only a few doors down from the agency. I'd already called to make an appointment, and when I pushed the intercom button and announced myself, I was instantly buzzed up.

No sooner had I entered the office than a stout little dumpling of a woman rushed from behind her desk to wrap me in a tight embrace. "You poor thing," she said, her words muffled by my shoulder.

I stiffened, half wondering if a knife was about to be plunged into my back. After all, I was here because I suspected the agency could be connected to a murder. Instead, the woman, who I assumed must be Tambria Callahan, buried her face in my chest and squeezed me tight. From the quick glimpse I caught before the unexpected hugfest, Tambria sported a dowdy mom haircut, an embroidered pastel sweatshirt, and a thick daub of frosted baby pink lip-gloss. Not at all what I expected from the daughter of the elegantly groomed Lois Gorman and mother of the stylishly disheveled (and admittedly pretty good-looking) Carson.

"You'll have to forgive me," she said, pulling a crumpled Kleenex from her sleeve. Her eyes were reddened from crying. She gestured for me to take a seat in the vinyl-covered chair next to her desk. "I've been a mess since yesterday. I'm broken up about Jeremy's death." She seemed to shake herself. "Where are my manners? We haven't even been properly introduced. I'm Tambria Callahan, but only my mom calls me that. Everybody else calls me plain old Tami."

"Delilah O'Leary," I said.

"Of course. Mom told me about you and Miss O'Leary finding Jeremy's body. That must've been awful. Your poor aunt. She's a firecracker, but she's got a big heart."

I was surprised to hear this generous and surprisingly accurate assessment of my aunt from a stranger. By now, I knew all about my aunt's reputation as an intimidating teacher, and I was aware that she could appear demanding and sarcastic. But Tami was spot-on. Auntie Biz wore a suit of armor, but she loved fiercely and deeply. Her students were scared of her only because they didn't want to disappoint her.

As I settled into my chair, I took stock of the office. Flowery wallpaper, gold-colored lamps, wood-veneer furniture.

There were two desks, laden with file folders. Each sported a vase of fake flowers and a coffee mug. Tami's mug said World's Best Mrs. I assumed her husband had the adjacent desk with the World's Best Mr. mug. The office was comfortable, but deeply unfashionable, a bit like its proprietor. Not exactly the villain's lair I'd been picturing, where Lois Gorman and her evil progeny conspired to murder Jeremy. The only thing fishy about the place was an actual fish tank perched between the front windows.

I heard footsteps on the stairs and the door opened to reveal a squat, silver-bearded man carrying a bag from one of the downtown pastry shops. He looked like a life-sized garden gnome. "Hello, you must be Ms. O'Leary," he said, in a flat-voweled Upper Midwest accent. He put his free hand on his chest. "Irv Callahan." He set the bag down, sat on his rolling desk chair, and scooched it toward us. "You and Miss O'Leary doing okay? We've been so worried." He shook the bag he'd brought. "Would you like a mini muffin? The banana nut are scrumptious."

"Um, no, thanks," I said. The combination of their gentle sincerity and the mini muffins made me feel like I'd somehow ended up at a church coffee hour. They seemed to be encouraging me to unload some emotional baggage, but I was determined to stick to my agenda: get the scoop on them, their family members, and Jeremy. I shifted in my chair. Touchy-feely heart-to-hearts gave me the jitters, and I couldn't let these people's oozing empathy gum up my mission. "You said you had some caregiver profiles for me to review?"

"Of course, dear. I'm sure you're anxious to get someone in place to help with your aunt." Tami seemed slightly taken aback by my abrupt pivot to business talk, but she recovered quickly. She flipped through the stack of folders on her desk, plucked one out, and handed it to me. "We think Lorna could be perfect, don't we Irv? Lorna cared for a very sweet gentleman for the last, oh, what is it, Irv? Five years?"

Irv nodded. "Would've been five years in July."

"He just passed just last week, poor dear."

I flipped through the folder. It reminded me of an online dating profile, detailing Lorna's age, hobbies, habits, and references.

"Do you have these kinds of files on all your employees?" I asked.

"Yes. In fact, that nice police detective was here this morning, asking for a copy of Jeremy's file," Tami said. "Have you met him? Very handsome gentleman."

"Brought us Starbucks," Irv added.

Apparently, I wasn't the only one getting the good cop treatment from Detective Capone.

"Lorna looks great," I said. "How does this work? Do I interview her? I'm not sure what the process is."

"Well, we do our best to match our caregiver with the person they're going to be caring for. We like to explore one or two options at a time, since this can be an overwhelming process. So much of it is about personal chemistry, especially for a potential live-in situation. It has to be the right fit."

I continued to page through the file. "It must be hard to attract good people to this kind of work, huh?" I asked.

"We do our best," Tami said. "It's true that the pay isn't as high as we wish it could be."

"And the work can be demanding," Irv agreed. "You've gotta love it."

"You really do." Tami reached out and put her hand over her husband's. They looked at each other and smiled.

"Did Jeremy?" I asked. "Love it?"

"Oh, heavens, yes. He'd been with us for nearly ten years. Since we started," Tami said. "He took care of my own grandmother after her stroke. Nursed her right up until she died."

"He was one of our very best," Irv agreed. "So devoted."

"Must be a tough business," I said.

"I suppose it could be, for someone who didn't love the work," Tami replied.

"But I suppose there are other benefits. As the owners, you two must do all right," I probed, hoping they wouldn't see through me as easily has Sonya had. "In a business like this? I've heard there's a lot of money in nursing homes."

"Maybe in some of those big whoopty-woo national chains that want to squeeze every penny from their poor clients," Tami said with a chuckle.

"Or I suppose the chichi places up in Madison that charge big bucks and have white tablecloths and trips to the opera and such," Irv speculated. "Maybe *they* make a lot."

"But we're not like that here," Tami said. "No, no. Irv and I get by okay, but we're not in it for the money. Before we started Glacier Valley, I was a social worker, and Irv here was a Lutheran minister."

Irv picked up her train of thought. "Tami and I saw a need for quality, affordable senior care in the community, and that's what we aim to be. We got the idea when Tami's dad got sick. She and her mother both had to quit their jobs to nurse him. She's an only child, so it all fell to her and her mother. He was sick for years before he died. Kidney cancer."

"My dad had the same thing. It was hell." I hadn't intended to share that. I was here to grill them about a murder for heaven's sake. What was this town doing to me? "It was quick for him, though," I continued hastily. "Six months from diagnosis." Despite my wish to keep up a neutral front, my voice trembled with grief.

Tami and Irv were quiet for a moment, seeming to sense my roiling emotions. Tami pushed a box of tissues across the desk.

"After Daddy died," Tami said quietly, "we didn't want other families to struggle the way we did. This can be a hard time of life for seniors, and sometimes it's every bit as hard for the families who have to watch them struggle. This business has helped us, too. It was such a relief to have all this in place when Grandma Dorothy had her stroke a few years ago."

"Grandma Dorothy was a wonderful woman," Irv explained.

Tami nodded. "But very set in her ways."

"Tami and her mom—you know Lois, right?—well, they couldn't care for her by themselves. Toileting, bathing, and such is difficult with anyone, but Grandma Dorothy was especially particular about how things were done. She never wanted to go into a home."

"My mother never would've let that happen," Tami said. "They were close as two peas in a pod. She was killing herself trying to care for Grandma until Jeremy came in and took over the heavy lifting. He was a lifesaver for our family."

I stuffed those details in my mental case file.

"We both feel this is a calling more than a business," Irv said. "That's why Glacier Valley is set up as a not-for-profit company."

"And that's why we're so grateful to you for hiring Carson," Tami said. "He wants his own car so badly, so he doesn't have to borrow the minivan anymore, but Irv and I just can't afford things like that. You know how it is for boys that age, especially in Geneva Bay where so many people are well-to-do. Carson wants to have all the latest gadgets and doo-dads, like his friends have."

"We hope he's been doing a good job for you?" Irv said, his face expectant.

Even if Geneva Bay was turning me into a softie, I couldn't quite manage to say anything positive. Still, I had to give myself credit for not going with my first thought: *He's a lazy, worthless little punk, and I would take enormous plea-sure in watching him be consumed by flesh-eating beetles.*

"Um, is Carson your only child?" I asked.

"Yes, he is," Irv said. "We'd been married for more than ten years when he was born. Doctors had told us we couldn't have children. Then our little boy came along."

"Our little miracle," Tami said.

I made a shape with my mouth that I hoped resembled a smile. I was beginning to understand the family dynamic a little better. Irv and Tami obviously hated the idea of anyone suffering or struggling. They'd long prayed for a child, and they were "blessed" with their precious Carson. I could almost hear the whirling rotors of helicopter parent-ing. Equally, though, I began to wonder if some of Carson's swagger was a kind of desperate performance. Geneva Bay had mega-rich kids aplenty. If he'd spent his life trying to fit in with them, having overly involved older parents who said things like "doodads" and ran a nonprofit senior care com-pany probably wasn't a ticket to Cool Town.

"You two didn't come to the soft opening," I observed. "But your mother did. I'd told the staff they could invite their families." I hadn't thought much about it at the time, but now that I'd met them, I wanted to know more about their ab-sence. Carson brought his grandmother, but not his parents.

"Carson didn't mention the invitation to us," Irv said. His expression moved from confusion to hurt as he glanced at Tami.

"I thought your aunt had invited Mom." Tami blushed, as we all seemed to realize simultaneously that Carson had purposely overlooked them. "Oh, that type of thing isn't really for us anyway. Big, fancy parties and such."

"We wouldn't have wanted to cramp Carson's style. You know teenagers," Irv added. His smile didn't quite camou-flage the hurt in his eyes.

"And how's Carson taking all of this?" I asked, trying to move the conversation past the awkward moment. "He must've known Jeremy through Grandma Dorothy. How terrible for someone he knew to be killed when he was right there."

A shared look of worry passed between them. "He's not taking it very well," Irv said.

"He's hardly left his room all day." Tami shook her head. "It's so silly, but he keeps saying that what happened with Jeremy . . ." she paused, seemingly unable to get the words out.

Irv took her hand and the two of them looked at me with wide, desperate eyes. "He keeps saying that it's all his fault."

CHAPTER 11

I walked slowly back to my car, mulling over my visit with Tami and Irv. I'd grilled them about Carson's insistence that Jeremy's death had been his fault, but they seemed as clueless as I was about it. They chalked his reaction up to posttraumatic stress and survivor's guilt. If I wanted to find out more, I'd have to find a way to talk to him myself.

My phone buzzed in my purse. Sonya's contact flashed on my screen, a goofy picture of her glammed up as Elvira, Mistress of the Dark, a few Halloweens ago. I put the phone to my ear. "Hey, Son, everything okay?"

"Peachy," she replied. "But the battery on Biz's hearing aid conked out, and I'm getting hoarse from shouting at her because she can't hear me, and deaf from her shouting at me because she can't hear herself. Can you swing by her place and see if the police are done scouring it for clues? She said she's got a couple of spare batteries in the kitchen drawer. Apparently, it's the drawer with the cookie cutters and crocheted potholders."

I smiled to myself. Biz's methods of organization were notoriously higgledy-piggledy. "You got it."

"Do you have your key to her place? I looked in Biz's purse, but I can't find hers."

"That's weird. Did you ask her where they are?"

"She dozed off," Sonya said.

"Well, I've got mine. I'll take care of it." I paused. "But we should try to find her keys. I gave her a spare to my apartment and the restaurant in case I ever got locked out. I don't like not knowing where they are."

I started toward my car again, but then pivoted away. The late afternoon weather was glorious, and I needed some time to clear my head. I headed down the sidewalk toward the lake, deciding to take the shore path to Auntie Biz's instead of driving. Quickly heading out of downtown, I passed the immaculate piers and grand verandas of the nearby lakefront houses; many of the inhabitants already seemed well into the cocktail hour. Some lolled on their patios and screened porches. Others were readying boats for sunset cruises. Most waved a friendly hello as I passed or raised a champagne glass in greeting. Even though I could no longer lay claim to being one of Geneva Bay's upper-crust homeowners, the delights of the shore path were still mine to enjoy. In a strange quirk particular to Geneva Bay, the homeowners whose land the shore path traverses maintain their own sections, but the public can freely access the entire circuit. Walking the path gave an intimate glimpse into the pampered lives of Geneva Bay's well-heeled residents. As I passed Sam's house, I walked more quickly, trying not to dwell on the fact that up until yesterday, I was inches away from being one of those well-heeled mansion owners.

In less than thirty minutes, I'd arrived at Auntie Biz's cottage. The cottage was one of the few modest-sized homes in this part of Geneva Bay. It had originally been built as a summerhouse for one of the mega-mansions, a lakeside spot where the ladies could change into their bathing suits and tea could be served without guests having to make the long trek up the manicured paths to the main house. Biz had bought it for a song decades ago when the property was split up and sold off to pay back taxes.

The tiny, two-bedroom cottage was dwarfed by the Greek Revival mansion that stood about three hundred yards up a gentle rise. The mansion's owners—an investment manager from Chicago and his Barbie Doll wife—had planted an imposing row of cypress trees between their property and Biz's, presumably so Biz's modest, slightly ramshackle house wouldn't spoil their orderly aesthetic. While the main house used a tasteful terra-cotta palate, Biz's place was painted the color of an overripe lemon. The paint peeled in places, and the screened porch—a later addition to the original summerhouse—seemed to tilt slightly leeward. Massive weeping willows dominated the yard, their branches making the property feel sheltered, even hidden. To one side, the small, untidy garden still hadn't been cleared of the debris of last year's vegetable crop. Beyond the garden stood a rickety wooden shed.

As I approached the cottage, a knot of shame tightened in my throat. When I was younger, and my sister and I used to hang out in town, we would often lie to other kids we'd meet, telling them our aunt lived in the mansion, instead of the modest house behind it. A few times, I even had dates drop me off at the gate of the main house. I'd stand outside and wave until they drove out of sight, then I'd scuttle down to Auntie Biz's. One time, she'd been out in her garden and had caught me in the act. She never said a word about it, but the pained look in her eyes that day spoke volumes. I'd seen the same look in Irv and Tami Callahan's eyes when they realized that Carson had been embarrassed to invite them to the soft opening.

A Geneva Bay police car and a black Dodge Charger I recognized as Capone's were parked along the long gravel drive that connected Auntie Biz's cottage with the main house's driveway. As I approached the house, another police car pulled up and parked behind the others. A young, female officer with angular features and a no-nonsense bun stepped out.

"Hi," I called. "I'm Delilah O'Leary, Miss O'Leary's niece."

"Laura Rettberg," she said, giving my hand a firm shake.

"I came to see if I could pick up some extra hearing-aid batteries for my aunt. They're in a kitchen drawer with the cookie cutters and potholders," I explained.

She eyed me warily. "I'll have to ask Detective Capone."

I stood in the driveway, feeling awkward. After my mom died, my sister, our dad, and I had moved every couple of years, and I'd changed schools half a dozen times. Dad had been unsettled by the sudden loss, and could never quite put down roots anywhere or stick with the same job after that. Summers at Auntie Biz's had been our one constant. The key to Auntie Biz's front door, the same key I'd had since I was a kid, was right inside my purse. But suddenly, I had to ask permission before I could enter. The wind kicked up, blowing my long chestnut hair loose. I shivered. Daylight was fading, and on cloudless late-spring days like this, the night's chill could creep up quickly. Through the waving willow branches I saw a speedboat buzz past, cutting a tight ring of doughnuts into the lake's surface. It mirrored my mood. Yesterday, the path to happiness shimmered ahead of me. Now, I felt like the speedboat, still going full pelt, but spinning in circles.

"Ms. O'Leary." Capone's deep, reassuring voice called from the front door. He held out his palm, revealing two minuscule silver discs. "This what you're looking for?"

"Thanks." I gestured toward the cottage as he dropped the batteries into my hand. "Still at it?"

He nodded. "For a small house, this search has been slow

going. Your aunt certainly has a unique way of organizing things."

"I never will understand how she can put together such amazing meals in that kitchen. Cooking requires precision. It's like Mary Poppins' carpetbag in there," I said.

Capone chuckled. "I get that. My son is training to be a surgeon, but his apartment looks like a bomb site," Capone said.

"How are you that old?" The words tumbled inelegantly out of my mouth before a thought had even formed in my brain.

"I'm forty-two."

"Sorry, I meant, I didn't know you had an adult son."

Although Capone had a trim physique and only the merest hint of laugh lines, I'd already guessed he was a few years older than my thirty-five, based on the fifteen years he said he spent with the Chicago Police Department prior to moving to Geneva Bay. I knew nothing about his personal life, so the fact of him having a son shouldn't have come as a shock. Still, a son who was old enough to be doing medical training and living in his own apartment? How could that be? Was his son some sort of child prodigy?

Capone must have registered my unintentional rudeness, but he let it float past. "C.J. He's in his third year at Northwestern Medical School."

"You and C.J.'s mom must be very proud," I said, hoping my fishing expedition wasn't totally obvious. Capone didn't wear a wedding band, and I'd assumed he was single. If I was wrong, it was probably for the best. Earlier that day, I'd been strategizing about winning Sam back, and now here I was shamelessly sizing up my prospects with Capone. I silently took a vow of celibacy.

While I had been wrestling with my libido, Capone's face had taken on a faraway look. "I am proud," he said. "C.J.'s mother and I never married, though. We were teenagers when he was born. She drifted out of our lives a long time ago, but he's a good kid."

Before I could bait my hook to fish for more information, Officer Rettberg came out of the house with two other uniformed officers.

"We're pretty much done inside, sir," she said to Capone. "Just the shed to go."

"Go ahead," Capone said. "I'll be right behind you." He turned to me and explained, "Your aunt had said that Jeremy took the shed keys away to keep her from accessing the firearms inside. I thought we might find a spare set somewhere inside, but no dice. Officer Rettberg ran back to the station to check Jeremy's keys out of the evidence locker. I didn't want to force the door if we didn't have to."

Once again, I was surprised at Capone's thoughtfulness and courtesy. And by that drop-dead gorgeous face and those incredible, pillowy lips. If I had to be under a cloud of suspicion, I was glad it was his cloud.

"Find anything interesting inside?" I ventured.

"You know this is an ongoing investigation, right? And that you and your aunt are suspects in a murder?" Capone replied, with a smirk.

"I had to try," I said. "Patience isn't a virtue in my book."

Capone sighed. "Mine either. Working for a small-town police department has its disadvantages when it comes to an investigation like this. This is our highest priority, trust me, but we don't have the manpower to do everything all at once. Geneva Bay has great cops, but most of them are blessed not to have much experience with this kind of thing. This is Rettberg's first major crimes case." He nodded toward the serious-faced young woman. "She only joined the force last year. She was a school resource officer until the chief reassigned her to help with this investigation."

I turned toward a clattering sound, which was followed by pounding footsteps.

Officer Rettberg ran up, breathless. "Sir, you're going to want to see this."

Capone walked swiftly behind her. Without any conscious intention, I tagged along in their wake. The door to the shed opened wide enough for a riding lawn mower to cruise in and out with ease, so even in the failing light, I could see the contents as soon as I rounded the corner of the house. Cob-webbed garden tools, a couple of ceramic pots. And on the floor, a small suitcase, laying open. Packed to the top with cold, hard cash.

CHAPTER 12

Once the cash in the shed was revealed, the police shooed me away like a stray dog. Capone was uncharacteristically curt, not offering so much as a goodbye as he directed Officer Rettberg to escort me back to the shore path.

"I can find my own way," I protested as she approached. I knew she was only doing her job, but I refused to be frogmarched from Auntie Biz's cottage. I glared at her until she backed off and then stalked away through a cut-through in the trees. Shadowy twilight had begun to descend, and for a moment, my eyes struggled to adjust. Still reeling from the shock of seeing heaps of money sitting incongruously next to my aunt's rusty lawnmower, I almost failed to notice a rapidly retreating figure a few yards ahead of me.

My first thought was that a tourist had wandered from the shore path. Most people respected the commandment that walkers could peep all they wanted at the big houses from the vantage point of the path, but that they were forbidden from trespassing. Occasionally, though, some brazen vacationer would try to bag a closer look, or rowdy teenagers would dare each other to steal a dip in one of the grand houses' pools.

"Hey," I called out. "This is private property."

At the sound of my voice, the figure accelerated into a full-out sprint. It wasn't until the man disappeared out of view that I registered the stylishly unkempt hair and loping, athletic gait. Carson. I was sure of it.

I froze for a moment, uncertain about what I should do. No way could I catch up to Carson. My curvy figure was not built for speed. Should I go back and tell Capone? By the time I went back and alerted the police, Carson would be long gone. Besides, Capone had his hands full with the discovery of the money. Trespassing, even under suspicious circumstances, wouldn't provide enough evidence to link Carson with Jeremy's murder. I'd tell Capone next time I saw him. Maybe by then I'd have a chance to talk to Carson and find out for myself why he was skulking around Auntie Biz's cottage and why he bolted when I saw him. I relished the thought of interrogating the little punk.

As I headed back to town to collect my Jeep, the sun sloped toward the horizon, until all that was left was a faint purple-blue sky. By the time I walked past Sam's, the house stood in darkness. I could tell that Julio and the other workmen were long gone. I still had a key, but I resisted the urge to take one last tour. Better to yank my heart away from it fast and hard. I hurried past the fence that shielded the pool from the shore path, and it crossed my mind to text Julio about nixing some of the landscaping trees. When they grew, the bur oaks the landscaper had suggested were likely to block the view of the external security cameras that had been installed the day before. Sam wouldn't have considered how all the pieces would fit together, and the issue probably wouldn't get corrected if I didn't handle it. *Not your problem anymore*, I reminded myself.

I pulled out my phone. Better to delete the house's security app now than to become some kind of crazy stalker ex, peering through the video footage of property that wasn't mine. At Auntie Biz's suggestion, we'd set up a separate system with a different company at the restaurant so I could deduct the cost from taxes, but they both worked similarly. My finger hovered over the Delete button, but before I could press it, my heart skipped a beat. I clicked into the app. Had Julio said that the cameras were active as of yesterday? They'd catch anyone making their way along the shore path or along the road in the front of the house. Anyone walking from Auntie Biz's cottage toward town.

I scrolled through the time-stamped footage. If he'd hustled, Carson would've come this way ten or fifteen minutes earlier than I had. I zipped through images. Families and couples out for a stroll. An elderly couple walking their dog.

Bingo. The footage was grainy in the dim twilight, but as I zoomed in, Carson's lanky figure came into view. I took a few screen captures of the close-up, and saved the video clip to show Capone later. Finally, something to back up my suspicions about the weasely server.

When I finally reached town and climbed behind the wheel of my car, my thoughts shifted back to my ex's whereabouts. That was another on my list of mysteries to solve. I could see why Sam's sudden disappearance planted him on Capone's suspect list, but I was certain of his innocence. I was mad at him, sure, but Sam didn't have a violent bone in his body. He hated conflict. The bigger the conflict, the more he retreated. Yesterday's fight was our biggest ever, so I supposed it made sense that he'd retreat further and more completely than he ever had before. I just had to figure out where he'd gone.

I cast my mind back to the fight we'd had the previous day, trying to rewind the mental play-by-play for some clue. I'd initially assumed he would go to the mansion for a few days to cool off, but something about that didn't sit right. A little detail niggled at my brain. I thought through our fight, grimacing at the memory of the awful things we'd said to each other. I remembered Butterball's mournful green eyes. Then Sam started packing. Yes. There it was. As he'd stomped from room to room, he'd walked to the dresser and taken his passport from the top drawer. If Sam wanted to get as far away as possible, a passport would help.

Instead of taking a left onto the road that led back to the restaurant, I headed north toward the Grand Bay Resort and Spa. Capone had said there had been no hits on Sam's credit card, and I knew Sam never carried large amounts of cash. So, if he'd left the country, he didn't go by car, train, or commercial airline. Any of those options would've left a paper trail.

I'd always liked how discreet Sam was when it came to his wealth. We'd dated for months before I had an inkling of just how bottomless his bank account was. He'd asked me to join him for a festival of New Age music. Don't judge. In those days, I was so smitten with him that I agreed to attend just about every whacky granola, crystal worship-y, patchouli-addled event ever conceived.

That day, I hadn't even thought to ask Sam where the festival was, assuming it was within driving distance. When Sam took me to an executive airport outside Chicago and told me we were flying to Tennessee for the day, I felt like I'd fallen into one of the *Fifty Shades of Grey* novels, minus the kink. Sam had an account with a private jet company, the kind of outfit that believed swiping credit cards was for mere mortals. They only serviced approved account holders, who were billed directly.

Why hadn't I thought of it before? If Sam had skipped town, he would've used Jet-a-Porter, his rich-guy rent-a-jet service. The Grand Bay Resort had the nearest executive airport, and was the preferred means for Geneva Bay's tony part-time residents to zip into town for the weekend. Sam and

I had even used the airport a handful of times when we were shopping for our, make that *his*, house.

I knew from my limited, vicarious experience as a jet-setter that Sam would likely have had to summon a plane from Chicago or another larger airport. Small terminals like this one remained open limited hours or by appointment, and didn't house a stable of at-the-ready jets. Given the hour, the small airport building was deserted, and the parking lot held only a dozen or so cars. Sure enough, Sam's white Tesla was tucked in among them. Eureka.

I took out my phone and looked up the number for the jet rental service.

"Jet-a-Porter, this is Gemma. How may I assist you?" the woman who answered my call purred.

"This is Delilah O'Leary. My fiancé, Sam Van Meter, has asked me to join him at . . . his destination. He left yesterday night from the Grand Bay Resort in Geneva Bay. I'd like to book a flight on his account. Same route. Departing ASAP."

"Certainly, madam." I heard the clicking of keys. Even before I'd met Sam, I'd been around plenty of rich people in my restaurant jobs. I hoped I'd absorbed enough to successfully mimic a sense of haughty entitlement. "I see your name listed on Mr. Van Meter's account. Can you please confirm the account passphrase?"

"Neutral Milk Hotel," I said without hesitation. Sam used variations of the same password, the name of his favorite band, for everything. He'd tried repeatedly to get me to like the alt-rock group. I'd given it my best shot, but truth be told, their music made my ears want to shrivel up and die.

"We can have a Gulfstream IV sent from Milwaukee, arriving at Grand Bay airport at eleven this evening. Will that suit you?" Gemma asked, with Siri-like efficiency.

"Yes. While I have you, would you be a dear and look up the weather at my destination? I want to be sure I've packed appropriately. The weather there can be so changeable this time of year," I said.

"In Costa Rica? Mild and sunny, as always," Gemma replied, sounding a little baffled.

I cringed. Costa Rica was renowned for its picture-perfect climate year-round. Whoops. "You know, with climate change . . . and El Niño," I mumbled. "It's about a seven-hour flight, right? Can you remind me what time Mr. Van Meter left Geneva Bay yesterday? I just got back from St. Tropez and I'm still all muddled with the time zones," I said.

Gemma's keys tapped in the background. "Looks like it was around ten p.m. We had to send a plane all the way from Louisville."

"Oh! I've just realized that I can't possibly fly tonight. I have a facial appointment in the morning with Sebastian . . . Paddington-Bear. He's the best there is. His asphalt and cardamom micropeel is to die for. I'll have to ring back tomorrow after my appointment to rearrange the flight."

I ended the call before she could reply. Sebastian *Paddington-Bear*? That was awful, but my impression of an arm-candy girlfriend had been convincing enough to get me the information I wanted. I had to hand it to myself. I was getting pretty darn good at this detective stuff.

CHAPTER 13

Sonya and I sat at my kitchen island sipping a crisp rosé. Okay, Sonya sipped; I guzzled. Auntie Biz was already tucked into bed. Butterball zoomed around the living room, consumed by his regular evening burst of energy. He rushed headlong from the living room to the kitchen and back, suddenly stopping in his tracks and making an ungainly flying leap onto the coffee table. He froze—mesmerized by a hair elastic I'd left there.

We both stared at him, watching as he batted the hairband as if demons had suddenly possessed his paw.

"Anywhoo . . ." Sonya said, widening her eyes at the cat's crazed antics. "Sounds like you had quite the day."

"Yep." Before Butterball distracted us, I'd filled her in on my visit to Glacier Valley Senior Care, the cops finding the cash in Biz's shed, my near run-in with Carson, and my discovery about Sam's whereabouts. I took another drink, allowing the bright acidity of the wine to coat my tongue. Veronica Tanaka had chosen this vintage, and suggested we encourage customers to pair it with our fiery Eggplant Nduja or Asparagus and Prosciutto pizzas. I'd been skeptical, thinking a rosé would be too cloying for pizzas that contained cured meats, but we'd done a tasting session a few weeks before, and her choice had proved to be spot on. Turned out, it also paired well with Triscuits dipped in ranch dressing, my dinner for that night. Sonya and Biz had already eaten by the time I returned. Sonya had "shopped" in the restaurant kitchen and prepared a Moroccan lamb dish using the authentic earthenware tagine she'd bought me as a birthday present the previous year. Even though they'd left plenty for me, I'd been too mentally wiped out to even microwave a plate of leftovers.

"Maybe Capone should hire you. You're a natural." Sonya cast a glance at the closed bedroom door. "You're sure the money in the shed isn't hers?"

"I can't picture Auntie Biz hoarding cash like that," I said. "When my dad was going through his treatments, she tried to send some money to help out, but he refused to take it. He said she was barely scraping by on her pension. She lives modestly, but her property taxes and the maintenance on the cottage are a huge drain. Plus, the amount she'd been trying to send was a few hundred dollars. What was in that suitcase looked like thousands. I honestly think if she'd had that kind of money, she would've given it to us. Dad was like a son to her. Besides, would she have handed over the only shed key to Jeremy if she'd been storing a Brink's truck's worth of cash out there?"

"So I guess it must have been Jeremy's," Sonya said. "That certainly thickens the plot."

I downed the last drops of my wine and poured myself another glass. "I forgot to ask, did you get anywhere with Officer Stanhope?"

"Operation Flirtation?" She batted her eyes and playfully flipped her hair away from her face. "The main thing I discovered is that he's been very happily married for thirty-two years."

"Oh. So I guess he didn't succumb to your feminine wiles." I grimaced.

"After what happened at Quotidian, my feminine wiles should be surgically removed and locked in a concrete vault," she said, with a touch of bitterness. "Stanhope and I had a nice, normal chat. He's friendly enough, and he really appreciated the food we've been taking out to him and Torvald. I did manage to wheedle out one nugget of intel."

I raised an eyebrow.

"He confirmed that the gun that Biz was found holding was hers," she said. "Duly registered. Ballistics confirmation of the bullet will take a little longer, but all the preliminaries point to her gun being the murder weapon."

I swore under my breath. I'd been holding out hope that Auntie Biz ending up with her gun in her hand had been a bizarre coincidence.

"He also asked me if we were missing any wine glasses from the restaurant."

"Wine glasses? Why?" I asked.

"Dunno. I got the impression that the cops found some broken glass near the crime scene, but he wouldn't tell me more," Sonya replied. "It could be unrelated, though. A lot of people like to stroll along that path in the evenings with their sunset cocktails."

"We should do an inventory to see if we can figure it out," I said. "Since last night was the first time we used the new glasses, we might be able to nail down if any went missing." As I took another swig of wine, my phone buzzed in my pocket. A video call from Melody and Daniel flashed up on the screen.

Their faces appeared and Sonya leaned over my shoulder to put herself in the frame on my side of the call.

"How goes the Menomonie fact-finding mission?" I asked.

"It's going fantastic," Daniel said. His words slurred slightly and even in the dark, he looked a little glassy-eyed.

They were sitting in Melody's Honda, in what appeared to be a parking lot.

"Has someone come forward saying Jeremy spent his holidays with them?" I asked, allowing my hopes to rise.

"No," Melody said. "But we're making progress. Menomonie is pretty small. We canvassed most of the restaurants today and now we've moved on to the bars."

"Yes, bars. We're showing Jeremy's picture to the local people on our phones to see if anyone recognizes him," Daniel explained. "By tomorrow or maybe the next day, we'll have covered every hangout in Meemom . . . Moomuneenee."

Melody nodded. "If Jeremy spent time here, somebody should have seen him."

"Are people suspicious? Do they want to know why you're asking questions about him?" Sonya wondered.

"*Pfft.*" Daniel blew a raspberry, dismissing Sonya's suggestion with a wave of his hand. "The people in Meemom . . . Momomininny are so friendly. They won't stop talking to us everywhere we go." Daniel's voice was much louder than it needed to be, considering they were calling from a quiet car. "They buy us drinks in every bar."

Melody shot him an amused look. "The local *women* buy *you* drinks in every bar. I'm the designated driver." She turned back to the screen. "We're telling people that I'm Jeremy's daughter and I need to clear up some things with his estate. It seemed like a good cover story and people seem to buy it."

"She's doing a great job," Daniel said, giving Melody a haphazard pat on the head. "Who knew that this sweet farm girl could be such a good liar?"

Melody beamed back at him.

"Good work, you two. I'll let you get back to Operation Needle in a Haystack. Maybe you should hit a coffee house next instead of another bar," I suggested, ending the call.

"Well, they might not find anything, but at least Melody will get to spend some quality time mooning over Daniel," Sonya said, taking a sip of her wine.

"So you noticed her crush, too?"

"My blind uncle Mortimer would see it, and he's been dead for twenty years," she sniffed.

I topped up my wine. "Hey, there's something that's bothering me. About Melody," I said. "What if she really is a good liar? Now that we know that Biz's gun was more than likely the murder weapon, we can be pretty sure the murderer was in the restaurant last night. The gun was in Auntie Biz's purse at the start of the night and in her hands at the end of the night. So that probably rules out Irv and Tami Callahan as suspects, along with anyone else who wasn't at the party.

"I'm sure Biz didn't kill Jeremy," I continued, "which means someone inside the dining room at the party must've gotten it out of her purse, used it to shoot him, and then placed it back in her hand after she passed out. My aunt specifically mentioned that Melody wheeled her out when she was marooned against the wall. I went back through all the footage from that night. The people that I know left the restaurant at the same time as my aunt and Jeremy were you, me, Carson, Veronica Tanaka, and Melody."

"No," Sonya interrupted.

"I didn't even finish my thought," I protested.

"You were going to ask me if I think Melody could've done it, and the answer is no. Actually, my full answer is hell to the N-O."

"How can you be sure?" I asked. "We've only known her for a couple of weeks. Yes, she seems like a sweetheart, but Ted Bundy fooled a lot of people, too. Apparently he was very charming right up until he murdered all those people."

"My certainty isn't based on the fact that she's likable."

She crossed her arms, her face taking on a schoolmarm expression. "Remember, Dokters are born lawyers. Melody was never out of my sight for more than a few minutes. She kept picking up the slack for Carson, which didn't leave her enough time to sneak down to the dock and back. When I went out to the patio right after you left, she was coming back in with a stack of plates. Usain Bolt couldn't have run down to the lake, shot Jeremy, and then gotten back to the patio and gathered all those dishes in the amount of time it would have taken. Even if she's managed to hoodwink us all with a Tony-winning naïve farm-girl act, she literally could not have done it. A killer needs means, motive, and opportunity. If she pocketed Biz's gun, that would give her the means, sure, but nothing else."

"You're right. Even if she took the gun, there was no opportunity for her to commit the murder," I said with a sigh.

"Besides," Sonya continued, "what would her motive be for killing Jeremy?"

"Pure homicidal mania?" I ventured, half smiling.

"Right, and Butterball was her accomplice. The two of them are a modern-day Bonnie and Clyde." We laughed at the mental picture. "More than likely, that shed full of cash plays into the motive," Sonya concluded.

"But even if that connects to Melody somehow, you're right. Now that I think about it, she was probably still in the restaurant when I heard what I thought was a car backfiring. The sound we now know was the gunshot. She had no opportunity to get down to the crime scene before I did."

I played back the mental images of the party again. Who else had access to that gun? I'd pushed Biz's wheelchair out of the way briefly when Jeremy brought her drink. Then she'd wobbled a little and . . . *I'd asked Carson to bring her chair over.* I remembered now. I'd had to shout to get his attention and he shuttled her chair over to where we were standing.

"I need to talk to Carson," I whispered. "He was probably the last person to touch the wheelchair other than Jeremy and Biz herself. Maybe he saw the gun in her purse and pocketed it then. He slipped away just before the shooting. So there's your means and your opportunity."

"What about motive?" Sonya asked.

"That thing he said to his parents about being responsible for Jeremy's death, I don't think that's something he'd just *say*. There has to be a reason. He knew Jeremy from when he used to look after Carson's great grandmother. Maybe they have some kind of beef going back to that time."

"Wouldn't he have been just a kid then?"

"Kids can have beefs. Also, why would he be lurking outside my aunt's house if he wasn't up to something?" I paused. "I want to talk to Lois Gorman, too."

"That's probably the first time in history anyone has ever uttered the phrase 'I want to talk to Lois Gorman,'" Sonya quipped.

"Jeremy cared for Lois's mother Dorothy for months. Tami told me her mother and Grandma Dorothy were extremely close. Lois must've gotten to know Jeremy at least a little bit during that time. Tami said they adored Jeremy, but maybe that's not the whole story. At the very least, maybe she can tell us more about his past," I said. Butterball nudged my foot and I leaned over to scoop him into my arms. He purred as I pressed my forehead against his.

"I didn't even get a chance to ask you with all this chaos," Sonya said, leaning over to give the cat's ears a scratch. "What did you and Sam decide about Butterball? Is Sam going to let you keep him?"

Truth was, I hadn't even allowed myself to think about it.

A hard knot formed in my stomach. I could accept the loss of my dream house, but my sweet kitty? Sure, Butterball had originally been Sam's cat, but for the last three years, I'd been the one to feed him, patch him up after his fights, deal with his hairballs, and take him to his vet appointments. He'd been by my side all through my father's illness. *Could Sam just take him from me?* I blocked the thoughts, like a child closing her eyes during a scary movie. "We didn't really talk about it," I said. "Sam left so quickly."

"My cousin Sylvia's a custody attorney. She does pet cases all the time. Last year, she did two llamas and a mongoose. Say the word and she'll be at your service."

I mustered a smile. "Thanks."

Sonya drained the last of her wine and clapped her hands on her thighs. "Time to call it a night. Stick a fork in me, etcetera." She stood and kissed my head, then Butterball's. "Adieu, my dah-lings."

After Sonya left, I fed Butterball and, even though I was exhausted, dragged myself to the shower. The grunge of the day's stress and frantic activity covered me like a slimy blanket. The soothing jets of hot water lulled me into a stupor. I soaped my entire body, from my toe tips to the crown of my head. As I rinsed, a dull thump sounded from somewhere nearby, followed by a thunderous crash that rang out like a shattering windowpane. I hastily turned off the shower, wrapped a towel around my dripping body, and rushed out into the main living space.

Semidarkness softened the outlines of the furniture and kitchen cabinets. All was still. "Auntie Biz?" I called out softly. My voice trembled. No reply. I left a sodden trail of footprints as I padded through the kitchen and living room, heart pounding. My brain sent red-alert signals rocketing down every nerve fiber. *Why wasn't Biz answering? What if the killer had returned?* Maybe Biz had been his target all along.

I could scarcely take a breath as I creaked open the bedroom door. Inside, Biz snoozed in my king-sized bed, seemingly undisturbed by the commotion. I watched the rise and fall of her chest for a few moments, to reassure myself that she was okay. I moved back into the living space. All the windows seemed intact. Maybe something had happened out in the parking lot? I couldn't be sure where the sound had come from. As I moved into the kitchen, though, something sharp sliced into my foot. I cursed and flicked on the light switch. That's when I saw the pottery fragments of my beautiful Moroccan tagine—the one Sonya had used to make dinner than night—scattered like blown leaves all across the kitchen floor.

Shoot. Butterball was notorious for knocking into valuables. He hadn't done it lately, so I had gotten lax about clearing tables, dressers, and countertops of fragile items. Looked like he was up to his old tricks.

I hobbled back into the bathroom, cleaned and bandaged the gash on my foot, and then threw on my bathrobe and slippers. The mess extended across the length of the kitchen and beyond. I'd tracked in water from the shower. Sonya hadn't cleaned the tagine, so its death throes had flung bits of couscous and lamb everywhere. And my sliced foot had somehow managed to splash blood around like a PETA protester. My mind struggled to comprehend the gruesome acrobatics that had allowed blood from my foot to splatter onto the countertop. How was that even possible?

I donned rubber gloves and mixed up a solution of diluted bleach. So much for my early night. Strangely, I looked forward to tackling the chaos. Although I knew cooks who dreaded cleaning, it had always been one of my favorite parts of being a chef. Seeing my kitchen sparkle at the end of a night's service filled me with a sense of well-being. Tonight especially, I felt that by mopping up every shard of the broken dish and bead of couscous, I was working to wipe away the wreckage of my life.

I pitched everything into a garbage bag and headed out to bring the remains down to the dumpster. As I approached the door, though, I saw a dim crack of moonlight. The door hadn't been shut all the way. My heart pounded anew. In my survey of the apartment, I realized that Butterball hadn't been in evidence. Now I raced around the apartment, searching for him, still clutching the garbage bag. He was a big presence, and his portly body wasn't easily concealed. I checked his usual haunts to no avail and ran back to the door. Had I locked it behind Sonya when she left? I honestly couldn't remember.

The opening in the door wasn't wide, but it was definitely large enough for Butterball to have slipped a paw in. He'd been known to take off like a flaming arrow when he was scared, and the noise of a smashing dish would definitely have spooked him. I also wouldn't put it past him to slink out to avoid the consequences of his actions, knowing that he would be in trouble. Either way, it seemed he was on the loose.

After his string of kitty altercations and injuries when we first moved, he'd been confined to the apartment. Since then, he'd only been outside when closely supervised by me or Sam. Would he even know where he was? What if he ran too far and got lost? I hurried down the stairs and tossed the trash bag next to the dumpster.

The moon wasn't quite full, but between its glow and the illumination from the security light fixed on the side of the restaurant, I had a reasonably good view of my surroundings. To my left was the dumpster and the back entrance to the restaurant; to my right was the parking lot. I walked in that direction. The lot was empty, save for two police cars, which sat a few spaces away from my Jeep. Police cars. I'd forgotten all about our minder. But why two? Surely one cop could handle babysitting me and Biz. Maybe the officer on duty—Torvald or Stanhope or whoever was stationed here tonight—had seen Butterball. I hustled over to the cars, but my heart sank when I discovered they were empty.

"Butterbaaaall!" I paced the parking lot in my slippers, pulling my robe more tightly around my body. I doubled back on myself, making a slow circuit of the building. By now, I was gripped by a full-on panic. Butterball had no collar. I thought I remembered Sam saying that the animal shelter had microchipped him before he was adopted out, but with Sam out of the country and incommunicado, how would anyone even know who to contact?

"Butterbaaaall!" I yelled again and again, my voice growing rawer.

I crossed the parking lot toward the small patch of woods that separated the restaurant from town. Before his home confinement, when Butterball had free rein to wander, his favorite pastime, other than brawling, had been bird hunting. He'd never been a good hunter, but the occasional bloody, feathered offering he used to bring in was yet another reason he was now kept entirely inside. Old habits died hard.

I called out again, trying to keep back the tears. I was nearing the deserted dock area, almost to the spot where I'd found Jeremy's dead body just one night earlier. As I stepped onto the shore path, the crunch of sand and gravel bit into my brain, calling up the memory of that gruesome discovery. The wind whispered in the trees, and the waves thumped rhythmically against the shore.

Instead of being lulled by the lake's gentle noises, I was on the cusp of a nervous breakdown. The police had taken down the caution tape from the crime scene earlier that day, but my mind still screamed *Caution!* with each step I took.

In the trees, close by, came a rustling noise. Had something moved, or had my fear totally hijacked my senses? The rustling became more frantic and a chorus of screeching and hissing emanated from the trees.

"Butterball?" I whispered, barely able to form the sounds of his name. Only the discordant chirps of nighttime insects replied. I cleared my throat. I needed to get ahold of myself, for Butterball's sake. Whispering and cowering wouldn't bring him home. "Butterball!" I called. A large, dark animal shape rocketed out of the trees, sending my heart clashing against the walls of my chest.

A moment later Officer Mustache aka Officer Torvald, staggered through the trees like a lumbering Yeti. In his arms, he cradled a large, butterscotch-furred bundle.

I ran over to them and melted, sobbing, against them. I took Butterball from Torvald and cradled him in my arms.

"Thank you," I managed to blubber.

"He's faster than he looks, 'n so?" Officer Torvald said with a laugh.

The trees rustled again, and another police officer with graying hair and eyes as green as Butterball's crashed onto the shore path. He pulled a few burrs off his uniform and then stuck out a hand. "Lee Stanhope."

I greeted the officer. "How did you find him?"

"Chased him all the way here," Stanhope said. "We'd been talking by our patrol cars, getting ready to change shifts. I thought I heard something, and when I looked up, I saw this big guy come flying down the stairs." He patted Butterball's rump.

Torvald nodded. "We figured he must've escaped from your place, so we pursued him. We saw him encounter another feline and there was an altercation."

"Took us a second to realize what was going on. That other cat was a mighty big fellow, too." Stanhope patted his slightly paunchy midsection and then patted Butterball again. "I know how that is," he chuckled.

I ignored the jab at my cat's weight. I was overjoyed to have him back, every last ounce of him. I looked off in the direction they indicated that the other cat had run and clicked my tongue. "It's that Maine Coon again, I bet. The one with the pointy ears who looks like the devil."

"Sounds about right," Stanhope agreed.

"I can't thank you enough," I said. "I doubt the Chicago PD would've bothered to run through the woods after a cat."

"Luckily, we don't get many murders in Geneva Bay, so we get pretty good at chasing stray pets and finding stolen bikes," Torvald said.

"Are you hungry? I can make you something." Food was my go-to means of expressing gratitude. Well, of expressing any emotion, really.

"No, thanks, ma'am. I've got to get on home to the wife," Stanhope said.

"And I'm still working through what's left over from what you sent out for lunch," Torvald said. "Those calzones were out of this world. And that dip, the green stuff?" He kissed the tips of his fingers.

I beamed, squeezing Butterball to my chest. Few things gave me more joy than seeing someone well fed. "I'm glad you liked it. I used the same ingredients we put in our curried cauliflower pizza, but I thought you'd want a more portable version, so I made it into a calzone," I explained. "We serve it with a chunky green tomato and mint chutney. I blitzed that into a dipping sauce."

"Well, whatever that was, I'm tempted to arrest you because there must be addictive drugs in it," he said with a laugh. "At the station, they all thought this was a bum assignment, sitting out here all night staking out you and Miss O'Leary. But when we told them about the perks, suddenly they're trying to trade shifts."

CHAPTER 14

I woke up with a start, accidentally launching Butterball from where he'd been nuzzled next to my feet. He screeched his displeasure before sauntering off to his litterbox. My sleep had been fitful, not only because I'd given up my bed to Auntie Biz and slept on the couch again. My dreams had been strange and disturbing—full of the confusion and fear that characterized the last few days. Something felt off.

Outside, the garbage truck grumbled up to the back of the restaurant. It beeped into reverse, and then the machinery of the truck began to squawk and hiss as it maneuvered into place. There were definite disadvantages to living over the restaurant. Good thing I could make do with very little sleep. Between the late-night closings and early morning deliveries and noisy garbage pickups, my windows of undisturbed slumber were bound to be short. *If the restaurant ever even got off the ground*, I reminded myself.

I tried to quiet my breathing as I looked around. Dull, gray light penetrated into the room through the balcony doors. Rain drummed steadily on the windows. My kitchen sparkled from the thorough scrubbing I'd done the previous night. Still, something wasn't right.

At last, the dissonant clatter of trash bins being emptied

signaled that the garbage truck was ready to depart. That's when I heard it. A soft moan from the bedroom.

"Auntie Biz?" I called, as I hurried to the door. Inside, Biz lay on the carpet, doubled over and shivering. I gasped and dropped to the floor next to her. "What's wrong?" She was curled in a fetal position, her muscles twitching. I put a hand to her clammy forehead. She opened her eyes just long enough for me to observe how dilated the wide, black circles of her pupils were. "Oh, God," I whispered.

Scrambling to my feet, I raced back to the living area. Phone. Phone. Where was it? I found it next to the couch, and, with shaking hands, dialed 9-1-1. Time slowed to a crawl as the phone rang. Even during the last year of Biz's worsening health, I'd witnessed nothing remotely like this. She'd often been sleepy and confused, never rigid and unresponsive.

Once an ambulance had been summoned, I raced downstairs. I didn't even feel the raindrops. I pounded on Torvald's car window, jolting him from a doze. "My aunt. Please, hurry." Together, the two of us raced upstairs.

He tested her pulse and shined a small flashlight into her weirdly dilated eyes. He repeated the test and his brow furrowed in confusion.

"What?" I demanded. "What's wrong with her?"

His voice tightened as he continued his rapid assessment of her condition. "It's . . . nothing." He shook his head again. "I just thought . . . Nothing. Sorry. The ambulance will be here soon." He directed me to get a blanket to wrap my aunt's shivering body. I wrapped it around her and cradled her like a child, stroking her feather-soft white hair as we waited the interminable minutes for the ambulance to arrive. This couldn't be happening. *Hadn't I lost enough?*

Officer Torvald, in his patrol car, followed the ambulance to the hospital, and he sat in the waiting room with me after the doctors whisked my aunt away for tests. I didn't have the wherewithal to make conversation or to sip the coffee he'd bought from the vending machine for me. He patted me on the arm. "It'll be okay," he said. "Your aunt's a tough lady. Me and both my brothers had her for homeroom. Didn't dare be late for Miss O'Leary's class."

I mustered a weak smile. Where I'd grown up, a lot of kids were raised to avoid cops. Even though I'd come from a law-abiding family and had always tried to walk the straight and narrow, that attitude had rubbed off on me. Being in a place where the police found lost cats and brought Styrofoam coffee cups to worried family members would take some getting used to.

A South Asian doctor in teal scrubs came into the empty waiting room and sat across from us. She looked about twelve years old, with wide, black eyes and a thick mop of curls.

"Miss O'Leary, I'm Dr. Sittampalam."

"How is my aunt?"

"Stable. Can I ask what medications your aunt has taken in the last forty-eight hours?"

"Um, I can't remember exactly. There are a lot. About a dozen different bottles." I gasped. "Oh no. I forgot to tell Sonya to give her her pills before bed last night. She was already sleeping when I got home. She missed her evening doses, and I can't remember if she took the dose she's supposed to take during *Jeopardy!* I didn't even think . . ." I put my head in my hands. "This is all my fault, isn't it?"

The doctor shook her head. "Do you remember the names of any of the medications your aunt was prescribed?"

"Oxysomething and dexasomething else. Something zolem." I shook my head. "I'm sorry. The last few days have been so crazy, I wasn't paying attention. Her caregiver died suddenly without leaving any instructions, so I just did what it said on the bottles. You know, if it said give twice a day with food, that's what I did. I should've called her doctor to double-check. You must think I'm a complete idiot."

"No," Officer Torvald soothed. "Youse've had a lot to deal with."

"There were a few pills I recognized from when my dad was sick," I recalled. My voice quivered, but I was determined to keep control of my emotions. Crying in front of strangers was not in the O'Leary playbook. In fact, crying was not in the O'Leary playbook, period.

"And what was he sick with?" Dr. Sittampalam asked.

"Cancer. Kidney cancer," I sputtered.

Dr. Sittampalam and Officer Torvald exchanged a look.

"What?" I demanded. "Please don't tell me she has cancer, too." I bit my lip. Hard.

Dr. Sittampalam gave a vigorous shake of her Shirley Temple curls. "Thankfully, no." She paused, leaning closer to me. "But the drugs you're describing are usually reserved for very painful conditions, things like spinal-disc degeneration, end-stage cancer pain, things like that. I believe the doses she took were high, too." She paused. "Your aunt seems to be suffering from opiate withdrawal."

"Opiate withdrawal?! Auntie Biz?"

The doctor nodded.

Torvald sighed, resting the fingers of one hand on the end of his blond mustache. "I suspected, but I didn't believe my own eyes. Told myself Miss O'Leary couldn't be dopesick," he said. "Unfortunately, we see a fair bit of it nowadays. Happens when addicts can't get a hit."

"Auntie Biz isn't a junkie," I huffed. "Those were prescriptions. She needs someone to help her take her medications, so she wasn't even taking them by herself. She probably had a bad reaction to one of the pills."

"I'm afraid not," Dr. Sittampalam said.

"Rabbit asked me something about her having problems with pain," I paced up and down the small room, remembering the conversation I'd had with my newly hired dishwasher. "He noticed the pills when he was in my apartment yesterday. I didn't think anything of it. I just assumed that older people have aches and pains and take a lot of medications."

"Rabbit? Rabbit Blakemore?" Torvald asked. A furrow of concern creased his pink forehead.

"You know him?" I asked.

Torvald nodded and rose to his feet. "I'm going to step out real quick. Make a couple calls," he said.

What could this have to do with Rabbit? I wondered.

Sonya burst through the waiting room door, her normally perfectly coifed bob ruffled and her flawless red lipstick noticeably absent. "Oh my god, Dee. I came as soon as I saw your text." Before I knew it, she had plowed a path toward me. I collapsed into her embrace. She stroked my hair and made a shushing sound, easing me into a chair.

With shuddering breaths, I managed to summarize the story for her.

Dr. Sittampalam waited until the volume of our blubbering had lowered and then said, "We've already tried to contact Miss O'Leary's doctor. Unfortunately, his office is closed until Monday, but his answering service will try to reach him. Once I've reviewed her medical record, I'll have a better idea of what's going on with her."

"Will she be okay?" Sonya asked.

"She's stable," Dr. Sittampalam repeated, without elaborating.

"Oh, Dee, I'm so sorry," Sonya said. "I should've thought

to give her the medications last night. Biz and I were having a whale of a time. We played some Boggle and she kicked my butt, as usual. Then she got sleepy and I helped her to bed." She hung her head. "I'll never forgive myself if something happens to her."

"This isn't your fault. I never told you to give her the pills," I said. "I didn't expect that I'd be gone all day." I knew Sonya would never have endangered Biz. She'd spent dozens of weekends at my aunt's house over the years. The three of us would stay up into the wee hours, tasting each other's culinary inventions, drinking cocktails, and concocting elaborate feasts. Some of those dishes had made their way onto the menus of the high-end Chicago restaurants where Sonya and I worked.

"It may be for the best that you didn't give her any medications," Dr. Sittampalam said. "Something doesn't add up. Overall, she seems to be in reasonably good health for a woman of her age, and yet you describe a dozen daily medications. The pharmacy of a very sick person. I'd like to see for myself what she's been taking."

I sprang up. "I can go home and get her pills for you. That might be faster than waiting for the doctor's office to send over the records."

Dr. Sittampalam nodded. "That could be helpful. Leave them at the front desk and have them page me."

Sonya and I hopped in her car and hurried back to the restaurant. The rain continued steadily. Geneva Bay hadn't yet fully awakened. Tourists tended to rise slowly on the weekends. The parking spots in front of the Egg Harbor Cafe were all filled, but downtown was otherwise deserted. Sonya and I barely spoke a word. It was the heaviest stretch of silence in our nearly twenty-year friendship.

When we arrived back at the restaurant, I took the stairs two by two. By the time Sonya caught up with me a moment later, I was standing in the kitchen. Instead of gathering up Auntie Biz's pill bottles, though, I was rooted to the floor, dumbfounded. The counter was empty. The pills were gone.

CHAPTER 15

I stood in the kitchen blinking, as if I could close my eyes and magically summon the vanished pill bottles. "They were here, right?" I asked, turning to Sonya, who stood behind me, panting from running upstairs.

"Could Biz have moved them?" she asked. "Let's check the bedroom."

The two of us searched the apartment. Given the size of the space, it didn't take long to determine that the pills were gone.

I shook my head, my brain misfiring like a faulty engine. "They're not here."

Butterball meowed his hellos and sidled up to Sonya. She scooped him up for a cuddle.

I slapped my hand against my forehead. "Poor guy skipped breakfast again this morning. I can't believe what a basket case I've been. That's, like, the third time in the past couple of days I've forgotten to feed him. And Biz's medications. I know I gave them to her at lunchtime, and I'm almost positive I put them right back, but after that, I just can't remember. I feel like I'm going crazy."

Sonya pulled a can of tuna from the cupboard and cranked

it open. "Dee, you can't expect yourself to be as on top of everything as you usually are. You've barely slept, and you've had more drama than a cineplex in the last few days. You've got to cut yourself a break." As she spoke, she dumped the tuna into a bowl, mixed in some dry kitty kibble, and placed it on the kitchen island.

Butterball stood on his hind legs, stretching his forelimbs longingly against the cabinet below the tuna. He began circling the island like a prowling shark. He took a few steps back, as if preparing to leap up, but stopped midstride and resumed his impatient orbit.

I watched him for a moment, realization landing in my stomach like a brick. I scooted the bowl closer to the edge. "C'mon Buddy," I urged. Butterball again prepared to jump, and then instantly thought better of it. He sat down and turned accusatory green eyes toward me that seemed to say, *Why are you teasing me?*

Sonya looked at my face. "What's going on?" she asked.

"He's too fat to jump up here."

"Don't tell me you're going to put him on that weird raw wildlife diet that Sam found online. I, for one, refuse to butcher a chipmunk. Where would we even get a steady supply of dead chipmunks? Pretty sure Big Dave and Sujeet don't carry chipmunk meat." She grabbed the food bowl and set it on the floor, where Butterball dove for it. "See? Problem solved." She scratched his ears. "You're beautiful just the way you are."

I held up my hand. "Shh. I have to think." I didn't really have to think, though. The truth was right in front of me, but I needed a moment to stare it in its ugly face. If Butterball couldn't get onto the counter himself, there's no way he could have knocked over the tagine the night before. There was only one possible conclusion—someone broke into my apartment last night and stole Biz's pills. Only maybe they didn't break in. Auntie Biz was convinced that the murderer had rifled through her purse to get her gun. Maybe her keys weren't lost. Maybe they'd been stolen, too. I groaned inwardly. Her keys included conveniently labeled spares to my apartment and the restaurant.

Someone had stolen her keys on the night of the murder and used them to break into my house. Whoever it was must've broken the tagine, and the noise probably sent the robber rushing out, leaving the door ajar and allowing Butterball to escape. My heart crashed around my chest like a demented bumper car.

I needed to talk to Capone.

Capone picked up my call on the first ring. Turned out that Torvald had already brought him up to speed on my aunt's condition and everything that had happened that morning. If Capone was surprised to hear about the break-in and the stolen pills, his voice didn't show it. I supposed he didn't want to dwell on the fact that the officers who were supposed to be guarding/jailing me had let a thief slip by them and then gotten distracted by my errant cat. I didn't want to dwell on it either. Not while there was still a murderer on the loose. After my initial feeling of disquiet about being watched by the cops, I'd actually begun to take some comfort in Torvald and Stanhope's presence. I didn't know for sure if the murderer and the burglar were the same person, but either way, it seemed that having my own personal police patrol within spitting distance had done little to deter criminals.

"Torvald is still at the hospital," Capone told me. "He'll let your aunt's physician know that she'll have to try to find out what she'd been prescribed a different way. Hopefully, they'll reach your aunt's primary care doctor. If not, Glacier Valley might have records. I'll swing by with a CSI to collect evidence from your place. Usually, we can't afford to put crime scene investigation resources into domestic robberies, but in this case, I think it's justified."

I groaned. "Bad news. I cleaned the whole place, and the trash has already gone to the dump. I heard the truck this morning."

"From what you described—the blood spatters that were hard to account for from your foot injury—it sounds like the thief may have cut him or herself on the broken dish, too. We may be able to pull some DNA," Capone said.

"Clearly, you've never seen me clean." I slumped onto the couch and pulled Butterball into my lap. "I can't believe I sabotaged the crime scene. This could've been the break we needed to catch whoever did this." I shifted the phone to my other ear. "I should bring you into the loop with a few other things, while I have you.

"I know where Sam is," I explained. "Well, kind of. His car is at the Grand Bay Resort. I'm pretty sure he flew from there to the Costa Rica on a Jet-a-Porter jet around ten p.m. on the night of the murder, so he couldn't have done it."

"The time of the murder was around nine twenty. You're saying he suddenly left the country right *after* the murder, and that proves his innocence?" Capone's skepticism was evident.

"Hear me out. The jet company had to send a plane from Kentucky. It would take at least a few hours to get that organized. He probably called the company right after our fight that afternoon, but couldn't leave until the jet got there. I bet he hung out in the hotel café until it arrived. Maybe someone will remember seeing him there."

"Well, I'll grant you that at least now we have more to go on to try to establish his whereabouts. I don't want you going rogue trying to track him down yourself," Capone said.

I opened my mouth to tell him about catching Carson on the security camera, but I decided now wasn't the time. The security footage didn't actually prove anything. Capone was clearly irritated with me, and I couldn't risk going off half-cocked.

"I was hoping my tip about Sam would make up for me destroying all the robbery evidence," I said.

"I'll let you know when we're square," he replied.

"Can I ask you something?" I said. "I noticed Torvald's ears perk up when 'opiates' and 'Rabbit' were mentioned together. Do I need to be worried?"

"Cops who've been around awhile know Rabbit pretty well," Capone said. "He dabbled in prescription drug 'repurposing' back in his heyday."

"Ah, so that was the drug offence he mentioned on his résumé," I said.

"As to whether you need to worry, yes, you should. There's a murderer on the loose and someone broke into your apartment. Rabbit was never been involved in anything violent before, but prison can change people. I'll be having a conversation with him, and soon. In the meantime, let us do our jobs, okay? No more amateur sleuthing. You seem to have forgotten that you and your aunt aren't in the clear. Any sloppy evidence gathering by someone so closely involved in the investigation could set us back."

I wanted to be reassured by his honey-smooth baritone, but, as I hung up the phone, I couldn't help feeling that the dark forces in the background were moving a lot faster than the police investigation. Despite Capone's warnings and my missteps as an amateur sleuth, I had to keep trying.

"Well?" Sonya said, taking a seat on the couch next to me. "I was doing my best to eavesdrop, but Capone's a low talker. Did he say something about Rabbit?"

I nodded and filled her in.

"What do you think? Would Rabbit have done it?" Sonya asked.

"I want to give the guy the benefit of the doubt. He and
Auntie Biz seem genuinely fond of each other." I hesitated.
"But I barely know the guy, and he did just get out of prison.
He seemed like he wanted to get on the straight and narrow,
but if he's an addict, best intentions could easily go out the
window. I can't deny that his eyes landed on the pills the second he walked in."

Sonya clicked her tongue. "Doesn't look good, does it?"

"No. Capone said they're going to have a chat with him."

"Something tells me Capone might not be quite as gentle
questioning an ex-con as he was questioning an eighty-year-
old schoolteacher and a pretty local restaurant owner," she
said. "The good news is if Rabbit stole the pills that would
make it less likely that the robbery and Jeremy's murder were
connected. He wasn't at the party."

"So I can take comfort that I was burglarized by an ordinary drug fiend and not a murderer?" I said.

"Exactly."

CHAPTER 16

Sonya and I had barely finished our conversation when a car whooshed into the restaurant parking lot, breaking the steady rhythm of the rain. I walked to the window, where I saw a beat-up Ford Focus of indeterminate color—greige, maybe?—rumble to a stop. "That's Rabbit's car," I gasped. "I forgot he said he was coming in this morning."

"Guess the Five-O haven't gotten to him yet," Sonya said. "Do you want me to call Capone?"

I thought for a moment. "Yes, but wait about ten minutes. I want to talk to Rabbit myself."

"Didn't Capone explicitly tell you to back off the Nancy Drew act?" Sonya said.

"Rabbit is my employee. I can't throw him to the wolves without talking to him first. I've dealt with a lot of shady characters. I've got a pretty good sense when someone is trying to pull the wool over my eyes."

Sonya chuckled. "That's an understatement. I'll never forget when that vendor at Kyōten tried to pass off Oklahoma Angus for Kobe beef. Remember? He was so scared, he accidentally called you 'mommy' at one point while you were haranguing him."

I threaded my fingers together and cracked my knuckles. "Let's hope I can live up to my reputation."

I ran down to unlock the restaurant, glad I hadn't yet given Rabbit his own key. If he turned out to be guilty, that would be one less thing to worry about. Rabbit entered the kitchen a moment later, while I was still toweling the rain off my face. He, too, was sodden. I threw him a kitchen towel.

"Thanks. Cats and dogs," Rabbit said, wiping his face. When he finished, he turned to me. "What's on the agenda for today, chef?"

"Follow me," I directed. I walked through the swinging door into the dining room and indicated that Rabbit should sit at one of the tables. No sense in beating around the bush. I sat down opposite him. "I need to know if you stole my aunt's pills."

Rabbit's eyes widened and his brow creased in confusion. "Miss O'Leary's pills?"

"Yes. The pills you saw on the counter yesterday. You seemed very interested in them. They've gone missing. Did you take them?"

"No!" Rabbit practically fell out of his chair in his scramble to deny the accusation. He took a breath and repeated, "No, ma'am."

I leaned closer, pressing my forearms on the table between us. "Do you deny that your eyes went straight to those pills yesterday?" Here, I saw some hesitation. Rabbit's eyes flicked around the room like lightning bugs in a jar. "Well?"

He hung his head. "No, I don't deny it."

"Why were you so interested in the pills?" I demanded, raising my voice a notch.

Capone seemed to have perfected the good-cop persona. That wasn't my style. I'd clawed and scraped to the top of my profession in overheated, macho kitchens. "Nice" never won anyone a Michelin star.

"I didn't take them. I swear it on my daughter," he pleaded.

"So, you just have a casual interest in pharmaceuticals?" I asked.

"Force of habit, I guess," Rabbit replied. His head hung. "Those kinds of pills. I could see straight off what they were. Oxy, percs, benzos."

"Go on."

Rabbit shifted in his chair and planted his eyes on the table. "After my first conviction, for when I burned down that old warehouse out by Route 50 when I was seventeen, I couldn't find no work once I got out. I got into trouble. Owed some bad people money." His eyes met mine, his expression stony and serious. "A lot of money. I pushed pills for them. One of the guys had a girlfriend who worked in a nursing home. She'd skim the pills from the old folks and we'd resell them. They also had someone who'd forge prescriptions for us to fill. They had another guy who worked at a pain clinic, too. You'd go to him and he'd write you a script. It changed all the time. People would get cold feet, or get arrested, skim off the top, use with the product they were supposed to be selling, steal from each other. The players were always changing."

I thought back to Capone's description of "dis-organized crime." That seemed to gel with what Rabbit was describing.

"So you weren't an addict?" I asked.

"Alcohol has always been the demon I wrestle with," he replied, with a flat, slightly haunted look in his eyes. "The pills were pure business. You can sell oxycodone on the street for twenty, twenty-five bucks a pill."

I thought back to the veritable pharmacy I'd had on my kitchen counter. "Twenty dollars for one pill?"

He nodded. "When I saw all those pills, it brought back the memories, is all. I noticed they had a few different doctors' names on them and a few different pharmacies' names, too."

Now that Rabbit mentioned it, I remembered noticing the same thing. Some of Auntie Biz's prescriptions had been filled from pharmacies as far away as Janesville, forty miles away. I had considered it a little odd at the time, but I hadn't ascribed any sinister motives.

"It also worried me a little when I saw what kinds of stuff she was taking," Rabbit continued. "Sometimes a pharmacist would start asking questions when you brought the fake script in, you'd have to say you had a real bad back pain from a car wreck or something. Those pills that Miss O'Leary had were no joke. Most doctors don't just give prescriptions like that for any old thing. I thought maybe she was real sick with something. But you said she ain't sick, so that's a relief."

"She wasn't sick yesterday," I muttered. He looked at me quizzically, but I waved his unspoken question away. If I started talking about Auntie Biz being in the hospital, I'd shatter my tough-guy facade. "One more question. Where were you last night?"

"With Everleigh at my mom's. The custody hearing went good, so the judge upheld my right to see her. I got every other weekend for now, but maybe more in the future. Everleigh came home with me straight from the hearing, since her mom hadn't let her come the last couple weekends I was supposed to get her. Me and Everleigh made pancakes together this morning. She's an early riser, like her old man." He smiled, his eyes soft.

I leaned back in my chair. If Rabbit was lying, he'd done it extremely well. I'd looked for all the usual tells—hesitation, weird eye movements—but I'd seen nothing. His explanation made sense. His alibi, however, was going to be hard for him to prove. Even if his mother and daughter vouched for him, it wasn't the most airtight explanation for his whereabouts.

"Thanks for answering my questions. Detective Capone is going to be here soon," I said. "He wants to question you, too."

Rabbit's eyes filled with terror. "The cops? I thought you'd at least give me a chance to prove myself." He put his hands over his face. "They'll take me back to jail. I'll lose Everleigh for sure."

"I wasn't trying to get you in trouble," I said, softening my tone. I suddenly felt like some kind of reverse King Midas. Instead of turning everything to gold, I cast suspicion on everyone who crossed my path.

Rabbit looked up, a glimmer of hope in his eyes. "You believe me? That I didn't take Miss O'Leary's pills?" His brow furrowed. "Then how come you told the cops I took them?"

"I mentioned your name, that's all. The cops took it from there."

He shook his head, looking frightened and queasy. "They won't care if I did it or not. They start questioning you and twist your words. Then you're a goner."

"Rabbit, you're innocent this time. It won't be like the other times."

He put his face in his hands. "What am I gonna do?" he murmured, over and over.

"Hey, I've got your back, and I know you won't make me regret it. This is your chance at redemption. Earn it."

Rabbit peeked over the tops of his fingers. His vulnerability made me wish I were the kind of person who could make people feel better with a word or a hug. Tough love was the best I could muster. "If you're as open with Capone as you've been with me, he'll be reasonable."

My eyes drifted out the huge plate glass windows where, through the rain and mist, I could make out the shore path, a little snaking line that disappeared into the trees. The scene of Jeremy's murder lay just beyond.

"I'm sorry you got dragged into this," I sighed, my tone softening. "Believe me, I know how it feels to be in the wrong place at the wrong time."

CHAPTER 17

I directed Sonya to stick close to Rabbit and make sure he didn't get bullied or enticed into saying anything incriminating. Well, anything more incriminating than the actual truth. She assured me that a veritable stable of cousins and uncles could be called upon to swoop to the rescue if need be.

Even though I hadn't intended it, with Capone on his way to the restaurant to question Rabbit, events had conspired to give me a clear shot at talking to Carson and finding out why he was snooping around outside my aunt's cottage. Finally, I'd get my chance to pin that little jerk to the wall.

I had his address from his employment application. I cruised past the Frank Lloyd Wright–inspired library building, past downtown's charming shops and restaurants, and past the lakefront park with its picturesque Victorian-era band shell. Tourists under umbrellas or wearing ponchos scuttled from place to place, trying to wring some enjoyment out of the rainy day. As I headed out of town, the tree-lined boulevards and quaint buildings gave way to a teeming tangle of modern vacation rental condominiums, which became cheaper and lower quality the farther I drove from the lake.

I pulled up at the address—a modest, brick split-level in a neighborhood on the unfashionable side of Highway 12. An older-model minivan hunkered in the driveway, the car that Carson was so desperate to replace he'd deigned to take a job waiting tables at my restaurant. In a circle of white rocks sectioned out from the front lawn stood an iron bench surrounded by kitschy statues. A little Dutch boy and girl in wooden shoes and wide-brimmed hats smooching one another, a stone corgi, a decorative flagpole festooned with a flowery banner that read "Happy Spring!" I could picture Tami and Irv sitting there in the evenings, probably holding hands, waving as Carson rolled up in the passenger's seat of one of his cool, wealthy friend's cars.

I cringed, feeling a wave of sympathy for the young man. For someone so status conscious, parents like Tami and Irv, with their dweeby good cheer and their keenness to be involved in their son's life, would cause deep embarrassment. No, I reminded myself. This was the kid who looked you square in the face and said you should hire a busboy to wipe down tables because it wasn't in his job description. This was the kid who'd requested to leave early on Saturdays— our busiest nights—so the job didn't interfere with his social life. Plenty of kids would give their eyeteeth to have supportive parents like Tami and Irv, even if they were card-carrying dorks.

By the time I rang the doorbell, the rain had slowed to a drizzle. It was only eleven a.m., but I felt like the day had already been at least a week long. I waited for a moment and then rang again. Heavy footsteps thudded down the stairs and the door creaked open to reveal Carson, stylishly unkempt in striped pajama shorts and a vintage band T-shirt. Even half-asleep, he looked fashionable. Ah, the blessings of youth. If I were similarly attired, I'd look like I lived under a bridge.

Carson's eyes widened when he saw me, and he ran a hand through his sleep-tousled hair. "Oh, hey, Delilah." He left the screen door closed between us, and eyed the street, as if trying to gauge whether I'd come alone.

"May I come in?" I asked.

"Uh, now's not a great time," he said, flashing a tight smile. "I just woke up."

I opened the screen door and pushed past him. "I don't mind." We stood for a moment in a small entryway. I sized up the house. Tami's apparent fondness for wallpaper and fake floral arrangements wasn't limited to the offices of Glacier Valley Senior Care. I eased past Carson and made my way into the formal living room furnished with a shiny mauve couch and love seat. On the wall hung embroidered samplers with inspirational mantras and a large gilt-framed portrait of a middle-school-aged Carson.

Yapping sounded from elsewhere in the house, getting closer until an ungainly brown and white corgi burst into the room. Although the dog continued barking, I could see by the frantic wag of its tail and ecstatic gyrations of its plump little body that the noise was borne of excitement rather than menace.

I stooped down and held out my hand. "Hi, sweetie. What's your name?"

As I stroked the dog, Carson murmured something I couldn't quite make out.

"What was that?" I asked.

"Honey Bunny," Carson repeated, through gritted teeth. "His name is Honey Bunny." He nudged the dog aside with his foot. "And he's a pain in the butt."

Carson scooped up the dog and stomped upstairs with him. When he came back he said, "I put him back in his crate."

"You didn't have to. I love animals."

He picked a piece of fur off his dark-colored T-shirt. "He

slobbers and sheds everywhere. He used to be Nana Dorothy's. We got him when she died."

I mentally recorded another strike against Carson. No one was a bigger neatnik than I was, but I would never be unkind to an animal because of it. Butterball was a shedding machine, but I loved every fuzzy bit of him.

"Nana Dorothy was your mom's grandma, right? Were you close to her?"

He shrugged.

"Your parents aren't home?" I asked. I planted myself on the couch and motioned for Carson to take the love seat. He stood for a moment, rigid as one of his mother's decorative statues.

"No. They go to brunch with people from church on Saturdays." Carson edged toward me warily, arms crossed over his chest and hands tucked tight into his armpits.

"Take a seat," I ordered. "You knew Jeremy from back then, right? When he was your grandma Dorothy's caregiver."

"I mean, I knew who he was, but I didn't, like, *know* him. He was just the weird guy who took care of Nana," he replied. "Nana didn't like me to see her all sick like that, so I didn't go over there much once Jeremy was in the picture."

"Why do you say he was weird?" I asked.

He shrugged again. "You know, he was just so, 'Anything I can get for you, Dorothy?' 'Do you want another cracker, Dorothy?' It was over the top."

"But that was his job, right? To take care of her?"

"I guess, but he didn't have to be so creepy about it. It got so she depended on him for everything. Like she had to ask his permission to breathe. It was weird. And he was cagey."

"Cagey? Do you mean he had secrets?" I asked.

"I mean, obviously. Everybody has secrets."

"Did you suspect Jeremy of something?"

"I don't know what you're getting at," he said, keeping his hands stubbornly tucked into his armpits. "You know this is, like, my personal house. You have no right to be here." Getting no reaction from me, he continued, "This is an invasion of privacy."

"You know what else is private property? My aunt Biz's house. You want to tell me why I caught you trespassing there yesterday?"

He twitched. "I don't know what you're talking about."

"Really?"

He scrunched his face into a mocking smile. "Really."

The temperature of my blood ratcheted from a simmer to a boil. I pulled out my phone and called up the screen shot I'd captured of him walking down the shore path. "So this isn't you walking away from my aunt's house last night?"

He shrugged, but I sensed a subtle shift in his posture. He'd moved from offense to defense. "Last I checked, it's a free country," he said. "People can walk on the shore path."

"You know you're fired, right? I don't like shirkers, and I especially don't like shirkers who lie."

He uncrossed his arms and threw up his hands. "Fine by me. I never wanted to work at your stupid restaurant anyway."

That's when I saw it. A white ribbon of gauze wrapped around his left palm. I'd thought his arms-crossed posture was simply sulky, but it seemed that it was also evasive. Remembering the unexplained blood spatters in my kitchen, I said, "I guess you don't need to work for tips anymore. Not when you can sell stolen prescription pills and make a lot more money." Carson flinched as if I'd hit him, but said nothing. I pressed my advantage. "I know you took the pills. They're worth a lot of money, so that makes sense. What I don't understand is why you killed Jeremy."

Carson jumped to his feet. "I didn't kill him!"

"You disappeared down to the dock moments before he was shot."

"I was with Veronica," he said. "She vouched for me. Ask the cops."

"You and Veronica Tanaka are close?" I asked, incredulity creeping into my voice.

"Very."

This was an interesting tidbit of information. Veronica had made it sound like Carson was following her around like a smitten puppy. Carson was hinting that they were a couple. I tended to believe Veronica. Even if I conceded that Carson was good-looking, the coupling didn't compute. Carson was nineteen; Veronica was probably ten years his senior. While she hobnobbed around high-end restaurants and event venues in her late-model BMW, he drove a battered minivan and lived with his parents. She seemed smart and accomplished, not to mention drop-dead gorgeous. I supposed it was possible that she'd been wearing a very thick pair of wine goggles on the night of the party and hooked up with him for lack of better options. Stranger things had happened.

"Where were you two, exactly? I don't remember seeing you in the crowd when everyone rushed down to the dock," I said. Truth was, the aftermath of finding Jeremy's body was such a blur, I probably wouldn't remember if the pope had been standing there in his full clerical regalia. Still, I thought I'd try my luck at getting a more complete alibi.

"We were in the back seat of her car, getting better acquainted," Carson said. He puffed his chest, as if daring me to challenge him.

Yuck. I was glad I'd had to skip breakfast that morning. But his explanation just didn't have the ring of truth. Various scenarios spun through my head, until one in particular landed smack in front of my face.

"Even if I bought that, it doesn't let you off the hook at

all," I said, developing the idea aloud even as I spoke. "In fact, that makes it more likely you were involved."

Carson raised a smug eyebrow. "How so?"

"Maybe you don't know," I said. "Jeremy and Veronica were friends. She knew him, but she kept it from the cops." I realized that I, too, had failed to mention the connection to Capone. Whoops. With the rapid-fire developments of the last twenty-four hours, Auntie Biz's revelation that she recognized Veronica had slipped off my radar screen.

Carson shook his head. "Why would Veronica hang out with that loser?"

"Maybe she has a thing for losers?" I suggested, raising an eyebrow.

"I think you'd better leave," Carson snapped. I'd expected an angry reaction, but he looked confused, off-balance.

"Not until you tell me the truth. Where were you when Jeremy was shot?"

"Like I said, Veronica and I were hooking up. We left the party at around nine or nine-thirty and went out to her car. We were there until everybody rushed down to where Jeremy was killed. When we saw that the party was over, she left."

"How did she get home?" I asked. "Her car was parked at the restaurant all night."

"She walked. She'd had a couple glasses of wine and didn't want to drive."

"How did you get home? I don't remember seeing your minivan in the parking lot that night."

He mumbled something.

"I didn't catch that," I said.

"My mom picked me up because the stupid van isn't running. I told the cops already," he snapped.

"What's to say that you and Veronica didn't kill Jeremy together?" I countered. "Or maybe you were jealous of Veronica and Jeremy's friendship."

He scoffed. "You think I was jealous of that guy?"

Again, I was struck by the unlikelihood of a Veronica-Carson pairing. She hooked up with a guy who needed to get a ride home from his mom?

"Say I choose to believe that you didn't kill Jeremy. What about the pills? Whoever broke into my apartment left evidence behind. Blood. Probably from a cut on his hand." No need to mention that I'd bleached that evidence into uselessness. "How did you cut your hand?"

He paused. "I was fixing my car."

"You mean your mom's old minivan that she lets you drive?"

He rolled his eyes.

I drummed my fingers on the arm of the couch and gave Carson a hard look. He turned his eyes to the opposite wall.

Of all the weaselly little lies he'd ever told me, this was among the hardest to swallow. My dad had been an amateur mechanic, spending countless weekends tinkering with misfiring engines and wonky transmissions in our driveway. My dad was meticulous, hardworking, and not afraid to get his hands dirty. He was everything Carson was not. If the image of Carson romancing a glamorous sommelier was a stretch, the idea of him splayed out under a decrepit old minivan downright snapped the rubber band.

Carson had dug deep into his defensive position—deny everything. I had to lure him out. "It sounds like you've got an alibi for the murder, and an explanation for the cut on your hand. And you've sworn to me that I was mistaken about seeing you at my aunt's house yesterday, right?"

"That's right," he said.

"Well, I'm sorry I bothered you." I stood up.

Carson looked perplexed. "You shouldn't go around accusing people," he ventured, seeming unsure why I was suddenly letting him off the hook.

"Why don't I give you your pay and we'll go our separate ways?" I said. "I'm sorry things didn't pan out with you working at the restaurant. I have your money in my car." The last bit was true. Even if Carson turned out to be a thief and a murderer, I wasn't going to let that stop me from being an honest businesswoman. I'd always find a way to pay my employees, no matter what. My eyes fluttered to the empty finger that used to hold my engagement ring.

I snapped my attention back to Carson as he shuffled his feet into a pair of Nike slides and followed me out to my Jeep. The rain had stopped and tiny slivers of blue sky were beginning to crack through the clouds.

I reached into my purse and pulled a few bills from the wad of cash I'd gotten from the pawnshop. I'd have to sit down with Auntie Biz later and figure out the accounting side of paying employees with sticky wads of cash from a pawned engagement ring. It definitely didn't seem like a topic she would've gone over with her accounting students. Oh well, an audit was the least of my concerns right now. I was on to this knucklehead, and I finally had a chance to catch him in a lie.

I stretched across the seat and released the lever that popped the Jeep's hood. "While I've got you here," I said, "I wondered if you could take a look at my CV joint? Since you know about fixing cars." I walked around to the front of the car and propped the hood open. "Mechanic wants to replace it, but my owner's manual says it should go another few thousand miles." I pointed to a small U-Bend in the engine's complex architecture. "Does it look all right to you? Hard to know who to believe in a situation like this. You know how mechanics are. Some will just straight up lie to your face."

Carson peered under the hood, hands on his hips. He made a show of pulling out the oil dipstick and unscrewing the lid to the coolant reservoir. He wiped his hands on his pajama shorts saying, "Yeah, the CV joint seems okay. I'd say you've got a while longer before you need to replace it."

"Thanks." I smiled tightly, handing him his cash. I slammed the hood shut and slid behind the wheel of my car. As I watched him make his way through the immaculate tackiness of his front yard, my smile broadened. I'd spent enough time looking over my dad's shoulder while he worked to know that the CV joints are part of the car's axles, connecting the wheels to the driveshaft. They're nowhere near the engine. *Gotcha, weasel.*

CHAPTER 18

I returned to the restaurant after my confrontation with Carson. A van marked Crime Scene Investigation was parked near the stairs to my apartment. Another search. Capone had mentioned that he was sending someone over to scour the place for evidence related to the break-in. Nothing was private anymore—not my love life, not my finances, not even my home. My life felt like a giant yard sale, all the pieces laid out on the lawn for anyone to pick through. As I glided into a parking spot between Rabbit's jalopy and Capone's sleek black cruiser, Sonya flew out of the restaurant's front doors. Her face was red, her mouth formed a tight line of apprehension. With her full skirt swinging and retro hairstyle flying, she looked like a crazed Beatles fan.

She was talking before I was even fully out of my car. "I don't like the way the questioning is going, Dee. I tried to tell Rabbit to clam up and wait for my cousin, but he's a nervous wreck. He agreed to be questioned, and now he's worried that he'll look guilty if he backs out and says he wants a lawyer. Capone's not even being particularly hard on him. Rabbit went all squirrely at the mere sight of his badge. It's like he's got cop-ophobia, which is understandable based on his history with law enforcement. But still, I'm worried that if he's in there much longer he's going to confess to the JFK assassination and kidnapping the Lindbergh baby. Guy has no poker face whatsoever."

"Why isn't your cousin here? I thought you were going to call him at the first sign of trouble?" I said, following Sonya to the door.

"Seth can't get up here until this afternoon. His daughter's supposed to start violin lessons and he's in some kind of dispute with his ex-wife about it. She's a lawyer, too, would you believe? He's over there this morning with *his* lawyer trying to get his ex to sign . . . I don't even know what. A violin contract for a six-year-old? And my uncle Avi popped his Achilles tendon playing pickleball this morning, so he's no use. My mom's at the hospital with him." She took a deep breath. "Anyway, I'm glad you're here. Capone wouldn't let me stay with Rabbit during questioning, so I've had to keep coming up with excuses to go in and check on them. One of which actually allowed me to get some quality investigating done. Do you remember the cops mentioning something about broken glass? Well, I inventoried the glasses in the bar, and it turns out we're missing two champagne glasses."

"I wonder what that's all about," I said. "My aunt and Jeremy didn't take any glasses with them. Why would the killer have? And why take two? Weird." I shook my head. "Did you tell Capone?"

"Yes, he made a note of it. Then he told me to get lost." She blew air up through her bangs. "Any update on Biz?"

"Dr. Sittampalam called when I was on the way back. Auntie Biz woke up briefly, but she was so agitated they gave her something to take the edge off. I guess they're worried about her heart. Even in young patients, withdrawal symptoms can be serious. She's unconscious again. They're hoping to keep her sedated so she can sleep off the worst of the effects." My voice shook. "I can't believe my eighty-year-old aunt is in detox."

Sonya squeezed my shoulder. "She'll come through it. The O'Leary women are tough."

I bit my lip. "I know," I said, feeling about as tough as a newborn kitten.

"Speaking of tough O'Leary women, have you called your sister?" she asked. "Maybe she'll want to come."

"No way. You know Shea. I sent her a vague text, but I played down the seriousness. If she comes it'll become the Shea Show."

I reached for the door handle, but Sonya pulled me to one side of the glass doors. "Whoa. You may be going into battle here. You can't go in looking fragile. Gird your loins." She pulled a tube of lipstick out of her skirt pocket and ordered me to pucker. She applied the color and then smoothed my unruly hair with her hands. Lastly, she eased the V-neck of my blouse down a fraction and nodded approvingly. "Loins girded."

"Operation Flirtation?" I asked. "What happened to feminism?"

She shrugged. "Feeling more confident can't hurt, right? And if you end up getting arrested, you'll take a better mugshot." She patted my arm. "Good luck. I'll go around through the kitchen door and spy from there. There's some schmo upstairs searching your apartment."

"Yeah, I saw the van," I said.

"I heard him tell Capone there was no sign of forced entry, so either we accidentally left the door unlocked or the thief had your aunt's keys. I also heard the crime scene guy cursing quite a bit. Apparently, he's seen professional hit men who didn't clean a crime scene half as well as you. I don't think he's found a shred of evidence. Not a fingerprint. Not a hair."

I frowned. "Guess I'll have to look for the local chapter of Neatniks Anonymous."

As I entered the restaurant, I was still gathering my thoughts about Sonya's revelations and figuring out what I was going to say to convince Capone to lay off of Rabbit. The restaurant's dining room still sparkled from the deep clean Rabbit had given it yesterday. A man after my own squeaky-clean heart. The tables were set, everything poised and ready. It looked like we were about to throw the doors open for the lunch crowd. Overhead, the faces of the Chicago luminaries beamed and the oversized gangsters loomed.

Whether by coincidence or intention, Detective Capone was seated directly under the canvas bearing the image of his infamous forbearer. The Al Capone toddler carica-ture emphasized the mob boss's doughy jowls and reced-ing hairline. Three generations later, the DNA had morphed into something altogether different. Capone Version 3.0 was strong jawed, caramel skinned, and solid as a stone wall. Only the thick black eyebrows and perfect Cupid's bow lips were conserved. Rabbit sat across from the handsome detec-tive, twitching and sweating like he was about to give birth to an electric eel.

"Everything okay?" I called out.

"Mr. Blakemore and I are just about finished," Capone said, half rising to greet me.

I gestured for him to keep his seat and joined them at the table.

"I told him the truth, chef, but he thinks I'm lying, I can tell. If I get arrested, I'll be in violation of my parole. I'll lose Everleigh for sure, whether I'm guilty or not." Rabbit's voice shook so much he could barely get the words out. He seemed on the verge of tears. "I can't go back to jail," he whispered.

"I need to speak to Mr. Blakemore alone," Capone said. His tone wasn't unkind, but some of its characteristic warmth had cooled.

"Is he under arrest?" I asked. "Because if not . . ." I raised an eyebrow.

Seeing that I wasn't budging, Capone continued, "Delilah, you're dangerously close to interfering with an investigation."

"I can't sit idly by," I countered.

"If you can't restrain yourself, I'll need to take Mr. Blakemore to the station to finish questioning him," he said.

"No!" Rabbit and I yelled simultaneously.

I jumped out of my chair. "There was no robbery. Nothing was stolen."

Capone looked at me like I'd sprouted horns. "Is that right?" Capone said, crossing his arms over his chest. "So you made a false police report this morning?"

"I was mistaken. I got confused in all the commotion." I raised the back of my hand to my forehead, Scarlett O'Hara–style. "It's been a very trying time. Before Auntie Biz went into the hospital, she told me she threw all her pills into the lake."

"Really?" Rabbit said, looking bewildered.

I gave him a reassuring nod. "There was no theft. Your own crime scene investigator can't find any evidence of a break in. So you have to let Rabbit go. There's no crime to charge him with." I kept my face impassive. First, I'd interfered with the investigation. Now I was blatantly lying to a cop. I didn't expect Capone to believe me, but I had to pray he'd go along with my bluff.

"Mr. Blakemore, would you mind waiting in the kitchen while I talk to Ms. O'Leary?" Capone asked. His voice was steady. A steady boil. He waited until Rabbit was out of the room and then turned to me, his amber eyes steely.

"I understand you want to help. That doesn't mean you get to swoop in and question suspects and witnesses before I get a chance, and it definitely doesn't mean lying to me about the robbery to get Mr. Blakemore off the hook."

"He didn't steal the pills," I pleaded. "He swore to me on his daughter's life. Doesn't that mean something?"

He frowned. "With detective work like that, the citizens of Geneva Bay will be relieved to know you're on the case."

"He can't mess up his parole," I said.

"Robert Blakemore is a convicted felon," Capone said. "Convicted for something almost identical to what happened here. I'm a fair man. I hope I've proven that to you. But I wouldn't be doing my job if I didn't make sure his story checks out."

"Did he tell you about Auntie Biz's pills? How they were from a bunch of different doctors and pharmacies? That seems pretty fishy, doesn't it?" I asked.

Capone nodded. "Raised a red flag for sure. That kind of pattern fits with prescription drug trafficking."

"Why would he have told me all that, admitting that he'd paid close attention to the pills, if he was guilty of stealing them?" I asked.

Capone tipped his chin. "You've got a point."

"Now that Rabbit told me about how that whole world operates, it seems pretty obvious that something weird was going on with those pills. I didn't register it at first, but that's not exactly my bailiwick. Why didn't you guys notice it when you packed Auntie Biz's overnight bag?" I asked.

"This is Officer Rettberg's first major case. She's pretty green. Stanhope asked her to pack your aunt's overnight bag. He had your aunt as a teacher and the idea of choosing delicates and denture cream for her scared the pants off of him," he explained. "Still, Stanhope or I should have checked through the bag before releasing the contents. I wish we had. Then maybe your aunt wouldn't be in the position she's in."

"It's not your fault." I took a deep breath and blew it out. "And it's probably for the best that it all came to light. For my aunt to go into withdrawal like that? Clearly, someone had been giving her too much strong medication. I can't understand why, though. Was she being poisoned? She doesn't have much in the way of assets. She's ornery, but seems to be well liked. What does any of this have to do with Jeremy or Auntie Biz? The prescriptions, the cash in the shed."

"The break-in?" Capone offered the addition to my list with a sardonic raise of his eyebrow.

"What break-in?" I responded, pressing my hands together angelically.

"In all seriousness," Capone countered. "You've got to stop taking matters into your own hands. I need you to understand that this is not a game. You're not playing Clue. A man was murdered—shot through the head—a few yards from where we're sitting. That murderer might have a key to your apartment."

I grimaced, both at the mention of Jeremy's gory death and the realization that I hadn't yet told Capone about my visit with Carson.

"What?" Capone demanded.

"If you didn't like me talking to Rabbit about the pills, you're really not going to like what I have to tell you now. I think I have evidence that Carson Callahan is involved in Jeremy's death."

"You can prove it?" Capone asked.

"Well, I can't *prove* it, but I have a hunch." The dark look on Capone's face grew even darker. "A very serious hunch."

"I'm glad it's a 'very serious hunch.' That should be plenty to convince twelve jurors," Capone retorted. He leaned back and spread his hands wide. "Well? The floor is yours. Let's hear what you have to say."

"I went to drop off Carson's wages this morning. He has a cut on his hand, and he lied to me about how he got it. I can think of only one reason why he'd lie about something like that." I quickly summarized my encounter with the former server.

"You think he stole the pills and cut himself on the broken tagine." Capone finished my thought.

"Yes, if the thief cut himself, it would explain the extra blood that I saw." I stopped myself. Even though Capone and I both knew I was lying about there being no break-in, I had to maintain the fiction that I'd been mistaken or Capone would have enough cause to drag Rabbit in for questioning. "*If* there was a theft and *if* I saw blood."

Capone rolled his eyes.

I continued, "I can also prove that Carson was snooping around my aunt's place yesterday evening when you guys were searching it. I saw him in the trees, and when I called out to him, he ran away," I explained.

"You're sure it was him? It was getting dark by the time you got there," he said.

"I've got video," I offered, pulling out my phone and zooming in on the image on the screen.

"That does look like Carson Callahan, but it doesn't look like your aunt's property," he said.

"Well, no. It's outside Sam's house. Carson was on the shore path around the time I saw him, probably making his way back to town," I said.

"That's not solid enough. And as for seeing him near your aunt's house, an eyewitness account from you isn't going to

convince anyone. You could be covering for your aunt or trying to throw suspicion off yourself," he said.

"You think I'm lying?" I asked. "I mean, about this, not
the break-in."

"Would I be crazy if I did? You just told a straight-up
whopper about your aunt throwing her pills into the lake,"
Capone said. "I don't like being lied to."

"Me, either. I only lie when it's absolutely necessary to
keep someone from losing custody of their kid," I said. "Or
similar circumstances."

He leaned closer, and folded his hands on the table. "I appreciate that," he said with a frown. "Regardless of whether
I believe you or not, I don't think I could get a warrant based
on your say-so or video of Carson at a location that's more
than a half mile away from your aunt's cottage. We have no
idea what he was doing there, and no evidence that he did
anything wrong, except perhaps trespassing. None of this
would hold up in court."

"But . . ." I began. I had to make him listen somehow.

His expression softened as he raised a hand to cut me
off. "You've got good instincts, and I know you're trying to
help. But you've got to realize that two days of scattershot
gumshoeing doesn't trump my two-decade law enforcement
career. I have hunches, too, but being a detective is about meticulously building a case, gathering admissible evidence,
cross-checking alibis. It's the difference between throwing a
dinner party and running a restaurant kitchen."

Now that I'd played all of my cards, I realized how poor
my hand must look. I'd been proud of my sleuthing, but Capone had to think of how things would look to a judge and
jury. He was right. None of the evidence that I'd given him
was real proof.

"Delilah," he said, a line of worry creasing his forehead.

"If you're right, and Carson is the killer, you put yourself in serious danger by confronting him alone. Take care of your aunt. Take care of yourself. Leave this investigation up to me. That's an order. You're a chef, so I know you understand an order when you hear one."

CHAPTER 19

I mulled over Capone's words as I punched through the swing door into the kitchen. I felt like a naughty child who'd been scolded. Part of me fumed at Capone's condescension. Despite having zero experience investigating murders, I'd made some significant progress and felt like I deserved at least a little credit. I wished I'd stood up for myself better. I had to admit, though, that Capone wasn't wrong in pointing out the missteps I'd made along the way. That made his reprimand all the more frustrating. I hated being in the wrong.

I was so caught up in my thoughts that I'd forgotten Sonya and Rabbit were in the kitchen, doing their best to look busy as they tried to eavesdrop. Sonya, it appeared, had several batches of deep-dish pizza dough tucked away in the proofing cabinet and Rabbit had chopped button mushrooms and onions into microscopic shrapnel.

"So, he's not gonna drag me downtown?" The words were out of Rabbit's mouth before the door even stopped swinging.

"Not now, and not at all if I can help it. I meant it when I said I'd look out for you," I said. "Capone knows I'm lying about the break-in and the missing pills, but he's decided not to call me on it for the time being."

Rabbit leaned heavily into the counter to steady himself. "Praise the Lord," he said. "Thank you for doing that. You could've gotten into a lot of trouble lying to him like you did."

"Don't mention it," I said. I surveyed their efforts. "Didn't Capone wonder what you were doing, making all this food when the restaurant was closed? He must've known you were trying to spy."

Sonya patted a ball of dough. "I'm one hundred percent sure he was on to me. That guy's sharp. He told me that Stanhope and Torvald mentioned we've been feeding them. I think that's why he let me stay in here even though it was obvious what I was doing. He also said not to forget there are hungry officers down at the station who would probably work better on full stomachs."

"Bribery, eh? We can fill that order. Least we can do since Capone has cut me about ten miles of slack. I was also thinking I need to take a pie or two over to the hospital. Dr. Sittampalam and the nurses have been such sweethearts."

I turned to Rabbit, whose cutting board held an array of finely diced vegetables. "I see you've taken your nervous energy out on those poor innocent vegetables." I could identify with the impulse. I'd been known to tenderize meat into a fleshy pulp and pound dough into flaccid submission when I was angry or stressed. "You've got Everleigh with you all weekend, right?" I asked.

"Yeah, my mom's watching her now so I can work," Rabbit replied.

"Why don't you go home and spend some time with her?" I suggested. "There's not a whole lot to do around here, except apparently make pizzas for the entire Geneva Bay police force."

"You sure?" he asked. "Me and Sonya could get this done while you go over and sit with Miss O'Leary at the hospital."

A loud "Ha!" escaped from Sonya's lips. She put her hand over her mouth.

"What?" I demanded.

"Sorry," she said. "It's a nice thought, but the idea of you sitting quietly and keeping a calm bedside vigil . . . ?" She let out another barking laugh.

"I can keep a calm bedside vigil," I protested.

"Really? Like when your dad was in hospice?" She turned to Rabbit. "She rewired the lamps in all the rooms on his floor."

"I installed a few dimmer switches," I explained. "The lamps were too bright and a lot of the patients had conditions that made them prone to headaches."

"And she repotted the plants in the solarium," she continued.

"They were drooping! Nobody wants the last days of their life to be spent looking at a bunch of droopy ferns!"

"I'm pretty sure they had to replace the linoleum in the hallway floor because of the rut she wore in it pacing back and forth with all her *calm vigil keeping*," Sonya said, making air quotes around the last three words.

I hip-bumped her aside and picked up the dough ball she'd been working with. "You, alleged best friend, go feed Butterball and then call a locksmith. If someone has my spare keys, that means we're going to need new locks on the apartment and the restaurant."

"Ten-four, Boss Lady," Sonya said, with a wink and a mock salute.

"And after you've got that underway, go home to get changed." I could tell by her less-than-perfect coiffure and makeup that Sonya had flown straight out of bed to get to the hospital that morning, and I knew she wouldn't feel like herself until her hair was slicked into place, false eyelashes were rooted to her lids, and peachy white powder refined her complexion. I turned to Rabbit. "You, my friend, should go and spend time with your daughter. If anyone needs me, I'll be here, keeping a very calm vigil with this dough."

Sonya had already made a good start on basic deep-dish crust and tomato sauce by the time I took over the cooking, which made it easy for me to pick up where she'd left off. My Red Hot Mama Pizza was usually a crowd pleaser, and I figured it would go down well at the police station.

I adore spicy food, and when I'd first tried the Red Hot Mama recipe out on friends, I'd calibrated the heat level to suit my atomic palate. By the end of that night, some of my most macho pals were daring each other to make it through a whole slice without drinking water. They'd laughed as beads of sweat formed on their temples and the heat rose through their faces like lava spilling over the rim of a volcano. I'd since toned down the heat to make the recipe a little more palatable for the average restaurant goer, but it still came with a warning on the menu that the Red Hot Mama wasn't for the faint of heart or the timid of tongue.

I separated the basic sauce into two pans, seasoning the spicy batch with a heaping teaspoon of red pepper flakes. I assembled the toppings: house-made pickled jalapeños, zesty chicken sausage that I'd spiked with garlic and paprika, and crumbled bacon. Once I took the pizza out of the oven, I'd hit it with a topping of sprinkled blue cheese and a drizzle of creamy ranch sauce.

Looking at the mounds of finely diced veggies that Rabbit had prepared, I was inspired to invent a new recipe. I fished around in the meat section of my fridge. Hidden among the prosciutto and Parma ham, I noticed a slab of guanciale, a cured meat product made from pork jowls. I'd somehow failed to make the connection that Rocco Guanciale, the former owner of this building, shared a name with a succulent cured Italian meat. I pulled guanciale from the fridge and chopped it into miniature cubes, the same size as Rabbit's mushrooms, onions, and multi-colored bell peppers. The fat from the meat would coat the veggies as they cooked, giving a salty, buttery heft to the flavor. Guanciale tastes like the essence of bacon—pork distilled down to its fatty, umami gorgeousness.

The rainbow of tiny toppings lent itself to the name Rocco's Rabbit Food Pie—my tribute to Geneva Bay's criminal element. Time would tell if it would make it into my standard pizza repertoire, or if the recipe would need further refinement.

I put together a few of my favorite old standard pizzas to be sure there would be something for everyone. It felt good to be back in the kitchen, confidently doing what I was best at, instead of floundering in the confusing and dangerous world of criminal investigations. My mind felt calmer than it had in days. Still, even here in my inner sanctum, thoughts about the case crept in. Capone was right—I had to look at the investigation in terms of hard evidence. I mentally reviewed my list of suspects.

Personal feelings aside, Sonya, Melody, and Daniel were off the list for sure. They were nowhere near the crime scene and had no motive. Auntie Biz, on the other hand, looked like an obvious suspect. She owned the murder weapon and was found holding it at the crime scene. She admitted to Capone that she didn't like Jeremy. But she would have had a million and one chances to kill Jeremy. He'd been with her all day, every day, for months. Despite whatever mental slippage she'd had in the past year, she was sharp enough to think of something less obvious than shooting him with her own gun while they were alone on the shore path. Still, the mystery surrounding the heavy-duty prescriptions she was taking remained. How had all those pills been prescribed to her and why? And why was someone so determined to get their hands on them that they'd break into my apartment? Much as I hated to admit it, it was hard to see how the police could cross her off the list.

Rabbit had come onto the scene the morning after the murder. Suspicious timing, for sure. He certainly had a stronger link to the world of crime and prescription drug misuse than anyone else in my orbit. I knew next to nothing about him. He worked hard and kept his head down, two important virtues in my book. Although Auntie Biz had liked and trusted him, I couldn't rule him out entirely. But where was the motive? The connection to Jeremy? And why take a job at the scene of the crime when it would put him right in the crosshairs of the cops? Possible, but unlikely.

I spun the wheel of suspects again and landed on Sam. I felt a pang in my chest. My anger about our fight had begun to ebb away, and I was left with a sense of regret. For three years, he'd tried his best to calm my raging storms and I'd tried my best to spur him into getting his act together. Despite the clear mismatch in our temperaments and ambitions, we'd really tried to make it work. Sam had some undesirable qualities. He was aimless, unable to deal with misfortune (his or anyone else's), and occasionally clueless about the struggles of ordinary people. But he didn't have a violent bone in his body. He apologized to doors if he slammed them too hard. Not exactly the personality of someone who would go to extraordinary, almost psychotic, lengths to sabotage his fiancé's opening night. To me, the timing of his flight to Costa Rica further proved his innocence. If he'd planned a violent act in advance, he was smart enough to have made sure his getaway flight was at the airport waiting for him as soon as he'd pulled the trigger. The fact that he'd booked the jet in a huff right after our fight seemed like a clear indication that his decision had more to do with hiding from the wreckage of our relationship than going on the lam after committing a crime.

My mind went back to those last few hours of my engagement to Sam, and I assembled ingredients for another brand-new recipe—spinach, onions, and nutty, sweet Gouda cheese. I'd always processed my emotions best while I was cooking, so it was fitting that I should cook up an homage to the ill-fated debacle of Sam & Delilah's restaurant. I snagged a taste of the toppings and let the flavors meld in my mouth. The grassy tang of the spinach intermingled with the cheese's unctuous depth and the onions' honey sweetness. Even if the real-life Sam and Delilah were never meant to be a couple, the toppings on my new invention were a perfect marriage. A few more tweaks—maybe a scattering of toasted pine nuts?—and Deep Dutch Pizza would be a surefire hit.

As I popped the pizzas into the oven, I thought through other possible suspects. Lois Gorman was unlikeable, and her family had a history with Jeremy. Her daughter and son-in-law could be a connection to the prescriptions, having extensive access to my aunt's personal information. Still, I couldn't believe that Irv and Tami would be a party to anything criminal. If they were part of a drug ring, why did they live such a modest lifestyle? By Tami's account, she and her mother both adored Jeremy and were grateful to him for caring for their loved one. I tried to figure out if they could have conspired together, but the connections all seemed too vague. If Lois killed Jeremy, what linked her to the pills? And if Irv and Tami were linked to the pills, what linked them to the murder? They weren't at the party and it seemed improbable that they could have gotten ahold of Biz's gun and then lain in wait for Jeremy.

Veronica Tanaka—now there was a woman who had something to hide. Auntie Biz, in one of her increasingly rare moments of clarity, swore she recognized Veronica as one

of Jeremy's "friends." She and Carson had disappeared right
before the murder, and they shared a dubious alibi. I'd have
to think up an excuse to talk to her again without running
afoul of Detective Capone. Despite the dressing-down he'd
given me, I couldn't give up on trying to find the truth. I wasn't
constitutionally capable of giving up, or of letting people tell
me what to do. I'd just have to be more careful about how I
went about investigating.

I couldn't outright dismiss the possibility that one of the
other partygoers, or even a complete outsider, had killed Jeremy. The more evidence that accrued, though, it seemed like
the murderer had to be someone who'd known Jeremy and
was somehow connected to Auntie Biz and the pills. Even
as my mind clicked over all the possibilities, I kept circling
back to Carson. The guy was a proven liar. More damning,
there was a mismatch between his desire for material goods
and his work ethic. That combination provided rich fodder
for greed and easy-money schemes to take root. The unexplained cut on his hand potentially linked him to the stolen
pills, which linked him to taking my aunt's keys out of her
purse, which linked him to the murder.

By the time I finished my ruminations, I'd munched my
way through half a wedge of Gouda, four slices of bacon, and
a stick of pepperoni. Realizing it had been a couple of days
since I'd eaten a vegetable, I ate a red pepper to round things
out.

Again, I'd skipped meals and ended up gorging on whatever food crossed my path. I had to get more disciplined about
my eating habits or Butterball and I would end up wearing
matching muumuus. Worse still, I could tell that the extra
weight was starting to affect my work. Practically every day
since I was sixteen, I'd worked a fourteen-hour shift on my
feet. My joints were starting to feel the strain. If I kept on
like this, I wouldn't have the stamina to make it through.

After I'd boxed up the hot pies, I adjusted the seasoning on the ranch sauce for the Red Hot Mamas and poured it into a couple of to-go sauce containers. Drizzling it at this stage could make the crust soggy.

Despite devouring a large helping of my pizza toppings, I'd still managed to turn out eight large deep-dish pizzas—two Deep Dutches, two Red Hot Mamas, two Rocco's Rabbit Food Pies, and two plain cheese. Plenty to feed the hungry cops and nurses of Geneva Bay. Good thing the town wasn't larger or I would bankrupt myself giving away free pies . . . faster than I already was bankrupting myself, that is.

CHAPTER 20

I loaded the pizzas into the back of my Jeep and pointed my car in the direction of the Geneva Bay Police Department. A phalanx of flagpoles and aggressively landscaped flower-beds greeted me as I pulled up in front of the stately brick building. I decided to make my trip a quick one. While I'd been making the pizzas, I'd also been cooking up a plan to do more investigating, a plan I knew Capone would not approve of. I told myself that my white lies and attempts at misdirection were in the service of the greater good, but Capone's scolding had gotten under my skin. I wasn't sure if I could count on myself not to let on what I was planning.

I ducked inside the building and dropped four of the pizza boxes at the reception desk with a scribbled note to Capone: "Humble pies, compliments of the chef. Hope they earn me a slice of forgiveness." The desk sergeant laughed at my puns and tried to make small talk, but all I could manage was a tight-lipped smile in return. I didn't want to open my mouth, fearing that my guilty conscience would give me away.

I hustled back to the parking lot. My mind was so distracted that I almost walked directly into the path of a car that was turning into the parking lot from the road. The driver hit the brakes hard, and then rolled down the window.

I looked up, ready to apologize for my carelessness. Instead, my eyes locked onto a familiar face, a face that was gaping at me. I gaped right back.

"Delilah?"

"Sam?"

My former fiancé pulled his white Tesla into a parking space and ran out to throw his arms around me. I was too befuddled by his unexpected reappearance to fully return the hug, so I stood there with my arms bent and my head tilted to one side like a crash test dummy. Part of me wanted to sink into his arms and stay there all day, breathing in the familiar minty, citrusy smell of him. But another part of me, namely my fists, wanted to land a couple punches on that fine-looking face of his. How dare he dump me and disappear during the worst few days of my life, and then resurface without warning and act like nothing had happened?

"Are you okay?" he asked, pulling out of the embrace to look me over. "When I picked up your messages, and all the messages from the police"—he swallowed—"I went to the apartment and Butterball was the only one there. The restaurant was closed and you didn't answer your phone."

"I was driving," I said. "I must've had the Bluetooth off." I took my phone from my purse. Sure enough, I had two missed calls from Sam.

"When I couldn't reach you, I came here to see if the police knew where you were. I didn't know what to think." He glanced over my shoulder toward the police station. "Were you . . . were you arrested?"

"No," I said. "Why on earth would you think—?" I shook my head. This was no time to pick a fight. "I was dropping off pizzas." I took a step back, taking stock of the man who, up until a few days before, was my betrothed. Sam's long hair was loose, cascading down his neck and shoulders. His skin was tan, his posture relaxed. Other than the crease of worry in his eyes, he could've passed for a surfer version of Jesus. "Where have you been?"

"I was at a silent meditation retreat in Playa Hermosa." He gestured with his open palm toward a small stone bench in front of the station. He put his other hand on the small of my back, guiding me gently to take a seat. His touch felt calm and reassuring. I remembered this feeling—how nice it was to have someone who believed everything would always work out for the best. Someone whose very fingertips radiated tranquility. He sat down next to me. "After our difference of opinion the other day, I was hurt. And what was worse, I knew I'd hurt you. I felt so awful about what I'd said to you and about ruining your big night."

"So you disappeared? Sam, I was worried."

"I'm sorry. I had to cleanse my heart chakra. Take stock and really reconnect with myself. My whole energy was"— he made a face of disgust and waved his hands over the center of his chest—"gummy." He sighed. "No phone, no technology. Just let it all go. You know?"

"No, I don't know," I said. I remembered this feeling, too—how maddening it was to have someone who had a hard time understanding the troubles of mere mortals like me. Someone who thought it was normal to zip off in a private jet to Central America for a little quality one-on-one time with himself. "I've been here dealing with the aftermath of a murder. Auntie Biz is in the hospital. We almost lost Butterball. Someone broke into our apartment. The restaurant is closed because after you left, everything was in limbo." I paused. "I needed to talk to you and you were totally AWOL."

"I'm so sorry. I didn't know any of that. Guru Brian said to leave our phones at home." His eyes fell to my hand. "Hey, where's your ring?"

"I had to hock it."

"What? Why?"

"Sam, you left me with no access to money. Everything is in your name. I couldn't pay the staff. I couldn't pay the bills. I couldn't open the restaurant because you own the building. All the vendor accounts are in your name. With us being broken up, I didn't know what I was supposed to do."

"Broken up?" he repeated. He turned toward me and his eyebrows knitted together. "I'm sorry I said that. I don't want to break up. I was . . . disquieted."

I suppressed the urge to laugh. After all the "disquiet" he put me through by ghosting me, he was waltzing back and expecting to pick up right where we left off. I had to admire that about him. He was so sincere in his belief that everything always worked out.

I sighed. Staying mad at Sam was impossible. "I'm sorry, too," I said. "I've been acting more like your boss than your fiancée. My chakras were pretty gummy, too."

"You look so radiant today," he said, giving me a shy smile. "I can tell you've been cooking. You always look radiant when you've been cooking."

I looked down at my outfit. I'd showered and changed into a button-front linen maxi dress while the pizzas were baking, even taking a few minutes to de-frizz my thick hair. *Just in case you ran into Capone at the station.* I blushed. *Shut up, subconscious.*

"You look great, too," I replied, sorry for my earlier anger. Maybe it was wrong of him to skip town without telling anyone, but he was right about his blissful ignorance. How could he have known what would happen? And for someone who'd always had an endless cushion of cash to fall back on, the idea that his leaving might strand me with a negative bank balance probably hadn't even occurred to him.

I rose. "Sam, I'm so glad you're safe. You had me genuinely worried. And believe it or not, I've done some soul-searching,

too. You were right about a lot of the things you said. A lot
has changed in the last few days, though. Too much is going
on right now for me to take a time-out to work on our relationship. You need to go in there and tell the police where
you've been, and I need to get over to the hospital to see
Biz." He reached out to take my hand. He squeezed my fingers, then brought them to his lips. The sweet way his lips
brushed my skin still gave me butterflies.

"I'm truly sorry, Dee."

"Me too," I said, giving his hand a squeeze. "We'll talk
soon, I promise, but right now there really are more important things than our relationship. I don't mean the restaurant,
either. This is genuine life-or-death stuff."

Before he could say another word, I hightailed it to my car,
forcing myself not to look behind me. I still loved Sam, but
the past few days had laid bare all the cracks in our partner-
ship. There were so many things we needed to talk about, but
I needed time to think, and that wasn't going to happen any
time soon.

I drove to the hospital, where I unloaded my pizza offer-
ings at the front desk, explaining why I'd brought them.
Luckily, they'd stayed hot in their insulated bag. The woman
sitting at the desk greeted me with a wide smile, her white
hair billowing up behind a chunky headband of black ribbon.

"Oh, my lands!" she exclaimed, peeking into one of the
boxes. "These smell heavenly. I'll take them straight to the
staff breakroom. I'll have to make sure to put a piece or two
aside for Dr. Sittampalam, otherwise our interns and residents
will devour these. They're like piranhas." She looked at me
quizzically. "Did you say you're Miss O'Leary's niece?"

"That's right." I nodded.

"I was so sorry to hear about her being in here," she said.
"Both my boys had her for personal finance in high school.

My older one became an accountant because of her." She sighed. "This is so sweet of you to bring us food. My husband and I can't wait for your restaurant to open. Such a perfect spot, right there on the lake."

I smiled, even though her words felt like a kick in the gut. Perfect. It was a perfect spot. Sam was back, which potentially solved one major challenge, but until Jeremy's killer was found, a cloud of suspicion still hung over all of us. And there was no way I could think about opening with Auntie Biz so sick. Opening day was still miles beyond my grasp.

The front desk woman pointed me toward the ICU. I followed her directions, taking the elevator to the second floor and heading left down the corridor, my sandals squeaking on the shiny linoleum. I approached the door with a growing sense of dread in the pit of my stomach. I'd spent the last year trying to ignore my aunt's declining health. *What if she . . .* I wouldn't even let my brain complete the thought.

As the door slid open, a pretty nurse with short, springy dreadlocks came out of the dimly lit ICU to greet me. "Hello, Miss O'Leary. Your aunt's friend just arrived for a visit, too."

"My aunt's friend?" I repeated. I wondered if Sonya could've decided to come over here after all.

The nurse, who introduced herself as Kinzy, directed me toward my aunt's bedside, where the curtain was partially open, offering me a glimpse of her small body lying in the large hospital bed. I'd spent time in the ICU in Chicago—too much time—when my dad was sick. This hospital's unit was an altogether different beast from the cavernous wards in a university hospital in a major city. Geneva Bay's ICU was a small, five-bed ward, with each patient's bed able to be sectioned off by a curtain. There was only one other patient in the unit, an elderly man hooked up to a respirator. Kinzy left me and went over to tend to him.

Even though I could only see a sliver of Auntie Biz's body through the opening in the curtain, her frailty hit me smack in the face. She was totally helpless. I walked toward the bed, and over the grating rhythmic *beeps* and *whooshes* of the other patient's life-support machines, my ears tuned into the sound of a familiar voice.

"I'm sorry," the voice whispered. And then again, "I'm sorry."

I pulled the curtain back to reveal Lois Gorman sitting in a chair, holding my aunt's hand. Lois's wig looked as lofty and glossy as ever, but her face seemed ashen and hollow. Auntie Biz, meanwhile, lay in the bed looking much as she did when I'd left her—muscles twitching, forehead slick with perspiration, her skin the color of dirty linen.

"Delilah," Lois stammered, clearly startled by my sudden entrance.

"What are you doing here?" The words came out of my mouth as a demand rather than a question. Lois and her family were still firmly on my list of suspects. I knew she and my aunt weren't close friends, at least not in my aunt's opinion, and I couldn't think of a good reason why this woman would be visiting.

She rose and smoothed her blouse. When I first opened the curtain, Lois looked fragile, almost pitiful. Now, in a flash, her face transformed into a mask of indignant reproach. "I brought some flowers," she huffed. "I didn't like to see her lying there alone. Now that you're here, I'll be on my way."

"Not so fast. I heard you say you were sorry. What are you sorry for?" Politeness be damned. I didn't trust this woman, and I didn't like her being alone with my comatose aunt. Especially when said aunt had been the only person present during Jeremy's murder—other than Jeremy himself and his killer, that is.

"I was saying I'm sorry that Elizabeth is sick of course,"

Lois replied. "No one wants to end up in a hospital bed, left all alone."

"That's not what it sounded like. It sounded like you were apologizing for something you'd done wrong. Did you hurt her?" I shunted her aside and looked Biz over, but couldn't see any obvious marks. I turned my icy glare back on the woman, who by this point was literally clutching her pearl necklace in shock.

"Hurt her?" She looked aghast. "How dare you. I was keeping her company. You were nowhere to be found. She shouldn't be alone in here. Anything could happen to her."

I ignored her insinuation that I wasn't a sufficiently devoted niece. "How did you even know my aunt was in the hospital?"

Lois bristled. "This is a small town. Judy, one of the girls from the bridge club, was here visiting her new baby granddaughter. She happened to be walking past the elevator and saw your aunt being wheeled out. She texted all of us to let us know. I offered to bring over flowers and a card from the group." She gestured to the side of my aunt's bed. Sure enough, a tasteful arrangement of yellow and pink roses adorned the side table.

"Thank you," I said, my tone returning to civility, "but Biz wouldn't want you to see her in this state."

"What's wrong with her? Judy didn't know, and Kinzy said she wasn't allowed to tell me because of patient confidentiality, even though I know her entire family from church." Lois said the last part extra loud, casting a frosty glance across the room at the young nurse, who was still tending to the other patient.

"A bad reaction to medication," I answered. True-ish. Knowing the town's propensity for gossip and Lois's propensity for sticking her nose where it didn't belong, I wasn't sure my aunt would want me to be one hundred percent honest.

"Will she be okay?" she asked. Her forehead creased in a look of concern, causing little fissures to appear in her thick layer of foundation makeup. The concern seemed genuine, but I had to wonder: was it concern that my aunt might die or concern that she wouldn't? If Lois were the killer, surely it would be more convenient for her if my aunt were out of the way? Maybe I was overreacting, but there was something out of whack about this whole situation.

"She'll be fine. She just needs rest, and to be left alone," I replied. I was sorely tempted to twist Lois's arm behind her back and frog-march her out of the room, but I realized that this might be my only chance to quiz her one-on-one about Jeremy.

"You must've been through this before," I said, gesturing to Biz's bed. "Tending to a sick relative? Tami said your mother Dorothy was ill for a long time."

Lois nodded. "She was never in the hospital, though. She wanted to stay in her home until the end. It's important to be there for your family when they can't take care of themselves, and respect their wishes." Her voice fell to a whisper. "My mother was a wonderful person."

"It's hard," I agreed. Despite my suspicions, the empathy in my voice was real. Caring for a dying parent—I'd been there, too. "Lucky for you that Jeremy was able to step in and lend a hand."

"Hired help has its place, but there's no substitute for family," she countered.

"That's an interesting perspective, considering the business your daughter and son-in-law are in. Tami said you were all very fond of Jeremy."

Lois fell quiet. Her eyes drifted to Auntie Biz's bed, and for a long moment, the two of us watched the shaky rise and fall of my aunt's chest. At last, Lois said, "I won't speak ill of the dead." She snatched her purse from the seat next to her and rose to her feet. As she moved past me, she stopped and said, "Don't leave your aunt alone like that again. Anything could happen." She leaned close to my ear. "Anything," she hissed.

CHAPTER 21

I stood next to my aunt's bed for a moment, stunned. I was tempted to run after Lois and try to wring more information out of her, but my short career as an amateur detective had made me realize that once the person you're questioning turns hostile, there's rarely much more to be gained by continuing to press them. After all, I didn't have the option of locking up uncooperative witnesses like the actual police did.

I texted Capone. *Lois Gorman came to visit my aunt in the ICU. Creepy, no?*

A moment later his reply came. *I don't like that either. Torvald is getting some food. I'll ask him to stick around and keep an eye on her.*

I beckoned Kinzy over and asked her to check my aunt's condition. As the nurse looked over all the machines and readings, I watched my aunt's eyelids flick back and forth restlessly.

I asked, "No one hurt her or did anything to her, did they?"

The nurse jerked her head back, offended.

"No, not you. I mean, could someone, a visitor, say, have done anything bad to her? You'd be able to tell, right?"

She looked at me sideways. "Do you mean Mrs. Gorman? She's been the only visitor. She taught my stepdaughter's confirmation class at St. John's."

I waved my hand to dismiss the thought. This wasn't going well. Geneva Bay was too darn small, and it wouldn't do for me to appear to be spreading rumors about Lois trying to harm my aunt. "Just, you know, anyone. My aunt witnessed a murder, and I want to be sure that she's safe in here. I don't want any more visitors unless I approve them, okay?"

"Of course. I'm sorry I didn't call you to ask about Mrs. Gorman visiting. She said she was a friend of your aunt."

"It's okay," I said. "I'm just a little high-strung right now. I'd rather know before anyone else comes in."

Kinzy nodded. "Absolutely. Your aunt is improving, by the way," she said. "I know she doesn't look well, but her vital signs are much better." She squeezed my shoulder. "She's going to be okay." She smiled and left, pulling the curtain closed behind her.

I forced myself to sit down and take hold of my aunt's hand. It felt as delicate as a hummingbird.

"Hi, Auntie Biz," I whispered. "It's me, Delilah."

I thought I saw her eyelids flicker, but I couldn't be sure.

I sat there for a few moments, feeling utterly helpless and on edge, trying to remember some of the calm, centering exercises I'd learned in the yoga and meditation workshops Sam had dragged me along to. The first thing that came to mind was my feeling of supreme antsiness at the memory of having to sit still in those stupid workshops and do nothing for hours. Hours that could've been spent *accomplishing* something. I tried again. *Breathe.* Now my brain presented a running replay of the horror and confusion of the past few days. Someone I knew was probably a killer. I had to find out. No use thinking about that now. It would just make it even harder to sit here calmly if I let myself think about all the investigating I should be doing. I pushed the thought aside and tried to go to my happy place. My kitchen. I wished I was there now. Maybe I could make some of Auntie Biz's favorite foods and freeze them for when she got better. My kitchen, in my restaurant. Maybe I should talk to Sam and figure out how I was going to open the restaurant. *Ugh.* I could feel my blood pressure rise at the mere thought of that inevitably difficult conversation.

I heard the curtain draw back as Dr. Sittampalam, along with Officer Torvald, slid into view on the far side of my aunt's bed. I hadn't even heard their footsteps. Maybe I was getting better at meditating after all.

"She looks real tiny in this big bed, 'n so?" Torvald said quietly, removing his hat as one would for a passing casket.

"Small doesn't mean weak," Dr. Sittampalam replied, giving Auntie Biz's hand a gentle squeeze. The doctor herself couldn't have been much over five feet tall.

"How is she?" I asked. "Kinzy said she's getting better."

"If all continues to go well, we'll keep your aunt here for a few days and then, with luck, she can go home. Putting her in the ICU is a precaution, really. She doesn't need assistance breathing or a feeding tube. She just needs time and some medications to help her rest. Honestly, none of us has ever detoxed such an elderly patient before. It can be a very difficult process, even with young, strong people. The more she sleeps through, the better."

My phone jingled inside my purse.

"Please, take the call," the doctor urged. "There's not a lot you can do here."

"No, I should stay," I said, thinking about Lois's warning.

"I'll be with her," Torvald said. "She'll be safe." When I still didn't budge, he added, "You go home and get some rest."

"Thank you," I said, remembering that I was supposed to make Torvald and Stanhope aware of all my movements. But my next move was definitely not to head home for rest. "I will. I just have to run a quick errand on the way," I said, hoping I'd be forgiven for using a very broad definition of "errand."

"Sure," he said. "I promise we'll call you if anything changes."

Despite the grim surroundings and Lois's strange quasi-threats about watching over Auntie Biz, their words lifted my spirits. Sonya had been right: keeping quiet bedside vigils was not my mission on this earth. It wasn't for lack of love, but rather a question of constitutional makeup. I was a doer, a goer. God had permanently wired my internal switch into the On position. It had taken every ounce of my willpower to sit at Auntie Biz's bedside for even twenty minutes. Torvald and the doctor had sensed that and released the chains of my guilt.

"Thank you for the pizza," Dr. Sittampalam called as I hurried toward the exit.

"I had some, too," Torvald said. "That one with the spinach and onions was real good."

As I hustled down the linoleum hallway, I picked up the phone to find Daniel and Melody's faces flashing up on a video call. Melody waved excitedly when I answered.

"Tell me you've had a breakthrough," I said. "I need some good news."

"Big breakthrough. Huge," Daniel said.

"I think maybe we have." Melody nodded agreement.

"We were ready to give up," Daniel said. "We were packing the car to leave when Melody had a moment of genius. Tell her," Daniel prompted, giving Melody a nudge with his shoulder.

"It wasn't genius." Melody blushed. "I just all of a sudden remembered from my Wisconsin history class in high school that we learned about all the state's different Native American tribes, and how the groups who survived are now living in tiny pockets of tribal land. There are the Ho-Chunk and the Chippewa and the Potawatomi, who were the original settlers around Geneva Bay," she explained. "And I remembered that one of the tribes was named the Menominee, you know like the town, only spelled different. And I wondered if there was more than one Menomonie, maybe. I looked it up on my phone and saw that there was a Menominee Casino Resort outside Keshena. Like two hours east of Menomonie the town. It seemed like it was worth a shot to go by there real quick. We didn't want to come back empty handed."

"We're there now," Daniel cut in. He panned the phone's camera to give me a view of the neon signs and flashing gaming machines in the background.

"The very first waitress we showed Jeremy's picture to knew him." Melody smiled shyly as she described their success while Daniel nodded encouragement. "She didn't want to talk at first. She thought he owed us money or something."

"But I convinced her," Daniel said, raising his eyebrow rakishly.

I rolled my eyes at him as Melody continued the story. "She told us that he used to come by here a lot."

"Jeremy played big. When he won, he would pass out big tips and brag like a squash," Daniel said.

"Brag like a squash?" I repeated.

"You know, *se lució el chayote*?" He mimicked a braggart puffing out his chest and looking down his nose. When Melody and I shook our heads in bafflement at this pantomime, he shrugged. "It's what you say in Puerto Rico when somebody is a show-off. *Se lució el chayote.* Like they're being puffed out like a squash."

"*Eso no se traduce, hermano.* Doesn't translate," I said.

"Not important." Daniel dismissed the impromptu Spanish lesson with a flick of his hand. "Anyway, the waitress said when Jeremy lost, he turned mean. A few months ago, he had a bad streak. His behavior got so bad, they put him in the black book."

"Black book?" I asked, confused. I'd only heard the term "black book" used with the word "little" in front of it on a TV show about an infamous Hollywood madam.

"The casino has a database of people who are banned," Daniel explained. "They call it a black book. I guess it goes back to the old days in Las Vegas. It's a list of all the people who've been caught cheating or doing something else really bad."

"Wow," I said, processing this new information. I'm not sure what I expected them to find, but it wasn't this. Clearly, I wasn't the only one who had a knack for amateur sleuthing. Auntie Biz had called Jeremy a phony, and it seemed she was spot-on. Jeremy had been living a secret life. I'd been sure the cash in the shed would somehow connect to illegal prescription pills, but now that wasn't the only possibility. Maybe it was tied to his gambling. "Great work, guys," I said.

"Are you going to call Detective Capone?" Daniel asked. "Maybe this can help the police figure out the motive. Seems like he might've owed someone money."

"About that," I said, grimacing. "Capone told me that if I interfered in the investigation again, I'd be in hot water. I'm guessing sending you two on a trans-Wisconsin detective mission probably counts as interfering."

"That *is* a problem," Daniel said, his handsome face taking on a pensive expression.

I thought through the options. "Maybe I could send an anonymous email?"

"They can track which computers emails come from. He'd know it was you," Daniel countered. "What about leaving a letter outside the station?"

"Then they'd really know it was me," I said. "Capone's seen my handwriting, and I'm sure they must have cameras outside the station door."

"Maybe do that thing where you stick the newspaper letters together to make the words, and then disguise yourself when you drop it off?" Daniel suggested.

"Perfect. For the disguise, I'll wear a creepy clown mask so I look like a psychopath dropping off a ransom note," I replied with a frown.

Daniel shrugged, unfazed by my snide remark. "Hey, I'm the beauty of this operation, not the brains."

Melody furrowed her brow and bit her lip. "I've got an idea." She waved it away. "It's probably too complicated."

"No false modestly," I commanded, even though I was pretty sure her modesty was in no way false. Her self-confidence wouldn't fill a thimble. "You've got good ideas."

"Well, my cousin Angie's boyfriend works as a nine-one-one dispatcher for the county. He knows all the cops. I can tell Angie that I came up by the Menominee Casino with a friend and mentioned Jeremy's death in front of our waitress. I'll tell her what the waitress said about his gambling. I'm sure Angie will tell her boyfriend, or maybe even call Capone directly. She loves spilling juicy gossip and showing off that she's in the know. She'll take the bait, for sure." She paused. "She's a real *chayote*."

Daniel burst out laughing. "*Perfecto, mija*."

"That could work," I said. It was one hundred percent true, which tempered my guilt about sneaking around, and it would probably seem natural for Melody to talk about the murder considering what big news it was in Geneva Bay. Best of all, Melody's plan put several degrees of separation between this clue and me. "Do it," I said.

Now that they had their marching orders, I had my own investigating to do.

CHAPTER 22

Although it was the weekend, Veronica agreed to meet me for coffee at the café restaurant of the Grand Bay Resort. I'd enticed her with the promise of a sizeable down payment on the consultancy fee I owed her. The main lodge of the resort's impressive collection of buildings lay before me as I wound my way up the curving drive. In addition to the airport I'd visited a few nights before, the Grand Bay boasted two golf courses, a ski hill, and a spa, and the property was dotted around with communities of owner-occupied villas and townhouses. The lodge itself was low-slung, with flourishes designed to echo Frank Lloyd Wright's Prairie-style architecture. Wright and his disciples had been active in this area, taking private home and civic building commissions all over northern Illinois and southern Wisconsin. The sophisticated exterior concealed the building's slightly risqué origin as a hotel that had formed part of Hugh Hefner's Playboy empire.

Out of habit, I piloted my Jeep toward the valet parking stand, before remembering my financial situation and veering into the Ordinary Joe parking at the far end of the entrance. After thirty-plus years of being a working-class scrimper, my three years with Sam had quickly accustomed me to all the niceties that go along with being rich, or in my case, rich-adjacent. Ah, Sam. I'd have to decide what to do about our relationship, and money wasn't going to have any part in the verdict. I'd either choose to be with him because I truly believed he was my soulmate, or I was going to have to strike out on my own. I sighed. At least returning to the proletariat would up my daily step count.

As I took a few steps toward the hotel, I was shocked to see Veronica's BMW pull in just a few spaces away from me, at the very furthest reaches of the parking lot. Surely, she had enough money for valet parking. I waited for her to emerge.

"Hi," she called, giving a graceful little wave.

"No valet for you, either?" I asked.

"Nobody touches my baby if I can help it," she said, patting the side of her car with maternal affection. "I always park Beemer as far as I can from other cars. Don't want to get dinged by a stray shopping cart or have somebody open their car door into us." She chirped the door locks shut with the remote and fell into step beside me. I took note of the way she spoke about her car as if it were an extension of herself.

"Delilah, don't you look cute today," she observed.

"Thanks," I murmured, looking down at my "impress Capone" dress.

Her compliment made me feel gawky and embarrassed, and not just because I'd subconsciously gotten dressed up for Capone. How to respond? "You remind me of my sickeningly perfect sister, Shea, and every cheerleader I ever burned with jealousy over in high school" probably wasn't sufficiently gracious. I was more secure in my self-image as an adult, but Veronica was exactly the kind of trim, elegant woman who still intimidated me. Sure, I could probably dunk on her if we were shooting hoops and I'd definitely annihilate her in a tug-of-war, but those things rarely came up in day-to-day life.

Inside the café a few minutes later, Veronica made a bee-line for the best table, a two-top in a cozy nook by the large stone fireplace. Floor-to-ceiling windows afforded a view of the resort's man-made lake and the plush-looking fairway beyond.

"I forgot that you've been doing some work here," I said.

"Yes, they hired a new chef last fall. He redesigned all their menus, and they're doing a total revamp of their wine list to match. It's a fun project."

By "fun," I guessed Veronica meant "incredibly lucrative." Considering the price she commanded for putting together our little wine list, I could only imagine what she earned on a contract like this. Still, I didn't begrudge her her success. I'd worked with a lot of sommeliers in my career, many of them with egos and reputations that far outstripped their skills. Veronica had a rare palate and an uncanny sense of what customers would buy. Talent like that should be re-warded.

A striped-aproned server sidled over to take our orders. "Hi, I'm Dylanne," she said, pointing to her nametag. "What can I get you ladies?"

"I'll have a green tea with a little glass of ice on the side. You're espresso, right?" Veronica said to me. When I nod-ded, she continued with a wink, "I *thought* that was your poi-son of choice."

Considering that I'd wanted to meet her to discuss Jeremy's murder, her choice of the word "poison" unsettled me, as did her eerily accurate memory of my preferred form of caf-feine. I'd made drinks once or twice at the restaurant when she and I met to discuss her suggestions for the wine list, and apparently, she'd recorded my preference in her mental fil-ing cabinet.

"I'm glad you asked to meet," Veronica said, once the server had dashed off to make our drinks. "There aren't enough female entrepreneurs in Geneva Bay, and networking with other women is so important if we're going to stay competitive. I really admire what you've been able to achieve with the restaurant. It's a great concept and the menu is to die for."

I flashed a half smile, wondering if her macabre puns were deliberate. It was tough to take the measure of this woman. Her cascade of thick black hair, her tanned, toned figure—she seemed flawless, like she'd been retouched in Photoshop. I couldn't tell if her flattery toward me was genuine or calculated to achieve some end. I'd never been proficient at the schmoozy side of owning a business and words like "networking" always made me shiver, but clearly, it all came naturally to her.

"I appreciate you giving me some extra time on the invoice," I said. "Like I explained on the phone, the cash flow is tight right now, so I can't pay you in full." I dug in my purse and handed her what remained of the rubber-banded stack of grubby bills I'd gotten from the pawnshop.

She managed to look only mildly disgusted as she clutched the cash wad between her manicured fingers and dropped it into her purse. "I understand. Starting a business can be a struggle. I was lucky when I started my consultancy firm that I had a little bit of a cushion."

"Oh, really? Family money?" I wanted to figure out what made her tick, but I also wasn't averse to throwing her off-balance with a bold question, even one that bordered on rudeness.

She smiled demurely. "Similar circumstances to you, I suppose. I had a generous boyfriend. Maybe generous for different reasons, though. Mine was married. Wife, kids, the whole bit. I was living in L.A., struggling to find work as an actress, and I relied on my boyfriend completely. He paid for my whole existence."

I bit my tongue. In my younger days, I'd judged trophy wives and freeloading girlfriends, never imagining how anyone could let themselves end up in that position. Now I understood it all too well.

"When I found out about his family," she continued, "I think he expected me to just accept it, but I didn't take it very well. He was afraid I'd spill the beans to his missus." She rolled her eyes. "I wouldn't have done that, but he gave me some money to get out of Dodge. I took it, but I promised myself that would be the last time I'd ever rely on a man for anything. I've learned that the only person you can count on is yourself," she said.

Our server returned and placed our drinks on the table. "Thank you, Dylanne," Veronica said, flashing the girl a wide smile. Based on the picture that was forming in my head, it didn't surprise me that Veronica was the kind of person who remembered the names of servers and shop attendants.

"So no romance for you?" I asked. "You seem a little young to have resigned yourself to single life."

She shook her head. "Once bitten, twice shy. Besides, I'm married to my work."

"So your thing with Carson was a one-night stand?" I pressed.

"Thing with Carson?" she repeated, looking bewildered for a moment. "Oh, that." Her spine stiffened.

"He made it sound like you two were an item," I said.

"Well, I didn't say I was a nun," she countered.

"I guess I'm surprised that Carson of all people took your fancy. It seemed like he was annoying you with his attentions on the night of the soft opening."

"You know how it goes," she said primly.

"Not really," I replied. "Honestly, it surprised me to hear that you and Carson were hooking up in the back seat of your car. He seems like the type to do something like that, but you don't."

Her arm twitched and she knocked her purse off the table. She scrambled to the floor, picking up her wallet, her phone, and the wad of bills I'd given her. "Where's Beemer's key?" she said, sounding frantic, like a child who'd lost her security blanket.

I scooted my chair back to help her search. Spying her key on the floor under my chair, I bent down and picked it up. "Here you go," I said, holding it out. "Beemer means a lot to you," I observed.

"That car was the first big purchase I made with my own money. I saved for four years," she explained, snatching back her key.

"A symbol of independence," I said. I was struck by a sudden feeling of déjà vu. *Her purse, the car*, my mind seemed to whisper.

"Something I earned." As she placed the beautiful Louis Vuitton bag back on the table, her eyes turned steely. "I hate it when a nice place like this forgets the little details. With these round-backed chairs, there's no place to hang your purse. Obviously designed by men."

My questions had clearly put her on the defensive, and I realized I needed to ease off. Better to try to keep her on my side for the time being even if it meant it would take longer to get my answers. Capone didn't seem to have this problem. Being questioned by him was like having your brain massaged.

"I feel the same," I said, pushing aside the strange murmurings in my head. "It's always seemed ridiculous to me that at a nice restaurant, women are expected to set their purses on the floor or hold them in their laps the whole time they're eating. And it's bad business to let coats and bags take up seating that could be used for paying customers."

"I noticed that you put purse hooks and coat racks every-where at your restaurant," Veronica said. "It's a nice touch." She pushed the plunger on her carafe of tea, and poured the grass-colored brew into her cup. She brought the cup to her face and inhaled deeply, but didn't drink it. I watched in fas-cination as she extracted two ice cubes from the extra glass Dylanne had brought, added them to her cup, gave it a stir, and at last took a slow sip.

"How's your tea?" I asked.

"Nice. They source it from the southeast coastal moun-tains in Japan. Very smooth, good mouthfeel, and the floral notes aren't overpowering," she replied. "It would probably be better boiling hot, but I can't risk damaging my palate." She nodded toward the glass of ice. "I've never tried their espresso."

"Maybe a teensy bit underextracted, but decent," I said, now slightly self-conscious that I liked my coffee hot enough to melt my lips. "Good beans, I'd say, but an inexperienced barista." It had been a while since I'd compared flavor pro-files with anyone except Sonya. It felt so good to talk shop that I almost forgot I was here to question a potential murder suspect. Time to get back on track. "Not much seems to get by you," I noted.

"I try to be observant. Clients like it when you remember little things like their favorite vintage. And obviously I have to keep my flavor memory sharp to do my job."

"From what I've seen, you're always on the ball. It struck me as odd that you were so inattentive the night of the party."

She nodded and sipped her tea.

"You didn't notice anything worth mentioning to the po-lice. You had a few glasses of wine, went out to your car with Carson, and the next thing you knew, the police were there, right?"

"That's what we told the police," she replied. Her fingers

tightened around her teacup. Interesting how once again her choice of phrasing skirted my question.

"Strange that you didn't hear the gunshot."

She shrugged in reply.

"Then you walked home because you 'didn't want to get in the way' of the investigation?" She kept her lips clamped shut, and we sipped our drinks.

My eyes once again fell to her bag, and the whispering in my brain increased. Something, some bit of information, was trying to work its way to the surface. "You left the restaurant without your purse that night. Seems like a big thing to forget, since your phone and car keys were in it." I sipped my coffee. "Caught up in the moment with Carson, I guess?"

"I hate to cut this short," she said, casting a theatrical glance at her watch, "but I've just realized that I double-booked myself."

Looked like I'd pushed her too far. Playing the good cop clearly wasn't my strong suit. Oh, well. Bad cop it was.

"I know you know Jeremy," I said.

She fiddled with the clasp on her purse. "I'm sure I've seen him around. It's a small town."

"My aunt saw you come by her house to visit him a number of times. Why did you lie? Were you friends with him? Or maybe you had a fling with him, too, like you did with Carson?"

She flinched as if I'd kicked her. "Me and Jeremy, hooking up?" She laughed bitterly. Her voice deepened as all pretense fell away. "You have no idea who that man was."

"I know he was leading a double life. I know he had gambling debts," I said. "Did he owe you money? Is that how you knew him?"

She slammed her teacup into its saucer with such force that I thought it would shatter. "You let a viper into your aunt's life. Whoever killed him did you both a favor." She reached into her bag and pulled out the wad of money I'd given her as a down payment on my debt to her. She peeled off a few bills and threw them on the table. "On me. No need to thank me." She bared her teeth in a twisted smile, and then swept out of the room.

CHAPTER 23

I sat in the café, feeling fired up. Dylanne, the server, came over to clear away Veronica's teacup. I ordered another shot of espresso, a chocolate chip muffin, a turkey club, and a slice of quiche Lorraine. I had thinking to do, and after days of slapdash meals, I wanted to do it on a full stomach and a fully caffeinated brain.

I now had a clear admission from Veronica Tanaka. Not only did she know Jeremy, she hated him. A new theory was percolating in my mind. Perhaps she'd decided to kill him and convinced Carson to do her dirty work for her. She was certainly beautiful enough to play the femme fatale role. But what could have caused her to hate a man that much? Even though I'd suggested to her the possibility that she and Jeremy were lovers, it seemed wildly improbable. Carson, at least, was cute enough to make the idea of a casual fling somewhat plausible, and his attentions toward Veronica could, by some measures, have seemed flattering after a few glasses of wine.

But Jeremy? He wasn't exactly Mr. Universe, and by the accounts Melody and Daniel had gotten from the casino, his personality could be singularly unpleasant. So what connected Veronica and Jeremy? The dodgy prescription pills?

A gambling debt? Money clearly meant a lot to both of them—Jeremy because he needed it to pay for his destructive habit, Veronica because she prized her independence. While Jeremy had kept his money lust well-hidden, Veronica displayed hers for all to see. The stylish clothes, the blingy jewelry, her designer purse, the car. *The purse, the car.*

The restaurant around me seemed to fall suddenly quiet as a latent memory finally shoved its way to the front of my brain. If Veronica had left her purse inside the restaurant, that meant she'd left her keys inside, too. The security video I'd shown to Capone showed no one going back into the restaurant after the partygoers had stampeded down to the murder scene. At least, not until after the police had arrived and swept the place. What would have been important enough to lead on-the-ball Veronica to do something flaky like that? And then to skedaddle before she could reclaim her bag?

The day after the murder, Veronica showed up in an Uber to collect her purse. She'd taken her car key out of her purse right in front of us and used it to unlock her BMW. I'd failed to notice that crucial detail this whole time. If her key had been securely tucked away inside her purse, that meant her car had been locked when she left the restaurant on the night of the murder. There was no way she and Carson could have been making out in the back of it as they'd sworn in their alibi.

I flipped through other scenarios. Could she have left the car unlocked, and then locked the doors manually after she and Carson concluded their tryst? Not likely. Geneva Bay was a safe town, but with the constant stream of tourists, it wasn't the kind of place where everyone left their doors unlocked. I'd seen for myself when we arrived at the resort that Veronica locked her car doors out of habit. She took care of her BWM like it was a pet.

Time to call Capone. As wary as I was about another

dressing-down from him, I'd kept quiet about my suspicions about Veronica for long enough.

I dialed his number and waited. *Come on, Capone, pick up.* I hung up and tried again. The ringing seemed to echo throughout the café.

"I thought I warned you about amateur sleuthing," a low voice said, simultaneously sounding in my ear and over my shoulder.

I jumped out of my chair and spun around, landing face-to-face with the handsome detective. He lowered his phone from his ear.

"I wasn't sleuthing. I mean, wait, what are you doing here?" I sputtered.

He wagged his phone back and forth. "Let me guess. You were calling me with information about Veronica Tanaka."

"How did you know?"

"Well, we just loaded Ms. Tanaka into the back of Stanhope's squad car. She's on her way to the station. I need to head over there, but I'll give them a few minutes to book her in. Then maybe a few more minutes to let her sweat it out."

"Book her in? You arrested her?" I asked.

"Yes."

"But I haven't even given you my evidence yet," I said.

It was a lame response, but I was reeling from the shock of his revelation. I'd been so frustrated, thinking the investigation had been moving at a snail's pace this whole time. I'd thought I was holding crucial evidence that would finally bring a break in the case. Yet somehow, the whole thing had fallen into place without me even being aware of what was happening. I could hear Sonya's voice ringing in my ear: *"You have to stop thinking you have to do everything alone."*

"Evidence, you say?" Capone raised his eyebrow. "So you *were* sleuthing."

"Not technically. I had a business meeting with Veronica. I owe her some money from her work at the restaurant, and I was making a down payment." I looked down at my phone, which was still in my hand. "Hold on, how did you know I was here? Do you have a tracker in my phone or something?"

Capone sat down in the chair Veronica had formerly occupied.

"No, we're not tracking your phone," he laughed. "Although I'm thinking about it. Now is a good time to remind you that you promised to check in with Torvald or Stanhope before going anywhere. Apparently, you told Torvald you were 'running a quick errand'?"

"In a manner of speaking," I replied.

"Well, I was here because we were following Veronica Tanaka. I saw your car parked outside next to hers," he said. He leaned in. "Tell me about your evidence."

"I discovered that Veronica knew Jeremy. My aunt recognized her from her visits to the house. Veronica admitted as much just now. She also said that she hated him."

He nodded, his expression neutral. Either he had the world's best poker face, or I was telling him information he already knew.

"I had suspicions about her since the very beginning," Capone said. "I saw to her on the night of the murder. One of the other officers was collecting everyone's contact information, but as soon as I pulled up, I could see that out of all the partygoers standing there, she was unusually agitated. Most people get upset when they end up in close proximity to a murder. This was more than that. I only saw her for a moment, but her eyes that night . . ." He shook his head. "She was like a caged animal. There wasn't any evidence or other obvious connection between her and the victim, though. Plus, she had an alibi from that Callahan kid. I had nothing to go on other than a hunch."

"Detective work isn't about hunches." I echoed his words back to him.

"Well, not *technically*." He echoed my words back to me. "I've been at enough crime scenes to know the usual range of reactions you get from witnesses. Something about her demeanor was off. Strange enough that I did some further digging into her past. It turns out, she has a lot of secrets."

Our server made her way over, shouldering a tray. "Here's your muffin, your coffee, and your quiche, and your club sandwich," she said, naming each dish as she set the plates on the tiny table that stood between Capone and me.

"Brain food," I said, blushing. "Do you want something?"

"I wouldn't pass up half a muffin." He shrugged. "You know, for my brain."

I smiled as I slid the plate across to him. "Veronica told me she lived in L.A. and tried her hand at acting," I said. "I got the sense there was more to that story."

"Your gut steered you right," he said, biting into the muffin. "She moved to L.A. when she was sixteen. She did some racy modeling. Way too racy for a teenager, if you catch my drift. When she was in her early twenties, she got ahold of some money somehow—maybe stole it—booked it out of town and invented this whole new persona."

"I don't think she stole the money," I said. "She told me it was a hush-money payment from a married lover. I believe her. I could tell she wasn't proud of it."

Capone nodded. "You've got good instincts. We haven't been able to turn up any complaints or charges against her, and that would explain it."

"So you had a hunch because she was acting strange, and it turned out she had an unsavory past that she kept hidden.

That still doesn't explain what evidence you used to arrest her. Were you able to crack her alibi open?" I asked, crossing my arms.

"From the know-it-all look you're giving me, it seems like maybe *you* were," he said, with an amused raise of his eyebrow.

I hadn't meant to come across as a smarty-pants, but a teensy part of me did feel robbed of the dramatic, triumphant reveal I had pictured.

"As it happens, I was. The alibi she gave—that she and Carson were in the back seat of her car—couldn't be true. Her keys were inside the restaurant the whole time. If you check the security video, you'll see that she never went back inside after she left. She left her purse inside, and it stayed there until the next day."

From the way he furrowed his brow, I could tell this was new information to him. "That's not bad detective work," he said. "Especially for someone who wasn't supposed to be doing any investigating."

"Hey, I can't help it if clues just find me," I said, flashing a *Mona Lisa* smile as I took a bite of quiche. It was better than I expected, with velvety eggs and pleasantly salty little chunks of ham.

Capone popped the last piece of muffin into his mouth. "I met your fiancé this afternoon. Nice guy."

I was momentarily taken aback at the prospect of Sam and Capone meeting. *That's silly*, I chided myself. *Your probably ex-fiancé and the detective investigating your aunt's caregiver's murder talked to each other. It's not weird unless you make it weird.*

"Is he in the clear now?" I asked.

"I never say anyone's in the clear until the killer has been tried and convicted." He frowned. "And sometimes not even then. But if you're asking whether I'm going to arrest him as an accomplice to Veronica Tanaka, the answer is no. His story checks out."

"What did you and Sam talk about?" I asked.

"Yoga," he said. "I used to take my granddaughter to one of those Baby and Me classes." He laughed. "I learned that I am *not* flexible. I lurched around like Frankenstein in there."

"I didn't realize you have a granddaughter," I said, struggling to keep the astonishment out of my voice. "How old is she?"

"Audra. She's two."

He took out his phone and flipped to a photo of a cherubic girl with Gerber baby dimples and an Afro-puff hairstyle.

"She's an absolute doll," I said, hoping my honest reaction to the girl's sweet, little face hid my shock at the revelation that Capone was a grandfather. I'd just about come around to the idea of him having a son old enough to be in medical school. Now a granddaughter, too?

"Thanks. She's a handful, but she's our angel. My son, C.J., married his high school sweetheart, Joy. She died of a spinal tumor not long after Audra was born." He took in a deep breath. "When C.J. got into med school, we knew it was going to be rough for him to take care of Audra by himself in the city. So she lives up here with me and my mom during the week. Then, when my mom goes into the city to sing on the weekends, she takes Audra to be with C.J. It's a juggling act, but it's worked out so far."

"I'm so sorry for your family's loss," I said.

I found myself wondering if I could take on a challenge like that. Or if I could take on a man who took on a challenge like that. *This isn't a date, Delilah. Capone's personal life is not your concern. You're here to discuss a murder investigation.*

Dylanne came over to clear our plates. "Can I get you anything else?" she asked.

I shook my head. I'd somehow made my way through the mountain of food I'd ordered.

"So, back to the case," I said, once she'd moved out of sight. It was time for me to put aside my attraction to Capone once and for all. Across town, there was a handsome fiancé ripe for the (re)taking. Why was I being such a ninny? "If you hadn't disproved Veronica's alibi, what led you to arrest her?"

"We found texts on Jeremy's phone. Screen shots from films and magazine spreads that Veronica had appeared in, back in her younger days. He was demanding increasingly large sums of money to keep those images to himself. Several of the blackmail demands match up with dates when Veronica's cell phone data showed she was in the area of your aunt's house. Her bank records confirm that she withdrew funds before each of those meetings. And then, two days before the murder, Veronica withdrew ten thousand dollars in cash."

"Was that the cash you found in my aunt's shed? All the blackmail payments?"

"No way to match the bills up exactly," Capone said. "But it's a pretty straight line to draw. Jeremy demands cash, which we can prove with the texts. Veronica makes withdrawals in those amounts, which we can prove with her bank records. They meet up, which we can prove with her cell phone location data, and now your aunt's testimony. Cash materializes in your aunt's shed, which we can prove because"—he put his hands up—"we have a shedload of cash."

"What about the pills? Were you able to prove that the two things were connected?

"Yes." He paused and a dark look came over his face.

"What?" I asked.

"You might not want to hear this."

"You should know by now that I'm not going to wilt if you tell me something shocking," I replied.

"I'll grant you that," he said. "Jeremy was part of a drug racket, piggybacking off of your aunt's prescriptions. His job was the perfect cover. He had a variety of mechanisms for getting pills—forgery, bribery, and at least a few doctors who were careless to the point of negligence. All the same kinds of tricks that Rabbit and his crew used to pull. These dealers." He shook his head in disgust. "It's like playing Whac-A-Mole. You pull one guy off the street and three more pop up to take his place. You bust up one supply line and they figure out another one.

"Based on Jeremy's texts," he continued, "as he tightened the screws on Veronica, he coerced her into helping to distribute pills to some higher-end clients. She could move more easily in those circles than he could. She went along with it—briefly. But a few days before the murder, she told him she was done pushing pills for him and done being blackmailed. She would pay him one last installment, and then it was over. Her exact text was '*Come what may.*'"

As Capone explained the nature of Jeremy's operation, a hard coal of anger caught fire in my chest. Once he'd finished speaking, there was a moment of quiet. The first few words that came out of my mouth after that were very unladylike and very, very descriptive. Capone didn't so much as blink, though. I supposed chefs, cops, and sailors were roughly on a par when it came to colorful language.

"Jeremy was drugging my aunt, wasn't he?" I spat out the question, but I already knew the answer.

"I believe he was," Capone said, confirming my fear.

How had I missed the signs? Once Jeremy came on the scene, her fatigue, her memory lapses, her paranoia, her strange bouts of dizziness and illness—it all got worse instead of better. And once he moved in, she grew even more out of it. Whenever he was away and I was alone with Auntie Biz, she gradually improved. I'd self-importantly ascribed those upturns in her health to my presence. I thought she'd just been so happy to see me, or perhaps she was putting on a bit of a show of wellness for my benefit. But in truth, she was feeling better because that lowlife wasn't around to sedate her.

"Your aunt is a very sharp cookie," Capone said, "and she was probably catching on to his behavior. Some of the providers he got prescriptions from, her own primary care provider for example, were legitimate, and probably wrote prescriptions for her in good faith. She was present for a number of those doctor's appointments and if she'd been at her full capacity, I'm sure she would have signaled that something was wrong. He kept her drugged enough to keep her under his thumb."

"But he was diverting most of her pills to sell them," I said, picking up his train of thought. "So when I suddenly started giving them all to her at once, and then accidentally took them away by missing several doses, I threw her system for a loop."

We were quiet for a moment, and I recalled Veronica telling me that whoever killed Jeremy had done me a favor. I was coming around to the idea that she was right. If she wasn't in jail, I might've made her a thank-you dinner.

"So blackmail and illegal prescription pills," I said. "That must be how he supported his gambling habit."

Capone raised an eyebrow, and I realized that I'd gone one step too far in connecting the dots.

"Gambling habit, huh?" Capone said. His amber eyes twinkled with amusement. "I wondered if the little birdie who gave me that tip might be part of your flock."

I bit my thumbnail, remembering the elaborate smoke-screen I'd created to have Melody transmit the information about Jeremy's gambling to Capone via her cousin's 9-1-1 dispatcher boyfriend. "Can I plead the Fifth?"

"If you keep those pizzas coming, you can plead any amendment you want to. I almost had to break up a fight at the station over the last slice of that spinach one."

Even though I'd now had half a dozen conversations with Capone in the past three days, I still couldn't get over how easy it was to talk to him. Here we were discussing a murder and an illegal drug ring, and it was as natural as if I were talking to Sonya about the week's produce orders. I felt like I'd known him all my life.

"So was Veronica the one who broke into my apartment?" I asked, pivoting the conversation in the hopes he wouldn't quiz me further about my role in the casino tipoff. "If she wanted out of the whole drug scheme, I don't understand why she'd want to steal the pills. To destroy them because they connected her to Jeremy? Or maybe to sell them herself, since she'd seen how lucrative that could be?"

"Honestly, that's one of the details that's still bugging me," Capone replied. "Veronica was here on the night of the break-in. She had dinner with the food-and-beverage manager at the restaurant, and they were seen by a dozen witnesses. They stayed until closing, meaning she was nowhere near your apartment when the robbery took place."

"Could she have had an accomplice? Carson was willing to lie about her alibi, and he was definitely lying about how he cut his hand." I paused, remembering a clue that up until now hadn't made much sense. "The missing champagne glasses. Maybe that's how he cut himself."

"Great minds think alike," Capone said, tipping his head in my direction. "Still, that's a confusing piece of evidence, wouldn't you say? If the two of them planned to commit a murder together, why would they bring champagne glasses?"

"To toast their success in killing Jeremy?" I ventured, knowing it was a far-fetched theory.

"I've known all kinds of killers in my time," he replied. "Even a stone-cold hitman wouldn't stand over a body for a toast. Later, in the privacy of their home, maybe. But nobody brings cocktails to a crime scene. Well," he continued with a shrug, "let's hope Carson Callahan can shed some light on it. Officers should be at his house as we speak. We're going to serve a warrant for giving a false statement and see if that's enough pressure to make him flip on her. Kid doesn't strike me as a murderer, and frankly, I don't think he would have been smooth enough to pull it off. Young guys like him are the sloppiest of killers, too amped up on testosterone to be methodical and too arrogant to think they'll be caught. He's not even a very good liar. You and I both saw through him from a mile away.

"Still," he continued, "I don't want to see him rot in jail if Veronica tricked or coerced him somehow. We'll know more once we question him."

I tried to picture Carson Callahan, weasel extraordinaire, in prison—washing in a communal shower next to some tattooed goon, eating cafeteria slop from a tray, using a shared metal toilet with no seat. I expected the image to be satisfying, but other thoughts crowded in. Thoughts of Irv and Tami visiting with their "miracle baby" across a hard plastic table bolted to the floor. Them keeping every detail of his room exactly the same until he got out. Tami sitting in that room at night crying.

Ugh, if I weren't careful, Geneva Bay would turn me into a sentimental ball of mush.

Capone leaned back in his chair. "Am I to take it that you're now admitting that your aunt didn't throw her pills into the lake? Or does this whole conversation also fall under your Fifth Amendment plea?"

"I'll have to check with one of Sonya's cousins. I'm sure she's got a constitutional lawyer tucked away somewhere in the family tree," I replied with a sly smile.

CHAPTER 24

Two weeks since Veronica's arrest, and the restaurant was finally set to open. For real this time. I passed a last swipe of gloss across my lips and leaned into the bathroom mirror for a closer inspection. Not half bad. For years, Sonya had been trying to give me tips for my eye makeup, and I'd finally caved. Was this the start of a new, less-controlling Delilah? Probably not, but I had to admit that her techniques and color choices did accentuate the dusky blue color of my eyes. Butterball, as usual, had established a sentry post on the side of the sink. I nudged him aside as I pinned one last stray strand into my chignon. He meowed his approval. Even though I'd be on kitchen duty tonight, wearing my white chef's jacket, black pants, and clogs, I planned to come out for a few passes through the dining room to greet my guests and wanted to be sure to look the part of a successful restauranteur.

I scooped my fur-baby into my arms and poured myself a glass of rosé. We headed out to the small patio, where Auntie Biz was taking notes from an issue of *Food & Wine* and enjoying the gin fizz that Daniel had brought up for her earlier. Butterball and I settled into the deck chair next to hers. Other than the steady thrum emanating from Butterball's chest as I stroked his back, we were all quiet, peering out over the lake from our second-floor perch.

I sighed, giving Butterball a scratch on the head.

"That didn't sound like a sigh of contentment," Biz observed.

"I should be content, right?" I asked. "My dream is finally coming true."

As if to underline my point, a postcard-perfect family with four small children waved up at us as they tootled past on their pontoon boat. Across the water, the crisp spring green of the foliage stood out against the cobalt blue. Even though we were only just beginning the tourist season, the warm early June weather made it the ideal day on the water.

"So what gives?" Biz asked.

"Maybe it's some kind of PTSD reaction, but I keep thinking that this isn't over. That some other bad thing is going to happen," I said.

"Bad things are always going to happen," Biz replied, turning back to her magazine. "That's life."

"Thanks, for those inspiring words. You should get a job writing Hallmark cards."

"Shouldn't you be downstairs cooking? I thought you said the doors were opening at five o'clock sharp," Auntie Biz said, ignoring my sarcasm.

"I'll head back down in a minute. I needed to freshen up. We're in surprisingly good shape, though. Rabbit does the work of ten men. He got all spiffed up tonight in case he has to fill in at the front of house, since we haven't found a new server to replace Carson."

"Any news on that little punk?" Biz asked.

"Nothing new. I still can't believe he got away by jumping out of his bedroom window when the cops came to arrest him. That's got to be a ten-foot drop."

"He must've been desperate," Biz said.

I nodded. "That's the last anyone's seen of him—hopping his back fence and running away. Tami and Irv came by this morning to see if I'd put up a missing-person's poster. Carson doesn't have the resources to pull a disappearing act like Sam did. They have to be wondering if he's . . . if he's not alive anymore."

"Maybe the idea of prison was too much for him to handle." Auntie Biz tsked.

"Last time I talked to Capone, he said they were combing the woods and lakes around here." I shook my head and took a shaky breath. "Tami and Irv were beside themselves. Poor them. Poor Carson."

"Since when do you have sympathy for a missing weasel?" she asked, raising an eyebrow. "Especially one who's wanted as an accomplice to a murder? It's almost as if your heart's not made of stone."

My mouth formed a sad smile. "You can't tell anyone, or I'll snitch and let them know yours isn't made of stone either."

She laughed, a strong, robust guffaw that gave me a glimpse of the woman I'd known before Jeremy infiltrated her life. Those glimpses of her former self were becoming more and more frequent as she slowly recovered from her ordeal. "What makes you think it's not?" she asked.

"Just a hunch," I said. "Lord knows you've never let on. How's your drink?"

"Not strong enough," she replied.

"That's intentional. You're supposed to be taking it easy," I scolded. "What with your history as a junkie."

Biz rolled up the magazine and swatted me with it. "Sass mouth."

I leaned over and squeezed her arm. "Seriously, I'm so happy that you're okay. You had me worried."

"Well, I'll be out of your hair soon, now that that punk Jeremy isn't drugging me into helplessness," she replied. "I'm glad I can help out that little blond girl by letting her stay with me."

I bit my tongue and sipped my wine. Dr. Sittampalam expected Auntie Biz to have a long, slow road to recovery, but Biz was determined to move back into her own house ASAP. I'd been fretting about it since she was discharged from the hospital. She'd been willing to stay with me for the time being, but it clearly wasn't a workable long-term solution. My place only had one bedroom and a steep set of stairs, and, frankly, between Biz's stubbornness and my type-A personality, the likelihood that we'd end up killing each other was high.

A solution had presented itself earlier in the week when Melody's basement apartment had flooded during a downpour. She needed a cheap place to stay on short notice. Biz, meanwhile, had a spare room in her cottage. Now that, as Biz put it, "that punk" wasn't drugging her anymore, she would need only minimal help around the house, which Melody was all too happy to provide in exchange for rock-bottom rent. We'd presented the arrangement to Biz as if she'd be the one doing Melody a favor, even though it was more the other way around. The combination of Melody's unsinkable cheerfulness and Biz's hardscrabble acerbity was bound to be . . . interesting. I hoped it would be like combining sweetness and acid to get something tasty—strawberry balsamic vinegar, maybe. Most importantly, though, it gave me a measure of confidence that Biz would have someone trustworthy looking out for her.

In the weeks that had passed since Veronica's arrest, a lot had changed. After many all-night discussions, a few of which ended up turning into another, more pleasant kind of all-nighter, Sam and I had finally agreed that we were best off as friends. We had a deep bond of affection, but in the time we'd spent apart, I realized that I'd never really thought about what kind of future I'd have as Mrs. Sam Van Meter. Living off Sam's money. Tolerating his weird hobbies. Nagging him to set some goals. It wasn't me. At least not the me I hoped to become—Delilah O'Leary, independent woman, successful chef, goddess. Okay, maybe that last one was over-ambitious, but I was well on my way to the other two.

Sam had generously agreed to pay all of the restaurant's bills up until we opened, and then continue to cover payroll for the first three months. He'd lease the building to me at a reasonable monthly sum. It was enough of a boost to get me off to a good start, but the restaurant's ultimate success or failure would be mine alone.

The separation had been easier than I'd anticipated, perhaps because Sam was so passive and I was so decisive. I'd proposed arrangements in a detailed spreadsheet that took me three nights to finish; he glanced at it for five seconds before shrugging and saying, "Sure, whatever you think." The only point of contention had been custody of Butterball. Neither of us could imagine life without our portly kitty. For a few heartbreaking days, I thought Sam might draw a line in the sand and insist that Butterball be his alone. After all, he'd been the one to adopt the cat a few months before he and I started dating. Even Sonya's cousin Sylvia, the pet custody lawyer, wasn't sure I had a very strong case. Ultimately, though, we'd worked it out without any legal help. I agreed to strictly abide by Sam's chosen "wellness" plan for Butterball in exchange for fifty-fifty custody.

Thinking about how close I'd come to losing my precious fur-baby, I hugged him extra tight and buried my face in his golden fur. He purred like one of the motorboats gliding across the lake.

"You spoil that cat," my aunt said.

"Not anymore," I said. "His new diet starts tomorrow. Sam took him to some homeopathic shaman or something and came away with a whole list of recipes that are supposed to promote weight loss. I've decided to improve my eating habits, too, in solidarity." I pressed my forehead to Butterball's and said, "Isn't that right, Butterbutt? You and Mommy are going to be unstoppable."

A knock sounded and I rose to answer the door. Butterball padded along in my wake. I wondered if it was Daniel coming up to freshen our drinks. Instead, I opened the door to find Capone cradling his dimple-cheeked granddaughter.

"What a pleasant surprise," I said, inviting them in. I'd almost gotten used to how handsome Capone was, but the vision of him holding an adorable toddler made my heart do an extra somersault. *Stupid biological clock.* "You must be Audra."

The girl nodded and then pointed to Butterball. "Kitt-eh!" she squealed, her round, black eyes lighting up.

"We have a cat, too." Capone explained.

"Brujo, right?" I asked.

"You remembered," Capone replied with a smile. "Yes, Brujo and Audra are best friends, even though as a rule Brujo hates everybody."

"Butterball's great with kids. He lets Sonya's nieces put American Girl doll outfits on him." I knelt on the floor. "Audra, this is Butterball."

"Bub-ba," she repeated, nodding solemnly.

"Do you want to show Butterball his feather wand? He likes to try to catch the feather on the end." I demonstrated the toy for her, and Capone set her down to wave it around for the cat to chase.

"I hope we're not interrupting," Capone said. "You must be busy getting ready for the big grand opening tonight."

"Not at all. Biz and I were just taking a moment to relax on the balcony before the craziness starts. Every table is booked from open to close. I guess the extra publicity from the murder did us some good." I shrugged.

"People can't get enough of crime," Capone sighed. "I can't tell you how many times I've thought about changing my last name, especially since I moved up here and everyone has a story of a grandpa or great uncle who had a run-in with my great-grandfather, or John Dillinger, or one of the other mobsters who used to hang around Geneva Bay."

"You can try out O'Leary, if you don't mind being compared to a cow," I said, remembering Capone's reference to the famous Chicago legend.

I thought I detected a slight blush in his honey-colored skin. "I hope you don't think I was comparing you to a cow when we first met," Capone said. "You're a little bull-headed, maybe, but never cowlike."

"Whatever, Son of Scarface," I laughed, giving him a playful punch on the shoulder. "Hey, I know I said we're packed, but I can make space for you and Audra, if you want to join us for an early dinner? On the house."

"I wish we could. My son is in town for the weekend, and my mother cooked for us all. She's Cuban, and when she cooks, she goes all out—picadillo, fried plantains, okra stew. I think if she hadn't become a singer, she'd have been a chef. You remind me a lot of her. I should introduce you."

Introduce me to his mother, eh? Our eyes locked. I'd never noticed how his amber irises held little flecks of molten gold. My knees went rubbery. He licked his pillowy lips and opened his mouth to speak.

"Bub-ba!" Audra screamed, laughing as Butterball lunged at his toy.

Capone cleared his throat and the momentary enchantment dissolved. "I came by to wish you luck, but I also wanted to give you an update on the case."

"News on Carson?" I asked.

"Afraid not. But I did want to set your mind at ease about Veronica's guilt. Set both of our minds at ease, really."

"I just don't want to be responsible for helping put an innocent woman behind bars," I said.

"I understand." His eyes went to Audra, but she was wrapped up in playing peek-a-boo with Butterball. He lowered his voice. "The video your security cameras took on the night of the party shows Veronica leaving almost immediately after your aunt and Jeremy. Carson follows them a few seconds later."

I nodded. "That doesn't prove much, though. They'd already admitted that they left the restaurant." I'd been too upset on the night of the murder to watch the entire thing played back. Capone's expression remained grim, his face bearing the weight of further revelations. "There's something else," I said. "Isn't there?"

"There were bloodstains on the dress Veronica wore to the party that night. It came back as a match for Jeremy's blood," he said.

I exhaled. "How does she explain that?"

"She doesn't. She insists she didn't kill him, but she won't say anything more. I don't know if that's her lawyer's choice or hers. Either way, we're not getting anywhere with her."

"Dang it. I still have so many questions." I enumerated them on my fingers. "Was Carson her accomplice? Did she plan the whole thing in advance? Who broke into my apartment? What happened to the stolen pills?"

"Sometimes we can't dot all the i's," Capone said. "It bugs me, too. We don't have everything in this case, but we have more than enough. The bad guy doesn't always confess. We have to hope we've built a strong enough case to convince a jury."

"I just wish I could convince myself," I said quietly.

Many times over the previous weeks, I'd replayed my

interactions with Veronica Tanaka in my mind. Perhaps I was feeling the heavy weight of being the one who helped provide evidence of her guilt, but I'd begun to have doubts. When I'd discovered that Jeremy was no good, the information confirmed suspicions I'd had all along. But finding out that Veronica was a murderer still didn't sit right. When I'd told Capone about my doubts, he'd reassured me that we had to let the evidence speak for itself. The blood on the dress was just one more nail in Veronica's coffin.

Capone knelt down and scooped up his granddaughter. "Come on, pumpkin pie, we'd better hit the road and let Miss Delilah get on with things. This is a big night for her." He tipped an imaginary hat to me. "It's been a pleasure working with you. I'll miss trying to keep you from going rogue."

A lump rose in my throat. I'd gotten used to chatting and texting with Capone, and had come to think of him as a friend. Maybe more. It suddenly hit me, though, that our relationship had been, essentially, business. Now that Veronica was behind bars, there would be fewer and fewer reasons for us to interact.

"I appreciate you stopping by," I said, doing my best to smile.

Audra flapped her chubby little fingers at Butterball. "Buh-bah, Bub-ba."

"Oh gosh, you're taking half a cat's worth of fur with you," I said. They were both wearing dark clothes, which were now heavily decorated with yellow cat fluff. "Let me get the lint roller."

Capone laughed. "It's fine. Like I said, we have the same challenges at home." He picked at Audra's shirt. "Although maybe not to this extent." He bent down toward Butterball. "Buddy, you've got to get better at choosing gifts. This isn't the kind of fur coat anybody wants."

I closed the door behind them and leaned my back against

it for a moment, exhaling deeply. Time to get to work. I walked over to the kitchen island, where I'd set a pair of small gold earrings, the shape of knives, that I intended to wear that night. On a typical night in the kitchen, I avoided wearing jewelry. Bracelets, necklace, rings, and the like were too prone to getting caught up in the frenzy of a busy dinner service. Tonight, though, I decided a little celebratory bling was in order, and picked the earrings, which had been a thirtieth-birthday gift from Sonya. I put the first one in my ear.

A knock sounded and the door immediately opened, startling me. The other earring flew out of my hand and onto the floor. I cursed and held my hand to my beating heart.

Sam stepped in. "Sorry, did I scare you?"

"A little. I dropped an earring." I moved to my hands and knees and began to search for the missing jewelry.

Sam knelt on the floor next to me to aid in the hunt. Butterball sauntered over and presented his head to be petted. "Hey, Buddy," Sam said, pausing to stroke the cat's fur. "You get to come home with me tomorrow. Julio is making you your very own room, with a big, sunny window to lay in and watch the lake." He looked at me. "I know you've got to get to work, but I wanted to make sure it's okay to write a check to the meat guys. Melody said they dropped off another invoice."

"Yes, that'd be great. They delivered our order this morning." I leaned back on my haunches and rested my hand on his arm. "I can't thank you enough for everything you've done. It's really great of you to zero out all of the restaurant's accounts before opening. I can't tell you how much it's going to help to start without carrying all that debt."

He smiled and settled into a full squat, his elbows resting on his knees, something I was nowhere near flexible enough to pull off. "I wish you'd have let me do more. I'm not only doing this because you were my fiancée, you know. I believe in you. Remember that I tasted your food before I ever set eyes on you. This is what you were meant to do, Dee."

"Thank you," I whispered, my voice catching.

We stayed quiet for a moment before I turned away from him and busied myself searching the floor. If I was going to stand firm on my decision to break up with Sam, I had to resist the urge to throw myself into his arms. Butterball edged his way around the counter and then stopped, pawing furiously at an invisible enemy near the baseboard. Out of the corner of my eye, I saw a glimmer.

"Wow, he found my earring." I gave the cat a congratulatory pat as I plucked the tiny golden knife from the floor and fastened it into my ear. "Good kitty." Butterball ignored me and continued to swipe at the baseboard. "What is it, Bud?" I leaned closer and ran my fingers under the bottom edge of the cabinetry until my fingertips met a small, jagged piece of pottery.

"What's that?" Sam asked, as I pulled the tiny fragment from its hiding place.

I stood up and held the shard in the light. It was the color of clay and about the size of a laptop keyboard square. "It's a piece from my smashed tagine. The one the thief shattered when he broke in."

Sam moved next to me, and the two of us peered closely. "What's the dark stuff?" He asked, pointing. "Dried blood?"

"I think so. Looks like we might be able to dot one of our i's after all."

CHAPTER 25

Melody zipped through the kitchen door, cheeks pink with exertion, her curls bouncing. "Dr. Sittampalam is here with some friends from the hospital. They want to congratulate you on the opening. They wondered if you had a minute to come out and say hi."

The kitchen had been slammed all night, but Sonya and I had managed to keep pace. Melody was flying around the front of house like a blond tornado, with Rabbit backing her up as busboy and giving the occasional assist as a back waiter—the "invisible waiters" diners rarely notice who fill glasses, clear plates, and help carry orders for large groups. Daniel kept the liquor flowing, leaving his post to serve as maître d' if he saw Melody getting too overwhelmed shuttling plates back and forth. All in all, despite being down a server, we were nearing the end of service and had somehow managed to keep the train cars on the rails. My muscles were taut, my feet were aching, and the heat of the oven was making me sweat like a turkey at Thanksgiving, but I was in control. I almost had to pinch myself every time I realized that this was my restaurant.

"You good in here if I go out and greet her?" I asked Sonya.

"Girl, please," she replied, with a dismissive wave. "I've churned out four hundred cheese soufflés in under three hours with Jean-Philippe Frenet screaming in my ear." She had a point. Although opening a restaurant was surely one of the most stressful undertakings a chef could inflict upon herself, it was an altogether more rewarding kind of stress compared to many of the pressure-cooker situations we'd been through earlier in our careers. Sonya threw open the oven door, and a blast of hot air hit my face.

"I'll bring the doctor's group their pizza while I'm at it," I said. "Save Melody a trip."

I patted the sweat off my face with a clean towel, popped on some oven gloves, and used special metal tongs to remove the group's order—tonight's bestseller, the Deep Dutch— from the hot oven. I inhaled the sweet, garlicy aroma. Perfection.

Threading my way through the packed dining room, I tipped my head toward Sam, who was seated at the bar, sipping on a cucumber-and-basil infused mineral water—an off-menu drink Daniel made just for him. I was glad to see he'd taken me at my word that he'd always be welcome at the restaurant. I recognized Geneva Bay's mayor and a number of other local luminaries. I smiled at them and made my way out onto the patio.

Night had fallen, and a plump half-moon hung low, its white glow reflecting off the water. I stopped for a moment, allowing my eyes to adjust to the lower light of the crisscrossing suspended outdoor lights. The vibe was altogether different out here—still busy, but with fewer tables and no walls to amplify sounds, it was almost peaceful. As my eyes got their bearings, my smile shriveled when I noticed Lois Gorman seated with several women from my aunt's bridge club. I could happily have lived my life without ever having to see her again, but Geneva Bay was small, and it seemed that she would continue to turn up like a bad penny.

"Delilah," one of the ladies called, fluttering her fingers in the air. I recognized the woman as Judy, the big mouth who'd told everyone Auntie Biz was in the hospital. When I tried to pretend I hadn't heard her, she stood and called again, "Delilah."

I made my way to their table. Seemed I wouldn't get out of saying hello, even though I was lugging a flaming hot, extra-large pizza that weighed almost five pounds. Although I didn't want to admit it, I was also lugging around about five pounds of guilt—misplaced, but unshakable—about what had happened to Lois's grandson. What if Carson had killed himself because of the evidence I'd gathered against him?

I flashed a tight smile. "Thanks for coming," I said.

"Oh, we wouldn't have missed this for the world," Judy said. "We snagged the last reservation of the evening. I never eat this late, but we had to make an exception."

"Eating this late gives me indigestion," one of the women, a stout septuagenarian with hair the color of a sweet potato, complained. "I always eat at six."

"So take a Tums," another woman snapped. "This is Elizabeth's grandniece's opening night."

"I remember when Rocco Guanciale owned this place," Indigestion Lady said, fiddling with her napkin. "No respectable person would have come here."

"I was here every weekend!" Tums Lady shouted, and her companions burst into laughter.

"We're just so sorry that Elizabeth couldn't come downstairs to join us," Judy continued, once the uproar had died down. "I called her to let her know we were coming, but she said she wasn't feeling up to it."

"How is she?" Indigestion Lady asked.

"Getting her strength back, little by little," I replied.

"Please give her our regards," Tums Lady insisted.

I glanced around the table. I realized with embarrassment and shame that I'd written these women off as interchangeable bores—a phalanx of elderly chatterboxes with mints in their purses and white sneakers on their feet. I hadn't even bothered to learn their names when I'd taken my aunt to her bridge club. In fact, they were funny and supportive and clearly cared about one another. I'd avoided them for the same reason I'd stayed detached from Jeremy and Biz's arrangements. I didn't want to hear about this one's wonky hip or that one's faulty hearing aid or how cutting the grass had become overwhelming. I didn't want to deal with the frailties that accompanied illness and aging.

Their faces were all turned toward me with looks of expectation and concern. All except Lois Gorman, who, despite the smile plastered on her face, looked like a corpse that had been microwaved on low for thirty seconds. Her glossy wig still adorned her head, but even it looked deflated. Her usual mask of makeup was absent and she wore a blouse and jacket in funeral black.

Judy seemed to notice the direction of my gaze. "We couldn't lure Elizabeth out to join us, but we managed to drag Lois along tonight, didn't we, Lo?"

Lois managed a half-hearted nod.

"They'll find him, hon," Tums Lady whispered, squeezing Lois's hand.

"They will," Judy said. "He's probably laying low until this all gets cleared up. I'm sure he had nothing to do with it."

I didn't have to ask who they were talking about. "Good to see you. I need to deliver this pizza," I said. I wondered how much any of them knew about my part in putting Carson into the firing line of the investigation. "Thanks again for coming, I'll tell my aunt you said hello."

I stepped over to the table next to the bridge ladies, the table closest to the lake, and set the Deep Dutch pizza down. I greeted Dr. Sittampalam and her companions. "Thank you all so much for being here."

"This is a great view," the doctor said. She laughed. "Well, it's pitch dark, but it's fun to sit under the stars and watch the lights on the passing boats."

"For you, only the best table in the house will do," I said. It was corny, but true. I'd seen Dr. Sittampalam's name on the reservation list and made sure Melody seated her group at a table with primo lake views.

One of the interns, a slightly built Black guy with a hipster beard, pointed to the menu. "Delilah and Son. I didn't know you had a son. You never brought him to visit at the hospital."

I laughed. "You're the first one to mention it. It's actually Delilah and *Soh-n*, as in my sous chef, Sonya Perlman-Dokter. Now you're in the know, but you have to keep it a secret from the tourists. It's how we'll know you're a local." I winked at him as I used a spatula to extract cheesy slices of deep dish from the pan and began to pass them around. Because of the density and high-moisture content, deep-dish pizza retains a lot more heat than thin crust, so servers usually dish out the first pieces with gloves or oven mitts to avoid guests burning themselves.

"Keeping us fed the whole time your aunt was in the hospital was really kind, but it was also a great marketing ploy, like giving free samples in the grocery store. Now all my residents and interns are loyal customers," Dr. Sittampalam said, gesturing to her companions. "I think I would've had a mutiny on my hands if I hadn't brought them here on opening night."

I laughed. "I can't thank you enough for all you did for Biz when she was in the hospital. We're really grateful."

"How is she?" one of the interns asked. "She still owes me bridge lessons."

"Getting stronger. She'd love to see you, but I don't think she's up for visitors. Even she had to agree that tonight would be too much for her, but I hope that before too long she'll be lending a hand in the kitchen now and then."

"It's good that she's resting," the doctor said. "It must make you all breathe a little easier to know that the killer is behind bars."

"I'll feel better when the trial is over," I said. "Just a few hours ago, I found another piece of potential evidence up in my apartment. It seems like this will never end."

"Evidence?" Dr. Sittampalam repeated.

"What, like a stolen letter or monogrammed handker-chief?" the hipster-beard guy said, with a sly twinkle in his eye.

One of his companions punched him on the shoulder. "This is real life, dude. Somebody broke into her and Miss O'Leary's apartment, like, while they were in there."

"It's okay," I said, waving my hands. "I'm all for gallows humor. It's the only thing that's kept me halfway sane the past few weeks. Anyway, the evidence is bagged up on my kitchen counter and ready to drop off at the police station to-morrow morning."

"Ahem." I turned around to find the source of the fake cough. Rabbit stood behind me. "Sorry to interrupt, chef," he said. "There's a supplier on the phone for you. Says it can't wait."

I excused myself and followed Rabbit through the dining room toward the kitchen. "A supplier? At this hour?"

"That's what he said. He's just the driver. It was hard to understand him, but he said his boss told him he's gotta drop some fresh cheeses off before the end of his shift tonight and needed you personally to sign for it."

I glanced out the windows as we passed. The parking lot was packed with cars. "No way is he going to back a delivery truck in here," I said, raising my voice both out of annoyance and to be heard over the clamor of the restaurant. "He'll get stuck and hem everyone in." I groaned. "It has to be some kind of screwup. Nobody in the industry does evening deliveries, and we have everything we ordered. I double-checked the invoices against the deliveries myself."

Rabbit shrugged. "Maybe it's a new driver?"

We walked into the kitchen where the phone receiver stood on the counter next to Sonya. She wiped her saucy hands on a towel and slipped another pizza pan into the searing oven. "The guy hung up on me," she said. "I told him I'd come out and get whatever it is, but he mumbled something and hung up."

"Want me to go out there?" Rabbit asked.

"No, Melody's still slammed out there. Can you give her a hand? There are a few tables on the patio that need their drinks topped up." I slipped my apron off over my head. "Whoever made this screwup is going to have hell to pay on Monday. But for now, I'll get this truck driver off my back and out of my parking lot."

Melody flew in through the door. "How're the Deep Dutch and Eggplants coming for table twelve?"

"Two minutes," Sonya replied.

I slipped out the back door amidst the clamor. As the door shut behind me, it felt like I'd entered a different world. I could still hear the murmur of voices and distant clinking of dishes from the diners on the patio, but compared to the noise of the kitchen, this seemed like an otherworldly calm. Compared with Chicago, where stepping outside for a break meant stepping into a grimy alleyway frequented by rats, this would be yet another benefit of my new gig. An owl hooted in the distance as a gentle breeze stirred the trees.

Between the moon and the lights around the building, I could see most of the parking lot and make out the dim outlines of the road. Not a delivery truck in sight. Maybe the driver had come to his senses and realized there was no way to back a truck into the packed lot?

I took a few steps forward, intending to check that the truck wasn't parked farther along the road where the trees blocked my view. Instead, I became aware of a figure looming in the darkness just behind me. I inhaled sharply as something cold and hard was rammed against my back.

"Walk," a familiar voice commanded.

CHAPTER 26

My panicking neurons struggled to form an understanding of what was happening. The voice was deeper, rougher than I remembered, but I knew it instantly—Carson Callahan. He must have been hiding behind the restaurant. He grabbed my shoulder with one hand and pressed the metal object against my body again. A gun. Carson Callahan was holding me at gunpoint. The delivery had been a ruse to get me outside. How had I been so gullible? Rabbit had never met Carson and wouldn't have recognized his voice. That's why the caller had hung up when Sonya tried to quiz him.

"Come on, move," he repeated, more forcefully. "We need to talk."

The acrid smell of accumulated sweat rose off his body. I turned my head and managed to catch a glimpse of his greasy hair and wild eyes before he nudged me forward with the gun. This agitated, filthy man bore little resemblance to the carefree, stylishly slapdash server I'd hired a few weeks before.

"I don't know what you think you're doing," I said, trying to keep the quiver out of my voice. "All I have to do is yell and a whole restaurant full of people will come running to help me. Sonya is right behind the door."

He nudged me with the muzzle of the weapon. "Do you really want to call more people over?"

"Carson, your grandmother is here eating with her friends. She's worried about you. Your parents are a wreck. Whatever you're thinking of doing, don't do it," I said.

He hesitated. Adrenaline coursed through my body. He was kidnapping me, leading me Lord knows where for Lord knows what purpose. Now was the moment to fight back. He wasn't much bigger than I was, and I knew I had at least a fighting chance to overpower him if I moved quickly. Coming here and intercepting me just outside the restaurant on opening night clearly meant he was desperate, though. The thought that by struggling I could draw others toward him, toward a crazed man with a loaded gun, stopped that train of thought cold. I couldn't risk it. I had to pray that once we got farther from the building I'd have another chance.

Carson gave me a shove with the muzzle of the gun and I lurched forward. We skirted the parking lot near the road, sticking to the shadows of the trees that ringed the property. I hoped that, despite the darkness, someone might spot my white chef's coat and raise the alarm, but no one came into or out of the packed parking lot during the few seconds it took for us to cross it. Surely, Sonya would soon realize I was missing.

We advanced wordlessly until we reached the patch of woods where Butterball had run away to, and where, I recalled grimly, Jeremy's killer had hidden in the moments before the murder. Carson steered me toward a gap in the trees. Various scenarios wheeled through my brain. Could Carson have been the mastermind of Jeremy's murder all along? Did he do it to impress Veronica? Was he leading me back to the spot where he had killed Jeremy? Would he shoot me in the same place? My steps halted.

"Move," Carson growled.

This could be my last chance to escape. I pinwheeled toward him, arms flailing, giving him everything I had. I landed a heavy blow on his body and got in a good kick to his shin. With him momentarily stunned, I took off running back toward the restaurant. I got only a few feet before Carson's footsteps thundered up behind me. He lunged, tackling me around the legs. I staggered forward and came down hard on my hands and knees. Damn my curvy, top-heavy figure.

Carson grabbed me by the arm and yanked me to my feet. "I don't want to hurt you, Delilah. I just want to talk. Don't try that again." His voice was raspy, winded. He pushed me through the gap in the trees. A faint path, a diagonal cut-through, had been trodden, but within a few steps, the tree canopy blocked out the light so completely that I could barely see the ground. I stumbled over tree roots as we hurried along. My knees ached; I was pretty sure I'd gashed them both when I'd hit the ground. My palms felt like they'd been dragged across a box grater. Carson propelled me forward and kept me upright with a painfully firm grip on my arm.

Before I knew it, we'd reached the end of the trail, the place where the trees opened onto the shore path. Carson craned his neck to check that the coast was clear of passers-by and then shoved me toward the dock. A few speedboats were moored there, along with a pontoon and a bowrider that looked to be about twenty-five or thirty feet long. Carson hustled me along the dock and used his weapon to point toward the boat.

"Climb aboard," he ordered. The boat loomed up in the darkness. Although I couldn't make out all the features, I knew enough about boats to realize that this was an expensive model. The kind with plenty of cockpit space for a well-to-do family to use for tubing and days out on the water. I also knew that boats like this usually had small cuddy cabins, with a head, or toilet compartment and an adjacent, enclosed sleeping and lounging area. Surely, he wasn't going to force me belowdecks? I gulped. When I failed to move, Carson stepped toward me. "Climb aboard," he repeated. Then added, "Please."

With shaking hands and aching knees, I made my way up the ladder and flopped gracelessly over the side onto the deck of the boat. I clambered to my feet as Carson climbed in after me. I expected him to untie the rope that bound the boat to the dock and take us out onto the lake, but instead he just stood there, a line of concentration creasing his brow.

"Where are you taking me?" I demanded.

"I'm . . . not sure," he replied. His voice quivered. He suddenly sounded less Clint Eastwood, more kindergartener.

"You're *not sure*?"

"Give me a minute," he snapped. *Was he crying?*

I realized then that this was as far as his plan had extended. He'd been desperate to get me out here, alone and away from the restaurant, and now he didn't know what he was going to do with me. Why go through all the trouble of kidnapping me if he had no plan?

The floor of the boat's cockpit was illuminated with a row of embedded LEDs. Carson's momentary show of weakness allowed my mind to recalibrate. This quivering wreck of a person was no criminal mastermind. He was a terrified, desperate kid. And not a very sharp-witted one at that. In this brighter light, I saw what had eluded me up until now—the weapon Carson was carrying wasn't a pistol. The muzzle was far too wide to be an ordinary gun, and, most tellingly, it was painted safety orange.

"A flare gun?" I said, my voice rising.

"Flare guns can be dangerous at close range if they're loaded," he countered. "But I couldn't find the flares."

"It's not even loaded?" Dear Lord, I'd let this idiot kidnap me with an unloaded flare gun.

Carson looked around. "Shh! I can't think when you yell at me."

I stormed toward him and grabbed the gun out of his hand. He put up no resistance as I tossed it over the side of the boat into the lake. It hit the water with a *galloop*, and for a moment ripples smacked faintly against the side of the boat. Once the sound faded, Carson and I were left to stare at each other. His shoulders slumped, and he tucked his hands into his armpits.

"What was all that about?" I asked.

"I saw it in a movie."

"Carson, do you realize how much trouble you're in? The police have a warrant out for your arrest. Your parents and your grandma are afraid you might be dead. Kidnapping me isn't going to help your situation," I said.

"Kidnapping?" he repeated, mouth agape. "No, no. I was just . . . I needed to talk to you alone, okay?"

"Doofus," I muttered under my breath. "Taking someone at gunpoint, even if the gun is a flare gun and even if you saw someone do it in a movie, is kidnapping. You hurt me. I was scared."

"I'm sorry, okay," he replied peevishly, wiping his nose and eyes with the back of his hand. "I needed to talk to you. I've been trying to call the restaurant for days, but Sonya or Melody kept picking up. I was afraid they'd recognize my voice."

"What phone were you using? The police have a trace on yours. They said no calls had been made."

"Majid leaves one on the boat." He bobbed his head toward the door to the cuddy cabin.

"Who the hell is Majid?" I asked, finally looking around to get the full measure of my surroundings. Even in the low light, the boat gleamed. Boats take a lot of wear and tear. Clearly this one was little used and meticulously maintained.

A few details, however, clashed with the impression of a pristine watercraft. The deck of the cockpit was littered with empty Red Bull cans and Power Bar wrappers, the door to the cuddy had been pried open, and the whole boat stank like unwashed socks.

"Majid's this Saudi kid I met last summer. When his dad has business in the city, his mom and him and his little sister come up here. They've got a place by the Wrigley mansion. Like twenty bedrooms. We went out on the boat together a couple of times with some other guys, so I knew where he kept the key and everything." Perhaps sensing the death rays of judgment shooting out of my eyes, his tone became defensive. "It's, like, morally wrong that they barely use the house and only take the boat out a couple times a season, you know? I remembered him saying they usually have a guy bring the boat out of storage and get it ready before they come," he explained.

"So you've been righting this 'moral wrong' by squatting on this guy's boat since you ran from the cops?" I asked.

"Uh-huh. I hid out in the woods for a couple nights, but I knew I couldn't last like that. And then I remembered that Majid said they're usually here from mid-June to the Fourth of July, so I snuck over to their dock, and sure enough, it was there. They left some emergency supplies in the stowage."

"If you needed to talk to me so bad, why wait until opening night, when the restaurant is jam packed?" I asked.

"Like I said, I tried to talk to you sooner, but I couldn't reach you. Then earlier today, I saw Majid's family's Benz pull into the driveway. It was only a matter of time until they wanted to use the boat and found me."

"So you stole their boat under cover of darkness. Great solution. I guess now you can add 'grand larceny' to your rap sheet," I said.

"I'm going to put it back before they notice," he whined.

"And I had no other way of getting over to the restaurant without being seen."

I pressed my fingers to my eye sockets and exhaled. It wasn't even worth pointing out that Majid's family were unlikely to miss the obvious signs that someone had been squatting in their boat. "Okay, Carson. You have my attention. What did you need to talk to me about so badly that you were willing to abduct me and pirate this poor kid's boat?"

He sucked in a deep breath, and slumped onto the bench seat at the stern of the boat. "I need your help. I need you to tell the police I'm innocent."

CHAPTER 27

"You're innocent?" I repeated Carson's assertion, my hands balling into fists. I closed my eyes, trying to contain my rage and draw calm from the sound of the waves lapping gently against the side of the boat and the cool evening breeze. No dice. "Innocent of what exactly?" I barked. I gestured to my torn pants, bleeding knees and hands, and the garbage that littered the deck of the boat.

"You know"—he waved his hands around his head—"the murder and stuff."

"Tell the cops yourself," I said. "They definitely want to talk to you."

"They won't listen! They arrested Veronica, and she's totally innocent. I need you to, like, negotiate my surrender, or whatever. You can talk to Capone for me."

I took a seat in the captain's chair and swiveled it to face him. I leaned forward, elbows on my thighs. "What, exactly do you want me to say? That I'm sure you're a really great guy even though you tricked me, kidnapped me, and stole a boat? After how you evaded the police? News flash: they don't love it when people do that. Not to mention how you repeatedly lied about where you were and what you were doing on the night of the murder."

He rose to his feet and paced, dragging his fingers down his face. "Veronica and I were together when Jeremy was shot. Why won't anyone believe that?"

"Because that's already been proven not to be true."

He shook his head. "What do you mean?"

Carson had apparently been cut off from the news, living like a vagrant on this boat, having escaped before the police could question him. He probably had no idea the jig was up on his alibi. "Carson, the cops already know that Veronica's car was locked at that time you said you were with her. You couldn't have been in there. Plus, they found Jeremy's blood on her dress."

He sat back down, crossing his arms over his chest. "Well, the making out in the car part was maybe not that true," he mumbled.

"Come again?" I said.

"I made that up, okay?" he huffed. "Veronica agreed to go along with it."

"Why would she do that?"

He hung his head. "Because she needed me as her alibi. I *was* with her when Jeremy got shot. That part was God's honest truth."

"But you weren't getting busy in her car."

"No." His voice cracked, making him seem even more like the teenager he was. He shuffled his feet and cleared his throat. "I saw her leave the restaurant and I followed her. I was going to ask her to come see my friend's band. You probably think I'm dumb for thinking I had a chance with her, but we have a lot in common."

I didn't say what I was thinking—that they'd both allowed their vanity and status consciousness to lead them astray.

"I caught up to her when she was coming back up the path. She looked really upset. I asked her what was wrong, but she wouldn't tell me. That's when we heard the gunshot."

"You're telling me that the original story about you being together was a lie, but this new story about you being together is the truth." I struggled to keep the sarcasm out of my voice.

"Yes," he said. "You've got to believe me. We were walking together, almost all the way back to the parking lot, when Jeremy was shot. We ran back down the path toward the sound of the shot, and when we got there, Jeremy was dead. Veronica went over to him to make sure. That must be how the blood got on her dress. Your aunt was slumped in her chair. We thought she was dead, too."

"And you didn't check on her to make sure? You just left them there?" My voice went shrill. Carson was asking for my help. He was desperate, no doubt having spent days running on adrenaline and Red Bull, trying to cobble together a plan using his limited mental resources. Still, the thought that he and Veronica had left Auntie Biz alone without even trying to summon help infuriated me.

"I would have called nine-one-one, but Veronica was scared," he said. "She started crying and freaking out. She, like, fell into my arms. I practically had to carry her back. She said she'd been arguing with Jeremy and she was afraid everyone would think she killed him. She needed me to be her alibi, and she wanted to put some distance between us and the crime scene."

"You didn't see the killer?"

He shook his head. "No. I think whoever it was cut through the path in the woods."

"How did you know that path was there? It's hard to see unless you're looking for it," I said.

"All the locals know about it," he explained. "It's one of the only places where you can get from the shore path to the road without going on to private property or having to jump a fence."

"So you cooked up the idea of you guys being together in her car?"

"Yeah," he said, suddenly very interested in a spot on the floor. "She went along with it because we didn't really have time to make up another story. She was kind of a wreck. I offered to have my mom drive her home, but she said she needed to walk to clear her head. Her whole body was shaking. She just kept saying her life was over if anyone connected her and Jeremy."

"Did she explain her connection to Jeremy?"

"Not really. It seemed like he had something over her, like from her past."

"He was blackmailing her."

He shrugged. "I guess so. She said she needed to get something. Something she'd given him that could lead back to her. I offered to do it for her. She didn't want to let me, but I convinced her that it would look too suspicious if she got caught, since she and Jeremy had a connection." He swallowed. "There's something else I need to tell you. I lied to you."

"No kidding. Which time?" If the mood hadn't been so deadly serious, I might have laughed at his "confession."

"About being in the woods by your aunt's house that day. It was me."

This was no great revelation. I'd been convinced the figure in the woods was him as soon as I saw his lanky figure loping off down the path. The words *well, duh* nearly escaped my lips, but I managed to say instead, "What were you doing there?"

"Veronica said the thing she needed to get was in your aunt's shed."

"The money," I said.

"Money? No." He looked confused. "She assumed the money she gave him had been spent already. The suitcase the money was in was what she wanted. She thought it might have her fingerprints on it. She was afraid it would lead back to her."

"And that's when I saw you lurking by my aunt's house. You went to get the suitcase," I said.

He nodded. "I waited until it was almost dark to go, but when I got there, the cops were searching the place. I had planned to go the same night as the murder, but the stupid minivan was broken down and I couldn't ask my mom for a ride without her getting suspicious. That van is a piece of garbage."

"Yeah, that's how you told me you cut your hand, right? Fixing the minivan?" I crossed my arms over my chest and arched an eyebrow, waiting to see if he'd come clean or double down on his previous lie.

He hung his head and said nothing.

I took it as an admission of guilt. "So how did you really cut your hand?" I prompted.

"It doesn't matter," he mumbled.

"It kind of does. Did you, for example, cut it stealing pills from my house?"

"What? No. I already told you, I don't know anything about that. I cut it on a champagne glass the night of the murder. I was holding the glass in my hand and I crushed it in my hand when the gunshot went off." He picked at some invisible thread on the seam of the bench seat's cushion. "It was really loud and it surprised me."

"You cut it on a champagne glass?" I said, retaining my skeptical pose.

"Yeah, when I went out to meet Veronica, I brought two glasses of champagne. You know, for me and Veronica."

"What made you think she wanted champagne?"

"It's romantic." He shrugged.

I felt my blood pressure spike. "You're only nineteen."

"I know, okay? You don't have to rub it in," he sniveled.

"You're underage," I said. "You could've gotten my restaurant shut down by serving yourself alcohol."

I knew Carson had much bigger problems than underage drinking at that stage. But it was one thing watching him trash his own life; endangering my business was another matter. Between his admission about leaving Auntie Biz for dead and this, I was struggling to suppress a strong impulse to chuck him over the side of the boat along with that ridiculous flare gun. I couldn't believe I'd ever felt sorry for him.

"Your restaurant got shut down anyway," he replied, his lips forming a petulant pout.

Touché. The little brat had a point. Thinking back to what Officer Stanhope had told Sonya about finding broken glasses in the woods and the bloodstains on Veronica's dress, the evidence did match up with Carson's story. The pieces fit. Still, his reactions were further proof that the kid's DNA was pure weasel.

"Even if I said I believed you, what do you want me to do about it?" I asked.

"Get the cops to believe me," he said.

I rose. "Here's what I will do. I'll call Capone and let him know where you are." I turned to the cockpit console and removed the boat's key, slipping it into my pocket. "You can spend the next few minutes until he arrives cleaning up Majid's boat. Then, if you still have time, maybe clean yourself up a little. You smell like a gangrene toe that's been left in the sun."

"You're not going to stay and help me?" he said. His mouth hung open.

"No. You're lucky I'm not, because then I'd have to tell the cops about how you forced me here at gunpoint."

"It was a flare gun! It wasn't even loaded!" he protested.

"Listen, you little . . ." I dug my nails into my palms and

took a deep breath. "That's the one scrap of mercy you get from me, okay? And you should be grateful."

"But, don't you believe me? I'm telling the truth. You need to get me out of this." His voice rose in pitch and his nose and eyes streamed.

"Not happening. You threatened me. You injured me. I was terrified, Carson. I thought you were going to kill me."

"But you wouldn't have listened to me . . ." he began.

"Believe it or not, I'm helping you." I surprised myself at how measured my tone remained. My soul glowed a little as I realized I was channeling my own mother. No way would she have raised a kid like Carson. "I know you're used to being bailed out, but you're an adult and you need to start acting like it. You've made some poor decisions, decisions that have serious consequences."

"Aren't you afraid I'll run away again if you leave me?" he said.

I shook my head. "We both know that you've run out of options. It's time to face the music. You want to impress Veronica? Man up, tell the truth, and hope it's enough to get her out of jail."

CHAPTER 28

I dialed Capone's number as I hobbled down the shore path toward the restaurant.

"Sorry to interrupt your family time," I began when he picked up, "but I thought you'd want to know that Carson Callahan is hiding out on a stolen boat—a thirty-foot Regal bowrider—at the dock next to the restaurant. He's unarmed. He's as repentant as he's constitutionally capable of being, by which I mean that he feels sorry for himself, although I think the magnitude of the harm he's caused still escapes him."

"Can I ask how you know all this?" Capone said.

"Probably better if you don't," I replied.

"Pleading the Fifth again?" Despite the seriousness of the situation, a ripple of amusement coursed through his deep, silky voice.

"Something like that," I said, picking twigs out of my disheveled hair.

"Don't suppose he confessed to a role in Jeremy's murder?" Capone said.

"No, and he also swears Veronica is innocent," I said.

"Do you believe him?" he asked.

"I suppose I do. I don't know." I let out an exasperated sigh. "I moved here to get away from it all."

"Well, I've got news. *It all* is here, too."

"Don't I know it. Hey, can you call Carson's parents and let them know he's okay? I really don't want to get involved."

"That's a first," he quipped.

"I swear, this time I wasn't looking for trouble. Trouble went way out of its way to find me," I said, remembering how smoothly the night had been going up until my abduction.

"All kidding aside, you sound a little shaken up. Everything all right with you?" he asked, concern warming his tone.

"Never better," I deadpanned.

I hung up and continued on my way, breathing a sigh of relief a moment later as the restaurant came into sight. Even though I'd only been a few minutes' walk away during my ordeal, I felt like an astronaut returning from a moon mission. I'd have to cut through the parking lot so none of the diners on the patio would see me. It really wouldn't do to have the chef limping out of the woods looking as if she'd just gone ten rounds with a rabid badger.

I zigzagged through the parking lot, trying to stay in the shadows. Luckily, we were nearing closing time, and the crowd had thinned out considerably. I pictured the kitchen. This was the part of service when the adrenaline would fade. Feet would be aching, muscles would be coiled into tight knots, and ears would be buzzing from the constant clang of cookware and shouts of "Order!" "Fire!" "Picking up!" I hoped Sonya managed to get through the last of the reservations without me. After the nine-o'clocks put in their orders, there would have been a few more straggling pizza orders, but the tickets would have downshifted to things like shared apps and bar snacks. Daniel would probably be in the weeds with cocktail orders for a little while yet, but the kitchen would be starting clean-up and next-day prep.

As I rounded the back of a red Nissan, a remote key chirped and the car's headlights flashed. I let out a cry of shock.

"Delilah?" Lois Gorman clutched her chest and approached me, her look of surprise melting into concern. She slid her car key into her purse. "Good lord, look at the state of you!" She leaned closer to inspect my knees. "Your pants are all torn, and your hair is just, well, it looks awful. What happened?"

"I . . ." I waved my hands, searching for a way to explain my appearance that didn't involve telling her that her grandson had kidnapped me. "I fell."

"You *really* look awful," she emphasized, clicking her tongue.

"I'm fine, thanks for your concern," I said, through gritted teeth. "I need to get cleaned up and change."

I began to ease past her when I heard the distant wail of a siren and realized that the cops would most likely be pulling into my parking lot any minute. It was the closest parking to the dock where Carson was hunkered down in his stolen boat. Although I was sure Lois would be relieved to discover that her grandson was alive and well, I was less sure that seeing him handcuffed and loaded into the back of a police car was the best way to reveal that information to her. *You owe her nothing. Let her see that little weasel spawn clapped in irons and horsewhipped. Not. Your. Problem.*

I took a few steps toward the restaurant, but my conscience dragged behind me like an anchor. I turned back toward Lois with a sigh. Deep down, I knew it was better to break the news about Carson to her gently and explain what he'd told me. Ugh. My conscience's voice had never been this loud when I lived in Chicago.

"Would you mind coming inside with me?" I asked.

"Inside?" she repeated. She clutched her purse and regarded me warily. "Why do you want me to come inside?"

"I'm not very steady on my feet after that fall," I explained. "I'd feel better if someone made sure I get in without further incident."

"Oh, all right," she said, relaxing her posture.

I walked across the parking lot toward the restaurant's back door, throwing in an occasional limp to keep up appearances.

"What on earth were you doing out here in the middle of your opening night?" Lois asked.

"It's a long story. What about you?" I asked, hoping to distract her by turning the questioning back on her. "You can't be finished eating yet, can you? I just saw your table's order come in right before I went outside." Theirs had been one of the last reservations of the night. I had no idea how long I'd been gone, but deep-dish pizzas take about thirty minutes to cook. I couldn't imagine how the bridge ladies would have gotten their food, eaten it, and paid in that space of time.

"It was chilly," she said. "I didn't want to catch pneumonia from the lake breeze. Maybe you should get some of those big heat lamps like they have at the nicer restaurants."

Nicer restaurants? My fists tightened into balls. *Last time I listen to you, worthless conscience.* I opened the kitchen door and held out my arm to usher Lois inside.

Sonya rushed over to me, taking hold of my hands. I winced when she made contact with the raw skin.

"Dee! Oh, thank goodness. I was just about to call out a search party." She took a step back, flipping my hands over so she could examine them. "Are you okay?"

Rabbit stood at the sink, wrist-deep in suds. He wiped his soapy hands on his apron. "Did you get into a fight?" he asked. He turned a wary glare on Lois.

"I'm fine. I fell," I added, realizing he was implying that Lois and I had been brawling out back. Taking a swing at the old gal had definitely occurred to me more than once, and heaven knew that I wasn't averse to throwing down when the need arose. If that had been the case, though, you'd better believe Lois would be the one looking like day-old roadkill, not me. "Lois was just making sure I got in safely."

"Well, I'd better be going," Lois said. "Now that you're safe inside."

"Could you hand me one of those paper towels?" I asked her, pointing to a stack on the far side of the kitchen. I needed to stall her until I could speak to her alone.

Lois crossed the kitchen and dutifully handed me a C-fold towel, which I wet in the sink and used to dab at my skinned knees. The jagged tears meant the pants were beyond repair. I'd have to get a spare pair from the office.

"I'm glad you're okay," Sonya said. "I got really worried."

Rabbit nodded. "When you didn't come back, we figured you'd gone back around to the patio or run into someone in the parking lot, but we couldn't find you."

I gave Sonya's arm a squeeze. "I'm fine. I got caught up with an old friend."

Outside, the sound of the siren drew close enough to be heard over the din of the kitchen.

"An old friend?" Sonya repeated, furrowing her brow. "And then you fell?"

Before I was forced to answer, Rabbit clocked the siren's high whine. "Hold on, is that the police? What are they doing here?" He stood on his tiptoes and craned his neck like an anxious meerkat, even though there was no earthly way to peer out the transom-height windows without growing wings. "It sounds like they're right outside."

"It's okay, Rabbit," I soothed.

I cursed myself. Why hadn't I told Capone to make sure they kept their sirens off? My restaurant was going to get a reputation as the O.K. Corral of Geneva Bay. Maybe I could bill it as dinner and a show.

Lois, who had been standing near the ovens, edged toward the door. "I'll be on my way. Leave you to your work," she said.

I pondered my options. I could still let her leave, let her learn about Carson the hard way. I pictured the scene: Lois, with her busybody tendencies, would definitely stick around to find out why the police had come. No doubt, the bridge ladies and the other patio diners would have their eyes glued on the activity as well. What a horrible shock Lois would get, seeing her grandson dragged into custody, filthy and pathetic, in front of half the town.

No. I needed to prepare her for what she might see outside. She already seemed on edge. I'd be doing the police a favor, too, by keeping her away. Last thing they needed was Lois Gorman launching into hysterics. Frankly, the restaurant didn't need that, either. My diners would get enough of an eyeful without her making a scene.

I cast a glance at the ticket rail. Miraculously, Sonya had the orders cleared. The last of the pizzas on order was already in the oven; the straggling app orders were plated and ready to go out. I handed a tray to Sonya and arranged the appetizer plates on it.

"Son, would you let Melody and Daniel know the kitchen is closed? Rabbit, can you start clearing the front of house? And keep everyone out of the kitchen, okay? Lois and I need to have a chat."

"A chat?" Lois repeated. Her face went pale, and I wondered if she had some inkling of the news I was about to share with her.

"Really?" Sonya cocked her head to one side. "You want to have a chat with Lois?"

I nodded. "It'll only take a few minutes."

Sonya shrugged an "it's your funeral" look. She shouldered the tray and headed toward the dining room, Rabbit following in her wake. I waited for the door to the dining room to stop swinging before turning to Lois. "We need to talk."

Her eyes darted to the door. "I really need to get going."

"There's something I've got to say to you first," I said. "And I'm afraid you're not going to like it." I took a step toward her to avoid having to shout over the noise of the ovens and the extractor fan. Lois jumped back, her eyes filling with fear. "What the . . . ?" I began, holding my hands up to try to soothe her. "I just want to talk."

"You called the police, didn't you?" Her words sizzled with accusation.

"Yes, I . . ." That's when I saw it. Yellow fur covered the lower part of her pants. "Were you in my apartment?" I asked the question, but the answer was obvious.

"No." She shook her head.

I pointed to her pants. "You're covered in cat fur. *My* cat's fur. I know it when I see it, believe me."

She looked down at her legs, where a telltale coating of Butterball's golden fluff stood out against the black material of her pants.

"Why were you in my apartment?" I took another step toward her. She darted toward the door, but I blocked her before she reached it. Adrenaline surged through my body. My brain sputtered like a filet hitting hot butter. If I believed Carson—and heaven help me, I realized I actually did—then who was left on my original list of suspects? Only Lois. How had I been so slow to realize it?

Her hands clutched her purse tightly and she drew it toward

her chest. "I popped up to say hello to Elizabeth. She didn't answer, so I let myself in. I was worried that something might've happened to her. You shouldn't leave her alone like that. I warned you."

CHAPTER 29

My eyes narrowed at Lois. She stood defiantly next to the gas range, shoulders thrust back, hands tight on the handle of her purse, a purse I suspected contained a Ziplocked shard of pottery with some telltale DNA on it.

"Warned me? If you laid a hand on my aunt, so help me God . . ." My voice pulsed with fury.

She straightened her spine. "All I've done has been to protect her."

"Let me see what's inside your purse," I said, closing the distance between us and grabbing hold of the bag's handle. "You heard me talking to Dr. Sittampalam about the evidence that was in my apartment, didn't you?"

She yanked her purse out of my grip. "I told you I went up to say hello to Elizabeth. Since when is that a crime?"

"You didn't go up there to see Biz. You went up because you knew there was evidence that could be linked to whoever stole the pills, which would link that person to the murder. If you didn't take it, why don't you let me look in your purse?"

"Because it's none of your business," she snapped.

My hands fell to my sides. What was I doing? Accusing an old woman of murder because she had cat hair on her pants? Her explanation that she'd gone up to see Biz was certainly plausible. Either I had to commit to purse snatching or I needed to draw her out some other way.

"Do you want to know why I fell?" I asked. "What I was doing out in the woods in the middle of dinner service? I was out there because your grandson kidnapped me." So much for breaking it to her gently. Another good-cop failure.

"Kidnapped?" she repeated, her eyebrows knitting together.

"Yes. He's terrified. He's been hiding out on a boat, trying to figure out a way to prove his innocence," I said.

"Carson's . . . okay?" she said. She stumbled backward, catching herself as she clattered into a stack of dirty pans on the work surface.

"Carson's alive, but he's not okay. He's in a lot of trouble," I said. "Until Jeremy's real killer turns herself in, your grandson will never clear his name."

"They arrested that Tanaka woman," she said, her jaw visibly tightening.

"She didn't do it. Carson is trying to get her freed," I said.

"No." Her head shaking became panicky, her movements jerky and disjointed. "No," she repeated. She dropped her purse on the floor and grasped at the sides of her head, as if to rein in whatever thoughts were swirling inside.

Outside, doors slammed. The police, most likely loading a frightened ex-waiter into a squad car. Maybe I could make a run for it, signal the police and get them to search Lois's bag before she had a chance to dispose of the evidence. But could they do that on my say-so, without probable cause and a warrant? I remembered Capone scolding me about shoddy detective work. I needed more. Maybe if she actually saw her grandson in a police car, she'd confess. It was worth a shot.

"If you'll come outside, you can see Carson for yourself." I reached out my hand to try to calm her. In a blink, she'd wrapped her fingers around the hilt of my ten-inch gyuto chef's knife, which I'd left lying next to a cutting board. The steel flashed as she brandished it toward me. I jumped back, my body going rigid with fear.

The gyuto was my go-to workhorse knife. I kept it razor sharp, ready to slice through the thick rind of a squash as if it were water, ready to carve up a mound of cauliflower as if it were air. Even a nick from that knife's edge could do serious damage to a clumsy fingertip, as I'd discovered on more than one occasion. I didn't want to find out what it could do to the rest of my body.

"I'm not falling for that. You think you can trick me into walking into the arms of the police? There's no way I'm going to let them take me," she growled.

I backed away, trying to see a clear path to the dining room. I didn't like my chances if I had to take the time to fiddle with the tricky knob of the back door. But if I could run through the swing door, I had a chance. Then again, who knew what this woman was capable of? Maybe she'd rush out after me. How long until Melody or Sonya or Rabbit stumbled in here, straight into her path?

"Those sirens we heard?" I pointed up in the air. "They're for Carson. That's what I wanted to tell you. They're coming to arrest him," I said.

She shook her head defiantly. "Carson wasn't involved. Once he explains that to the police, it will be fine."

"Veronica and Carson's fates are intertwined. He swears he was with her at the time of the murder. If she goes down, she's going to take your grandson with her. And, who knows? If he's successful in getting her freed, the whole thing could end up pinned on him. After all, they'll need to look for a new suspect," I said. "Carson's already lied about his alibi once. He could go to prison for Jeremy's murder."

A guttural sob rose from Lois's throat as she haphazardly

slashed the air with the knife. "It's not fair. I did the right thing."

Still racing through the mental calculus of my options, I said, "You think you're going to get away with killing me? The police are just outside."

"You think this is for you?" she scoffed, locking her fevered gaze on the glistening blade of the knife.

My mind raced. *Who was she intending to kill if not me?*

As if in answer to my question, she rotated the knife's tip until it was pointing at her own chest. She placed her left hand over the top of her right on the knife's hilt.

"Lois, what are you doing?" I asked, although the answer was obvious.

"How can he still be poisoning everything even after he's dead?" she screeched. She inhaled deeply and shut her eyes, keeping the knife's point aimed straight at her heart.

My body turned to stone. The clamor of restaurant sounds collapsed and faded until I could hear only my own panicked breathing. If I didn't do something, this woman was going to stab herself right in front of me. The knife hovered inches from her chest. There was no way to approach her without risking accelerating her death. She drew the knife back and squeezed her eyes shut as she prepared to plunge the blade into her chest.

"You can't save Carson if you're dead!" I cried.

"Everything is already ruined anyway. Tambria and Irv and Carson will never forgive me."

"They'll understand. They love you," I said.

She turned the knife's point back toward me and took a menacing step in my direction. Her eyes were wild, animal-like. "What would you know about it? I loved my mother, but it didn't matter. When she complained, I wrote it off because I was too busy with my own life. The longer I stick around, the more likely something like that will happen to me. I'll end up just like my mother, powerless, an easy mark for people like Jeremy. Becoming an old woman means becoming invisible. We're sent out to pasture. Forgotten. Nobody listens to you anymore. I'm not letting that happen to me."

"Tami and Irv won't let that happen. They've devoted their careers to helping elderly people," I said. "Jeremy took advantage of our trust, but that doesn't mean that will happen to you." I held my hands up as I backed toward the door to the dining room. "Tell me what happened," I said. "Please. You said you were trying to protect Biz. Warning me. What were you warning me about?"

"Jeremy," she spat his name, her voice shaking with emotion. "You can't let another person like Jeremy into her life." Her hand shook, causing the knife's blade to flash and tremble.

"He needed to die. You had to do it," I said, keeping my voice steady, as I tried to mirror her thoughts. Although my quick temper caused me to utter death wishes on a near-daily basis, the idea of actually being angry or hate-filled enough to shoot a man between the eyes . . . I could hardly process the thought.

"I had to do it," Lois repeated, zombielike.

"Tell me what happened, Lois. I'll try to help everyone understand. I promise."

The point of the knife dipped toward the floor as she slumped against the worktop. "That night. It was just an ordinary night. I only came because I wanted to encourage Carson. He'd been complaining about having to get a job, and I hoped a show of support would help motivate him." She squeezed her eyes shut, and I could see tears forming in the corners. She took a shaky breath. "At the bar, I saw him—Jeremy—pour some kind of powder into a drink. I confronted him about it. He told me it was medicine for Elizabeth. But I remembered . . . I remembered . . ."

"What? What did you remember?" I pressed.

"Mother. I saw him doing the same thing to her. He said she wasn't good about taking her pills and it was just easier that way. It never made sense to me, because he was always saying, 'It's time to take your medicine, Dorothy.' I never saw her refuse. So why did he need to slip something into her drinks? And there were so many pills. He was always saying Mother had this or that ailment, and needed more medicine. Suddenly, when I saw what he was doing to Elizabeth, it hit me like a thunderbolt. I swear, it was just like that." She snapped her fingers. "I saw the whole thing so clearly. He thought I was stupid. He thought he could pull the wool over my eyes again. But I saw what had to be done."

"That you had to kill him," I said.

She gulped air and nodded. "I'd had suspicions about him before, but I always told myself I was crazy. A couple of the girls at bridge club had pills go missing. Once, I thought I'd seen Jeremy reach into Carole Petty's purse and pocket something when he was there with your aunt." She pressed her eyes closed at the memory. "But I dismissed it, even later when Carole said she couldn't find the pain pills for her hip. Those stupid chairs at the resort don't leave you anywhere to hang your bag, so it didn't seem strange that the pills might've fallen out. She was worried because her doctor had told her to be careful with those pills. Anyway, I told myself there was no way Jeremy could do something like that. After all, what would it have said about me if I'd missed his true nature all the time he was caring for Mother? I'd recommended him to your aunt, for heaven's sake."

A lump formed in my throat. "I understand. Believe me."

She continued as if I hadn't spoken. "I should've seen the signs. I've known your aunt for years. She's always been the sharpest player at the club. A lot of spinsters are like that, since they have more time to focus on hobbies. I'm sure you're the same with this place." She gestured at the kitchen with the point of the knife.

I bit my lip. Even in the midst of a confession, she was true to form. She was lucky she was the one holding a weapon.

"Mother was very bright, too," Lois continued. "Until Jeremy came on the scene, Mother's problems had only been physical. Mother and Elizabeth both started downhill in just the same way. Elizabeth would be playing a hand of cards, and suddenly forget her bid. That wasn't like her at all. I've seen friends lose their memories, but the sleepiness, almost like she was floating, and then the jitters and the paranoia, even the ashen color of her skin—that was all just like Mother."

"Jeremy drugged your mother, too," I said. I glanced toward my pizza oven, hoping that son of a sea witch was roasting somewhere much hotter.

"Yes," she said. "I don't know how I missed the signs with Mother. He took me for a fool."

"He had us all fooled, Lois," I said.

"Well, I shouldn't have let myself be fooled, and I'll be damned if I was going to let him do it again."

I never liked Lois Gorman, but for the first time since I'd met her, I felt like she and I had a whole lot in common. If I'd found any of this out while Jeremy was alive, I truly didn't know what I would have done to him. But for the grace of God, our positions might have been reversed. "So, you followed Jeremy outside to kill him?" I asked.

She shook her head. "I don't know. Maybe. I think if he'd confessed and apologized, that might have been enough for me."

"But he didn't?"

"No." She spat the word. "When we were next to each other at the bar, I told him I didn't believe what he said about Elizabeth and the medicine in her drink. I confronted him about Mother. I still don't know all the details, but it was clear he was up to something with all of those pills. He didn't even bother to deny it. He said nobody would believe me and called me a senile old bat." Her expression hardened.

The missing elements in the story of that night began to fall into place. I remembered how Jeremy had disappeared for an unusually long time while getting Auntie Biz's drink. Then, when he materialized, he looked shaken. He must've realized that Lois was on to him. He'd seemed anxious to avoid Lois, which at the time, I took as a very natural reaction to the woman. But now, it took on an altogether different meaning.

"When I saw him leaving with Elizabeth," Lois continued, "I followed them down to the dock and . . ."

Even though she no longer seemed like an immediate suicide threat, the knife in her hand was shaking so violently, I was afraid that she might injure herself.

"You shot him," I finished her confession in a whisper to myself. The murder was finally, truly solved. Still, not all the loose pieces fit into the puzzle. "You used Biz's gun. How did you even know she had one, and that she carried it with her?" I asked. Before she could answer, I slapped my forehead. "No purse hooks. You saw it in her purse, didn't you?"

She nodded. "Like I told you, people's purses were always toppling over on the floor during bridge club. A few months ago, I picked hers up and I saw the gun inside."

"What about her keys?" I asked, remembering that whoever had broken into my apartment had let themselves in with a key. "Why did you take her keys?"

"I was afraid that if someone found out about what Jeremy was doing with the pills, it would come back on Tambria. The pills Jeremy was using were dangerous. That much was obvious. What if Elizabeth kept taking them and then she died? Glacier Valley Senior Care could be sued. I wanted to get the pills out of her house without anyone realizing," she explained.

"But the police moved them before you could get to them?" I asked.

"Yes, once I realized Elizabeth was staying at your apartment, I realized the pills were with her. I had to get them out. I hid in the bushes after dark, waiting for the cops to get distracted or fall asleep. When the shift changed and they were caught up yapping to each other, I took my chance. But then your cat scared me, and I cut myself. I nearly got caught." The frantic energy that had filled her body seemed to be draining away before my eyes.

Sensing that the danger had passed, I cautiously stepped forward and put my hand over hers. I gently pried the knife from her fingers. "You saved my aunt," I said. "I promise I won't ever forget that. But now, you've got to be strong, to prove Jeremy wrong. It's time for you to let the world know what kind of person Jeremy was, and to save your grandson."

Lois looked up at me. She set her chin in a firm line and nodded.

CHAPTER 30

At 4:15 sharp, Auntie Biz, who after more than a month of recuperation was finally feeling like her old self, slapped two potholders into my hands and tipped her head toward the large cast-iron pot on the stove. "Go," she commanded.

I dutifully took up the heavy dish of hot soup. She picked up an enamel pot that had been heating under the warming lamp and led me through the empty dining room, onto the patio, to the table closest to the lake. I set the pot down on a waiting trivet in the middle of a tabletop already brimming with deliciousness. Auntie Biz had insisted on making the "family meal," the free staff meal that restaurants dish out before or after service. Typically, our family meals were simple, perhaps some homemade pasta or another rustic, hearty dish.

Today, though, Auntie Biz had created a full-blown feast, showcasing the finest Wisconsin ingredients. A heaping platter of fried lake perch adorned with sunny yellow lemon wedges and ringed with ramekins of homemade pickles formed the centerpiece. On one side of the fish stood a dish of seasonal charred asparagus drizzled with a creamy horseradish sauce. On the other side, she set the dish she'd been carrying—traditional German-inspired spätzle flash-fried in butter and garnished with chives and fresh parsley. I removed the lid from the beer-cheese soup I'd been commanded to carry and dipped a ladle into the thick, orangey broth. I spooned out heaping bowls for Melody, Daniel, Sonya, Rabbit, and Auntie Biz and a smaller bowl for myself. So far, I'd managed to keep my promise to Butterball that I'd maintain a healthier eating plan in solidarity with his. I took my seat as Sonya handed me a basket containing slices of earthy, homemade rye bread. I took a piece and laid on a thin layer of local, Wisconsin butter.

We passed the dishes and joked around, enjoying the beautiful summer day. The area schools had let out the week before, and Geneva Bay's summer season was in full swing. Delilah & Son seemed to have caught on among both tourists and locals, and the future seemed rosy. Sam and I had even gotten into a good groove with Butterball's shared custody arrangement.

"I know we've had, like, a jillion different openings, but now that we're all together, this finally feels like the real, *real* opening," Melody said, popping a pickle into her mouth.

"Pteh, pteh, pteh." Sonya simulated spitting three times over her shoulder—her superstition for warding off evil. "Don't jinx it. We're never having another opening night, soft, hard, official, unofficial, or otherwise. No more shootings, no more crazed murderers with knives running around the kitchen. We make deep-dish pizzas and that's that."

"Here, here," I said, raising my glass of soda water.

"*Salud,*" Daniel echoed, raising a bottle of Orangina to the sky.

"Still, I wonder how Capone feels about you hooking Lois Gorman up with primo legal representation," Melody mused. "And Delilah and Biz promising to testify on her behalf."

"Well, he'll have to deal with it," Biz said.

"Capone will be fine. He's a *professional*." I inflected the last word with unintentional bitterness. I'd heard barely a word from Capone since Lois and Carson's arrests. Even though it was understandable that he wouldn't stay in touch now that the case was over, it felt a little like I'd gotten dumped after a promising date.

"How did he take it when you told him you'd be testifying on Lois's behalf?" Melody asked. "He must've been pretty upset."

"I didn't tell him, exactly. Sonya's cousin said we should relay communication through him," I explained. Maybe I'd owed Capone an explanation, but I owed Lois my aunt's life. "Lois is willing to admit what she did, and that's enough justice for me. I know she had her own reasons, but if she hadn't killed Jeremy, Biz might well be dead."

"It's not like she had much of a choice after they found the shard of the broken tagine in her bag," Daniel said. "She was caught with her hands in the dough."

I let his slightly wonky-sounding idiom slide. His literal Spanish translation of "caught red-handed" actually made sense in the context of an arrest in the kitchen of a pizza restaurant. "I don't see how any good can come from locking her up forever," I said. "It's not like there's a long line of people wanting justice for Jeremy."

"My cousin said this case is a defense attorney's dream," Sonya added. She waved her hand across an imaginary marquee. "Senior citizen takes revenge on pill-pushing abuser. His firm wants to get into more nursing home neglect cases. Thinks the 'Call the Dokters' shtick would be perfect for that. He says he might even get Lois off with time served and probation."

"I heard from Jeff at the Quik Stop that Veronica is going to testify against the ringleaders of the whole pill operation," Rabbit said. "That's why they dropped all the charges against her." He whistled through his teeth. "Hope she knows what she's getting into. Better her than me."

"Carson will probably avoid serious consequences, too," I said, shaking my head. I still wondered if I'd done the right thing by keeping mum about the kidnapping. "Drives me crazy how a poor Black kid from my old neighborhood would end up with years inside for a stunt like that. But a handsome white kid in this jurisdiction? He'll probably walk away with a wrist slap. I hope they'll tack on a few hundred hours of community service. Maybe it'll finally work some sense and humility into him."

Sonya was serving out second helpings to Rabbit and Melody a few minutes later when Capone's black Dodge Charger rumbled into the parking lot.

"The cop?" Rabbit said, looking around like he was trying to find the quickest exit route. I wondered if he'd ever lose that reflexive fear.

Auntie Biz put a calming hand on his arm.

"He looks mad," Melody whispered. "Do you think Lois Gorman escaped from jail or something?"

Sonya turned and punched Melody in the shoulder. "See? Trouble. You jinxed it by saying everything was finally okay."

"Stop talking or you'll make it worse." Daniel made the sign of the cross and threw the contents of Melody's glass of water on the patio floor. "To get rid of the *mala suerte*," he explained. Restaurant people are a superstitious bunch.

I held up my hands. "Chill, guys. Everything's fine."

I doubted my words of reassurance even as I rose to greet the detective. Since Carson Callahan and Lois Gorman's arrests a month earlier, I'd only seen Capone once when I happened to bump into him at the farmer's market. Now that our "business" was concluded, he, much to my disappointment, wasn't in the habit of stopping in. And Melody was right; he looked upset. His forehead bore a deep line of displeasure. He opened the back door of his car and pulled out a large box of some kind. By the way he had to heave it out of the car, I knew it must contain an unusually heavy load.

"I believe you know this hoodlum?" he said. He held up the box—actually a cat carrier—so I could see Butterball inside, pawing at the metal bars and mewing with fury. "He was in a fight."

I took the carrier from him and placed it on the patio, extracting my large yellow fur-baby. "He's supposed to be with Sam this week." I cradled Butterball and inspected him for damage. "Are you okay, Buddy?"

"If he got knocked around a little, he had it coming. I found him in my yard, assaulting our cat."

"No." I shook my head. "That's impossible."

Auntie Biz loudly cleared her throat.

Okay, maybe "impossible" wasn't totally accurate. Truth was, Butterball had been in more fights than Dennis Rodman. But he was never the aggressor, and he never came close to winning.

"Butterball only fights when he's provoked," I snapped. I had to bite my tongue not to add the other thought that was running through my head: *How dare you drop me like a hot potato the minute Jeremy's murder was solved—the minute I solved the murder!—and then show up after all these weeks accusing my cat of attacking yours?*

Capone crossed his arms over his chest. "He came into our yard. Brujo has a right to self-defense."

Sensing that things were getting heated, Sonya had sidled over and slipped in between Capone and me. "Cats will be cats, am I right? I'm sure Delilah is very grateful for you bringing Butterball back."

I shrugged one shoulder. A half admission. I wasn't going to forgive the insinuation that my cat was the aggressor anytime soon. "I'll text Sam and let him know, in case he's looking for him," I said.

"Why don't you join us, Detective Capone?" Sonya pulled out a chair.

"I should get going," Capone protested.

I set my chin in a firm line to match Capone's clenched-jawed expression. "He's a busy man. I'm sure he has better things to do than visit with us."

"Nonsense," Biz said, banging a serving spoon on the table. "I haven't cooked a full meal in months and I'm not going to see one crumb of it go to waste." She used the spoon to point at Capone and then at the empty chair. "He'll stay and eat."

Rabbit, still jumpy, sprang up and began setting a place for Capone. I took my seat across the table, still holding Butterball protectively in my arms.

"I bet he's acting out because of the separation," Melody whispered, rubbing the cat's head consolingly as I took my seat. "It happened with my nephews when my sister and her husband split up."

We sat in awkward silence for a moment. I felt a sharp kick on my shin and looked up to see Sonya tipping her head in Capone's direction. She raised her eyebrows and widened her eyes. I pursed my lips and gave a quick shake of my head. No way was I going to be the one to extend the olive branch.

"How's your cat?" Sonya asked, shooting me a flinty glare before she turned to the detective. "Did he get hurt in the fight?"

"Thankfully just a few scratches, but my granddaughter was out there and she almost got in the middle of it. I got there just in time."

"Ooh, that's bad," Melody said. From the way she flinched right after she said it, I guessed Sonya had shushed her with another well-placed kick.

"Butterball has some nerve to go up against a twenty-two-pound Maine Coon," Capone said.

"A Maine Coon, eh?" My eyes narrowed. "Is he black with pointy ears, by chance?"

Capone nodded. "That's why he's named Brujo. Black with orange eyes, looks supernatural. He probably weighs almost as much as this guy." Capone eyed Butterball. "Although Brujo's bulk is muscle."

"So now you're going to insult Butterball? When you needed him, it was all sweet talk and catnip, then you completely ghosted him, and now you storm in here like that? He thought you were friends. That maybe you had a connection. May I remind you that without Butterball, you'd still have the wrong person behind bars for Jeremy's murder?" I was on a roll now, hardly even stopping for breath. "He saved your bacon twice—once with stopping the break-in and again with the fur on Lois's pants," I fumed, rising to my feet. Butterball wriggled out of my arms and fled into hiding under the table. "He put himself in harm's way, and have you given him an ounce of credit? No, you made your arrests and then disappeared on me . . . I mean, him."

"I *was* grateful to Butterball," Capone said. "But I've been busy trying to clean up a very messy case and make sure the testimony and evidence a certain amateur detective gathered will be admissible. Maybe Butterball forgot that I'm still new here and that I have people to answer to. I put up with a lot of shenanigans because I thought we were all on the same side. Now, I find out through the grapevine that two of my main witnesses are testifying on behalf of the killer. That could bring down the entire case. I have to keep my distance from defense witnesses, so I can't be accused of witness tampering."

"Listen, buster," I said, leaning across the table and pointing an accusatory finger, "I'm on the side of justice, and testifying for Lois is the right thing to do. Speaking of justice, I've personally witnessed your cat taunting Butterball. He's the aggressive one. He's been at it for months, ever since we moved here. So you can take your messy murder case and Brujo's 'muscle' and shove them both up your—"

"Brujo's a good cat," Capone replied, cutting me off and standing up from the table.

"With all due respect, sir, I seen what happened with my own eyes." We all turned to find Rabbit fidgeting with his napkin, his eyes glued to his plate. I realized how much courage it would've taken for him to contradict Capone. "I was out for a smoke week before last and that big black cat went up to the dumpster out back and did his business right there in front of Butterball, keeping eye contact while he did it."

"See?" I said triumphantly. "That's Bullying 101."

"Then the black cat turned and started walking away," Rabbit continued. "Butterball went after him screeching like a Tasmanian devil and sucker punched him from behind. The black cat got his licks in, too, and they limped off their separate ways." Rabbit chewed his lip and cleared his throat. "I seen a lot of that kind of thing in prison. At the end of the day, both guys would say the other one started it, but they'd both get written up, you know?"

We all froze, rooted to our spots, chastened by Rabbit's words. I lowered my wagging finger to my side, and Capone and I sunk back into our chairs. Butterball leapt up on to the table. He looked around with wide-eyed confusion and let out a questioning *Mew?* No one even tried to stop him when he began to nibble at a piece of perch from the platter.

CHAPTER 31

After what seemed like an eternity of heavy silence, Sonya puffed air out of her cheeks and rose to her feet. "Welp, kiddos, I think we've had enough of today's episode of *Wild Kingdom*. We've got a service to finish prepping, and I think the chef and the detective have a few things to discuss." She tucked Butterball under one arm, grabbed a platter with the opposite hand, and headed toward the restaurant. "Great meal, Biz," she called over her shoulder. The others followed her in short order, clearing dishes away as they went. Even Biz was silent as she picked up the pot of soup and made her exit.

Capone rubbed his chin. "Look, Delilah—" he began.

I held up my hand. "I understand. That must've scared you to see your granddaughter almost get hurt right in your own backyard."

"No, I mean *yes* that was scary, but it wasn't your fault. Or Butterball's." He let out a long sigh. "I lost it."

The corner of my mouth curled into a smile. "I have to admit, I was a little shocked to learn that Detective Cool Hand Capone can get rattled."

He returned my smile and shook his head. "Truth is, I have a terrible temper, but I keep it in check . . . mostly. Got me into a lot of trouble when I was younger. Believe it or not, I wasn't always operating on this side of the thin blue line."

"Skeletons in the closet, eh?" I said, arching an eyebrow.

"Enough to fill a few closets," he said, the smile almost imperceptibly fading from his eyes.

The white sail of a boat drifted past, the laughter of the people on board carrying across the water. I tried to reconcile my feelings. Capone and I had had a very public shouting match just moments before. Neither of us had really apologized, and we were both still ticked off about it. I still believed I was right and he was wrong. That kind of thing happened all the time in the kitchens where I'd worked. Someone messed up, they got reamed out, you all moved on. Conflict had always sent Sam running for the hills. Capone, however, sipped his drink on the sun-soaked patio, seeming untroubled by the lingering discord.

"I know you don't think we're on the same side anymore," I said. "But I'm not trying to mess up your case. I know what Lois did is terrible. All I'm doing is keeping my promise to her that I wouldn't forget that her actions saved my aunt's life."

"I wish you'd respected me enough to tell me what you were doing," Capone said. "After everything we've been through, all the slack I cut you, I had to hear it from a lawyer?"

"I thought I was helping by staying out of your way, and honestly, I thought you were kind of over me," I said.

"Over you?" He raised an eyebrow.

"Over our friendship, I mean," I said, feeling my cheeks flush. "I guess I let the lawyers handle it because I was mad that you only seemed interested in talking to me until the case was done."

"I thought the same about you. Guess we got our wires crossed," he said. "When I get wrapped up in a case, while it's going on, that's my sole focus, but that doesn't mean I don't still care about my family and my friends."

"I hope I'm in that category," I said.

"You? Maybe. It'll be a while before I forgive Butterball, though."

"You won't be able to stay mad at him. Believe me, I've tried," I said.

"That might be something you and he have in common."

We fell into a companionable silence, sipping our drinks. I knew five o'clock was ticking closer, but I hesitated to draw our visit to a close.

"How's Carson?" I asked. "I heard they let him out on bail."

"Lucky, is how he is. That friend of his chose not to press charges about the boat. Carson happened to let it slip that he may have been involved in a kidnapping, but since no one has come forward about that"—he narrowed his eyes in my direction—"we won't pursue charges. He'll still have to pay for running away from us, but a kid of his age with those squeaky-clean parents and no record?" He shook his head and clicked his tongue. "He'll probably weasel out of any serious jail time."

I bit my tongue at his apt choice of verb. "And Lois? Is she holding up okay?"

"Surprisingly well. Released on home confinement pending the trial." He looked toward the lake, shading his eyes from the sun's glare. "Can I make a confession?"

I gestured to my chef's uniform. "Don't let the black and white fool you, I'm not actually a priest. Common mistake."

He chuckled. "Well, I won't expect absolution, but I'll hope for understanding."

"Chef's oath," I said. "I swear upon my cleanest apron."

He smiled and looked back at me, his amber eyes somber. "Being busy with the case wasn't the only reason I went AWOL on you after Lois was arrested. I was avoiding you because I felt guilty. I still feel guilty. I made a mistake, and it put you in danger."

"What are you talking about?" I asked.

"Remember what you told me Lois said to you that night? That being an old woman means becoming invisible? Well, I fell into that trap. I'd seen Lois when I reviewed the video on your security camera from the night of the murder. She went out the door not too long after Carson and Veronica."

"Well, I was so hell-bent on proving Carson had done it, I never seriously considered Lois a suspect, either," I said. "She had to pull a knife on me before I got the picture."

"But I'm a detective, and I pride myself on letting the facts speak for themselves. I'd discounted Lois as a possibility for the same reason I never really took your aunt seriously as a suspect—I thought they were both harmless old ladies. And because of that prejudice, you ended up in your kitchen with Lois holding you at knifepoint." He looked almost physically pained at the thought.

Two cars rolled into the parking lot. Our first reservations of the night. Capone tipped his head toward them and rose. "Well, that's my cue. I appreciate your understanding." He reached across the table and gave my hand a pat. The familiar rush of champagne bubbles coursed up my arm.

"For what it's worth, you have my absolution, too. We all have our blind spots. I consider myself a pretty good judge of character, and I let a drug-dealing gambling addict take care of my aunt and live in her house," I said. "You think I don't beat myself up every day about what could've happened to her?"

"Maybe we both need to cut ourselves some slack," he said. "After all, nobody's perfect."

I grabbed a stick of al dente asparagus, bit off the tip, and winked at him. "Speak for yourself."

RECIPES

DELILAH & SON CHICAGO-STYLE DEEP DISH

Yields: 4–6 servings
Prep time: 1.5 hours (including rising the dough)
Bake time: 30 minutes

Sonya here. Delilah & Son is built on quality, fancified deep-dish pies. When I said I wanted to adapt our basic deep-dish recipe so folks could make it at home, Delilah was, let's say, not super supportive. I think her exact words were, "I busted my butt for years honing my craft to get this recipe right and then invested every ounce of my being to make sure the restaurant was outfitted with the best equipment. You think Joe Public can just whip up *my* pizza on a Friday night using ingredients from the Piggly Wiggly and whatever bush-league garbage oven he has at home?"

I agree that it's hard to mimic restaurant food in a normal kitchen, but if you're game, let's give it a whirl.

First, let me say that Delilah has a dirty little secret. I'm not talking about her crush on Capone, which she thinks I don't know about. I'm talking about the fact that I'm actually better at making pizza dough than she is. To say Dee is a little competitive is like saying the pope is a little Catholic, so she was none too pleased in culinary school when I sailed through the Yeasted Doughs lesson while she struggled. Our instructor said her English muffins "bordered on impenetrable." She's gotten better since then, but she's not a natural. Personally, I attribute it to her kneading technique. If she's in a bad mood, she can be aggressive. Like Mike Tyson aggressive. Good dough requires finesse, not ten rounds in the boxing ring.

P.S. Don't tell her I told you about her infamous impenetrable muffins. It's a sore spot to this day.

The Recipe

This recipe will fill a **12-inch round deep-dish pan** and will feed 4 to 6 people. If you don't have a pan that big, you could use a 9-inch cake pan and either cut this recipe down by about one-third or keep the leftover dough for another purpose.

Dough

- 3 cups flour
- 2 tablespoons cornmeal
- ¾ teaspoon sea salt
- ½ teaspoon sugar
- 2 ¼ teaspoons (just shy of 1 packet) instant yeast

Did you notice that we're using instant yeast, not active dry? Okay, good.

- 3 tablespoons melted unsalted butter
- 3 tablespoons corn oil
- ¾ cup warm water (~110° F.)

Step 1: Make the Dough

Combine all the dry ingredients in the bowl of a stand mixer and give everything a little how-do-you-do with a wooden spoon. Add the butter, oil, and water and stir again until the dough just begins to come together. Do not over-mix or use boiling water here. Pop the dough hook on to your mixer and let that sucker spin on medium-low for about 6 minutes.

Quick tip: If you don't have a stand mixer, you can do all of this by hand. Make sure you use a B.A.B. (Big Ass Bowl), because you need a lot of room to maneuver. You'll probably need a slightly longer kneading time, too.

If the dough looks too wet, add one tablespoon of flour. Too dry? Add a tablespoon of warm water.

Step 2: Let It Rise

Form that bad boy into a ball and pop it into an oiled pizza pan (i.e., the pan you're going to cook it in). Make sure the pan is well-oiled, sides and all, and flip the dough ball once to coat it in oil. Cover the whole shebang with foil and throw a clean kitchen towel over it. Let it hang out in a warm spot for about an hour. On a cold day, you may want to heat your oven until it's just warm and then cut the heat off. Nestle your little dough baby in that cozy oven while it doubles in size.

If you'd like, you can start cooking your sauce (**Step 4**) while the dough is rising.

Step 3: Let It Rise Some More

After the first rise, unveil your dough. Set the foil aside; you'll need it again. Press the dough down to fill the pan and mold it up the sides. Fix any holes by sticking the dough to itself with wet fingers. Re-cover the pan with the foil and towel and let it rise for another 15 minutes.

Now is a good time to start **pre-heating your oven to 425° F**.

A couple of notes about the dough.

There's an active debate about whether cornmeal belongs

in authentic Chicago deep dish. We like it because it adds a nice yellow color to the dough and a little pleasant grittiness to the texture. Some of the big chains achieve a yellow color with food coloring, which . . . I mean, just why? If you want something to be a color, use ingredients that are that color. Don't get me started. Suffice it to say, we include a little cornmeal. The dough will come together okay if you leave it out because you're some kind of weird Gino's East cultist. Some places spread a dusting of cornmeal in the bottom of their pizza pan to add an extra crunch. You could go that route if it floats your boat.

We use corn oil in our dough. You heard me. Corn oil. It may not be the most fashionable of oils, but it's the best for this recipe. You can substitute olive oil if you prefer. It will change the flavor and color a bit, but the dough should turn out hunky-dory.

Don't use boiling water or it'll kill your yeast. The water should feel very warm to the touch, like a warm bath.

Sauce

- 2 tablespoons butter
- 1 small onion, diced extremely fine, or better yet zhuzhed in a food processor for about a minute (should yield about ½ cup)
- ¾ teaspoon salt
- 1 teaspoon dried oregano
- ¼ teaspoon crushed red pepper flakes
- 2 garlic cloves, minced
- 28-ounce can crushed tomatoes
- 1 teaspoon sugar

Step 4: Make the Sauce

Melt butter in a large saucepan over medium heat. Add the zhuzhed/diced onion. Toss in your salt, oregano, and red pepper flakes. Cook for about five minutes until the onion is translucent. Add the garlic, tomatoes, and sugar. Simmer on very low heat for 30 minutes or so. Taste for seasoning, and adjust as necessary. Let it cool slightly.

A couple of notes about the sauce.

You like spicy? Add more red pepper flakes. You like garlic? Throw in another clove. You do you, boo.

The quality of the tomatoes is super important. Probably the most expensive ones in the grocery store are gonna be your best bet. If you know an Italian person, ask them what brand they use.

Toppings

- 4 cups (32 oz.) shredded or sliced low-moisture mozzarella
- ¼ cup grated parmesan
- Optional: veggies and cooked meat

Step 5: Build Your Creation

Take the foil and the towel off your pan and behold your gorgeous dough. If the shape has gone funky during the second rise, press it back into submission.

Layer mozzarella directly on top of the crust. If you use sliced mozzarella, lay the slices out with a slight overlap, as if you're making a fruit tart. If you want to add sausage, veggies, or other toppings, now is your moment. Go nuts.

Pour sauce on top of the mozzarella then sprinkle the grated parmesan across the top.

A couple of notes about building your pizza.

If you're adding other toppings besides cheese, make sure the sauce covers your toppings.

We are using low-moisture mozzarella here. Don't use fresh mozzarella unless you want Delilah to personally come to your house and tell you how soggy and disgusting your crust is. Ditto with any other toppings you add. Don't add anything too wet, or you will regret it.

Super-Important Note: Deep-dish pizza layering goes cheese, then toppings, THEN sauce. If you do it the other way around, you're not making deep-dish pizza. You're making hot garbage and you have only yourself to blame.

Step 6: Baking

Pop your pan in the oven and bake it in a preheated 425°F oven for about 30 to 35 minutes. The crust around the edges should be lovely and golden brown.

Let the pizza cool for a few minutes on a wire rack. Slice, serve, and chow down.

DANIEL'S *EMERGENCIA MÉDICA* COCKTAIL

¡Hola, amig@s! This is my twist on the modern classic cocktail called Penicillin. Don't let the name fool you; this is a good kind of medicine. It cures anger, sadness, break-ups, you name it.

- 2 ounces blended Scotch whisky
- ¾ ounce fresh-squeezed lemon juice
- ¾ ounce honey-ginger syrup*
- ¼ ounce Islay single malt Scotch (I use Bow-more, since it isn't so strong with peat like some of the other Islay whiskies.)
- Garnish: candied ginger and a twist of lemon

This is what you do:

1. Add the blended Scotch, lemon juice, and syrup into a shaker with ice and shake. Put your hips into it if you want to get better tips from the ladies at the bar.

2. Strain into a rocks glass over fresh ice.
3. Top with the single malt Scotch. If you're making this for Delilah, and she's really angry, add an extra splash of whisky.
4. Garnish with a piece of candied ginger and lemon twist. If you want to get an even bigger tip, lean close to the lady you are serving and say, "For you, *mi amor*," as you pass the drink to her.

*Honey-ginger syrup: Combine 1 cup honey, 1 large (6-inch) piece of ginger, peeled and thinly sliced, and 1 cup water. Bring to a boil in a saucepan over high heat. Reduce heat to medium, and simmer 5 minutes. Place in the refrigerator to steep overnight. Strain with a cheesecloth. Save the remaining syrup for more cocktails or to add to your tea.

AUNTIE BIZ'S PISSALADIÈRE

I was never much of a traveler. Why go anywhere else when Geneva Bay's got a lake, ski hill, beaches, and woods? Still, I do like French recipes. Matter of fact, I bought a color television in 1966 so I could watch Julia Child's program, *The French Chef*, in full color. On my days off from teaching, I'd cook along with her. Anyway, enough chitter-chatter. Let's cook.

Prep time: 2.5 hours, including 1.5 hours rising time
Bake time: 25 minutes
Yields: 8 servings

Dough

- Approximately 3 cups leftover deep-dish dough, risen

OR, if you're a person who doesn't have continuous access to leftover deep-dish dough from your niece's restaurant:

- 1 ½ teaspoons active dry yeast
- ⅔ cup warm water
- 3 teaspoons olive oil
- 2 cups (250 grams) all-purpose flour
- 1 ½ teaspoons fine sea salt

Make the Dough

If you are using leftover dough, make sure it's brought to room temperature.

If you're making dough from scratch, put the warm water in a medium bowl and sprinkle in the dry yeast. Let it stand until foamy, about 5 minutes, then add the oil. In a large bowl, whisk together the flour and salt. Then stir the yeast-and-water mixture into the dry ingredients with a wooden spoon until combined. Turn the bowl's contents out onto a floured surface and knead until uniform and elastic, 3 to 5 minutes. Flour your hands if necessary to keep the dough from sticking. Transfer the dough to an oiled bowl. Flip the dough over, cover the bowl with a damp cloth, and let it rest in a warm place for 1 hour.

Filling

- ¼ cup olive oil
- 12 anchovy fillets
- 3 pounds onions, thinly sliced
- 3 cloves garlic, minced
- 1 teaspoon thyme leaves, chopped
- 1 bay leaf
- ½ teaspoon fine sea salt
- ¼ cup Niçoise olives, pitted

Make the Topping

While your dough is rising, make your topping. Heat the oil in a large skillet over medium heat. Finely chop two of the anchovy fillets. Add onion, garlic, thyme, bay leaf, and the chopped anchovies, then cover the pan and cook, stirring occasionally, for 20 minutes, until softened. Reduce heat to medium-low, stir in the salt, and continue cooking for 25 minutes, stirring occasionally. The onions should be pale golden and very soft; lower the heat if they start to turn dark brown at the edges or stick to the skillet. Remove the bay leaf, remove the onion mixture from the heat, and let it cool completely.

Roll Out the Dough

Lightly oil an 11×17-inch rimmed baking sheet. Working on a floured surface, roll the dough into an 11×16-inch rectangle, then transfer it to the oiled baking sheet and press the dough to the sides. Cover with a damp cloth and let it rest for 30 minutes.

Assemble and Cook

Heat the oven to 400° F. Spread the cooked onions evenly over the dough, and top with the remaining anchovies and pitted Niçoise olives. Bake until the edges and underside are golden brown, 20 to 25 minutes. Serve warm or at room temperature.

AUNTIE BIZ'S ORANGE SUPREMES WITH FENNEL AND ARUGULA

I like this salad because it's damn good. I'm not like one of those TV chefs who's going to tell you it's quick and easy. For a salad, it takes a long time to prepare. If you think life should be easy, then this recipe isn't for you. Go microwave a Swanson's. Cutting supremes is messy and boring, and shaving fennel takes precision, so if you want to whine about it, you know where the door is.

Prep time: 25–30 minutes
Yields: 4 dinner salads or 8 side salads

Salad

- 6 cups arugula, well washed and dried, tough stems removed
- 1 small fennel bulb
- 3 medium navel oranges

Garnish

- ¼ cup Greek feta crumbles (optional)

Orange Vinaigrette

- ½ teaspoon orange zest
- ½ teaspoon honey
- 2 teaspoons red wine vinegar or orange champagne Muscat vinegar (if you can find it). The Trader Joe's in Kenosha sells it.
- ½ teaspoon Dijon mustard
- ¼ teaspoon garlic, finely diced
- 4 teaspoon extra virgin olive oil
- Kosher salt, to taste
- Black pepper, to taste

The Salad

Did you wash and dry your arugula like I said? Good. Put it aside.

Wash the fennel bulb and slice it thinly using either a mandolin or a very sharp knife. Wash the slices and place them in a bowl filled with water until the fennel slices are covered, so they don't go brown. This will also allow any little bits of sand or dirt to be released.

Supreme the oranges. Don't know what that means? It means take all the membranes, pith, and rind off of it with a sharp knife. Don't know how to do that? Look it up someplace. What do I look like, a home ec teacher? Okay, fine. Sonya says if I'm bothering to write a recipe, I have to tell you the whole thing.

Cut off the tops and bottoms of the oranges so they stand flat on your cutting board. Using a very sharp knife and tracing around the curve of the fruit, cut the rind and pith off, being careful not to cut into the flesh. Now run your knife along the inner membranes, removing each section as you go. Then slice along the adjacent membrane until the cuts meet, releasing the segment. Transfer the segment to a bowl. Repeat. After all the segments are in the bowl, hold the membranes over the bowl and squeeze to juice.

The Orange Vinaigrette

Put the orange zest, honey, vinegar, and Dijon mustard into a small mixing bowl and whisk them together. Add the garlic, whisking to incorporate all the ingredients. While continuing to whisk, slowly drizzle the olive oil; set aside.

You are ready to put the salad together.

Drizzle the vinaigrette over the arugula, then toss well to lightly coat all the leaves.

Greens should be only lightly dressed. Don't drown them.

Place some of the dressed greens onto a salad plate or bowl then add some of the shaved fennel, orange supremes, and (if you want) Greek feta crumbles.

DEEP DUTCH PIZZA

Follow the recipe for Delilah & Son Deep-Dish Pizza. In **Step 5: Build Your Creation**, however, you'll make a few adjustments.

Toppings:

- 2 cups (16 ounces) low-moisture mozzarella cheese
- 2 cups (16 ounces) Gouda cheese
- 8 ounces (aka 8 handfuls) fresh baby spinach, cooked and very well drained
- 2 large red onions, thinly sliced and caramelized*

Heat 1 tablespoon of butter in a pan over medium heat. Add the spinach and cook until it's just wilted. Cool and then drain, squeezing out all the moisture in a clean kitchen towel.

Begin building your toppings with your cheese layer, as in Step 5 of Delilah and Son Deep-Dish Pizza (page 299). Next, add spinach and onions, making sure to nestle them all in a cozy blanket of sauce. The spinach will stay happy in its saucy blanket if it's well-covered. If you leave naked spinach on top of the pizza, though, it will burn.

Bake as directed in the basic recipe (page 300). Top with a scattering of toasted pine nuts, if desired.

*To caramelize an onion, thinly slice it. Melt 2 tablespoons of unsalted butter in a heavy-bottomed pan over medium heat. Sauté the onion in butter for about 15 minutes. Season with salt and a pinch of sugar. Sauté for an additional 10 to 15 minutes. Continue to cook and scrape, cook and scrape, until the onions are a rich, brown color. Add a splash of sweet white wine to deglaze the pan and cook for two minutes more until the liquid has evaporated.

RED HOT MAMA PIZZA

Again, you'll mostly follow the recipe for Delilah & Son Deep-Dish Pizza (page 295). In **Steps 4 (page 298) and 5 (page 299)**, however, you'll make a few adjustments. You will also add a few additional toppings to the cooked pizza.

In **Step 4: Make the Sauce (page 298)**, you will triple the amount of red pepper flakes to ¾ teaspoon. You will also substitute fire-roasted crushed tomatoes for the whole tomatoes and skip the zhuzhing in the blender step. Feel free to amp up the spice even more with a dash of Tabasco or Sriracha at the end if you think your guests can handle it. Remember, the Red Hot Mama isn't for the faint of heart or the timid of tongue.

In **Step 5: Build Your Creation (page 299)**, you will use the following toppings.

- 4 cups shredded (or sliced) low-moisture mozzarella
- Spicy chicken sausage or spicy Italian sausage
- ¼ cup grated parmesan

Note about the sausage.

Our meat guys, Sujeet and Big Dave, make our sausage to order, seasoned with smoked paprika, garlic, toasted fennel seeds, red pepper flakes, salt, and dried parsley. If you want to make your own, and you happen to have a food grinder and sausage casings hanging around your kitchen, knock yourself out. If not, substitute good-quality store-bought sausage with your preferred level of spiciness.

Once your pizza is cooked according to the basic recipe, remove it from the oven. Sprinkle it with:

- 2 slices bacon, cooked until crispy and chopped
- 2 green onions, thinly sliced on the bias

- 3 tablespoons crumbled blue cheese
- A drizzle of buttermilk ranch sauce*

*To make the buttermilk ranch sauce, mix the following ingredients together in a large mason jar with a lid:

- ½ cup mayonnaise
- ¼ cup buttermilk (in a pinch you can substitute sour cream)
- 1 small clove of garlic, very finely minced (or ¼ teaspoon garlic powder)
- ½ tablespoon snipped fresh dill (or ¼ tsp. dried dill)
- ¼ teaspoon dried Herbes de Provence
- Salt and pepper to taste

Screw on the lid and give everything a good, hard shake. Pop it in the fridge for at least 30 minutes prior to serving.